SHUTTLE

David C. Onley

SPACE SHUTTLE-COLUMBIA

Commander: Colonel Christopher Bishop III
Pilot: Lt. Colonel Dick Merriman

HYPERSONIC JET TRANSPORT-YORKTOWN

Commander: Lt. Commander Jack Lewis, Jr.
Pilot: Captain Robert D. Clark

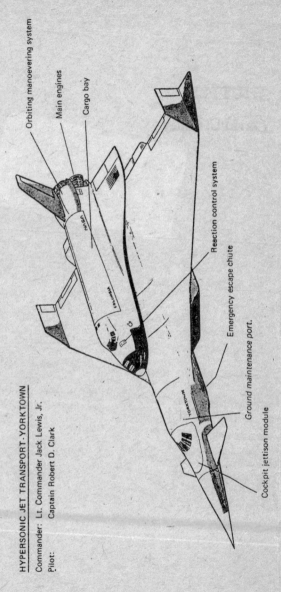

Orbiting manoeuvering system

Main engines

Cargo bay

Reaction control system

Emergency escape chute

Ground maintenance port.

Cockpit jettison module

ACKNOWLEDGEMENTS

If it is true that no man is an island, it is equally true that no novelist is the source of all knowledge, especially when dealing with the often complex and always changing world of technology. To make that world understandable and relevant is all the more difficult. Thus, I am indebted to many people who gave of their time and training, shared their experiences and offered generous assistance and advice towards the preparation of this book.

To attempt to list them all would inevitably exclude some and thus be unfair. However, certain individuals and organizations have been such an integral part of this work, I can say without hesitation that without their help this book would not have been possible.

First and foremost I offer thanks to the personnel of NASA's Johnson Space Center in Houston. In particular, I thank Milton Reim of the Public Affairs Office, Lonnie Cundieff of the Simulation Operations Directorate, John R. Smith of the Mission Control Complex and Flight Director Neil B. Hutchison. NASA's Industrial Communications Manager Bob Gordon was a constant source of help. Over the years Flight Director Donald Puddy continued to offer valuable insights. To Astronaut John Young, the Commander of the Shuttle Columbia, I also acknowledge my thanks.

Many others assisted along the way. These include Mr Roly Dodwell and Bill Turner of Spar Aerospace, Brien Grundy of IBM, Edward Gramauskas of Extramed Ltd., Vicky Hester of Redifon Simulations, William Dedecker and Bill McDonald of Flight Safety International and S. J. Reistetter of Pullman Kellogg Ltd. From Air Canada I thank Mrs G. Brocklesby, Co-pilot Peter Hodgins and Captain Frank Chowhan. I also wish to thank Lloyd Robertson of CTV and Randy Brown, Len Quinn and Mark Southcott for their advice and assistance.

Alex Markov of the University of Toronto's Institute for Aerospace Studies has my gratitude for his computations, calculations and critiques. The mistakes are mine, not his. To Mrs Chris McConkey, my typist, who made near illegible chicken scrawls appear on the page as neatly coherent text, I offer thanks.

I also thank my second 'family', the Williams, for their loyalty and encouragement. I thank my first family, especially my parents, for their support and love, without which the book would not have been completed, or even begun. The last word of appreciation goes to Bev Slopen, friend, literary advisor and agent, in that order.

David C. Onley
Ontario 1980

David C. Onley

Shuttle

Macdonald Futura Publishers

A Futura Book

First published by Futura Publications 1981

ISBN 0 7088 2087 5

Printed in Canada

Macdonald Futura Publishers Ltd.
Paulton House
8 Shepherdess Walk
London N1 7LW

PART ONE

Monday, May 11th

To the memory of my grandfather, Leslie Arthur Woolger, 1890–1977. In his lifetime he saw Queen Victoria's Diamond Jubilee, read about Charles Lindbergh's crossing of the Atlantic and together we watched men walk on the Moon. He considered the latter event, as just the beginning.

CHAPTER ONE

High above the Mojave Desert in California, a great bald eagle soared alone through the blue, cloudless morning sky. Farther from its rock-cliff eyrie than it had ever flown, the huge bird, searching, ever searching, studied the brown wastes below with an efficient predatory gaze. This territory, this vast wasteland of flat dry lakes and desert dunes, was new to it, and the air-currents, unnaturally strong for the time and place, buffetted and tested the creature's purpose, but to no avail. Muscles taut, winds whistling past, the bird wheeled on unflinchingly, towering over its expanding empire. There was no certainty of success in its hunting, yet the bird was instinctively confident of its ability to discover and thus to provide.

Suddenly the bird felt itself under attack. Reflexively, the bird's talons snapped to a menacingly defensive posture, its wings frantically beating the air. Desperately it searched for the foe. But the unseen attacker was embodied only in noise so unrelenting, so piercing that at last the bird abandoned its defiance, painfully twisted in mid-air, and with rapid, powerful thrusts of its great black wings, hastened to retreat. One last time the bird turned its head, screeching angrily, before it fled.

Far below, on Runway 22 of Edwards Air Force Base, the huge engines of the ominous black aircraft continued to blast their banshee scream across the desert. Flames spewing forth from the engines' exhaust ports first blistered the runway's surface into molten bubbles, then evaporated them, transforming them into torrents of gas.

Easily the most powerful aircraft in the world, the hypersonic jet's harsh geometric proportions challenged the senses. From its blunt aerodynamic nose along its pencil-like tubular fuselage, across its vast delta-shaped wings and up its jutting twin tail rudders, the vehicle conveyed a humbling sense of rude and awesome power. The ship rocked up and down in an angry agonizing dance, a mechanical confrontation between the irresistible force of its five jet engines and the unyielding resistance of its massive disc brakes. This brute of a vehicle, the hypersonic jet named *Yorktown*, was ready to fly.

Inside the *Yorktown*'s cramped cockpit, the two-man astronaut crew, in standard-issue powder-blue, high-altitude flight suits, manipulated a bewildering array of switches and dials with efficient, practised grace. Impatiently gripping their controls, they waited for the magic words from Houston's Mission Control: '*Yorktown*, you are clear for take-off and go for brake release'. But Mission Control had one final check-out to make before 'go' was given.

The final check-out was not with the crew of the *Yorktown*, but with the crew of the ship bolted integrally to the *Yorktown*'s back. The *Yorktown* was a carrier mother-ship. Its passenger, the second space shuttle ever built, the first ever to fly in space, was the Space Shuttle *Columbia*. The National Aeronautics and Space Administration had described their flight together as a proof of concept mission, a mission seeking to prove a bold hypothesis, which if successful, would forever change the lives of the crew, the future of NASA and that of the United States of America.

Check-out was confirmed. The Flight Director in Houston Mission Control spoke the magic words the crews had trained for eighteen months to hear, and the Commander of the *Yorktown* replied immediately, 'Roger, Houston! Hold on, *Columbia*! Here we go!' He released the brakes.

The raw fury of the *Yorktown*'s engines now fully unleashed, the black hypersonic jet with the *Columbia* on its back, rolled forward, slowly at first, then in seconds accelerating into a hurtling charge down the runway.

Straining mightily, the two mated vehicles crawled uncertainly into the sky, cleared the field and began a shallow climb. Correcting course to a southeasterly direction, almost parallel to that of the United States' Mexican border, and gaining speed every second, the *Yorktown*, *Columbia* on its back, disappeared into the sky. The Eighth Test Flight of NASA's Airborn Launch Development Project had begun.

NASA had scheduled the shuttle *Columbia*'s 'proof of concept' flight into space to last thirty-seven hours, twenty-five Earth orbits, before returning to land at the Kennedy Space Center in Florida. The *Yorktown*, after carrying the *Columbia* aloft, was scheduled to land near Houston within the hour.

Neither schedule would be met.

Neither ship would ever reach its destination. One would never return.

Within minutes, the lives of both crews, and indeed NASA's very future as an organization, would be in doubt.

CHAPTER TWO

FOUR HOURS BEFORE THE
YORKTOWN'S TAKE-OFF:

The Lyndon B. Johnson Space Center,
Houston, Texas

Twenty-five miles south of Houston, Texas, just to the east of the Gulf Freeway, the little town of Clear Lake had yet to prepare for a new day. Running off the Freeway on NASA One, the odd delivery truck and police car rolled by in the gray, pre-dawn light. The quiet atmosphere befitted that of an average small southern community. But further along NASA One, a big-city traffic jam lurched bumper to bumper in one direction – the Lyndon B. Johnson Space Center, the sprawling 1,620 acre nerve centre of the American Space Program.

Dozens of utilitarian, concrete buildings poured from the same architectural mould, and as gray as the clouded skies, suggested a modern suburban college campus whose major discipline was accounting. Inside the entrance, however, just past the kiosk with the uniformed guards checking the identities of the endless stream of drivers, a roadside display announced a higher purpose to the place than mere learning: full-scale replicas of the Mercury Redstone Rocket which had carried Allan Shepherd, the first American into space, a Titan B Rocket from Project Gemini, and the colossal third stage of the Saturn V, which sent twelve men to a rendezvous on the surface of the Moon, stood as mute monuments to past glory.

The physical layout of the Space Center conveyed the sense of perfect order: a consciously designed mechanistic interrelationship between the buildings, enhanced by wide separations of meticulously manicured grass and trimmed shrubbery, shallow reflecting pools, and cobbled brown pathways which connected the buildings' electronic circuits.

Each of the sixty buildings had a name: Administration Building, Simulation Operations Facility, the Shuttle Avionics Building. But to use the names themselves was to identify yourself as a visitor. NASA personnel, who dealt with numbers all day in their jobs, referred to the buildings by their designated number. Every building in the Space Center down to that kiosk sentry box at the front gate, was numbered. Administration, Building #1; Simulation Operations, Building #5; Public Relations, Building #2; and on to #60. The facilities were numbered with a purpose, and at the geographic core of the Johnson Space Center, sat Building #30.

Thirty. 30. In journalism the numerical symbol for The End. In the space business, it represented the Alpha and Omega of each manned space flight, the beginning and the end, and all in between: the Mission Control Complex. It had been claimed, and it was never denied, that 10,000 miles of cables coursed their way through the innards of the Complex. Ten thousand was conservative, count had been lost long ago. The colour-coded cables and wires were, of course, numbered, and ran through the building's two separate wings, through the Administration Wing with the smoke-black windows, to the second and third floor walkways and the main floor lobby connecting with the windowless Missions Operations Wing, with its exterior of gray chipped rock.

Like the nervous systems of the humans now filling the buildings, the cables began at the brain, the Real Time Computer Complex on the first floor of the Mission Operations Wing. Banks and banks of computers in a room larger than a football field, hummed and clicked and buzzed at decibel levels loud enough to force the human operators to wear headsets, to prevent ear damage and to enable them to communicate over the din.

And all of the cables, like roads to Rome, led to a single room on the second floor of the Mission Control

13

Complex, Building #30. All of the other buildings, whatever their number or name, and all of the theoretical, technological and human competence, the very purpose of NASA itself, was funneled into this one gray-walled, gray-carpeted room.

The red sign on the door spelled out MOCR in white block letters. Pronounced by the staff as Moe-kerr, understood to mean Missions Operations Control Room, it was known to the world as Mission Control.

Like every nerve-centre of historic decision-making, be it the Oval Office in the White House or the flight deck of a nuclear-powered aircraft carrier, the huge amphi-theatre-like room reeked of purpose and power. From the twenty-foot high, non-reflecting gray sidewalls, hung row upon row of colourful wooden plaques, insignias of past missions, dating back to the earliest days when national pride rode into the heavens with the six Project Mercury astronauts in their tiny capsules. Space history marched with the plaques, from the two-man Project Gemini to Project Apollo and the Moon, and the Skylab missions, through to the first Space Shuttle flights, and they hung like ancient battle flags over this present generation of Flight Controllers now assembled, remind-ing them that their duty as Flight Controllers carried with it the responsibility of upholding a tradition, a record of success and achievement.

The cables that had begun their journey at the Real Time Computer Complex, came to an end at four rows of computer terminal consoles on Mission Control's floor and its three ascending tiers. Like the sixty individually numbered buildings, each of the twenty individually numbered consoles had its own precise purpose. For eighteen months, the team of twenty Flight Controllers had trained for this morning, this 'proof of concept' mission with the hypersonic jet *Yorktown* and the space shuttle *Columbia*. They were mostly young, most in neat short-sleeved shirts and ties. All were intellectually gifted in their own right, and all were possessed of keen reflexes. If they seemed more intense than usual, if their concentration on their TV-like video display screens seemed excessive, it was because of an unspoken, but all-pervading awareness that within a few short hours, the lives of four astronauts in two ships, would rest in their hands. It was therefore no coincidence that of all NASA personnel, the Flight Controllers, the elite of a select few, were more sensitive to matters spiritual than the average person. Nor was it coincidental that whatever the level of faith, the incidence of shot nerves and flaming ulcers was higher than that of any other group.

This NASA machine of numbered buildings, colour-coded cables and human servant-master cogs, was in effect an organizational pyramid. The pyramid's firm foundation consisted of a global, five-continent network of tracking stations and research labs and a nation wide team of private contractors and sub-contractors who assembled the Space Shuttle itself. On the next level rested the actual NASA Launch Facilities: Edwards Air Force Base, California, the site for experimental flights, the Kennedy Space Center, Florida, the original 'launch pad', and finally, Vandenberg Air Force Base, California, NASA's west coast Space Shuttle Launch Facility. Above these came the Johnson Space Center itself, the Mission Control Building, the Mission Control Room, and the Mission Control Flight Controllers. The pinnacle of the pyramid, the capstone of the NASA machine, was one individual, the man who had hand-picked the Flight Controllers, the Lead Flight Director.

NASA's terse, two-sentence job definition, understated his authority: 'The Flight Director provides overall management and authority for flight execution. All other Mission Control positions report to the Flight Director.' Advanced degrees in engineering were, of course, technical prerequisites for the Flight Director's position. But because successful missions depended upon his Flight Controllers interacting as a team, being both independent and interdependent, the Flight Director required intimate knowledge of their roles, responsibilities, strengths and weaknesses. It required a man of discernment, wisdom,

15

judgment, tough nerves, mental, physical, and psychological stamina, a man whose intelligence was razor-sharp.

At the centre of the Mission Control Room, in the middle of the third row of computer consoles, sat Douglas Gordon Pierce, the Lead Flight Director for the Eighth Test Flight of the Airborn Launch Development Project. Lean and muscular, the Virginian's physique was impressive. Pepper-and-salt straight hair, cut short but not severely so, jaunty aviator-style glasses bracketing angular features, Doug Pierce's appearance belied his forty-one years. His confident unlined features were those of a contented bachelor, fulfilled in his work. While fate, chance or personal limitations trapped others in jobs of frustration and unfulfillment, Doug Pierce was exactly where he had wanted to be for as long as he could remember.

He was not merely a Flight Director of this particular team of Flight Controllers, but the Lead Flight Director of all NASA Flight Teams. He had not only chosen them, he had also chosen their designated colours: Blue, Red and Gold. The Blue Team shift ran from 2 p.m. to 10 p.m., its personnel to be replaced by the Red Team from 10 p.m. to 6 a.m. and Pierce's own team, now just about to begin their 8 hour shift at 6 a.m., the Gold Team.

His sense of patriotism would have preferred red, white and blue, but the framed scroll on the south wall of Mission Control to his left explained the choice. Apollo 13, 1970: the United States' only accident in space. The lives of Apollo astronauts Lovell, Swiggert and Haise, threatened in their broken capsule *Odyssey*. Tense days of feverish improvisation on what ironically had been Pierce's first Mission as a Flight Controller. And in the end, success. The Apollo 13 Command Module *Odyssey* returned safely to Earth, and the heroic competence of Flight Director Gene Kranz's men was rewarded. White had been forever retired as a team colour.

But that was in the past, a sequence of events Pierce hoped he would never experience again. And so he had chosen the symbol of purity, value, strength and malleability – gold. By all accounts, his Team was that good, and so was Doug Pierce.

As the countdown moved closer to 6 a.m. and the formal start of the Gold Team's shift, the Flight Controllers checked and rechecked tens of thousands of interrelated factors, and co-ordinated the data displayed on their screens with their 'bibles', the chronologically itemized Flight Plan. Their communications through small headset microphones proceeded with matter-of-fact crispness, an indication that the months of Missions Simulations, complete with scores of emergency scenarios, had brought them all to a finely-honed state of readiness.

Slowly Mission Control became increasingly quiet. Flight Controllers' voices fell to subdued, almost reverential tones. One by one, as if on cue, they glanced over their shoulders or turned in their orthopedically-designed padded, swivel chairs and looked towards the man at the centre console in the third row.

For one last time Douglas Pierce surveyed this room he knew so well before he began. On Mission Control's front wall the centrally positioned 21-foot wide, 8-foot high aquamarine World Map glowed comfortably. A bold yellow elliptical line, starting at Edwards Air Force Base and looping the world, confidently predicted the *Columbia*'s first orbit. On either side of the World Map, pairs of smaller 8-foot by 8-foot rear-projection display screens threw up ever-changing charts, graphs and data. Above the screens, white digital chronometers counted down towards various important targets and deadlines. The centre chronometer above the World Map occupied Pierce's attention: Five-fifty-nine-thirty a.m. Mission Control was about to go operational.

'This is it' he thought, pressing a button labelled 'P.A.' 'Eighteen months of work, and this is it.' Unconsciously unbuttoning his dark blue jacket, Pierce stood, scanned the sea of searching faces, then spoke in his resonant Virginian drawl, 'All right, everyone . . . we've come a long way. If you are all ready, let's have a good mission . . . and make some history while we're at it.'

Six a.m. One more time around the 'loop', the communications line throughout Mission Control. One by one, Pierce called out the title of the Flight Controller's position and one by one came the replies:

'Surgeon . . . Go.'

'Propulsion is Go.'

'Launch Vehicle Engineer – ready.'

'Trajectory . . . we are Go.'

There would be other Missions for Doug Pierce to lead, but not many. Advancing years would inexorably diminish his ability to cope with the Flight Director's pressure-cooker job of instant life and death decision making. If this experimental mission did work, his near-legendary record as Flight Director at NASA would continue unblemished and he would remain odds-on favourite to succeed his mentor, Dr Benjamin Franklin Fleck, and become the top man at NASA, the Administrator. And Pierce wanted this one to work, badly. But apart from Pierce's considerable private ambition, no other United States space flight, not John Glenn's first three orbits of the Earth, not Armstrong's first landing on the Moon, nor John Young and Bob Crippen's inaugural space shuttle flight, came close to the importance of this one, astutely billed by the media as the most important manned flight in the history of the United States Space Program.

The check-out continued:

'Communications, we are Go.'

'Computer Engineer, Go.'

'This is the Flight Director,' said Doug Pierce. 'We are Go.'

Mission Control was now operational. The final countdown for the Eighth Test Flight of the Airborn Launch Development Project had begun.

'Doug, let's take a look at the ships.' There was anticipation and excitement in the high-pitched voice of Lt. Commander Vince Torino, a dark-haired, swarthy, 38-year-old veteran astronaut, well-liked by his colleagues. Pierce pushed a console display button labelled 'Screen #4'. At the front of Mission Control, the far right-hand display screen flickered and snapped into focus, projecting an impressive picture of two unique aircraft. Torino shook his head slowly and bit his lower lip. 'Shit,' he muttered softly in disguised frustration.

Torino's position at Mission Control was that of Capcom, a position essential to the flight's success. A holdover term from the old days when Mission Control communicated with men in space 'capsules', the title of Capcom had remained the same, and so had the responsibility of maintaining constant communication with the crews and making certain they understood Mission Control's orders, while at the same time representing the crews' interest with the 'desk jockeys' in Mission Control.

But the peppery New Jersey-born Torino was not Capcom by choice. Eighteen months earlier, just after he had been chosen to be pilot of the space shuttle *Enterprise* for the next, the ninth, test flight of the project, fate had intervened.

While the shuttle *Columbia* would fly the 'proof of concept' flight today, Torino and Harwood had been scheduled even then to fly the *Enterprise* in the next week, in the 'confirmation of concept' flight. And then his heart, his damned heart, had picked up a slight flutter, and just like that, Vince Torino was out of it. No more the active astronaut, Torino had been grounded, replaced. Another colleague had been called off the bench, took his place, and left him on the sidelines.

To be left behind! It was all so infuriating! One stinking examination picking up a flutter that would not have grounded a commercial airlines pilot or even a professional football player, for God's sake, and that was it! He was dropped from the starting team.

Publicly, Torino had put on a brave face, a tough-guy nonchalance. Inwardly he was crushed, and on the day he had been informed of the Medical Review Board's decision, he had gone home and wept like a baby.

But that was past history. Torino had determined to be

the best damned Capcom going, to be so on top of it all, so indispensable to the Airborn Launch Development Project, that no-one, not one person, could even consider the hierarchy of the project without him. Vince Torino was a dedicated team player.

Even so, Pierce appreciated his friend's frustration. 'Some day, Vince, maybe some day.'

'Yeah, and when I do, I hope you are still running the show. You got us here, Doug.'

Pierce smiled, but said nothing, his silence discreetly confirming the accuracy of Torino's statement. Had it not been for Doug Pierce, this Mission and the whole Airborn Launch Development Project never would have taken place.

Torino stared at the screen, at the ships at Edwards Air Force Base, the audacity and implications of today's flight still amazing him. Far to the west, nestled on the edge of the Mojave Desert in California, Edwards Air Force Base was the home, both of the United States Airforce Test Pilots' School and of NASA's Pacific counterpart to the Johnson Space Center, the Hugh L. Dryden Flight Research Center. Situated on the vast expanses of Roger's Dry Lake, and well away from prying eyes, Edwards was the world's largest airport, either civil or military. Its surface was lined with a network of natural and man-made runways. To the north by the Control Tower called by the pilots 'Eddy Tower', Runways 15, 18, 23, 30 and 36 criss-crossed in a star pattern. To the south, aligned in a reverse 'F' pattern, were Runways 17, 22 and 25. Near Runway 22 were the objects of Doug Pierce's and Vince Torino's attention.

Two massive ships, one bolted to the other's back, sat inside a structure three-storeys high, painted dull burnt orange, built meccano-like of steel girders, an open-air garage, euphemistically called by NASA, the Mate-Demate Device. There, the smaller, white, upper-most ship, the Space Shuttle *Columbia*, had been lowered and bolted to the larger black vehicle, the *Yorktown* and were now said by NASA to be in a 'Mated Configuration'. The

Columbia was the first space shuttle to have flown in space, and the backbone of NASA's five-shuttle fleet. Illuminated by banks of Klieg lights in the pre-dawn desert air, its proportions were distinct. Over 122 feet long with a swept-back delta-shaped wingspan of 78 feet and with a single tail rudder stabbing 40 feet into the sky, the shuttle looked like a futuristic jetliner ready to carry passengers to another planet. Its black nose was rounded and only slightly tapered, in appearance rather like the nose of a 727 or a DC9. Extending up from the wings, the flat vertical sides of the fuselage curved gently to the middle, enclosing a hold called the Cargo Bay 60 feet long and 15 feet across, large enough to hold a Greyhound bus. In all, the *Columbia* was a purposeful looking vehicle, its intimidating 14-foot diameter rocket engines only hinting at its brute strength.

Half airplane and half space-ship, and despite its trouble-plagued beginnings, the shuttle had made space flight a routine and economic proposition, a part of the American experience – mom, apple pie and space shuttles in orbit. Unlike every one of its predecessors, the Mercury, Gemini and Apollo capsules which were worn out after one flight, the shuttle was re-usable, capable of conducting over one hundred missions. And again unlike its predecessors which parachuted into the ocean, the shuttle could glide to a conventional airport landing. The very term 'shuttle' had slipped into the language and was as familiar as the words 'satellite' or 'rocket'. Business around the world lined up to buy room in the shuttle's Cargo Bay, with the first four years of flight sold out before the shuttle had ever flown. Conducting industrial, medical and technical experiments in near gravity had become routine and, for the companies involved, highly profitable. Companies quickly discovered the profits to be made from products which could only be manufactured in the zero gravity of outer space. New alloys went into the construction of automobile engine blocks capable of lasting for 500,000 miles. Crystals grown in zero gravity were utterly free of flaws, a requirement critical to the communications industry. Developments in medical serums had been beyond the scientists' wildest expectations. Before the first shuttle had even been built, NASA had heralded the Shuttle Program as 'Man's Coming of Age in Space'. At the time the proclamation had seemed arrogant. Now it appeared an understatement.

Beneath the *Columbia* and attached to its flat underside, was a much larger ship, the harshly geometric midnight-black Hypersonic Jet *Yorktown*. Named after the redoubtable World War II aircraft carrier of the Battle of Midway, the *Yorktown*'s technically descriptive title 'Hypersonic' defined its capacity easily to exceed six times the speed of sound. The *Yorktown* and its sister-ships *Hornet* and *Liberty*, were the fastest aircraft ever built.

Unlike other jet aircraft, the *Yorktown* had two different and independent engine systems, located under its swept-back wings. The primary system consisted of five air-breathing turbine engines. Together the five engines enabled the *Yorktown* to travel faster and higher than Concorde, over 2,000 miles per hour at altitudes approaching 90,000 feet. Above that altitude the Earth's atmosphere becomes so thin that air-breathing turbine engines no longer function. It was the second propulsion system which enabled the *Yorktown* to soar to the fringes of space. At 90,000 feet five liquid hydrogen-powered rocket engines took over from the turbines and literally blasted the *Yorktown* to over 5,000 miles per hour, more than twice as fast as the fastest fighter jet, and allowed it to climb into the darkness, to altitudes up to 70 miles above the Earth. Its astronaut pilots, men sparing in their compliments, called the *Yorktown* the ultimate aircraft.

Seven times since the start of the Airborn Launch Development Project, Doug Pierce and Vince Torino had seen the *Columbia* mated to the *Yorktown* and, in alternate flights, the *Enterprise* joined to the *Yorktown*'s sister ship, the *Hornet*. This morning's Eighth Test Flight brought NASA to the project's culmination. But to both Pierce and Torino, the sight of a Space Shuttle mated to a Hypersonic Jet still looked odd, far from the traditional appearance of space shuttle at take-off.

All previous space shuttles had stood vertical on the launch pads of the Kennedy Space and Vandenberg Air Force Base, and had been blasted into space by rockets. The previous launch system's appearance included a bullet-shaped device, 154 feet long, 27 feet across, called the External Tank, secured to the shuttle's underside, providing the shuttle's three main engines with half a million gallons of propellants. Attached to the sides of the External Tank, a pair of solid-fuel rocket boosters 149 feet long, helped blast the shuttle from its vertical position on the Launch Pad to an altitude of 27 miles. The boosters, fuel spent, were then jettisoned, and parachuted back to Earth for refurbishing. The shuttle's three main engines continued to function drawing fuel from the External Tank until, after climbing to 69 miles, the tank itself was jettisoned, and tumbled back into the atmosphere, where it disintegrated.

A typical Apollo Moon Mission take-off had involved $100,000,000 of throwaway booster rockets. This largely reusable launch system, using external tank and two solid-fuel boosters, had slashed the costs of space shuttle flights to $20,000,000. But while the eighty percent reduction in cost had made such flights economic, it was still not cheap enough for what NASA had in mind.

NASA had long planned to use the space shuttle fleet to construct a network of orbiting solar power stations. Converting the sun's rays to microwaves to be beamed safely back to receiving dishes on Earth for reconversion into electricity, the solar power station concept appeared to be an ideal alternative to America's dependence on nuclear power. NASA's experimental station, Sol One, a demonstration project one kilometer square, had demonstrated the technological feasibility of orbiting solar power stations. But an inescapable problem remained: at $20,000,000 per flight, even the most generous cost-benefit analysis showed the construction cost of full-scale solar power stations, seventy-five kilometers square, to be wildly uneconomic, at least twice as costly as would be economically justifiable. Solar power satellites might provide the perfect answer to America's electrical energy needs, but they simply cost too much.

Doug Pierce, however, had come up with an imaginative solution. Known within NASA as an adventurous thinker, one not confined to traditional concepts, Pierce had realized that the answer lay in combining the potential of the hypersonic jet with the potential of the shuttle. His initial estimates had intrigued him and he conducted detailed computer analyses which confirmed the theoretical feasibility of a hypersonic jet carrying a space shuttle piggyback to a separation altitude of 70 miles. There, at the edge of space, the computer suggested the shuttle could separate and climb on alone into orbit, while the hypersonic jet returned to Earth.

The public had had enough of dependence on foreign sources of energy and reliance upon the time-bomb represented by nuclear power. NASA's Administrator, Dr Benjamin Franklin Fleck had proclaimed boldly to Congress, 'Give us the money and we will do the job.' What stirred both NASA and Congress into enthusiasm was the net cost per launch of this theoretical program – 9.3 million dollars, less than half that of a standard shuttle launch. If Pierce's project worked, then solar power stations would be economic. Congress responded with enough money for nine experimental flights, the number of flights NASA said would be required to prove the viability of Pierce's project.

It was very much Pierce's project and he took charge. NASA seethed with activity and renewed purpose. *Yorktown* and *Hornet* were removed from their scheduled high-altitude research projects and modified to accommodate a space shuttle. NASA pulled the *Columbia* and *Enterprise* off normal flight duty to be joined respectively to *Yorktown* and *Hornet*. A selection committee scoured the roster of the astronaut corps and submitted for Pierce's approval a list of the best who began an intensive eighteen-month training program.

Through it all, Doug Pierce's power and authority grew as he spurred on NASA, and pushed his team to their mental and physical limits. Breaking with tradition, he abandoned the committee process and himself hand-picked the teams of Flight Controllers. The project was that important.

One NASA tradition, however, was not broken: over the development of every new system, NASA crawled before it walked and walked before it ran. Accordingly, the nine manned test flights in the project were scheduled over eighteen months. The first two flights were conducted at subsonic speeds and below 20,000 feet, and tested the general air-worthiness and aerodynamics of a shuttle mated to a hypersonic jet. The third and fourth flights saw the shuttle blow free from the mothercraft at subsonic speeds, to check the separation system. On the fifth flight, the *Hornet* raced to over 2,000 miles per hour and climbed to 80,000 feet before the *Enterprise* separated and glided back to Earth. The sixth and seventh flights came closer to the ultimate goal, as the *Yorktown* went hypersonic at speeds of 4,000 then 5,000 miles per hour, at altitudes of 60 then 70 miles, before the *Columbia* separated. Seven flights into the air and none into space: Pierce's project was still just an idea.

This morning's flight was the ultimate test, the 'proof of concept' flight. The *Columbia* would separate from the *Yorktown* and attempt to climb on into orbit. If the eighth flight worked, then one week later the *Enterprise* and the *Hornet* would attempt a confirmation flight and if that in turn worked, then solar power stations could become a reality.

It was 7:13 a.m. Doug Pierce's team of Flight Controllers worked through the itemized countdown checkouts in the Flight Plan. At the Dryden Flight Research Center, Edwards Air Force Base, their counterparts conducted the physical preparations for the mission. If Mission Control, Houston, was the administrative centre of all operations, Dryden was the on-site operations field post for the flight, making certain all was ready for the *Columbia* and the *Yorktown*.

By 7:15 a.m., Houston time, the astronaut crew of the *Columbia* had finished breakfast, had received a final briefing, and had begun to don their bulky white spacesuits in the Suit Room, a room as clean and austere as a hospital operating theatre. Spacesuits were not usually worn by shuttle pilots during launches. Shuttle flights had become so routine that non-pressurized cotton uniforms were all that were required in the fully-pressurized cabin of the shuttle. However, this morning's mission was far from routine. The dangers inherent in the experimental flight prompted the use of suits able to withstand the vacuum of space.

The Commander of the *Columbia*, 43-year old U.S. Air Force Col Christopher 'Rusty' Bishop III was a man accustomed to danger. As the most experienced astronaut in the corps, Rusty Bishop did not so much live life as assault it. At six foot one, Bishop was the quintessential astronaut: articulate, witty, bright-blue eyes glinting with mischief, bright red hair. Had he been born in an earlier era, he would have been at home in the cockpit of a World War I Spad biplane, white scarf snapping in the breeze, guns blazing, cranking his machine into heart-stopping manoeuvres, only to return to base and buy drinks all round. When NASA required an astronaut for public relations, or for particularly difficult missions, Rusty Bishop topped the list.

He leapt from the table and swung his arms vigorously, testing the $250,000 suit's mobility.

'Well, wouldn't play golf in it, but I guess she'll do,' he grinned to one of the surgically-garbed, masked suit technicians. Pulling the man closer he said in a serious confidential tone, 'Get me an air sickness bag, will you? But don't let old Merriman over there know about it.'

Bishop winked, grinned again and glanced over to his colleague, the pilot and second in command of the *Columbia*, Lt Col Dick Merriman: 'Well, Dick old man, it won't be long now!' he said as the technician left on his curious errand.

Dick Merriman, a quiet-spoken Oklahoman with a flat scarred face and a nose obviously broken more than once, raised his eyebrows, snapped his gloves onto the wrists of his suit and nodded pensively.

'Don't sweat it, Dick – once we get up, it will just be like old times.'

Merriman smiled wrily. It had been two years since his jet crash and this was his first mission back into outer space. He felt he was ready, but lingering doubts inevitably remained. The crash, on a routine training flight, had left both legs shattered and with them, he feared, his nerve. NASA had placed him on 'temporary leave of absence flight status', primarily out of recognition for his contributions to the space program and his talents as a shuttle astronaut, because no-one at NASA had given Dick Merriman a snowball in hell's chance of ever walking again, let alone of flying into space. No-one, that is, except Rusty Bishop and Doug Pierce.

Before the selection for the Airborn Launch Development Project had begun, Bishop had cornered Doug Pierce in his Administrative Office and argued forcefully, 'We need his talents and his guts. He's got nerve like you wouldn't believe. If I had to choose one man to depend on it would be Dick.'

Pierce had appreciated Bishop's loyalty. 'You're going to have to depend on him. I've chosen you both to be the prime crew for the *Columbia*.'

And through two years of agonizing rehabilitation, Dick Merriman sweated blood and took every test and sweated more blood until the NASA doctors had but one recommendation. Dick Merriman's flight status returned to 'operational'.

Fully suited up, an ebullient Bishop and contemplative Merriman were eager to go. It was 7:45 a.m., two hours and fifteen minutes before their take-off.

Down the hall from the Suit Room, the twin, windowless light-blue crash doors were punched open by burly flight attendants in one-piece orange NASA jumpsuits. A small crowd of perhaps forty Air Force servicemen, Dryden Flight Research Center technicians, NASA and Edwards Air Force Base personnel formed a spontaneous receiving line to the transporter van, waiting to drive them to the *Columbia* in the Mate-Demate Device. Bishop and Merriman lumbered in their bulky suits out of the dim hallway into the bright clear California morning, each carrying a briefcase-sized airconditioning unit connected by coiling gold hoses, keeping them comfortable in their suits until they were on board the *Columbia* and plugged into the ship's life-support system. Applause from the observers, at first spasmodic, then contagiously louder, greeted the astronauts and cameras clicked, freezing a moment of history. The staid, no-nonsense engineers and military men waved and cheered like fans at a football game. These guys were their agents, damn it! Their work and sweat went for these guys! Heroes? Damn right. Bishop, always ready to play to a crowd, skipped a few steps and sang the first few lines of 'I Love a Parade', breaking them up.

'What's the matter?' he demanded innocently. 'You guys never seen grown men in snow suits in the desert before?'

The van rolled sedately past Mate-Demate Device #1, the open-air girdered garage housing the ships for the next test flight, the *Hornet* and *Enterprise*.

'The old *Enterprise*,' said Bishop with quiet respect.

'The first,' replied Merriman.

The *Enterprise* in many ways summed up the increased public interest in the space program. Originally it was to be named the *Constitution* in honour of the U.S. bicentennial, but NASA had been flooded with tens of thousands of letters urging that the first shuttle, the first true Space Ship, be named after the USS *Enterprise* of the TV series Star Trek. Overwhelmed by the spontaneous public demand, NASA gave way.

The *Enterprise* had been the first space shuttle to fly in the 1977 Approach and Landing Tests. Its initial role had been purely as a test vehicle never intended to fly in space, but the other four space shuttles could not handle the workload generated from private industry, so the *Enterprise* was overhauled, and pressed into service in outer space. It had not been the first shuttle into space – *Columbia* held that distinction – but the *Enterprise* was undoubtedly the most famous.

The van gently bumped to a halt and stopped at the base of Mate-Demate Device #2, a scant two hundred yards from the *Enterprise* and *Hornet*. Dozens of workers in hardhats and white NASA jackets scurried about. As first Bishop then Merriman stepped from the van with practiced care, work came to a halt and the workers cheered and clapped and waved.

'Jeez, just like the old days,' said Bishop as he and Merriman waved back in appreciation and looked up at their ship, the *Columbia*, perched atop the *Yorktown*.

The *Columbia*: the second space shuttle ever built, the first space shuttle to fly into space. Named after the Apollo 11 Command Capsule which had carried Neil Armstrong, Buz Aldrin and Mike Collins to their destiny, this new *Columbia* had been fueled for its thirty-seven hour mission and was almost ready to fly.

Bishop and Merriman strode purposefully to the base of the Mate-Demate Device where a steel-grated elevator waited to carry them up to the entrance hatch. An official greeting party of senior NASA personnel exchanged handshakes and backslaps with the crew. Then Bishop and Merriman stepped into the elevator, and with a final jaunty wave from Bishop they ascended to the *Columbia*'s main hatch entrance below the cockpit on the left. The elevator stopped with a lurch, and then transferred to a portable Clean Room separating the elevator from the Main Hatch, which was designed to prevent dust or debris from entering the shuttle and damaging its sensitive on-board equipment. The wind gusted dustily, and Bishop made a mental note that the Clean Room had served its purpose.

The *Columbia*'s main hatch, four feet across, opened

down and away from the ship like a round diving board, and even in ordinary clothes it took considerable dexterity to enter the ship without giving one's head a nasty crack. Bishop crouched and stepped into the hatchway, then stopped and looked back at Merriman pensively clenching and unclenching his hands.

'Dick? Tonight's paper: Headline! "Mission aborted! Bishop cracks helmet on entering shuttle!" '

'With that helmet, even you couldn't crack it,' Merriman replied. Merriman was right, of course. The clear fishbowl helmet looked thin but the heaviest major league baseball bat could be broken over it into kindling without even scratching the helmet's surface.

'I hope not,' replied Bishop. 'It was built by the lowest bidder, you know! Just like everything else,' he muttered to himself as he climbed through the hatch.

They stood in the *Columbia*'s lower-deck living quarters which were complete with food galley and storage space, sleeping bags and zero gravity toilet and then with some care, climbed the six-rung chromium ladder to the flight deck. Bishop, the Commander, took the left-hand seat, and Merriman, the pilot, the right. Disconnecting the portable airconditioning units, they plugged into the ship's life support system.

'Home again,' said Merriman with satisfaction.

'Home,' replied Bishop, cinching his belt and chest harness into place.

As they settled in, Bishop unfolded a small packet from his knee-pouch and handed it to Merriman.

'Dick? Me and the guys at Mission Control wanted to give you this.'

Merriman frowned, unfolded it and grinned broadly. It was an airsickness bag. 'My stomach and I thank you, Rusty,' he said, in feigned seriousness.

Like one in three of all astronauts, Merriman often became space-sick, a condition which after years of study and research NASA had been only partially successful in eliminating. Space-sickness was one of the dues to be paid, it seemed. Merriman, already keyed up, wondered if he would need the bag before they even took off.

Secured in their high-back chairs, the astronauts began the pre-launch checklist. They tapped requests on their centre console keyboards, starting up the space shuttle's five on-board computers. Directly between them on the centre of the *Columbia*'s control panel, three TV screens, six inches in diameter, were arranged in an inverted pyramid and the computers flashed back answers to Bishop and Merriman's requests in cool green numbers, charts and graphs.

The upper flight deck of the shuttle had far fewer dials and gauges than one would expect of a space ship because of those three screens, and because of the shuttle's computers. Instead of having to search visually across the control panel for data on dozens of separate dials and gauges, Bishop or Merriman had only to tap out a numbered sequence on their keyboards like a practised typist or keypunch operator, and micro-milliseconds later, six times as fast as the blink of an eye, the ship's computers displayed the desired information on one of the screens.

They worked through the checklist, reading it from their logs, confirming results with Pierce's Flight Controllers at Mission Control, and waited for the crew of the *Yorktown* to arrive.

At 8 a.m., T minus 2 hours, the Flight Controllers continued to report to Doug Pierce, and the Flight Director listened with care, scrutinizing his display screen for the slightest discrepancy which might endanger the launch. From the Instrumentation, Navigation and Communications Officer, known as INCO, Pierce had confirmation that the geosynchronous stationary satellites of the Tracking and Data Relay Satellite System, and the Ground Space Flight Tracking and Data Network were ready to provide total radio communication for the flight. From the Ground Resources and Network Manager, he had confirmation that the coordination of the operations in Mission Control and NASA's world-wide facilities was going smoothly. The Avionics Engineer, the man in charge of monitoring the *Columbia* and *Yorktown*'s Flight Control Systems, that is, the actual physical operations of the ship, reported all as operational. The Environmental, Mechanical and Electrical Systems Engineer established the readiness of the ships' electrical power systems, the Life Support Systems, and the mechanical systems. The Launch Vehicle Engineer in charge of the *Yorktown*'s overall functioning noted, however, some troublesome but minor anomalies appearing in the *Yorktown*'s fuel-line system. Pierce glanced at the chronometer, 8:10, and was almost relieved that that little glitch had appeared now and not later. He queried the Engineer further, and by pushing the appropriate button on his console examined the data on his own screen. The anomalies were there all right, but well within safety tolerances. Pierce told the Launch Vehicle Engineer to keep him informed of any changes. In the seven Staff Support Rooms surrounding Mission Control, dozens of technicians and Flight Control Staff members monitored the various mission systems, computers, avionics, propulsion, flight activity, instrumentation and communications flight dynamics and electrical, mechanical and environmental systems. Each man on each of the Staff Support Teams monitored their own console, tied in directly with both the Mission Control's Computers on the first floor of the building and the Mission Control room itself. It was a tightly integrated effort.

Doug Pierce ran his eyes down the chronologically tabulated Flight Plan, stopping at 8:15:30 – Navy Lt Commander Jack Lewis Jr and U.S. Air Force Lt Col Robert D. Clark. 'They should be leaving their Suit Room,' he thought. The van would take them to the orange Mate-Demate Device #2 garage, housing their ship, the Mission's mothership, the *Yorktown*.

Lewis and Clark were essentially the forgotten men of the mission, as their role in the flight, although critical, was brief – a short twenty-minute climb to the *Columbia* separation point at seventy miles altitude and then a quick return flight to Houston's own Ellington Air Force Base next door to the Space Center. Rusty Bishop's wisecracks had given the media enough to focus on from a personality point of view. Lewis and Clark had been relegated by the media to the status of supporting cast. But one writer, tracing the exploratory history of the space program for TIME Magazine, seized on the names of the *Yorktown*'s crew and compared their pathfinding role to that of the explorers who had long ago opened up the United States Northwest, and had dubbed today's flight 'The Second Lewis and Clark Expedition'.

NASA's Public Affairs Office, traditionally content to prepare informative, if uninspiring, NASA News Media Releases, jumped at the new label and pushed the analogy at every opportunity. Forty-two year old Robert D. Clark, *Yorktown*'s quiet-spoken articulate pilot, was the focus for the publicity. An amateur writer-historian as well as aerospace engineer, the ruggedly handsome astronaut was approaching the close of an eleven-year career with NASA. Most of his adult life had been tied up with the agency. Married after a year as an astronaut, he was involved in the record-shattering early years of the space shuttle program. After that, a best-selling book on NASA's impact on American history was followed by the death of his wife and two children in a car accident five years before. Add to this the constant training, the psyching up for each new mission, the let-down after each return to Earth: it added up to a great deal in eleven years. With the completion of this project, there would be time, time to reassess. The moment to change gear was approaching.

Rob Clark liked the analogy of the Lewis and Clark Expedition, and felt it appropriate to speak out, to re-emphasize what he had said in his book. A guest appearance on the Today Show, two weeks earlier, had given him that opportunity.

'The original Lewis and Clark expedition was a journey into the unknown. Our flight, the second Lewis and Clark expedition as some of the media have called it, is also a

33

journey into the unknown. Like the original, we seek information, we seek to increase human knowledge, and like the original we have no idea what the benefits of achieving our goals will be, except that they are inevitable. We do know this, and it surely is the lesson that history teaches about manned space travel. There *will* be benefits to all Americans, to all people, benefits far outweighing the costs involved.'

Now as he zipped closed his flight suit in the Suit Room next to the one Bishop and Merriman had dressed in earlier, Rob Clark, increasingly devout in the last few years, withdrew into introspective meditation – on himself, his flight and with his Maker.

'For God's sake, watch it! You nearly took my ear off!'

The angry voice of Jack Lewis Jr berating his suit technician for some unknown indiscretion shattered Clark's reverie. Clark stared at the chastened technician as he attempted to secure Lewis' helmet in place. 'Cool it, Jack,' he thought.

By all accounts, Lt Commander Jack Lewis Jr, 39, was a pain in the ass. He had chased after being Number One in everything he did for so long he had almost forgotten what he was trying to escape. Brilliant, opinionated, intense, sure of himself, his taut, tanned face, narrow gun-slinger eyes and blond brush-cut gave the Pennsylvanian an intimidating appearance. Berating subordinates who performed to less than perfection, moments after bestowing a compliment, was pure Jack Lewis. The nicest thing anyone could say about him as far as technique was concerned was that he was the best pilot flying. You wouldn't invite him to a party or out for a drink, you sure as hell wouldn't want your sister dating him, but if you had to place your life in one pilot's hands, damned if that pilot wouldn't be Jack Lewis.

His father had left home when Lewis was seven. His mother didn't care. Jack Lewis had fought his way through school, was bounced from college twice in a single semester and totalled the first car he had ever owned. Jack Lewis was a loser. But after the accident,

34

alone in the hospital in bandaged pain, he bit on the bullet, and determined to be a winner. Not just as a pilot in the Navy, but as a test pilot and the top of his class too. And not just as a test pilot, but as an astronaut, and the best.

The pursuit of Number One had itself become his escape, acquiring and possessing Number One, his sanctuary. In that haven, known only to himself, no-one could touch him. None could lay claim to his title, and the pursuit brought its own rewards: women who wanted no more of him than sex, and gave him no more than that either. The exception, briefly, was Charlene, who gave him much more. But he took and gave nothing in return. And now she was gone, used up like everyone else.

The only gospel Jack Lewis preached was that of pre-flight preparedness. 'Don't be afraid of anything. The only way to control fear while pursuing Number One is the constant exposure to increasingly difficult flight situations. A test pilot doesn't panic in a tight situation because with your engines flamed out and your control panel lit up like a Christmas tree, survival means thinking your way out of the mess.'

Just as quickly as he had erupted, Lewis had calmed himself and good-naturedly slapped the perplexed technician on the back.

'Just want it done right,' he said.

The humiliated technician left the room.

'No-one's perfect, Jack,' said Clark.

Lewis accepted the judgment with a nod.

'Just strive for it, that's all,' he replied, looking at the clock on the wall. 8:16, Houston time. 'Come on,' he said, 'we're late.'

The two astronauts, dressed in high-altitude pressure suits much easier to move in than the bulky space suits worn by Bishop and Merriman, but offering far less protection, left the Suit Room. The van that had taken Bishop and Merriman to the *Columbia* had now returned to take Lewis and Clark to the *Yorktown* where they rode the Mate-Demate elevator up to the cockpit door on the

35

starboard side of the *Yorktown*'s tubular fuselage, and climbed aboard.

Two 'Close-out Pilots', fellow astronauts assigned to assist them, helped Lewis and Clark into the cockpit seats. Even if both had not been over six feet tall and well-built, it still would have been a tight squeeze. The seat backs were reclined to a prone position and then Lewis and Clark straddled and inched their way forward in a waddle and sat down. The Close-out Pilots then pushed the seat backs up and locked them vertical. Lewis and Clark strapped themselves in, a mere sixteen inches from the network of dials and gauges on the *Yorktown*'s cockpit control panel. Unlike the relatively spacious flight deck of the *Columbia*, the *Yorktown*'s physical design sacrificed pilot comfort for function.

'Ever flown a VW Bug at 5,000 miles an hour?' said Lewis.

'The ship is fast,' thought Rob Clark, 'but the cockpit is like a coffin.'

Doug Pierce had long preached a variation of Parkinson's Law, so often in fact, that his Team in Mission Control had dubbed it 'Pierce's By-law', to wit: Tension increases as time to take-off decreases. Pierce's attention returned to an earlier problem. He looked ahead to the second row of consoles.

'Launch Vehicle Engineer,' he radioed, 'any further report on the fuel line anomaly on the *Yorktown*?'

'Negative. It appeared on the screen, then cleared up.'

'O.K. As soon as Lewis and Clark ignite their engines, though, have another look at it. It must be a hundred percent, or I won't let them take off.'

The engineer wondered if he had read his screen properly and worried momentarily that if Pierce was forced to scrap the flight before take-off, the inevitable investigation would prove that he had missed some indicator. 'No,' he reassured himself, checking his screen again. 'If something is wrong, the computers would have caught it.'

Columbia's five onboard computers and the *York-*

town's three, linked to Mission Control's Computer Complex, confirmed all systems as Go. At 9 a.m. the Flight Plan called for the *Yorktown* and *Columbia* to be backed away from the Mate-Demate Device by a convoy of powerful flat-bed diesel trucks. Both crews were ready, and at 9 a.m. on the dot, Pierce gave the order.

Inside the Mate-Demate Device a squat, cube-shaped flat-bed diesel truck attached to the *Yorktown*'s under-side, strained its engines, groaning in the agony of rolling the vehicles out of the garage. Imperceptibly at first, the *Yorktown*'s huge black landing-gear wheels responded to the diesel's efforts and Lewis and Clark felt a slight but distinct jerk as the reverse motion began. From their narrow gunslot-like cockpit windows, they watched the orange-girdered steel structure recede.

'Here we go,' said Lewis, tight-lipped.

Majestically the entourage of bright yellow trucks, engines growling in the bright blue morning air, escorted the two ships in slow régal progression across the tarmac towards the end of Runway 22. The procession stopped and the lead diesel flat-bed disengaged itself from the *Yorktown*'s nose-cone and wheeled away to join the other mechanical courtiers. For the first time, the *Yorktown* and the *Columbia* sat completely alone on the tarmac. The brilliant morning light emphasized the raw power of their starkly beautiful lines. It was 9:15 a.m., T minus 45 minutes.

Ten minutes of meticulous communications checkouts followed. Then the *Yorktown*'s commander, Jack Lewis gave a deep sigh and looked at his co-pilot.

'O.K. Rob, let's light 'em up.'

Clark nodded affirmatively, and Lewis radioed Mission Control, 'Houston, we are ready to turn engines One through Five.'

'We copy you, *Yorktown*,' said Pierce. 'You are go for Engine Turnover.'

'Ready for Engine Turnover,' replied Lewis, snapping open an eight-by-three inch metal plate on the control panel, designed to prevent an inadvertent engine start.

Five numbered toggle switches were revealed and Lewis pushed down on switch #1. The first of the *Yorktown*'s five engines whined to life. A green light glowed on Lewis' control panel.

'Turning One,' he announced. He depressed Switch #2 and waited for confirmation from a second green light, then repeated the procedure with Engines 3 through 5.

In Mission Control, the Propulsion Engineer and Launch Vehicle Engineer's consoles rapidly displayed five columns of numbers indicating that all five engines located beside each other on the *Yorktown*'s underbelly were firing perfectly.

'Houston? This is *Yorktown*. We have a normal start on all five engines,' said Lewis.

'Flight Director,' confirmed the Propulsion Engineer, 'we have a perfect burn on all five.'

'Anything amiss with the fuel line?' queried Pierce of the Launch Vehicle Engineer.

'Negative, Flight. Perfect numbers all round.'

Satisfied, Pierce adjusted his headset. '*Yorktown*, this is the Flight Director. You are clear to taxi out to Runway 22.'

'Roger, ready to taxi now,' replied Lewis, releasing the ship's brakes. The thrust of the *Yorktown*'s turbines rolled the ships forward. Fifty feet on either side of the *Yorktown*'s wingtip, two huge, yellow fire trucks equipped with fifty-foot long orange-painted boom cherry-pickers, manned by teams of firefighters in white asbestos suits, scanned the ships intently, looking for the first indication of trouble, ready to save the crews in case of fire or other malfunction requiring an emergency escape. Together, the entourage of ground, air and space vehicles rolled across the tarmac. The growl of diesel engines and the whining of the turbines echoed across the flats, out and up into the desert air, until the armada reached its destination, the end of Runway 22, the Benchmark.

Approaching from the rear, a squadron of sleek silver F24 Condor chase planes taxied single file along-side the *Yorktown* and *Columbia*, piloted by fellow astronauts.

Thumbs-up gestures and waves for good luck were flashed. The chase squadron would take to the air soon and join the *Yorktown* and *Columbia* later in mid-air, escorting them for the first phase of the climb, scanning the ships for troubles undetected by the crews. The sixth plane in line, identified as 'Chase Camera', had the task of sending airborne TV pictures back to Mission Control and to the millions of viewers throughout the nation and around the world. If the purpose of the Chase Camera plane was special, so was its crew, the crew of the space shuttle *Enterprise* still in Mate-Demate Device #1 atop the *Hornet*. And they hoped and prayed that today's flight went perfectly. Next week, they would have their own turn.

Col Austin 'Tex' Harwood, a red-faced, sandy-haired, Air Force colonel with a 'good 'ol boy' image, brought his plane to a halt forty feet to the right of the *Yorktown*'s fuselage.

'Ah, Chase Leader?' he drawled. 'Chase Camera here, we, ah, are taking a close-up checkout. Join ya'll upstairs in five minutes.'

'Roger,' replied the Squadron Leader, continuing with his squad down the runway.

'Awright, Brooksie,' said Harwood, looking over his shoulder to his co-pilot behind him. 'Turn your little Brownie loose, we haven't got all day.'

'Don't call me Brooksie,' chided Dr Adrienne Brooks with a smile, focussing her portable TV camera on the *Yorktown*'s cockpit windows.

'Awright, Dr Brooksie then,' chuckled Harwood. Brooks smiled and ignored Harwood's ribbing. She adjusted the sights of her camera again.

Many other women had preceded Adrienne Brooks as shuttle astronauts in space. They, however, had been non-pilots, called 'Mission Specialists' – she thought the NASA acronym of MS ironic – specialists conducting on-board mission experiments. But Dr Adrienne Brooks was different. As a medical doctor specializing in muscle kinesiology, the mechanics of muscles, she had expected

39

to use her medical background with the muscle research NASA conducted in the zero gravity of space aboard the shuttle. The notion of actually being a shuttle pilot, of being in charge of flying a shuttle, had been beyond her expectations, and certainly beyond those of the Astronaut Candidate Selection Committee, until she took routine training tests and scored high, revealing a natural aptitude for flying unparalleled in all NASA's history of testing. Her degree in computer sciences made mastering the shuttle's computerized flight controls easier, but it was her natural instinct, perfect vision, and blinding reflexes that left the Selection Committee in a conundrum. What were they to do with her? She was just too good to be anything less than a pilot.

Perhaps NASA was male-dominated, but the males that mattered appreciated top talent regardless of sex. One Flight Controller in the first space shuttle flight had been an eighteen-year-old girl genius, a Flight Controller at that age because she was the best. Another had been Chief Simulations Operator, the person who planned and ran the entire Mission Simulations Process, because she too was the best.

It was as if Adrienne Brooks' resume had been printed in red. The thirty-six-year-old Californian would have made it into space sooner or later. Capcom Vince Torino's heart flutter kicked her chance from later to sooner. While Vince Torino had wept in frustration, she had wept tears of joy. Dr Adrienne Brooks became pilot of the space shuttle *Enterprise*.

For eighteen months she too had trained with Tex Harwood, with Bishop and Merriman and Lewis and Clark, and now in one week she would become the first woman astronaut to fly, not ride as a passenger, but actually fly a shuttle into space.

She adjusted her camera on the *Yorktown*'s cockpit and zoomed in tight on Rob Clark's helmeted head.

'*Yorktown* pilot, Chase Camera here. Have you in focus. Looking good.'

Absorbed as he was in the countdown checkout, the

friendly familiar voice caused Rob Clark to smile and he squinted out of the narrow slotted window at the silver jet and the camera lense staring at him.

'Roger, Chase Camera,' he said. 'Thank you. Just keep it in focus. Got to give Houston some good shots.'

The nasal voice of the Flight Controller cut through. 'Chase Camera, clear for take-off.'

Tex Harwood lurched the Chase Camera plane forward and Brooks looked back at the rapidly receding *Yorktown*.

'Just remember the briefing,' she said to Clark.

'Noted. With appreciation,' replied Clark, watching Harwood and Brooks race into the sky.

The small briefing room had been crowded earlier that morning. There were the twelve Chase Plane astronaut pilots, some attired in bright orange and others in navy-blue high-altitude pressure suits, and there were NASA and Air Force officials and camera-men recording it all. In the first row of gray fibreglass chairs facing the lectern and blackboards, were Bishop, Merriman, Lewis and Clark wearing casual slacks and polo-type pullovers and they listened attentively as the little gray man with the coke-bottle glasses and the rumpled gray suit read off the last-minute details with all the enthusiasm of someone reading a shopping list. It was a routine ritual, weather reports of unusually gusty winds, minor alterations in scheduling, and other matters of pre-flight interest.

'And that, gentlemen,' he said, ignoring Adrienne Brooks, 'is that. Good luck and good flying.'

The scraping of chairs filled the room as the astronauts came forward for last backslaps, jibes and handshakes with Bishop and Merriman, Lewis and Clark. The schedule stopped for no-one, however, and in seconds only Lewis and Clark and Brooks remained.

'Come on,' said Jack Lewis impatiently. 'Let's get going.'

Brooks, her curly blonde hair off-setting her powder-blue suit, stepped forward.

'Jack? Good luck,' she said, shaking his hand.

Lewis' eyes darted up and down, drinking in the toned, gymnast-fit figure, 'Wouldn't mind at all,' he thought

'Thanks Adrienne,' he replied. 'Let's go, Rob.'

'In a minute,' said Clark, placing some papers on the lectern.

'O.K., but we're due in the Suit Room in four minutes,' Lewis said, leaving the room. The hydraulic door's mechanical air pump whooshed and the door clicked shut.

Brooks extended her right hand. 'Col Clark? I just wanted to wish you the best.'

'Thank you, Dr Brooks,' he replied, taking her hand in his, and grinning at their mock use of formal titles.

'Are you going to write another book? About this flight?'

'If I do,' he said, pulling her into his arms, 'you'll be the heroine.' He held her tightly and kissed her and she did not resist. Indeed, she encouraged the embrace for long, tender, timeless seconds.

'I love you, Rob Clark,' she whispered. 'You take care of yourself.'

He ran his fingers through her soft curly hair. 'And I love you,' he replied. His eyes stared deep into hers, then travelled across her oval face, her rich, soft lips, her flawless complexion.

'What are you doing?' she said with a smile.

'Just memorizing your face . . . your blushing face.'

He held her about the waist and she traced lazy, circling patterns across his chest with her fingers.

'Listen, I got a call from Dr Quinn at Rice yesterday,' he said. 'They want me to start this Fall.'

'Teaching?'

'Well, that too. How about running the whole Depart ment of Aerospace Engineering?'

'And?' she beamed.

'And, I said yes.'

'Fantastic,' she said, kissing him again. 'Tonight, back in Houston, we'll have steaks to celebrate.'

'Your place?'

'Our place,' she chided.

'Our's soon. Right now, it's yours.'

'O.K. Mr Puritan,' she teased. 'My place.'

'And if we time it right, we can watch the take-off on the news. They'll be your pictures – a double celebration.'

Clark smiled as he remembered kissing her again. Now he watched as her jet flew off into the distance, joining the rest of the Chase squadron. The years of emotional emptiness after his family's death in the car crash never had been filled, despite his throwing himself into his work. Adrienne, however, had filled it to overflowing, and he thanked the heavens for the faceless Selection Committee that had chosen them to work together on the project.

'Come on, Rob,' said Lewis, pointing to his countdown list. 'Time for the Flight Control checkout.'

It was now 9:58 a.m. In Mission Control, Vince Torino said, 'Two minute warning, Doug'.

Pierce smiled. Just as a football team entered the last two minutes of a game with a pre-planned set of plays requiring no wasted time in the huddle, Pierce's team at Mission Control had all of their actions pre-planned, practiced and perfected. Final execution awaited.

In two minutes, it would all begin. Two years of planning, eighteen months of rehearsal, endless hours of Computer Mission Simulations, seven preceding lead-up flights in the project and an infinity of checks and rechecks of every part of every component of the whole system, all leading to this flight, the Eighth Flight, the 'proof of concept' flight, proof or denial of Pierce's concept.

At T minus 60 seconds, Torino advised Jack Lewis and Rob Clark that they could begin to throttle up the *Yorktown*'s five turbine engines at T minus 30. Lewis made certain the *Yorktown*'s parking brakes were still secure.

'Roger, Houston, throttling up at thirty.'

He glanced at a pensive Rob Clark. 'Ready?'

Clark nodded vigorously, his eyes riveted to his controls. 'Ready.'

'O.K., Rusty and Dick?' radioed Lewis. 'I take it you're all set?'

Bishop, monitoring the *Columbia*'s computer screen, grinned at Merriman. 'Set?'

'All set,' replied Merriman.

'O.K. then, Jack!' cried Bishop eagerly. 'Let 'er rip!'

'O.K. We'll do her pretty quick,' said Lewis, gripping the *Yorktown*'s throttles with his right hand. 'Hold on!'

The green digits of the *Yorktown*'s countdown clock ticked backwards and Jack Lewis radioed Mission Control, 'Houston? Picking up the count at . . . 33, 32, 31, 30!'

He pushed the throttles wide open. 'Throttling up!'

Already roaring at idle, the *Yorktown*'s five turbine engines responded instantly, gulping hundreds of gallons of air into the intake ports. Screaming furiously, the engines blasted fiery orange streamers out of the exhaust ports, blistering the runway's surface. A hundred yards away the soundwaves battered the men in the convoy trucks and fire trucks, until they could feel their internal organs vibrating and they pressed their hands against their protective headsets in a vain attempt to shut out the head-splitting roar.

Now at full power, the *Yorktown* began rocking up and down, extending the landing gear to its full range of movement, while Lewis and Clark waited for Mission Control verification of engine performance. Lewis radioed Mission Control, confirming what Pierce could see on his own monitor screen. 'Houston? Perfect burn on all five! Ready to roll! Do we have clearance?'

Pierce hesitated for a moment, conducted one last check on the *Columbia*, then stood in his console, his hands defiantly on hips, stared at the T.V. display screen at the front of Mission Control and said, '*Yorktown*, you are clear for take-off and go for brake release.'

'Roger, Houston!' Lewis replied. 'Hold on, *Columbia*! Here we go! Coming up on 10 seconds to brake release . . . Mark! 10 seconds, 9, 8, 7, 6, 5, . . .'

Above in the *Columbia*, Bishop and Merriman tensed themselves, waiting for the neck-jerking leap forward . . .

'4, 3, 2, 1 – Brake release!' cried Lewis.

The raw power of the *Yorktown* now unleashed, the great black mothership with its small passenger shuttle lunged forward, slamming the crews into their padded chairs as it hurtled down Runway 22.

Capcom Vince Torino immediately updated Lewis and Clark in a clipped staccato barrage of instructions. 'One mile down-field, speed 300, get your flaps to 10.'

'Flaps at 10 degrees,' replied Lewis in a strained voice, adjusting the flaps for more lift. Faster and faster the *Yorktown* raced, pitting power against gravity, thrust against drag, to break free from the bonds of Earth. Rob Clark, eyes glued to his controls, watched the speed and distance indicator numbers trip off, too quickly even to keep count, so quickly he could only keep pace with the progression by spitting out linked numbers, the first being speed and miles per hour, the second being distance in miles down the runway.

'One-eighty at two,' he said. 'Two-twenty at three . . . two-sixty at three-five . . .'

Then that unmistakable feeling, the nose wheels rising, losing contact with the runway!

'Nose wheel . . . coming up!' Clark waited an anticipatory second, waited for the feeling of flight. 'There!' he thought triumphantly, and again as the rear wheels came free, 'Houston!' he cried, 'we've cleared the field.' A blast of wind, the gusty, high winds that had been battering the base for the last couple of days, hit the ships, and they lurched precipitously, dipping the left wing. Lewis winced and pushed the rudder hard right. 'Damn!' he thought, but the power of the *Yorktown* was more than sufficient. The ship stabilized and resumed its climb.

Pierce looked at the digital chronometer above the world map: thirty-one seconds past 10 a.m. Right on schedule. At 297 miles per hour, 3·8 miles down the runway, the *Yorktown* was airborn and with it the *Columbia*. They were on their way.

Two thousand feet above the field, the chase squadron screamed over the outer perimeter of Edward's Air Force Base and closed in alongside the *Yorktown* and *Columbia*. As they approached, Adrienne Brooks activated her T.V. camera, sending crystal-clear in-flight images of the roaring *Yorktown* and passive *Columbia* back to Mission Control.

Ninety seconds after take-off the *Yorktown* had soared its way to 20,000 feet, and was now over ten miles east of Edward's, heading in a south-southeasterly direction, almost parallel to the U.S./Mexican border.

Lewis stole a glance at the deserts of Nevada far below. Damn, it felt good! Perfect take-off despite the blast of wind. Perfect because he was flying it.

Three minutes, twenty seconds after take-off, 40 miles down range, all on schedule. In less than 20 minutes they would be 1,448 miles east of Edward's, 70 miles high, almost directly above New Orleans, and there the Columbia would separate and climb into space.

Before separation, however, Bishop and Merriman in the *Columbia* rattled through a myriad of pre-separation checkouts on the *Columbia*'s computers. All systems were Go.

The *Yorktown* approached 80,000 feet and the atmosphere quickly thinned of oxygen. Soon the *Yorktown*'s trump card would be played, the unique dual propulsion system would come into effect and its five liquid hydrogen powered rocket engines would be ignited. The turbine system would be shut down and with the flip of a switch the *Yorktown* would be transformed into a rocket-plane. Its speed, already at a supersonic 1,600 miles per hour, would jump, vault indeed, to hypersonic – over 5,000 miles per hour.

Back at Mission Control Pierce looked at the flight plan: Rocket Ignition at 82,000 feet. He scanned his display screen for *Yorktown*'s actual altitude, now 81,000 feet and climbing fast. All incoming telemetry, the computerized information informing Mission Control of the status of the ships, confirmed the *Yorktown*'s hypersonic hydrogen propulsion system as ready to fire. Pierce jabbed another display button: *Yorktown*'s trajectory path was on line, exactly. Check the altitude again – 81,500 feet.

'O.K., Vince, *Yorktown*'s go for rocket ignition.'

As Torino forwarded the authorization to the *Yorktown*, Pierce realized that the flight had reached another key hurdle. If the rockets failed, they were ready to abort the climb and return to base. But Pierce's mind was not on abort or failure, or another flight someday in the future.

'Roger,' replied *Yorktown* commander Jack Lewis. 'Confirm we are go for rocket ignition. Altitude now 81,700.' He glanced quickly at Clark, who nodded.

'O.K., Houston,' said Lewis, placing his hand on the ignition switch. 'We're on the mark, we are on the launch heading, we are now go for ignition in . . . 10 seconds, on the mark – Mark! . . . 10, 9, 8, 7, 6, 5, 4, 3, 2, 1,' Lewis pushed the button. *'Ignition!'*

The five rocket engines came alive, belching flaming contrails into the thinning atmosphere, jolting the ships forward and up, quickly pulling away from the chase planes. 'God! What a shot!' thought Rob Clark.

In Mission Control, Pierce's eyes fixed on the telemetry monitoring the rocket engines' performance. 'On the money,' he thought. The turbine engines were no longer necessary, the rockets had taken over.

He radioed Lewis and Clark, '*Yorktown*, we read a perfect burn. You are go for shutdown on turbines and clear to climb to the separation altitude.'

Jack Lewis' hopes surged with Pierce's order. 'Roger, Houston, we have shutdown on the turbines, we're going up.'

In seconds, the *Yorktown* had pulled away from the chase planes, leaving them far behind, like a racing car passing a stalled competitor on the track. Lewis' speed indicator leapt from 1,800 miles per hour to 2,500 miles per hour and thereafter continued in surges of over a hundred miles an hour every second.

The leader of the chase squadron shook his head in amazement. Though they were flying the fastest fighter jets in the world, he and his squadron were being left behind by the colossal power of the world's fastest aircraft, the *Yorktown*.

'They are saying goodbye to us,' he radioed his co-pilots. 'Houston? Chase Leader here. We'll leave Brooks and Harwood to take pictures, but we're breaking off and coming home.'

The pilot looked up and ahead into the deep blue heavens, at the quickly disappearing *Yorktown* and *Columbia*. '*Yorktown* and *Columbia*, this is Chase Leader – good luck and Godspeed.'

'Thanks for the escort,' replied Clark from the *Yorktown*. 'See you back in Houston in an hour.'

The chase plane squadron's five planes formed up into a V-wing alignment, and then one by one, like swallows, banked and dived to the left in beautifully symmetrical spirals, down, down and away, leaving the skies to the *Yorktown* and *Columbia* and to Brooks and Harwood in the camera plane. In no way could Brook's and Harwood's jet hope to keep pace with the *Yorktown*, but with their camera's telephoto capacity, they could at least keep the *Yorktown* in view.

'Just keep following them, Tex,' Adrienne said, increasing her magnification.

'Will do, Brooksie,' drawled Harwood.

In Mission Control, the propulsion engineer's screen continued to display rapidly changing numbers, numbers he would have described as beautiful, beautiful because the *Yorktown* was carrying the *Columbia* at precisely the rates the computers had predicted. *Yorktown*'s speed was now increasing so quickly that altitude was being expressed not in feet, but in miles, miles being eaten up in the climb to the *Columbia*'s separation point:

'Speed 3,100, altitude 22·3,' said Jack Lewis crisply.

'Roger, *Yorktown*, Trajectory has you on the money,' replied Vince Torino. 'You are 5 minutes 10 seconds from *Columbia*'s separation.'

In the *Columbia*, Bishop and Merriman's job was really about to begin. At 4,200 miles per hour, 33·5 miles altitude, the Earth's curvature had become distinct and the sky's blue was quickly yielding to the black of space. But their concentration on their controls was absolute and for a good reason. It was they, the crew of the *Columbia*, who would fire the explosive bolts holding the shuttle to the *Yorktown*. Bishop glanced at the separation switches. 'Five minutes,' he thought. In Mission Control, Brooks' pictures were so distinct, the sight of the two mated ships so magnificent, that the Flight Controllers longed to watch. But to their trained eyes the numbers and graphs on their console screens registered clearer, still more magnificent evidence no pictorial image could record. If nothing else, however, the television-viewing public were being treated to a spectacular display, to be climaxed in minutes with the breath-taking sight of the ships' separation and the *Columbia*'s climb into orbit.

Pierce monitored the incoming reports from his Flight Controllers with increasing satisfaction. The instrumentation and communication engineers' data showed that the three geo-synchronous satellites of NASA's tracking system were handling to absolute perfection all communications between Mission Control and the crews. The trajectory engineer reported to Pierce in an almost casual tone that the *Yorktown* after travelling over 1,000 miles and now over 45 miles up into the atmosphere, was off its pre-planned angle of climb by a mere one hundred feet. Inwardly, the engineer felt triumphant, and a slow smile crossed Pierce's face. They were going to do it.

The propulsion engineer faced a delightfully satisfying problem. The *Yorktown*'s use of hydrogen propellants was less than one tenth of one percent below the predicted rate. For a second he did not know whether to be pleased or disappointed, pleased because the *Yorktown* was using less fuel, or disappointed because he was off his projected target, albeit by less than one percent. He decided he was, overall, pleased.

By 10:19 a.m. the *Yorktown* had carried the *Columbia*

over 1,400 miles, and they were almost above New Orleans and closing on the separation point. For Lewis and Clark the mission was almost over. For *Columbia* astronauts Bishop and Merriman, the active phase of their mission was about to begin. In a mere sixty seconds Bishop and Merriman would ignite the *Columbia*'s three main engines and after confirmation of a good burn and after approval from Pierce, they would then hit the separation switch, freeing them from the *Yorktown* for their solo climb.

The clock ticked down relentlessly to the scheduled ignition of the *Columbia*'s engines. Yet unlike all other key events and manoeuvres in the flight, the actual moment of the *Columbia*'s separation from the *Yorktown* had no specific countdown time schedule. The separation of two mated aircraft even at subsonic speeds of four hundred miles per hour was, at best, a dangerous proposition, requiring steel nerves on the part of the pilot, a deft touch of the controls and total obedience to the actual separation procedure. The slightest mistake by man or machine, the tiniest deviation from the plan could result in disaster. But at hypersonic speeds of over five thousand miles per hour, the speeds the *Yorktown* and *Columbia* were travelling now, the separation manoeuvre required a precision far beyond the physical capabilities of the crews, a precision attainable only by the ships' on-board computers. An attempt by Bishop and Merriman to effect the separation manually would be pure suicide.

One NASA engineer once described the reflexes required of an astronaut to separate manually the ships at hypersonic speed. 'It would be as difficult as someone facing a golfer about to drive a golfball, reaching down as the golfer started to swing and pulling the golf tee out from under the ball just as the club made impact with the ball. Possible? Yes. Probable? No way. And the penalty for a mistake is severe.'

Therefore the computers, not the crews handled the bulk of the separation manoeuvre. Upon reaching the launch heading the computers would take control and verify that the *Yorktown*'s speed, altitude and angle of attack were exact. They would check that the *Columbia*'s engines were firing perfectly before separation, then confirm all of the *Columbia*'s systems as ready, double-check the entire program one more time and finally cause a green light on the *Columbia*'s control panel to glow. Bishop as commander would then hit the Auto Separation Switch, a round, flat button two inches in diameter, firing the explosive bolts of the Support Structure Assembly holding the two ships together. Then and only then would the *Columbia* be set free for its climb.

In the *Yorktown*, Lewis noted their speed and altitude: five thousand and seventeen miles per hour, 71 miles altitude.

'O.K. Rob, almost there,' he said. He radioed Bishop and Merriman in the *Columbia*. 'Rusty? We're coming up on the separation point. We're on the launch heading.'

'O.K., that's great!' bubbled Bishop. '*Columbia*'s ready. Thanks for the lift, guys.'

'*Yorktown* and *Columbia*,' announced Pierce in Mission Control, 'twenty-five seconds to *Columbia* ignition and, ah, the trajectory engineer has you still one hundred feet within our pre-programmed separation altitude.'

Lewis gripped the *Yorktown*'s control stock and allowed himself a smile. 'Close enough for us,' he said.

'As they say, close enough for government work, right?' quipped Bishop in the *Columbia*.

'Close enough,' chuckled Pierce. 'You're ten seconds to ignition.'

Miles below, far away from the *Yorktown* and *Columbia*, Adrienne Brooks held the image of the ships in view. In seconds her pictures would relay to Mission Control and to the world the raw power of a shuttle under full throttle. Fleetingly, she thought of Rob Clark in the *Yorktown*, now holding the aircraft on its steady climb. 'Way to go, Rob,' she thought.

The *Columbia*'s on-board computers had re-assessed the tens of millions of variables. All systems were go. The green separation indicator light on Bishop's control panel. lit up. In ten seconds the shuttle's three main engines would come alive, pouring on 1,500,000 additional pounds of thrust.

Bishop swallowed hard, inhaled and placed his right thumb on the *Columbia*'s Auto Separation Switch. He counted down to Main Engine ignition, 'Seven seconds to ignition,' he announced, '5, 4, 3, 2, 1, Ignition!'

The *Columbia*'s engines, conically-shaped and eight feet in diameter at the exit point, belched forth three violently orange flames, all the more startling by contrast with the blackness of near space. The roar worked its way through to the cockpit of the *Columbia* and, vibrating through the Support Structure Assembly, down into the *Yorktown*.

If exhilarating, the sensation of rapid acceleration, the vibration of power tingling throughout the ships, was also reassuring. It was a known and anticipated feeling. Just as a golfer feels the solid 'click' of a drive, and knows without seeing it that it is a perfect shot, the vibration of acceleration told the crews that all was well.

Even so, the crews were overwhelmed by the feeling, and the fact that the *Columbia* was now actually pulling the *Yorktown* up with it! The shuttle, hitherto an inert passenger simply taking a ride, had become the carrier!

The moment, the second of decision, had arrived for Pierce. Go or No Go, the choice was Pierce's, and Pierce's alone. He scanned his console. The indicators were all green, each screen Go, each said now!

Jack Lewis and Rob Clark waited impatiently in the *Yorktown*.

'Come on, Pierce!' muttered Clark.

Pierce prepared himself to give the *Columbia* the order to separate, but waited for one final confirmation of the *Columbia*'s readiness from the propulsion engineer. If the engineer confirmed a clean burn of the *Columbia*'s engines, they were away.

The engineer's confident voice came over Pierce's

headset. 'Flight? Propulsion. I confirm a clean burn by *Columbia* and we—'

The engineer's throat seized up. Pierce frowned at the jarring silence. A shiver shot up the engineer's spine. His console! The *Yorktown*! Red numbers flashed on his screen. 'The *Yorktown*'s fuel line! The numbers!' he thought in a panicky flash. 'They are all wrong!'

In the cockpit of the *Yorktown* and on the engineer's console, malfunction buzzers sounded in tones sickeningly flat. Pierce's eyes widened and he stabbed at his display button to see what the propulsion engineer saw. The buzzing droned through his headset. In the *Yorktown*, Lewis and Clark saw the print-up warning on their display screens and it chilled them. Instinctively, they held their controls more firmly.

'Houston!' snapped Lewis. 'We—'

Deep from within the mechanical innards of the *Yorktown*, came a dull thump. Then a terrible shudder shook Lewis and Clark. The ugly vibration transmitted itself through the *Yorktown* up to the support structure assembly holding the ships together and into the *Columbia*'s cockpit. Bishop and Merriman felt it and stared at each other. Their bodies were trained to feel, as much as to hear and see. They knew the vibration was horribly, and terribly, wrong.

But as suddenly as it had begun, the vibration stopped. Jack Lewis' voice was amazingly calm but the import of his words ripped through Mission Control like a grenade. 'Houston, we've just had a problem. Systems malfunction, engine fuel lines 1 through 5 inclusive.'

Lewis' message and its numerical confirmation on his console screen staggered Pierce.

A single tank in the *Yorktown* had failed, and with far-reaching consequences. At that moment, no-one in Mission Control, neither of the crews, knew exactly which tank had failed, but they could see the horrific results on their screens. The *Yorktown* was not out of fuel, but, almost as bad, the pressure needed to transport the fuel to the *Yorktown*'s engines was plunging, and rapidly. The engines still fired. The *Yorktown* still flew. But in minutes the pressure would collapse and the engines stop, and like an arrow reaching the top of its arc, the *Yorktown* would falter and fall back to Earth.

Pierce had to act. The flight was on the verge of being aborted. Lewis and Clark had minutes of fuel left with which to begin an emergency descent to an altitude where the *Yorktown*'s still operational turbine engines could be turned on again to land both ships safely. Their altitude was still 71 miles, 53 miles too high to activate the air-breathing turbines.

Fear swept Mission Control. Not one Flight Controller, not even Pierce, had ever dreamt that such an accident would occur, but each was acutely aware that an accident was only an unanticipated event, an event they, of all people, should have anticipated. There was no panic, no fumbling. Months and months of computerized mission simulations had drilled them in the precise procedure response to hundreds of disaster scenarios. This accident was no exception. Pierce's Flight Controllers and the crews of the *Yorktown* and *Columbia* knew exactly the steps required of them.

In the NASA Personnel Manual, the roles of the Flight Team are described. The Propulsion Engineer's function is to monitor the Hypersonic Jet *Yorktown* and the Shuttle *Columbia*'s propulsion systems. During a launch the Manual states that he is authorized to 'recommend aborts for major failures on hypersonic launch vehicle and space shuttle systems.'

But the decision was Pierce's. If the propulsion engineer's analysis confirmed that the *Yorktown*'s engines would soon stop firing from lack of pressure in the fuel line systems, Pierce would order a shift to a prepared contingency plan. If confirmation came, he would order the *Columbia* to shut down its engines. The two vehicles would remain mated. The *Yorktown* would begin an emergency descent until it reached an altitude low enough to allow its air-breathing turbine engine system to be reactivated. The *Yorktown* would change its course to the Kennedy Space Center in Florida, and there they would land.

The words PROPULSION ABORT flashed on Pierce's screen. That was his confirmation. There was no alternative. The flight had failed. He would give the order to abort the flight. The *Columbia* and *Yorktown* would return to Earth. Pierce's throat was dry, but he spoke clearly and quickly.

'*Yorktown*, *Columbia*, this is the Flight Director—'

A clanging warning sound stopped him in mid-sentence. More red numbers came up on his console screen. The *Yorktown*'s turbine engine system, the sole remaining source of power, had just been knocked out and with it the only way the *Yorktown* could effect an emergency landing.

On board the *Yorktown*, Lewis and Clark were awaiting Pierce's abort order when there was a ripping sound and a muffled thud. The *Yorktown* shook violently and their screens lit up.

'Houston,' cried Clark, 'we've just had a real bang, a—'

From the chase camera plane far below, Adrienne Brooks stared in wide-eyed horror through her lens.

'Houston!' she cried. '*Yorktown*'s underside!'

Pierce's concentration, like all of the Flight Controllers, had been directed to the numbers on his console and not the huge video-display screen at the front of Mission Control. When he looked up, he was sickened. A portion of the *Yorktown*'s underside had ripped away, exposing an ugly gash at least twenty feet long and four feet wide.

'Holy Mother of God!' he said.

Inescapable truths assailed the Flight Director. If the *Yorktown* descended to a lower altitude with such a hole in its belly, the denser atmosphere would literally rip the craft apart. For the first time in his career, Pierce was gripped by unbridled fear.

A terrified Jack Lewis, his heart rate at a startling one hundred and fifty beats per minute, spoke from the

Yorktown with the terse finality of a doomed man. 'Houston. Wholesale turbine system malfunction. We're losing fuel! Down to 50%, 40%, 35, 25 – 20—'

The propulsion engineer frantically cut through on Pierce's headset. 'Flight, we're losing it! Her fuel's plunging! There's nothing left to land with!'

Pierce was staggered. All the backups, the options, the rehearsals, were now of no use to him or to the crews. The accident had thrown them all into a nightmare world beyond their experience. For Lewis and Clark, the *Yorktown*, a responsive obedient ship whose performance was a reflection of their skills, had mutated into a wild runaway monster, a speeding auto, its steering crippled, its brakes gone, its throttle welded wide open. They did not panic, but their instincts coldly announced their fate.

It was all up to Pierce. The lives of four men rode on his next decision. He had mere seconds to act before the collapsing pressure in the *Yorktown*'s fuel line system would cause the engines to sputter, gasp and fade, leaving both ships coldly inert and on the point of a dive, from a height of seventy miles, into the ocean.

In Chase Six, Tex Harwood watched his own fuel gauge with increasing concern. The F-24 Condor was approaching its fail-safe point, the point beyond which a safe return to the Kennedy Space Center would be impossible.

'Houston, Chase Camera Plane at the fail-safe!' he reported.

'Screw the fail-safe!' snapped Adrienne Brooks behind him. 'They need the pictures!'

Pierce's order to the chase plane was blunt. 'Keep going,' he said.

Sweat beaded Pierce's forehead. There was one option, an emergency manoeuvre his team of flight controllers had simulated only once, and at that, unsuccessfully. The essential simplicity of the manoeuvre attracted him, but there was all too strong a probability that it would prove futile. It would not resolve the problem, but at worst it would buy time! Precious time! And if he did not try it, then his inaction would seal the crews' fate.

The ships could not land. The *Columbia* might be able to separate from the *Yorktown* and descend safely. But separation would leave Lewis and Clark in the battered *Yorktown* facing an unpowered descent. When the hypersonic jet with its exposed belly encountered the thicker atmosphere below, the ship would surely be torn to shreds. Separation might, just might, give Bishop and Merriman in the *Columbia* a chance, but it would kill Lewis and Clark. There were still seconds of life remaining to the *Yorktown*'s hypersonic engines. The two ships could not continue to fly together, but could they climb? Climb together into orbit? In simulation the manoeuvre had failed, but this was real.

Pierce's mind was made up. He gave the order.

'*Yorktown, Columbia*, remain mated! You are go for mated orbit – I say again, go for mated orbit! Bring your nose up and go for mated orbit!'

Capcom Vince Torino stared at Pierce in horror, dumbfounded by the Flight Director's seeming recklessness, before he grasped its essential logic. In the *Yorktown* Lewis and Clark absorbed the implications of attempting to go for a mated orbit with the *Columbia*, and so did their colleagues Bishop and Merriman.

'Let's do it, Jack! *Columbia* is go!' said Bishop.

'O.K.' replied Lewis. '*Yorktown* is go!'

'Roger,' bellowed Bishop in the *Columbia*. 'Roger! Nose coming up! Give us the numbers, Houston! Give us the numbers!'

The desperation in their voices carried through the Flight Controllers' headsets. Pierce's hand-picked Flight Team, the pick of a select few, responded. They prepared to exploit the full potential of the computer complex, and in seconds were calculating the precise altitude and speed the *Yorktown* would have to achieve to fling both ships together into an orbit that might last long enough to enable a rescue shuttle to be scrambled to save them. The Flight Controllers' fingers flickered across their keyboards. Orders flew to subordinate flight team members outside Mission Control. They all knew, as did the crews, that if the specific speed and altitude projected by the computers were not met, it would all be over.

Almost at once, the Real Time Computer Complex had responded and target numbers flashed onto Pierce's screen: speed, 17,500 miles per hour; altitude 99·317 nautical miles. That was it! Those were the targets! As Pierce jabbed at his keyboard, displaying the two numbers on the number one screen at the front of Mission Control, he radioed the crews.

'O.K. Here are your numbers. Speed, seventeen-five, altitude nine, nine point three one.'

'Copy that!' Lewis' voice was shaking slightly. 'Seventeen-five and niner, niner, three.'

The *Yorktown* and *Columbia* roared on, accelerated, climbing beyond certainty and hurtling toward space beyond the realms of theory and into the unknown.

Vince Torino read them their program. 'Your speed is 7,400. Your altitude is 79·9. O.K., speed now 8,000, altitude 84·5.'

The chase camera plane had passed fail-safe. The *Yorktown* was now no more than a speck in the lens of Adrienne Brooks' camera. Utterly despondent, she switched the camera off and bit her lower lip in frustration.

'That's it, Tex,' she sighed. 'Take us home.'

'If I can . . . if I can,' he responded. The F-24 banked into an emergency dive. Brooks and Harwood listened to the communications over their headsets with growing doubt and resignation.

'Dear God,' Brooks prayed silently, 'save them.'

Pierce's face was taut with concentration. It was now a matter of how long the fuel would hold out. If it lasted long enough there was a chance, if not . . .

Capcom Vince Torino's voice was low and fear filled as he looked at Pierce. 'Doug? They're falling short.'

'I know, I know,' replied Pierce. 'Keep giving them the numbers.'

'Your altitude is now 87·3, your speed, 10,000,' said Torino.

Jack Lewis spoke. 'Houston, we read 90 seconds pressure left in the fuel line!'

'Ninety seconds,' thought Pierce, 'they won't make it.' 'Roger, *Yorktown*,' Pierce replied. 'Keep it going!'

'Altitude 90, speed 12,300,' said Torino.

Pierce watched the two key numbers on the screen. The target altitude was 99·3 miles. The target speed was 17,500. If the *Columbia* failed to pull the *Yorktown* to that altitude and that speed, the orbit would decay within hours, the ships re-enter the atmosphere. Friction. Fire. The crews would be lost.

'O.K., *Yorktown* and *Columbia*,' said Pierce flatly, 'Trajectory has you on your target, your altitude is now 88 miles, your speed is 12,900 . . . a little higher, a little faster!' 'Too short! Too short!' he thought frantically.

'Houston, we have 60 seconds of fuel left . . .' Jack Lewis' voice trailed off. He did not have to complete the sentence. The unspoken message was understood by all. They would know their fate in a matter of seconds.

Vince Torino kept updating the numbers. 'Altitude, 92·9 miles, 7 miles to go, your speed is 13,800.'

'Houston, 30 seconds fuel left,' said Lewis.

The crews' heart rates had climbed over 160 beats a minute.

Torino continued. 'Speed, 14,800. Altitude 94·4. Your propellants are at 5%, 4% . . . Your speed is 15,000, altitude 94·7.'

Pierce stared at the target numbers on his screen. 17,500 miles per hour, 99·3 miles altitude.

Rusty Bishop's voice cut in. 'Houston! Engine shutdown! We are out of fuel. Orbit . . . orbit achieved!'

Pierce stared in disbelief at the huge display screens. Deathly silence descended upon Mission Control, as the Flight Controllers looked up. The target for a minimum safe orbit had been 99·3 miles. The screen said 94·7. The target speed had been 17,500 miles per hour. The screen said 15,100 miles per hour. An orbit had been achieved, but it was too low to be maintained for long. There was no doubt the *Yorktown* and *Columbia* would plunge back to Earth and burn up. The law of gravity would see to that. The only question was when. Pierce's gamble had bought some time. Would it be enough? And in a ship not designed to travel in outer space and holed into the bargain, how long could Lewis and Clark survive?

CHAPTER THREE

Bishop's last communication, 'Orbit achieved', echoed and re-echoed throughout Mission Control. Traditionally, the word signified both a successful launch and the beginning of a ship's journey in a planned Earth orbit. Now, however, the meaning was totally different – a grim acknowledgement of defeat. Doug Pierce and his team of Flight Controllers sat stunned.

The emergency had tested them to their limits. They had rehearsed almost every conceivable accident scenario during months of Mission Simulation runs, but no situation, no rehearsal could have prepared them psychologically for what had just happened. As Bishop's voice faded from his headset, Pierce began the agonizing transition from the relatively routine administration of planned procedure, to the trafficking in the unknown.

Pierce's face and armpits were soaked in sweat. His mind was racing. How long would the ships be able to stay in orbit? Was the support structure attaching the shattered *Yorktown* to the *Columbia* damaged? What if it was broken, or about to break? Were the *Yorktown*'s life support systems still working? Reluctantly he ventured on the unthinkable: were Lewis and Clark still alive?

Pierce swallowed and switched on the P.A. System to communicate with the assembled flight controllers of the Gold Team.

'This is the Flight Director,' he said. 'Everybody keep cool. Start compiling status reports, we'll need them soon.' 'I hope we'll need them' he thought.

As Pierce reached to his console to open a communication line to the *Yorktown*, he was overwhelmed by the very real probability that there would be no answer. Wiping the perspiration from his forehead he jabbed at the communications button. His throat was dry, his voice hoarse.

'*Yorktown*? This is the Flight Director. Do you read us, *Yorktown*?'

Silence.

Pierce's eyes darted to his left-hand control screen. The table of green numbers indicated that the *Yorktown*'s life support system was working perfectly, that Lewis and Clark had air to breathe. Pierce listened, anxiously. A sinking feeling gripped him. He cleared his throat and spoke again with anxious impatience.

'*Yorktown*, this is Houston Flight Director. Do you read?'

High over the Caribbean, the *Yorktown* and *Columbia* sailed silently, south by southeast, through the black void. Most of the lights on the *Yorktown*'s instrument panel were dead. Those still working flickered spasmodically, casting green, eerie, random patterns through the darkened cockpit. Red emergency lights on the panel pulsed on and off, maddeningly confirming the obvious. A buzzer droned.

In the commander's chair, Jack Lewis' blanched face was as still as marble. In the pilot's seat, Rob Clark's unfocussed eyes stared out through the *Yorktown*'s starboard forward window, across the ship's black nose and down upon the pale green waters of the mid-Atlantic Ocean. As an amateur weather observer, the four hundred mile-wide cloud, a white catherine wheel would have sparked his interest, but it did not register.

His alarm increasing, Pierce stared at the positive life support system numbers on his screen and waited for an answer. 'Maybe,' he thought, 'these numbers are wrong!' Anxiously he contacted the computer engineer only to be stunned at his reply: The *Yorktown*'s on-board flight computers and the Real Time Computer Complex beneath Mission Control were no longer co-ordinated with each other! The numbers Pierce and his Flight Controllers saw on their screens did not match what Lewis and Clark saw, if they still saw anything. The readings on Pierce's screen telling him Lewis and Clark had air to breathe were, in all probability, quite wrong.

In the *Columbia*, Bishop and Merriman were fully occupied controlling the flight path and altitude not only of the shuttle, but of the *Yorktown* as well. Still, they listened anxiously to Pierce's vain attempts to raise the *Yorktown*.

'Take the controls,' Bishop ordered Merriman. Merriman pulled back on the pilot's control stock, releasing minute wisps of gas and elevating the *Columbia*'s nose five degrees above the horizon.

'She's sluggish, Rusty,' said Merriman, 'we're really burning propellants.'

Bishop ignored the comment. 'If they can't hear Houston,' he replied, activating ship to ship communications, 'maybe they can hear us.' 'God' he prayed, 'let them answer.'

'*Yorktown, Yorktown – Columbia* commander calling – Jack? Rob? Do you read?'

Nothing.

Bishop and Merriman exchanged despondent glances. The most senior astronaut in the United States space program tried again.

'*Yorktown* – this is *Columbia* . . .' His voice trailed off, then he snapped angrily, 'Damn it, *Yorktown*, answer us!'

'I am,' thought Lewis, 'in a plane. I am in space. We cannot re-enter the atmosphere, we will burn up.'

'Answer them,' muttered Clark, staring bleakly at the flickering controls.

Lewis silenced the warning buzzer, shut off the flashing emergency light and swallowed what little saliva was left in his mouth.

'Houston? *Columbia*? This is *Yorktown*. We read you both. We . . . ah . . . Rob and I are in one piece.'

Audible gasps of relief broke the silence in Mission Control.

'O.K., *Yorktown*,' said an elated Pierce. 'Great to hear you.'

They were at least alive – for now. But by virtue of the

fact that the accident had distorted the co-ordination between Mission Control's computers and those of the *Yorktown*, Pierce and the controllers did not know the operational reliability of any of the *Yorktown*'s systems, nor even whether any of the systems worked at all. Pierce felt all the helplessness of a doctor attempting to treat a dying patient without being able to see or touch him, with unlimited technology at his fingertips, which he was unable to use. The accident had placed him in the worst imaginable position: a Flight Director, unable to direct, in charge of a Mission Control complex he was unable to control.

The immediate concern was the *Yorktown*'s emergency power supply – the Battery A System. If it was intact, if the accident had not damaged it, then and only then was there a chance that the *Yorktown*'s life support system could keep Lewis and Clark alive long enough to attempt a rescue. With no reliable telemetric data from the *Yorktown* on his console screens Pierce could only rely on Lewis and Clark for the necessary information.

'O.K., listen up, guys – *Yorktown*, you're going to have to read down to us your life support status – the accident knocked out our telemetry.'

'No telemetry? None?' asked Lewis.

'None,' replied Pierce.

Pierce heard Lewis' sigh of resignation over his headset. 'O.K., Houston,' he said, scanning the cockpit. 'Most of our controls are dead – ah, I'm still reading full power on Battery A – yeah, the life support system is still working . . . for now.'

Pierce sighed with relief. There was a chance. He could now inform Lewis and Clark of the first step towards home.

'All right, *Yorktown*. The Flight Activities Officer will contact Vandenberg Airforce Base and they'll have the shuttle *Atlantis* readied – we'll have her up there in twenty-four hours.'

Lewis and Clark greeted the news with silence.

'*Yorktown*? Do you read?' asked Pierce.

'Roger,' replied Lewis, 'we read. Twenty-four hours.'
'Jesus' he thought. 'Twenty-four hours? At this altitude?'
He looked at his altitude indicator in frustration.

'Do we have that long?' he blurted. 'How long will our orbit hold up?'

Taken aback, Pierce pushed his trajectory display button. All orbiting objects are governed by the pull of Earth's gravity, ultimately falling prey to atmospheric re-entry. An object five hundred miles above Earth will stay in orbit for centuries. Above two hundred miles the atmosphere is so tenuous, an object as big as Skylab may take several years before burning up. Between one hundred and fifty and one hundred and thirty miles, the increased thickness of the atmosphere increases the drag so that objects are doomed to re-entry in a matter of days. The orbital altitude of the *Yorktown* and *Columbia* registering on Pierce's screen, was 94·4 miles.

'I said – how long will it hold?' repeated Lewis.

The trajectory engineer listening to the exchange quickly flashed his preliminary analysis on the ships' orbital stability onto Pierce's screen – re-entry would occur on Thursday, at approximately 2 p.m. There would be enough time to make a rescue attempt.

'Thank you, Trajectory,' muttered Pierce, relieved to have a positive answer for Lewis and Clark. He informed them their orbit would hold long enough for the *Atlantis* to rendezvous with them. But Pierce also wanted Lewis and Clark to be aware of his flight controllers' determination to resolve the entire dilemma.

'Jack and Rob? We're moving at this end as fast as we can. It's a tight situation, I know that, but Vandenberg will have the *Atlantis* ready in time. We have a lot of good people down here working for you.'

As Pierce spoke, Rob Clark's eyes wandered across the *Yorktown*'s flickering control panel, trying to grasp the full extent of his predicament and drawing no solace whatever from Pierce's attempts to reassure them. Easy for him, Clark thought bitterly, he's not up here!

Clark found himself staring at his suit and suddenly he

felt a sinking feeling in his stomach. Like any pilot in a crashing aircraft, Clark's attention in those first frantic moments in space had been entirely upon keeping the ship intact. Now another problem forced itself upon him. Yes, their life support system was working – they had air. Yes, the emergency power supply in Battery A would keep the cockpit warm and keep the life support system working. Yes, the standby rescue shuttle, the *Atlantis*, would be ready to rescue them within a day, and yes, the *Yorktown* might hold together for another twenty-four hours. But . . .

'Oh God,' Clark muttered. 'Jack . . . our suits!'

'Just a minute, Houston,' said Lewis, interrupting Pierce. 'What did you say, Rob?' He looked at Clark's horrified face.

'Our suits!' whispered Clark. 'Our goddamn suits.'

Jack Lewis stared at his colleague's high altitude pressure suit, then at his own. 'Damn,' he said through clenched teeth, 'damn!' Angrily he snapped open the communication line to Pierce in Mission Control. 'Houston? Before you get the *Atlantis* up here, you guys better figure out how Rob and me are going to space-walk out of this bus over to the *Atlantis*, 'cause we're both wearing high altitude pressure suits and if we step outside of this baby with what we got on, we'll be dead in two seconds!'

Doug Pierce's mind reeled with competing problems. Each component of the mission jockeyed with the others for immediate attention. Each system, each aspect of the ships and of the Mission Plan, seemed to be of equal importance, yet some factors stood out. That Lewis and Clark's suits could not withstand the vacuum of outer space meant any attempt to transfer from the *Yorktown* to the *Columbia* or even the rescue shuttle *Atlantis*, was simply impossible – a crippling, perhaps fatal blow to Lewis and Clark's chances for survival. There was, however, nothing Pierce or anyone else could do about that, at least not now. He would have to buy some time, long enough to create a new set of logistics for a transfer from ship to ship.

Pierce began to think urgently about the *Yorktown*'s relative position to the Earth. Even at an altitude of 94·4 miles, there were sufficient quantities of minute atmospheric particles to offer frictional resistance of 'drag' to the ships' orbital flight path, thereby slowing their speed and increasing their rate of fall back into the atmosphere. The lower the orbit, the denser the atmosphere, the worse the drag, the greater the friction, until at an altitude of sixty-eight miles, the combination of those factors would cause both ships to burn up.

The laws of nature ensured an inevitable re-entry. There was, Pierce knew, no way to stop the fall back to Earth. But there was a delaying tactic. The time the *Yorktown* and *Columbia* stayed in orbit could be lengthened by Bishop and Merriman keeping both vehicles as aerodynamically trim as possible. If they simply allowed the two mated vehicles to drift, the drag would increase and the time to the burn up in the atmosphere would decrease – drastically.

Bishop, however, had already anticipated the suggestion Pierce had yet to make. From the left hand seat of the space shuttle's flight deck, the commander of the *Columbia* pulled back on his control stock and began muttering a string of obscenities. The *Columbia* was not responding as it should. His frustration centred in his knowledge of the capabilities and limitations of the *Columbia*'s engines.

The first and main source of the shuttle's power belonged to the three main engines positioned at the *Columbia*'s rear. But they had already done their job, had burned up 1,122 lbs. of liquid hydrogen and liquid oxygen propellant each second, generating the 1,400,000 lbs. of thrust needed to get the *Yorktown* and *Columbia* into orbit. No, the three main engines were useless.

Nor could Bishop rely on the shuttle's twin Orbiting Manoeuvring System engines, located at the base of the tail rudder – not yet. The two OMS engines had assisted the three main engines in the climb, each generating 6,000 lbs. thrust utilizing a hypergolic propellant, nitrogen tetroxide oxydizer and monomethyl hydrazine, as fuel, which ignited on contact with each other. Their 'punch' was much less than the power packed by each main engine, but equally critical to their crew's survival. If Bishop was tempted to use the Orbiting Manoeuvring System, he wisely resisted, knowing that he would eventually need every ounce of propellant to reduce the *Columbia*'s speed before attempting to land. Now he began to wonder if he would ever have that opportunity.

As he pulled back on the control stock, Bishop activated the space shuttle's third propulsion source – the Reaction Control System. Located on the top and the side of the *Columbia*'s nose were fourteen primary engines, and two vernier engines the size of a man's forearm. The engines offered 870 lbs. and 25 lbs. thrust respectively. On either side of the tail in front of the two OMS engines, twelve additional primary and two vernier engines gave additional propulsion. Together the fore and aft primary and vernier engines formed the Reaction Control System. Normally, this system would have allowed Bishop deft adjustment of the shuttle's position. Now, Bishop cursed aloud.

'Not responding?' asked Merriman.

Bishop glowered at the controls, perplexed and confused. 'You try it,' he said.

Merriman took hold of his own control stock and pulled back gently. The shuttle's nose rose, causing the horizon to appear to dip below them, but much, much too slowly.

'Jesus,' he said.

Pierce's voice came over their headsets. '*Columbia*, we'd like to advise you to keep your attitude as trim as possible—'

'We're already doing that!' said Bishop. 'But you'd better crank up the computers down there for propulsion adjustment. This bus is as sluggish as a pig in muck. We're not programmed to haul excess baggage!'

In the *Yorktown* Jack Lewis bristled at the reference. 'Look, Bishop! You can take your—'

'Sorry Jack! But the fact of the matter—'

'This is the Flight Director,' said Pierce, cutting off the strained exchange. 'Can the chatter! That's an order! Now, we're loading the computers to compensate for *Yorktown*'s weight factor and *Columbia*'s handling. We will uplink that data to you as soon as it's ready. In the meantime, *Columbia*, you will fly on manual, and your orders . . .' He paused and then went on. 'Your orders are to maintain your trim. Clear?'

'Clear,' replied Bishop.

'O.K. Now we have a lot to do. First of all, your numbers on your computers and the numbers here in Mission Control are out of sync. We have to co-ordinate them before we can give the *Atlantis* a target to aim at.' Pierce glanced at Vince Torino. 'The Capcom will start it off. Flight out.'

Pierce motioned to Torino and the Capcom set to on the checklist again, the same one he had run through barely an hour earlier. Only this time the numbers weren't matching. Unless they did, the rescue launch of the *Atlantis* would be literally a shot in the dark.

Pierce contacted the rest of the flight controllers. He pulled no punches. 'This is the Flight Director. We have a real mess on our hands and right now I have no idea whether the *Yorktown* and *Columbia* will hold together up there long enough for us to do anything but watch. But I do know this. If we screw up here we'll finish them off, so let's keep our cool. What I need is status reports on every system, every component of both ships. I need them now.'

Summoning all his authority, Pierce began barking orders like a Marine drill sergeant, the sheer tone and power of which established with the flight controllers that in the midst of this life-and-death battle, their leader was still in control.

Their response was immediate and unquestioning, born of confidence in Pierce and of the months of repetitive mission simulations. The computer engineer fired up the Dynamic Stand-by Computer in the Mission Control Complex as a safeguard against any possible malfunction with Mission Control's Real Time Computer Complex. As an additional insurance policy, the Goddard Flight Center in Greenbelt, Maryland, activated its computer complex and flight controllers were put on duty. If both the Real Time Computer Complex and the Dynamic Stand-by Computer Systems at the Johnson Space Center were knocked out, Goddard could take over the flight. The odds of such double failure occurring were next to none; but so, thought Pierce, were odds on the *Yorktown*'s accident and its results.

The trajectory engineer brought the full NASA tracking network into operation. The Tracking Data Relay Satellite System, with its three geo-synchronous communication satellites, already offered blanket coverage of the globe, making constant communications with the ships possible, but the land-based Satellite Tracking Data Network, a back-up system of tracking stations dotted round the globe, was hastily called into play, just in case. The flight activities officer quickly contacted the flight director of the Blue Team, scheduled to replace Pierce's Gold Team at 2 p.m., and asked for them to come in early. The operations integration officer contacted the Department of Defense to set in motion the activation of contingency landing sites for the *Columbia* and *Atlantis* at various military bases throughout the United States. Nothing was being left to chance.

The switchboard at NASA hummed as calls were placed to the contractors throughout the United States and Canada who had built the various components of the *Columbia* and the *Yorktown*, instructing them to get to the Johnson Space Center immediately to render whatever emergency advisory assistance the flight controllers and their staff could use.

Within minutes of the accident, an armada of scientists, engineers and technicians were winging toward Houston. Pierce had flung NASA into high hear. He had to – it was a race against time.

It was 10:40 a.m., ten minutes since both ships had limped into their decaying orbit. In ten minutes the mission had disintegrated. For a moment Pierce allowed depression to overwhelm him. The problems paraded like spectres. The orbit was perilous. The *Yorktown*'s sole source of air depended on batteries. The extent of the *Yorktown*'s damage was unknown. Vandenberg Airforce Base had yet to establish when the *Atlantis* could be readied, and even if the *Atlantis* could be launched in twenty-four hours and if the *Yorktown* held together that long, Lewis and Clark would still have to transfer out of the *Yorktown* into the *Atlantis* to be saved, and the suits they wore offered no protection in space.

Next step, thought Pierce, the next step. Automatically, he consulted the flight plan before him on the console. The bold-faced type read: '10:40 – SHUTTLE INITI-ATES ORBITAL STABILIZATION MANOEUVRE – YORKTOWN RECEIVES LANDING INSTRUC-TIONS – KENNEDY SPACE CENTER.' His flight plan, indeed all of the flight plans in Mission Control, were totally irrelevant to the present situation. The document, prepared over months and months, meticulously itemizing every step each flight controller and the crews should take in their proper co-ordinated sequence, meant nothing. With obsolete flight plans, the Gold Team in Mission Control were flying blind. The vast apparatus that was the world-wide NASA network of people, computers, systems, machines, was now without guidance or direc-tion.

High out over the Atlantic, off the coast of Florida, the F-24 NASA Condor chase plane, carrying astronauts Tex Harwood and Dr Adrienne Brooks, had begun its descent towards the Kennedy Space Center. Their frantic attempts to provide Mission Control, Houston, with video pictures of the *Yorktown*'s accident and their interception of the terse frightened exchanges between Mission Con-trol and the crews in space, had left both Harwood and Brooks shaken. They flew now in numbed silence.

Methodically, mechanically, biting back tears,

71

Adrienne Brooks stowed her camera away. The events of the past few minutes would not leave her mind. Over and over again: the *Yorktown*'s underside ripping away; the visible shuddering of both ships; Pierce's order for her to go to maximum magnification; and then, the helpless lost feeling as she watched the *Yorktown* and *Columbia* climb inexorably up and away, until nothing but blackness filled her lens. A feeling of despair overcame her. She had just watched astronaut Rob Clark, the pilot of the *Yorktown*, disappear from her life, pulled into space, gone.

Silently she had prayed as Pierce had attempted to re-establish radio contact, something she only did during moments of utter helplessness. 'How had it happened?' she asked herself. 'Pilot error? No, it could not be. Lewis and Clark, especially Rob, were simply too damn good, too proficient. Equipment failure? It had to be.'

'Equipment failure,' she concluded out loud.

'What was that?' asked Harwood, his eyes riveted on his plummetting fuel gauge.

'I said, it had to be caused by an equipment failure.'

'Either way, it'll be a long time before we fly our mission,' said Harwood, resignedly.

An investigation into the accident's cause was inevitable. Their flight, next week, the duplicate confirmation flight of today's disastrous mission, would just as inevitably be cancelled and with it, Adrienne's chance to become the first woman astronaut to pilot a shuttle. Even if the cause could be determined today, the whole program, let alone their flight, would be on an indefinite hold. The disappointment was bitter, but disappointment was part of being an astronaut. Pilot appointments to flights were often changed; you learned to accept it.

'It's a hell of a long way home,' said Harwood, watching his gauges.

She nodded in agreement and thought again of Rob Clark in the *Yorktown*. 'At least . . .' she swallowed hard, 'at least while they're still alive, there's a chance,' she declared. 'There's got to be a chance!' she thought.

'I don't mean them—' Harwood began to reply.

A warning buzzer sounded in the cockpit, interrupting the husky Texan in mid-sentence. Brooks' eyes darted to her own control panel. 'Fuel' she thought. Harwood silenced the buzzer with a jab of his meaty right hand.

'We burned a lot of juice getting Pierce his pictures, past our fail-safe point,' Harwood's voice reflected no fear, just cold reality, 'and we're still a long way out,' he said. Brooks looked at her fuel gauge again, thoughts of Clark, her flight and the program wiped from her mind.

'How much farther to Kennedy?' she asked.

'Twenty miles,' snapped Harwood.

'Can we get there?'

'Too close to call . . . Kennedy Control, Kennedy Control, this is Chase Six, we have a problem and request emergency landing on the shuttle runway. Our fuel is down to zilch.'

Before the flight controller could reply, Harwood told Brooks what he was going to do next. 'Adrienne? Dropping the wing tanks' he said, flipping open the jettison switch. The cylindrical tanks on the tips of the Condor's wings which had provided them with sufficient fuel to chase the *Yorktown* and *Columbia* across the United States and out over the Atlantic, were now empty, thus increasing both their weight and drag. Now the tanks snapped away, tumbling end over end into the ocean below.

'Chase Six, Kennedy Control here. The shuttle runway is clear for landing. With your fuel situation, if you want to ditch, the Coastguard is standing by.'

The prospect of ploughing the 20 million dollar aircraft into the ocean horrified Harwood. Forced landings on any body of water were tricky enough, but with the swells of the Atlantic Ocean just off the Cape – no thanks. One mis-cue and it would be all over. Far safer to eject, even at low altitude.

'No thanks, Kennedy – I'm not much of a swimmer. Besides we've got lots of film on board and Mission Control will need the pictures. You all just get your trucks ready, I may just bounce this baby in.'

73

Before the controller could reply, Harwood glanced up from his controls. 'There it is, Adrienne!'

Far ahead on the horizon, sat the Kennedy Space Center. An enormous white, monolithic cube, the world's largest man-made structure by volume – the Vehicle Assembly Building – stood out in stark contrast to the verdant swamps surrounding the space port. Once Saturn V Rockets had been assembled there for Apollo's journey to the moon. In recent years space shuttles had been mated there to their solid-fuel rocket boosters and external fuel tanks. Now it served Brooks and Harwood as a visual beacon.

Tex Harwood's concentration, however, focussed on the shuttle runway, a straight stony-gray ribbon slashed through the swamps. Twenty-seven thousand feet long, the longest runway in the world, the only runway ever built exclusively for a space ship, the curvature of the Earth prevented an observer standing at its centre from seeing either end. 'Twenty-seven thousand,' thought Harwood, 'we may need every foot of it.'

'Kennedy? Have you in sight,' he said.

Simultaneously, an orange light the size of a dime began flashing on both Harwood and Brooks' control panels, accompanied by a distractingly repetitive 'beep-boop – beep-boop' chime, alerting the two astronauts to the fact that the twin-engined F-24's Number 1 tank was almost empty. The beeping became a solid high-pitched whine – empty. The jet lurched at the loss of power.

'Number 1 out,' said Harwood. 'One left, two miles from touchdown.'

'Chase Six? Kennedy Control. Our trucks are standing by.'

Harwood blinked away the perspiration trickling off his brow. 'Roger, Kennedy. There's time to bail out, Adrienne, this will be rough!'

Brooks looked down at the green-blue waters below, seemingly close enough to touch. 'Screw you, Tex. I'm staying!'

'Lousy swimmer too, huh?'

A blue light the size of a quarter flashed on their screens, followed by a whining horn – they were one thousand feet from the runway.

'O.K., Kennedy,' said Harwood, '800 feet . . . down to 700 . . . 600 . . .'

With the port engine out, and the starboard engine still operational, Harwood fought the jet's tendency to veer left by compensating heavily with the tail rudders. The second orange light for the remaining engine's fuel supply came on; the 'beep-boop' chime followed.

'Three hundred feet out,' Harwood said. 'Too short! Too short!' he thought. 'O.K., gear coming down!' He waited till the last second to lower the gear, not wanting it to increase their drag any sooner than absolutely necessary.

At two hundred feet Chase Plane Six passed the runway's end marker. The earth rushed up to meet them. At one hundred and twenty feet the beeping became a solid whine. The roar of the engine died, and the silence was broken only by the whistling of air past the fuselage.

'No power!' cried Harwood.

Now Harwood's skills as a space shuttle astronaut came into play. Just as the shuttle glided to an unpowered landing, so too the F-24 approached the earth in a no-power glide. But there was a difference. The space shuttle had been designed to glide in, the F-24 had not. The slightest error on Harwood's part would prompt a stall, and slam the jet into a disintegrating pancake landing. Harwood gripped his control stock, keeping the nose low enough to prevent a stall and high enough to prevent the nose gear from crumpling on contact.

'Hold on!' he yelled. 'This is it,' thought Brooks, clenching her teeth.

Like a scarcely guided brick, the jet ploughed into the surface, ramming the landing gear's hydraulic shock absorbers up into the guts of the plane. The jet shook viciously, the tires smoked and screamed as the friction of contact transformed their solid black compound into a white gas. Brooks winced as the wrenching touchdown slammed her into her seat, shooting pain up her spine.

The F-24's nose bounced crazily up into the air then slammed down again. Harwood stood on the brakes, quickly bringing the racing jet to a manageable eighty miles per hour.

'That,' said Adrienne Brooks, 'was the worst landing I have ever seen in my life!'

'That,' replied Tex Harwood with a chuckle, 'was a good landing, 'cause we're going to walk away from it. We'll get this thing refueled and head to Houston.'

In Mission Control the World Map Projector Plotter traced the ships on their first orbit, the bold yellow line coursing southeast across the Atlantic towards Africa. The Mission Elapsed Time Chronometer above the world map read 10:15:15 – just over 15 minutes since orbit had been achieved.

The muscles in Pierce's neck and the small of his back ached from tension and he stood up and stretched to ease them. 'Vandenberg' he thought, 'the flight activities officer should know by now.'

Pierce walked quickly behind Vince Torino, still coordinating the computers in Mission Control with those of the *Yorktown*, and headed down the third row of consoles to the FAO – the flight controller whose job was unique. His specific duties included the integration of rescue launch procedures, the co-ordination of computer simulation runs for such launches, and the development of the crews' emergency activities. Unlike his fellow flight controllers, the better a flight went, the less the flight activities officer had to do. At Pierce approached his console, the officer had never been busier in his life. He saw Pierce coming and correctly anticipated the first question.

'Vandenberg will have the *Atlantis* ready for launch at 10:05 tomorrow morning he announced. 'Less than 24 hours,' thought Pierce.

The flight controller continued, 'As soon as the *York-*

town's first tank failed, Vandenberg started preparations for an emergency countdown.'

'Before we even got the men into orbit?'

'Before. It was a hunch on their part – said they were trying to buy us some time, and they will be ready to co-ordinate the countdown with us in forty-five minutes.'

Pierce nodded his approval. 'Very good – well done. Who's flying the *Atlantis*?'

'Lionel Gerber and Gordon Alexander.' Pierce nodded again with relief. The two astronauts had been the crew of the first flight to construct the experimental solar power station satellite.

'What about simulation practice times for them?' he asked.

'The simulations operations team here at the Space Center are loading the docking simulation run into their computer. We'll have it patched out by satellite to Vandenberg's simulation facility within an hour.'

'Not that they'll really need it,' said Pierce. 'They're experienced enough. Rendezvous shouldn't be too diffi-cult, even at such a low altitude.'

'There is one thing though . . .'

'What's that?'

'Gerber was in the control room at Vandenberg when I called. He wants to know how he and Alexander are supposed to get Lewis and Clark out of the *Yorktown* alive.'

'You mean their suits?'

'It was Gerber's first question.'

'I don't know – we'll have to get the status reports recorded here before we can turn to that one.' Pierce sighed and stared up at the world map. 'We've got to stay on top of this,' he said. 'We can't let it get away from us any more than it is now.' He turned to the FAO. 'The new flight plans? When do we get them?'

'On order. Be here any—' The flight controller stopped and pointed to the front of Mission Control. Four men came in, with armloads of thick blue binders – the new rescue flight plans.

'There they are,' he said.

Pierce returned to his console and interrupted Torino's conversation with the crews in orbit. 'Tell them we've got the flight plans. Now we can get moving.'

With the distribution of the new blue binders to each flight controller and the removal of the thicker, now useless original flight plan, the countdown to the rescue launch could begin. It was 10:55 a.m. Twenty-four minutes into the *Yorktown* and *Columbia*'s first orbit.

Pierce contacted his flight controllers. 'In five minutes, at eleven on the button, we'll co-ordinate the rescue flight plan with Vandenberg Airforce Base. Until them, keep at the status reports.'

The new flight plan's reverse chronological timetable of events was calibrated on a twenty-four hour countdown period, commencing at 24:00:00. The Vandenberg counterparts to the flight controllers in Mission Control had their own copies.

Moments before eleven a.m. Pierce spoke both to his team at the Johnson Space Center and to their counterparts at Vandenberg, California. 'We will be using the number five chronometer above the video display screen,' he said, looking at the digital clock above the now blank far right-hand screen at the front of Mission Control. Its white, digital numbers sat frozen at 24:00:00. It was now 10:59 Houston time. 'All right, Gold Team, and Vandenberg – we will commence rescue countdown in 5 seconds, 4, 3, 2, 1, now!'

The chronometer began ticking backwards, 23:59:59 – 58 – 57 . . . 'Now we have something to work from!' thought Pierce. 'Now at least we have a reference point!'

In conjunction with their own staff members in the computerized staff support rooms next to Mission Control, the flight controllers had preliminary status reports on the condition of the *Yorktown* and *Columbia* prepared by 11:30. The reports were tentative assessments of the situation – detailed analyses would take much longer – but upon those reports depended the future actions of the flight controllers, and most important, the decision as to whether a rescue was even feasible. Nervous anticipation swept the room. No single flight controller knew exactly what his counterparts had discovered. As each piece in the puzzle was presented the Capcom, Vince Torino, relayed the information to the crews.

For Pierce, the major continuing worry was the *Yorktown*'s life support system, the monitoring of which fell to the electrical, mechanical, environmental services engineer in the second row. Initially, Jack Lewis had confirmed the life support system's reliability. The engineer's report, however, cast new light. 'Flight? I've got some good readings. The *Yorktown*'s cockpit environmentals are still intact. The ship's fuel cells are still producing air, and as long as they have electricity, they'll have air.'

'What about their power?' asked Pierce.

'Well, uh, Flight, that's a different story. The *Yorktown*'s mechanicals are shot – we've got one dead bird up there on that score. She's on back-up reserve power – Battery A.'

'What's its reserve time?'

'Well, by diverting all power purely to the fuel cells for air, cutting back on the heat, communications and computers, we should be able to stretch Battery A's life to seventy hours.'

'We launch in twenty-three and a half hours,' thought Pierce. 'What about Battery B?' he asked.

'My readings are that Battery B is still intact – a lot of these numbers are still scrambled, but we could be able to shift to Battery B if we have to.'

'Could we stretch Battery B as well?'

'If we had to – yes.'

'O.K. Thanks. Now launch vehicle engineer. What do you have?' asked Pierce.

From the third row a wispy, bald man spoke in a soft voice. 'Flight, the world map flight path is accurate . . .'

Pierce studied the screen. The ships' flight path had extended elliptically across the south Atlantic Ocean and was now nearing the tip of South Africa.

Pierce glanced over the top of his console to the second

row of Mission Control and studied the hunched shoulders of the launch vehicle engineer. He looked like a defeated man, haunted by the memories of earlier that morning.

The engineer turned slowly in his swivel chair until Pierce could see the guilt and anxiety in the man's face. Pierce frowned for a moment, uncertain as to the source of his colleague's obvious discomfort. Certainly the entire team of flight controllers had been shocked by the accident, but the launch vehicle engineer's expression went beyond mere shock. Pierce's mouth opened slowly as he began to understand. The engineer had caught a discrepancy in the *Yorktown*'s fuel line earlier that morning, a discrepancy which had cleared up at the time, but one which in all likelihood was the actual cause of the failure of the *Yorktown*'s fuel line system. Moreover, it was a discrepancy the engineer might have questioned harder. The look of guilt on his face told Pierce the engineer believed he was at fault.

The engineer cleared his throat with a nervous cough, further humiliated by his inability to present Pierce with hard data on the *Yorktown*'s condition. 'God!' thought Pierce, 'the poor bastard!'

'Listen,' Pierce said gently, 'you gave me what I needed to know this morning. If anyone's at fault, it's me. You played it by the book. You did your job.' The engineer coughed again, nervously pulled at his nose, and pushed his glasses in place, relieved beyond belief that the man who could have had him removed from Mission Control had instead absolved him of responsibility.

'Thank you,' he said softly.

'No thanks needed,' replied Pierce, his impatience to discover the source of the accident replacing his concern for a subordinate. 'What I need is hard data. What do you have?'

The engineer sighed and pointed to his display screen. 'Dead numbers, Flight, nothing but dead numbers. I have no incoming telemetry from the *Yorktown*. The big bang knocked out its capacity to send us new data. All my numbers are frozen at the moment of the explosion. My numbers are history. Old news.' Now it was Pierce's turn to look defeated. No data from the *Yorktown*'s thousands of on-board sensors reporting to the launch vehicle engineer meant that their understanding of the *Yorktown*'s condition was maddeningly incomplete, like a jigsaw puzzle with dozens of the key pieces forever lost.

'Any probability of restoring telemetry?' Pierce asked tentatively.

'We're still trying, but as of now: negative.'

Pierce nodded, slowly accepting the verdict. 'Thank you,' he said. The Flight Director glanced at the world map at the front of Mission Control. 'Over the south Atlantic already,' he thought. He called on the trajectory engineer.

From the first row of Mission Control, known as 'the Trench' for its close proximity to the front-wall viewing screens, the trajectory engineer clipped out his report. 'Flight, as you can see, they're over the mid-Atlantic, they will cross the southwest African coast momentarily, intersecting with the Tropic of Capricorn. At the present, given their speed and altitude, given that the *Columbia* will be able to keep their attitude trim and minimize the drag, given—'.

'Given all the givens,' snapped Pierce, 'will they be high enough for a safe rendezvous tomorrow?'

'If Vandenberg is on line for tomorrow's rescue launch, the *Yorktown* and *Columbia* will still be up there with room to spare. The orbit will be a bit lower – down to, uh, 89.43 miles approximately, but they'll still be up there. But, ah, assuming that the *Atlantis* gets Lewis and Clark out safely and assuming that the *Columbia* then can separate from the *Yorktown* to return to Earth, uh, that leaves the *Yorktown* still up there and out of control, and our projections are that by Thursday at 1:30, the *Yorktown* will re-enter the atmosphere. I, uh, don't like to say it but I think we will have a Skylab scenario.'

'Not again' thought Pierce. 'Not if we can help it,' he replied. 'Flight Activities Officer, get your staff working on it right now. I want to know the feasibility of the

Atlantis towing the *Yorktown* up to a higher altitude, high enough that it will stay up there for years. *Columbia* doesn't have enough propellants to do it, but maybe the *Atlantis* can. Maybe we can take that ship apart piece by piece to find out exactly what happened. But one thing's for certain, we're not going to have another Skylab.'

'Roger, Flight,' replied the FAO, taken aback.

Pierce shut off his mike and turned to Vince Torino at his side. 'The last thing we need is a ship the size of the *Yorktown* coming in. Hell, at least we had some control over Skylab! But this, unmanned!'

He shook his head in disbelief at the ugly prospect. He was about to switch on his microphone, ready to call upon another engineer for another report, when his console rang with an incoming call.

Racing from the Kennedy Space Center towards Ellington Air Force Base next to the Space Center, Tex Harwood was on the line. 'Houston Flight Director, this is Chase Six. We are on our final approach to Ellington. We'll be with you in ten minutes.'

'O.K., Chase Six,' said Pierce. 'Get that film into processing and you and Brooks get your butts over here.'

Harwood brought in the F-24 to Ellington, and taxied to a halt. Waiting ground crew quickly slapped ladders up to the cockpit and Brooks and Harwood unfastened their safety belts and clambered down onto the tarmac.

Harwood grabbed the arm of a crew-member. 'We've got tons of footage in this baby. Get it out and over to the Space Center fast.'

The crewman nodded vigorously and pointed towards a nearby Huey Cobra turbine-powered helicopter with engines whining, a scant hundred feet away. 'They're waiting to take you to Control!' he cried above the roar of the engines.

'Good man, good man!' said Harwood, slapping him on the back.

Brooks and Harwood sprinted across the tarmac to the chopper and clambered aboard. 'Mission Control!' said Harwood to the pilot, 'and move it!' The limply hanging blades began slowly spinning into a straight blur and the 'copter climbed into the sky.

Adrienne Brooks slumped into a chair and shouted above the din, 'Pierce really sounded rattled!'

'Yeah, well, he's got some real problems,' said Harwood.

'Like their suits.'

'What?'

'Their suits! Jack and Rob . . . in the *Yorktown*!'

Harwood's face went blank. 'Shit' he thought.

In Mission Control, Pierce and the flight controllers listened to the report from the flight activities officer. Trained to deal in absolutes and givens, flight controllers had suddenly been flung, along with the *Yorktown*, into the unknown, where skills and abilities were useless in the face of broken machinery and plans. The reports did little to boost the dubious prospects for a successful rescue.

While the *Yorktown*'s life support system appeared to be in no immediate danger and while the *Atlantis* would arrive before the *Yorktown*'s orbit fatally decayed, the flight activity officer's final comment chilled his audience. 'There is, at this time, no contingency plan to transfer Lewis and Clark, with the suits they're wearing, safely out of the *Yorktown*.'

'For safely,' thought Pierce, 'read, alive.' It did not matter that the *Columbia* was operating perfectly, it was the *Yorktown* that mattered. And worst of all, the reports, the analyses of the condition of the ships, were only preliminary and superficial, sketchy outlines. A thousand and one variables, potentially cancelling out the initial findings, had yet to be determined. Hours of analysis were still required. Until detailed status reports could be compiled, Pierce's team could only take a rearguard defensive action. A growingly complex and increasingly unmanageable problem prevented the flight controllers from completing the desperately needed detailed analysis of the ships.

In a routine flight, Pierce's flight controllers would

have been fully occupied managing and monitoring the various systems of one ship – the shuttle. Now, with this anything but routine flight, the volume of the flight controllers' work-load had dramatically increased in both scope and dimension. Not only were they managing the flight of a space shuttle, but they were attempting to hold together the shattered hulk of a ship not built for space – the *Yorktown*. Frustratingly, their implements of operation – the Mission Control computers that normally would have absorbed such a work-load – had yet to be completely re-integrated with the *Yorktown* and *Columbia*.

There was more. Pierce could hear it in the flight controllers' strained voices. Although Vandenberg prepared the physical requirements of the rescue shuttle launch, Pierce's flight controllers also had to work out the intricate rendezvous docking procedures if the *Atlantis* was to meet up safely with the *Yorktown* and *Columbia*, a complicated series of events in itself, requiring almost as much time and effort of each flight controller as did the routine managing and monitoring of the ships' systems.

Daunted by their problems, Pierce's flight controllers still pushed on doggedly. Pierce wandered about the room tapping in on conversations, asking questions and proffering advice, and he began to fear that the flight controllers' brutal work-load would not only delay the compilation of detailed status reports, but might, at some point before the *Atlantis* could be launched, prompt a mental error, a harried mistake, which in the present circumstances could be fatal to Lewis and Clark, and perhaps even Bishop and Merriman in the *Columbia*.

There was one more problem, one more task with which he would have to burden some key flight controllers: creating the ship-to-ship transfer procedure for Lewis and Clark. Pierce stood, frowning worriedly.

He knew his team's calibre. They had shared many missions. He had hand-picked them, trained them. He knew their capacity, what they could do as individuals and as a team, and like other exceptional leaders, be they military, business or political, Pierce knew how far he could push them, how much they could take. Arms folded, he wondered whether they were already passed their own breaking point.

If he pushed them on he would find out, but could he take that chance? He had already shot the dice once before this morning in a gamble that the *Yorktown* and *Columbia* could achieve a mated orbit. Should he gamble again? Most certainly, the lives of four astronauts were at stake, not to mention his project, and indeed his future at NASA.

He looked at the chronometer at the front of Mission Control. Almost 12:00 noon. The second orbit was about to begin. No, he would not gamble. He had made his decision.

Standard operating procedure for space shuttle missions involved three separate teams of flight controllers, each with an eight-hour duty shift in Mission Control, giving NASA round-the-clock flight coverage. The lead team, Pierce's Gold Team, worked the 6 a.m. to 2 p.m. shift. The Blue Team, run by Flight Director Charlie Egerton ran from 2 p.m. to 10 p.m. and the Red Team headed by Flight Director Joe Gibbs took the midnight shift from 10 p.m. to 6 a.m. Three teams in twenty-four hours. It was one team too few.

'Vince? They are working their butts off. When Charlie Egerton's guys get in here at 2:00 they'll face the same problem, keeping the *Yorktown* in one piece, co-ordinating with Vandenberg and plotting the Lewis and Clark transfer. It's too much.'

'You have a plan?' inquired Torino.

'At 2 p.m. we, the entire Gold Team, move upstairs to the Reserve Control Room to plot the rescue. It's another shift, but at least Egerton's Blue Team will be able to concentrate on just keeping the *Yorktown* and *Columbia* intact and God knows that right now that by itself is enough.'

'That is, if I may say, an understatement,' replied Torino.

Still dressed in their flight suits, Adrienne Brooks and Austin Harwood strode quickly into Mission Control. The harried looks on the flight controllers' faces surprised them, and they slowed perceptibly.

'Kee-rist, do these guys look whipped,' said Harwood quietly.

'Probably haven't moved out of their chairs since 4 a.m.,' she replied.

Pierce, now on the line to the flight dynamics officer, waved and forced an unconvincing smile. They approached Vince Torino and shook his hand.

'Hi, Tex, Adrienne,' said Torino grimly. 'Heard you banged up your jet at the Cape.'

'Yeah, no fuel,' replied Harwood. He jerked a thumb in Pierce's direction. 'When the Flight Director says "climb" – you climb.'

'Well, you sure did some kinda flying to keep in range of the *Yorktown*, and your pictures, Adrienne – Pierce wouldn't have gone for a mated orbit without them.' Torino meant the words as a compliment but Brooks, unaware of all the facts, thought of her pictures as being responsible for putting Lewis and Clark in their predicament.

'Thanks,' she said. 'A lot!'

Torino missed the point. 'No, seriously – great pictures.'

'How are Jack and Rob?' she asked.

'Bearing up – second orbit.' He glanced at his console to make certain his line to the *Yorktown* was closed and then spoke in a confiding tone. 'The *Yorktown* is shot to hell. I don't know how it's holding together. We're running down the numbers on the computer.'

Harwood and Brooks exchanged a worried glance. 'Is it that bad, Vince?' she asked.

'Yeah,' he replied. 'Real bad.'

Having completed his call, Pierce pivoted in his chair, and interrupted the conversation. 'Glad you two are here. I take it you were briefed on the chopper flight over here?' They nodded in reply. 'Good. Now we have a couple of dozen problems needing answers all at once.'

'That's what we're here for, Doug,' drawled Harwood. 'You just tell us where you want us, and what you want us to do.'

'Have you got your films of the accident to the labs yet?'

'Yes, sir,' replied Brooks. 'The people at Ellington unloaded them out of the plane as soon as we touched down.'

'Good, and damn good pictures you gave us, Adrienne. Without them—'

'You wouldn't have ordered a mated orbit,' interrupted Brooks.

Pierce caught the trace of bitterness in her voice, perhaps even a feeling of responsibility. 'Your pictures, Dr Brooks, saved Lewis' and Clark's hides,' he said sternly. 'Without them I would have followed standard procedure, and they would have separated and descended. The *Columbia* would have made it back to Kennedy, but the *Yorktown* ... In the denser atmosphere, it would have been ripped apart.' Pierce waved his hand at the room. 'This place would have been empty right now, and we would be wearing black armbands. The responsibility for this Mission is mine – alone. Clear?'

'Clear,' replied Brooks, not chastened, but with her worries calmed somewhat.

'Now, Lewis and Clark are wearing high-altitude pressure suits, and can't withstand a transfer. Our top priority is developing a transfer procedure to get them out, and that is where I want both of you. The flight activities officer and his staff are plotting some optional transfer moves and we're really up against it at the moment. The *Atlantis* will be ready for launch tomorrow morning, but it won't make much difference, if we haven't figured a way to transfer them from ship to ship, so I want you to both work with the FAO on this problem. Any questions?'

'No, but a suggestion,' said Brooks. 'I'd like a crack at finding out what caused the accident.'

'What's the point of finding the cause of the accident right now?' asked Torino.

'We have to know what went wrong,' Brooks insisted.

'I know that,' replied Torino. 'But why right now? Why divert manpower and computer time when we have to get Lewis and Clark down alive?'

'Because I want to know what happened,' snapped Brooks. 'The computers can handle the load, so can the launch vehicle engineer and his staff. And right now they have nothing else to do but sit and watch. There's no launch vehicle to monitor, at least no launch vehicle that works. Besides, if we can get a handle on the cause of the accident, we can have a better idea on the extent of the *Yorktown*'s damage.'

Torino remained unconvinced. 'Next week's flight – your flight – has been cancelled anyway.'

'I know that,' replied Brooks. 'I just think it's a good idea to know what caused the accident.'

'So do I,' interjected Pierce. 'Maybe it would be an idea if you joined the launch vehicle engineer and his staff and tried to piece this thing together. Tex? You can work with the flight activities officer on the transfer.' Pierce looked up at the chronometer. 'We're running out of time. The *Atlantis* launch is at 10:05 tomorrow morning. By the way, at 2 o'clock the Gold Team here in Mission Control is moving upstairs to the reserve control room, so report to me there as soon as you have something.'

Brooks and Harwood made for the exit. It was 12:15, less than twenty hours before the launch of the rescue shuttle, the *Atlantis*.

Standard NASA operating procedure for Mission Control flight teams called for the oncoming team of flight controllers to be present in Mission Control a full hour before taking over the responsibilities of the outgoing team. Continuity of flight management and decision-making was ensured by the early arrival of oncoming controllers watching over their counterparts' shoulders, without interfering, but absorbing the essence of the preceding shift. The actual shift of teams took only a few minutes and each outgoing team prided itself on being able to hand over control of the flight so smoothly that the crews orbiting the Earth, unless otherwise aware of the time, would not realize that the flight team transfer had even taken place.

However, at 12:16, moments after Brooks and Harwood had left, the oncoming Blue Team of flight controllers, led by Flight Director Charlie Egerton, came into Mission Control. At thirty-four, Egerton was NASA's youngest flight director, a tall skinny man with a bushy blond beard, and an angular face. Egerton commanded wide respect for his ability to absorb wildly disparate factors, relate them to the problem at hand and choose the correct course of action. Even so, as Pierce and Egerton discussed the different actions the two flight teams would take after the 2 p.m. shift and Pierce briefed him on the events of the flawed flight, the sheer size of the problem overwhelmed the younger Egerton. Never, not even in the worst simulation, had he seen such devastation and confusion. He studied the notes in Pierce's flight log, shaking his head in disbelief.

By 2 p.m. the *Yorktown* and *Columbia* were twenty-nine minutes into their third orbit of the Earth, 94·3 miles above the western African coast. In Mission Control, Egerton's Blue Team had already plugged in their respective headsets, eager to get on with their shift.

The long hours, however, had begun to tell on the Gold Team. For Pierce in particular, the shift had been physically and mentally exhausting. He was hungry, his head ached from the ten hours of unbroken concentration, and the climactic time-stopping moments of life and death decision-making. The prospect of another eight-hour shift in the reserve control room seemed almost too much to take.

At 2:01 p.m., Egerton tapped Pierce on the shoulder. 'Any time, Doug,' he said, softly.

'O.K., Charlie,' said Pierce, making some notes, 'one final entry in my log.'

He logged the time, signed his initials to it and handed it to Egerton.

From the *Yorktown*, Lewis' voice came through on both Egerton and Pierce's headsets. '*Yorktown* Commander to Houston Flight Director.'

Technically, Egerton was now the on-duty Flight Director, but with a gesture he deferred to his senior, Pierce.

'Houston Flight,' replied Pierce.

'Flight, we know you guys on the ground like to shift teams without us knowing about it, but uh, we just wanted to thank you all for your work this morning – all of you.'

Above the *Yorktown* in the *Columbia*, Bishop chimed in. 'Yeah, and the *Columbia* thanks you, too, guys.'

Pierce, deeply moved, bit his lip. In the God-awful mess they were in, they still had time to thank him. 'Anytime,' he said. 'That's what we're here for. Just hang in there. Flight out.'

Pierce jabbed at the console, changing channels to the communication loops throughout Mission Control. 'Gold Team, we'll take a fifteen minute break and assemble upstairs in the reserve control room – Charlie and the Blue Team are taking over. Flight out.' He removed his headset, stowed it in the console drawer to his right, grabbed his jacket off the back of his chair and faced Egerton. 'It's all yours, Charlie.'

Pierce walked with Torino from Mission Control.

'I'd say we earned our pay for the morning,' said Torino.

'Yeah. Now we find out if we deserve the rest of the day's wages.'

Torino grabbed Pierce's arm, stopping him as they walked to the door. 'Doug? Can we do it?'

'We'll have to be good. And lucky.'

CHAPTER FOUR

The haggard members of Gold Team trudged out of Mission Control in silence, looking for all the world like a squad of infantrymen returning from a particularly bloody patrol full of ambushes. Strain was etched on their faces. Aften ten unrelievedly tense hours of duty they were mentally and physically sapped, but their day was by no means over, or even close to it. It had barely begun, and the next ten hours would make the first ten hours seem routine.

Pierce and Torino and the half dozen or so flight controllers crowded into the elevator down the hall from Mission Control and as the doors closed an anonymous voice muttered, 'If this bugger gets stuck . . .'

'If it does,' said another, 'Congress will cut the budget.'

Directly above Mission Control on the third floor of the building, was the reserve control room, an exact duplicate of Mission Control one floor below. On its gray walls hung plaques from other NASA manned missions. In fact, the only visible difference between the reserve control room and Mission Control (deliberately chosen to avoid confusion) was that the reserve control room had gray carpeting while Mission Control's was bluish-green. That there were two control rooms bore witness to NASA's standard of reliance on back-ups. If for any reason Mission Control became unusable, the entire management of any flight could be instantly transferred to the back-up control room. Now, though, the Gold Team would use the facility to plan the rescue.

At the front of the room a half-dozen folding tables had been set up, laden with sandwiches, carrot sticks, celery, fruit, tea and coffee. The ravenous flight controllers began devouring the spread.

'Vince?' said Pierce to Torino. 'Let's get some power in here.'

Torino nodded, walked over to a wall cabinet of circuit-breakers, opened it, and began flipping switches. Instantly the whines and hums of units and computer terminals rang through the room like an electronic symphony's tune-up. The world map flickered, then steadied. 'The third orbit,' thought Pierce, 'they're over India.'

The four display screens on either side of the world map came on, and through the P.A. system, Pierce's flight controllers could hear the voices of the Blue Team one floor below in Mission Control.

Pierce grabbed a beef sandwich off the table, poured some milk into a styrofoam cup, pocketed the plasti-pak of mustard and walked back to the Flight Director's third-row console. The rest of the controllers, including Torino, congregated around the tables at the front. Pierce was just as pleased. He needed the time to be alone, if only for a few moments. Some time to try to understand. He stared at his blank console screen, the magnitude of the disaster and the weight of the day's wildly unfolding events descending upon him.

The entire mission was a shambles. The Airborn Launch Development Project had been his idea. He had conceived the idea of an airborne launch for the shuttle, he had developed the idea into a concept, the concept into a plan and the plan into a project. He had hand-picked the key controllers, in some cases raiding them from other NASA projects in an attempt to put together the best possible team. Together they had guided the ALD project through seven increasingly complex missions, each an unqualified success. Now the eighth mission, the one which would have proved his idea, reared back and bucked with the mindless fury of an enraged animal. Now the whole project was on the line, and so were the lives of four colleagues.

Maybe the project would remain what it had been moments before take-off that morning at 10 a.m., an unproven concept. Maybe there would be no further

ALD test flights. Maybe the explosion which had shattered their hopes, had not been an accident. Perhaps some overlooked stress, some engineering factor had not been accurately assessed. Perhaps if there was another flight, the same accident would occur again. Maybe his idea was simply wrong.

He reached forward and turned up his console. Deliberately pushing buttons, he tuned the TV network's coverage onto one of the screens. He changed channels. 'Jesus,' he thought, 'all three networks are still covering the flight!' Intrigued, he turned up the volume.

'. . . have been in orbit since 10:31 this morning, Central Daylight Time. For those who missed the morning's tragic accident, we will now replay those frantic moments leading up to what is certainly America's worst space accident.'

Pierce stopped eating as the images of the *Yorktown* and *Columbia* came on. The TV announcer continued:

'These pictures were taken by Dr Adrienne Brooks from the chase plane flown by astronaut Austin Tex Harwood. Ironically, Brooks and Harwood were scheduled to fly next week's confirmation flight in the space shuttle *Enterprise*. Now, it was at this point, seventy miles up, that the space shuttle *Columbia* was scheduled to separate from the *Yorktown*. Watch closely to the underside of the black ship – the *Yorktown* . . . There!'

A large portion of the underside of the *Yorktown* ripped away. Pierce winced, munching slowly on his sandwich, reliving it all over again. 'The voices you are hearing are those of the astronauts, the Flight Director, Doug Pierce, at Mission Control, and the Capcom, Vince Torino.'

Enthralled, repelled, curious, Pierce watched the replay of the nightmare unblinkingly. 'Houston?! Do we abort?' 'We've just had a real bang!' 'Turbine fuel down to thirty percent, twenty percent!' 'I say again – go for a mated orbit.'

'Jesus! Did I sound like that?' thought Pierce.

'And now,' continued the announcer, 'the order to go

for a mated orbit has been given. The ships will quickly pull out of range of the chase planes.'

Pierce had heard enough, and killed the sound, but continued to watch intently. 'The whole world had seen it and heard it,' he thought. 'They must think we're idiots – the price we pay for openness.' Pierce had no beef with the TV media. They were, in fact, some of NASA's biggest supporters. Maybe it was that both businesses dealt with information, with knowledge and with technology – kindred spirits in a sense. Hell, why not? NASA's communication satellites had revolutionized TV. Live coverage from any point in the globe was accepted as a norm.

He saw the words 'orbit achieved' flashed on the screen, followed by still sketches of both vehicles in orbit, and raised the volume again to hear his own voice, 'Do you read, *Yorktown*?' Then Bishop's voice, 'Damn it, do you read?'

Pierce winced again, the nation had heard those exchanges too, and that was NASA's policy as well.

Not only did the space agency give the networks copies of the flight plan, but the networks received direct audio-visual feeds from Mission Control. Maybe that was why the media respected the agency as much as it did – NASA told them what they were going to do and when they were going to do it and then let everyone hear and see the results. The world had heard Armstrong say, 'That's one small step for man, one giant leap for mankind.' They now had also heard Jack Lewis say, 'You guys better figure out how Rob and me are going to space-walk out of this bus over to the *Atlantis*, 'cause we're both wearing high altitude pressure suits, and if we step outside of this baby with what we've got on, we'll be dead in two seconds.'

A sombre-appearing announcer intoned, 'As dramatic as these exchanges are, they underscore a brutal reality: four men are now trapped in space, their survival is still in doubt. We will return with our coverage in just a moment.'

A moronic advertisement for a toilet bowl cleanser followed and Pierce angrily snapped off the set. 'Still in doubt. What an understatement,' he thought.

Pierce looked up at the flight controllers now assembling at their consoles throughout the reserve control room, and tried to force the waves of uncertainty from his mind. His flight controllers knew what was expected of them, but he could not help but notice looks on their faces, expressions of disbelief and confusion.

Shock affects everyone, and these men despite their professionalism and training, were no exception. Pierce was no exception either, but like all truly superior leaders, he possessed the will to bury emotion, if only for a time, time enough to do the job in front of him. 'Worrying won't save them,' he thought. 'Action might.' He would allow no emotion, however natural, to interfere with the logical processing of the data and concepts necessary to save the crews. It was time to act. He crumpled the clear plastic that had held his sandwich, pitched it unerringly into a garbage can and slugged down the last bit of milk in his cup. Deliberately, he pulled on his headset and pushed the PA button. 'All right, everyone, let's get going.'

Moments later, he stood behind his console, tie loosened, hands on hips, and addressed his team. 'Gentlemen, we have very little time in which to compile and prepare a great deal of work. We all know what we face. Our goal is two-fold: first, co-ordinate the *Atlantis*' rescue launch with Vandenberg for tomorrow morning; second, find a way to get Lewis and Clark out of the *Yorktown*. Before we can do either, though, and especially before we can effectively work out a transfer manoeuvre, we need a more detailed status report on the *Yorktown*. Reports this morning were too superficial. I know your staff have compiled more data since then, so let's get to it.'

Again, the Gold Team swung into action. Again the battle was joined. Pierce watched the flight controllers call up information from the real time computer complex, their progress marked by the changing displays on the console screens. A sobering reality impressed itself on him, a reality forming at least a part of every flight controller's subconscious: if the lives of the crew were to be saved, reams of data would have to be processed into specific conceptual programs and those programs translated into precise and perfectly co-ordinated actions. The rescue attempt was in no way a random, seat-of-the-pants operation. Of course, to the world at large the very word 'computer' conjured up images of Big Brother, Big Government, depersonalization and incorrect billing for products never bought – a big, dumb calculator. When in doubt, blame the computer. To the flight controllers, however, the computer was more than a machine, it was a partner, a companion as necessary to the performance of their jobs as scalpels, X-rays and sutures were to surgeons. Without computers, space travel would have been not just difficult, but impossible.

Perhaps the public's reluctance to understand the computer was based on a failure to comprehend the harmonious functioning of the universe itself. Centuries before, Sir Isaac Newton had exposed the theoretical bedrock which now allowed the flight controllers to interact with that universe. On a theoretical plane, his three laws of mechanics were deceptively simple, but they were totally pertinent to the life or death of the four astronauts. The first law said that in the absence of an external force, a body will continue or be at rest, and if the body or object is moving, it will continue its motion in the same straight line direction at a constant speed.

The second law had been demonstrated by Rusty Bishop's attempts that morning to stabilize the ship's attitude in space: if a force is applied, the body will be accelerated in the direction of the force. And the third law stated: for any force applied in one direction, there is an equal force exerted in the opposite direction.

When the computers had given Pierce the speed the *Yorktown* and *Columbia* needed to reach a stable orbit, the numbers displayed on the screens were numerical representations of a further Newtonian axiom: to maintain a circular orbit, an object's centrifugal force trying to pull it away from the earth, had to be at least equal to the force of gravity. If the object's centrifugal force or its escape velocity was greater than the effects of gravity, an elliptical orbit would be achieved.

But the power of the *Yorktown* and *Columbia* had ultimately been less than the power of gravity. The ships had required an escape velocity of 17,500 miles per hour. They had achieved only 15,100 miles per hour, and thus further Newtonian laws had unavoidable relevance to Pierce's flight controllers: the larger an object's mass, the more the attractive force between it and the earth. Unless an object, be it a satellite, Skylab, or the *Yorktown* and *Columbia*, achieves escape velocity, gravity will inevitably pull it back to Earth.

As general statements, Newton's laws are immutable. But the assumptions upon which he based his statements were themselves built on the incomplete knowledge of the 1600's. Other forces were at work, modifying the general laws and requiring new tools of great precision for their very discovery and measurement. These forces, and their interacting relevance, were beyond man's calculation.

For instance, gravity is not constant, but varies with the earth's composition and geography. The velocity of earth's spinning rotation is not constant either, and not all celestial bodies such as the planets of the solar system, which to varying degrees affect orbiting vehicles, have a uniform mass, nor are they perfect spheres with their mass concentrated at their centres.

To calculate the criss-crossing and intimately interrelated forces affecting any space vehicle such as the *Yorktown* and *Columbia*, is an infinitely complex task. Because man's calculative competence is decidedly finite, space travel required a mechanical tool, able to assign a value to each conflicting universal force, a tool man could wield to reconcile the constantly changing forces affecting space vehicles: the computer was that tool – the tool which made Newton's laws operational and man's journey from the planet feasible, whose calculative abilities matched man's imagination and approached the infinite.

The thoughts of Pierce and the flight controllers were, however, not on a long-dead visionary, nor the latest advances in computer technology. As computations were calculated, as debates raged, as charts, graphs and columns of numbers were displayed on console screens, the Gold Team had but one desire: to complete the checkout of the *Yorktown* as quickly and as accurately as possible.

By 3 p.m. the flight controllers had completed for the first time detailed status reports on the condition of the *Columbia* and *Yorktown*. Pierce hoped desperately his team would have 'good numbers' for him – not just statistics, but the vital performance indicators of both ships, numbers which would let him and his men know whether Lewis and Clark in the *Yorktown* had a chance.

Although an optimist by nature, Pierce did not let the fact that earlier status reports had been somewhat positive, fill him with hope. They had, after all, been calculated without benefit of complete information due to the absence of co-ordination between the ships' and Mission Control's computers. He was not fearful, but he was concerned that if the indicators were too bad, he and his Team would be faced with an insoluble dilemma.

'O.K., trajectory engineer,' said Pierce over the communication loop in the reserve control room, 'we'll start with you.'

The trajectory engineer's staff support room had calculated that the *Yorktown* and *Columbia*'s orbit would remain relatively stable for three days, declining gradually through Monday to Wednesday from its present 93-mile altitude to approximately 83·176 miles. By Thursday morning, though, the decreasing frictional resistance of the lower atmosphere would pull at the ships fiercely and quickly. On Thursday morning the orbit would begin to collapse. The trajectory engineer's best calculations were a drop from 83 miles at 6 a.m. Thursday, to 68 miles by 2 p.m. Thursday.

Sixty-eight miles. The magic altitude was 68. Visually,

it seemed no different to 66 or 72 miles, or for that matter, 82 miles. But above it lay the vacuum of space, and below it were the first sensible traces of the atmosphere. And travelling at 13,000 miles per hour, the ships would hit it with all the grace of a racing car slamming into a brick wall.

The resistance would sear the ships, the wings would be torn from the fuselages, the rudders ripped away, the astronauts' bodies vaporized into non-existence. The trajectory engineer summarized his report with caution. 'Flight, we can only project the Thursday 2 p.m. re-entry time with 80% accuracy, within 48 hours. Right now, that 2 p.m. figure is not hard.'

There were too many variables, the ships' changing aerodynamic attitude as they lost weight through depletion of fuel being pre-eminent.

'O.K. But that's Thursday,' said Pierce. 'What we have to worry about is tomorrow morning, Tuesday, 11 a.m.'

'If the *Atlantis* launch is at 11:00,' replied the trajectory engineer, 'achieves orbit by 11:25 and can dock with the *Yorktown* by 12:30, the *Yorktown*'s altitude will be 90·352 miles. Even if the docking doesn't occur until late in the afternoon, the altitude will still be high enough for a safe transfer from ship to ship. But we still have to consider *Yorktown*'s eventual re-entry time. Assuming safe transfer of Lewis and Clark from the *Yorktown* to *Atlantis*, and no other problems, I presume the *Columbia* will finally separate from *Yorktown* and return to earth. That leaves the *Yorktown* up there, unmanned and uncontrollable. I mentioned this this morning, and I repeat it now. If she stays up until 2 p.m. Thursday, my staff support room projections indicate she'll break up, scattering a path of debris 1,000 miles long and 200 miles wide, and at this time we cannot predict with more than 70% reliability where that debris would hit!'

'O.K.,' said Pierce, 'with 70% reliability then, where would the debris hit?'

'The eastern seaboard – Boston, Hartford . . .'

The news silenced the reserve control room.

Pierce called the flight activities officer. 'What are the results of your analysis? Can the *Atlantis* pull the *Yorktown* to a higher altitude, high enough to forestall reentry until we have a chance to conduct an autopsy?'

'Flight, our calculations are that if the *Atlantis* can rendezvous before 4 p.m. tomorrow, that is, above 88 miles altitude, the *Atlantis*' power will be, I repeat, will be, sufficient to pull the *Yorktown* up to a stable altitude – a minimum three-year orbit.'

Pierce grinned at Torino in relief. 'No Skylab scenario,' he said, 'not this flight.'

'Yeah, sometimes you get lucky,' replied Torino.

Pierce called on the electrical, mechanical and environmental engineer, who delivered a terse report. The *Columbia* was in 'nominal' shape. That is, all of its electrical systems, environmental control, life support, auxiliary power units and hydraulic systems functioned at peak efficiency. That was the *Columbia*. The *Yorktown*? That was something else.

'I have four points to make,' said the engineer. 'First, *Yorktown*'s environmental, thermal and life support systems are, of course, on back-up seventy-two-hour reserve power. Second, we have detected a power leakage of as yet undetermined origin. If it drops out entirely, *Yorktown* will lose life support system power in twenty hours.' Pierce's eyebrows arched in surprise as he jotted the figure 20 onto his log, checked the time and projected twenty hours into the future. '12:20, Tuesday afternoon, awfully close to *Atlantis*' rendezvous time,' he thought fearfully.

The Engineer continued. 'Third, *Yorktown*'s auxiliary power units are out completely. The explosion had to be exceedingly severe for such damage. Fourth, what is not clear due to our lack of knowledge on the *Yorktown*'s structural damage is whether or not there are time-delayed effects at work.'

'Such as?' inquired Pierce.

'We know the explosion was bad, but we don't know if

any delayed effects may affect *Yorktown*'s life support system, or electrical power.'

'Will those systems hold together until the rescue?' asked Pierce.

The engineer at the extreme right-hand console of the row in front of Pierce turned in his chair and faced him. 'Flight, I think all of us would feel better if Lewis and Clark kept their helmets on and visors down.'

'So you don't know?' asked Pierce.

'Roger, Flight.'

Pierce covered the mouthpiece of his headset and leaned over it to Vince Torino. 'Call Charlie Egerton, have them relay that recommendation to Lewis and Clark. Check that. No recommendation, it's an order.'

Pierce looked straight ahead to the launch vehicle engineer's console one row in front of him. While physically identical to the other consoles – keyboard, call button, display screen – Pierce saw that the print-ups on the engineer's screen were disturbingly different. Instead of changing green numbers indicating up-to-date data, the numbers were red, fixed and unchanging.

He called the launch vehicle engineer. 'Do you confirm the possibility of delayed effects – an X factor at work here?'

The engineer responsible for monitoring the *Yorktown*'s propulsion system and propellant depletion was clearly uneasy at the only answer he could give. 'I have to confirm the analysis. Whatever the specific damage was, as you know, all I have are old dead numbers, and I have to confirm that while *Yorktown* used up its hydrogen propellant through leakage after the explosion and in the climb into orbit, we estimate that the *Yorktown* still has 4,000 pounds of turbine propellant in its tanks.'

Pierce was dumbfounded, 'Newton's third law', he thought. For any force applied in one direction, there is an equal force exerted in the opposite direction. If the *Yorktown*'s tanks ruptured, propellant could vent out into space. The force would be equal to a battery of thrusters gone wild, perhaps more powerful than the *Columbia*'s ability to counteract, and the two ships could very well cartwheel uncontrollably back into the atmosphere.

'Do you have a possibility or a probability factor on it, or when such venting might occur?' he asked.

The launch vehicle engineer looked at the dead numbers on his display screen and shook his head. 'No, Flight, not at this time. With no incoming telemetry from *Yorktown*, I don't think we could get a realistic fix on it even if we tried.'

'Then you have no fix on the tanks' reliability?'

'None,' replied the engineer flatly. 'All I can suggest, and it's outside my area of responsibility . . .'

'Give it to me,' said Pierce.

'What I'm thinking is Bishop or Merriman spacewalking out and eyeballing the damage to the *Yorktown*. It might give us something to go on.'

'Out of the question,' replied Pierce. 'I won't risk a space-walk under these circumstances. The risk is just too great. We'll have to take the chance that the tanks won't fail.' 'But what,' he thought, 'if they do?'

Then Pierce ordered the engineer to join Adrienne Brooks and his team of staff support personnel to continue the search of the telemetry tapes, trying to isolate the cause of the accident. For the engineer, the opportunity to find the cause was a chance, however slight, to restore his own shattered confidence in himself. Somehow it might help extricate his fellow flight controllers from the predicament they were in.

But as the reports continued, the magnitude of the disaster and all its ugly ramifications began to emerge. The initial status reports recorded that morning had been only a sketchy outline, hastily assembled. Now, colours, dimensions, perspectives slowly came into focus. The ground resources manager reported that NASA's worldwide offices, stations, labs and centres were on full alert, all in full co-ordination with Mission Control. That was to be expected. The instrumentation, navigations and communications officer confirmed that the tracking data relay satellite system of three geosynchronous satellites providing coverage of the ships, continued to keep Mission Control in touch. The back-up ground base flight tracking data network was on line as well, ready to provide communications over most of the globe should anything happen to the satellite system – not nearly as effective, but still a reassuring presence. The avionics engineer's report was incredibly brief, simply because all of the space shuttle's avionics (the two hundred black boxes which relayed orders from the computers and translated them into physical action, such as firing the shuttle's reaction control system thrusters) were working perfectly. The flight surgeon was predictably concerned, as only a doctor could be. The physical condition of Bishop and Merriman in the *Columbia* was, of course, excellent. Lewis and Clark? Unknown. The absence of telemetry to Mission Control meant no readings on their vital signs. Unlike Bishop and Merriman, the flight surgeon had no data on Lewis and Clark's heart, respiration and blood pressure. Thus, he could only listen to their voices, attempt to interpret and then make an educated but undeniably uncertain guess. On the whole he concluded that their condition was as good as could be expected: hungry and thirsty, but alive and fighting.

But balanced against this inherent optimism were the dark realities. Trajectory? Declining. Life support system? On battery reserve with a slow leakage. Lewis and Clark's transfer procedure out of the *Yorktown*? Yet to be developed.

Those key reports faced Doug Pierce with a painfully inescapable fact. The *Yorktown* was a fatally damaged aircraft. Its crew, Lewis and Clark were at the best living on borrowed time. Pierce and his colleagues knew that for Lewis and Clark, time might end in 24 hours, or in 24 minutes.

'Somehow,' thought Pierce, 'we have to hold the *Yorktown* together for 24 hours, get the *Atlantis* up there. That's all – just 24 hours.'

Twenty-four hours, long enough to get the *Atlantis* up and Lewis and Clark out. To do so required an extraordinary measure. A team of flight controllers trained to work as a cohesive unit was broken into three sub-groups, each attacking one potentially life-threatening aspect of the mission. It was only the second time in NASA history that an operational flight team had been broken out of their mould during duty and formed into specific sub-groups.

The first group, led by their flight dynamics officer, compiled and computed all logistical problems potentially preventing the *Yorktown* and *Columbia* from remaining operational, that might be encountered by the Blue Team's flight controllers below them in Mission Control. This troubleshooting group had their hands full, but if successful, the efforts of the second group would be rewarded.

The second group, headed up by the operations integration officer, assisted their counterparts at Vandenberg Airforce Base in California in co-ordinating the launch of the *Atlantis*. The co-ordination itself was a particularly critical task, because according to the rotation schedule of the three flight teams, it would be these same men, the flight controllers of Pierce's Gold Team, who would later conduct the Mission Control management of *Atlantis*' rescue launch.

Pierce, having divided up the responsibilities, served as grand co-ordinator for the entire effort. As leader of the third and final sub-group, if his efforts were not successful, the work of the other groups would be rendered useless. Their task was to create, invent or discover a method of getting Lewis and Clark in their standard high-altitude pressure suits out of the *Yorktown* and into the *Atlantis* alive.

In routine flights there was normally some leeway allowed in time required to complete assigned tasks, but now it was 3:30 p.m., barely 17 hours from the *Atlantis*' rescue launch. Pierce's group of flight controllers had huddled around his console. 'O.K. We have our work cut out for us,' he said. 'Now let's go.'

*

In other circumstances the view from the cockpit of the hypersonic jet *Yorktown* would have inspired both Jack Lewis and Rob Clark. The clouds below were like white puff-balls; the Himalayas jutted skyward, rust-brown and white-peaked; The Indian Ocean was bright blue. The earth's curvature was distinct and seemingly bordered from the pitch black of space by a spectrum of razor-thin blues and purples. However, the fact that the astronauts' view was from a hypersonic jet capable of withstanding the vacuum of space but incapable of surviving re-entry, made the view frightening, a sickening reminder of their predicament.

The physical set-up of the cockpit did nothing to provide psychological relief. Based on the aerodynamic design constraints of a jet capable of travelling at hypersonic speeds over 5,000 miles per hour, the *Yorktown*'s nose came to a needlepoint, its fuselage pencil-like. The cockpit was more cramped than a compact car. Its forward and side windows were mere slits, like a gunslot. Headroom was limited to a spine-bending crouch. The control panel was positioned 16 inches from their faces. The sides of the cockpit practically brushed against their shoulders. one man would have found it tight enough; for two men it was claustrophobic.

For over 5½ hours, Lewis and Clark had had no time to think of creature comforts. Instead they had maintained almost constant contact with Mission Control and Pierce's team in the reserve control room, feverishly working towards a solution.

'O.K. guys,' said Blue Team's Capcom Steve Whitimaker from Mission Control, 'that does it for now. Take a breather while we check things with the *Columbia*. I guess you guys can use the break, right?' he added with forced cheeriness. 'Right,' replied Jack Lewis in the *Yorktown*, incapable of optimism.

He exhaled a long breath and slumped back in his chair, leaning his head against the headrest, glancing out at the earth below. 'China' he said aloud. He shook his head in general disbelief and sighed.

To his right Rob Clark did not respond, but continued to stare out wistfully, frowning with concentration. 'Right now,' he said quietly, 'I betcha Pierce has them jumping through hoops in the reserve control room, and we're still stuck.'

Lewis' piercing blue eyes cut towards Clark wondering how he could even think of Pierce, or for that matter anyone else on the ground. He shifted his gaze to the Real Time Chronometer on his cockpit panel. Three-thirty-six, Houston time. It would take Mission Control another 14 minutes to complete the same instrumentations and communications check with the *Columbia* that he and Clark had just finished. The silence galled him. He hated waiting, and began punching numbers into the keyboard located on the 18-inch wide centre console separating him from his colleague.

Still fully suited up in their powder-blue pressure suits with white helmets and visors locked down in place, Lewis and Clark waited in relative silence as the minutes passed. The environmental system hissed gently as a mixture of oxygen and nitrogen gas circulated through the cramped, austere, mechanical gray cockpit. The computers monitoring the few remaining functioning systems of the broken aircraft, hummed gently in the background.

In their different ways Lewis and Clark both fought against shock and fear. Human nature waged battle against training and skill. Both men were test pilots – better than that, astronauts. Mental toughness born of natural disposition and nurtured by endless training, battled against their humanity. They were astronauts among the best; but they were also very, very scared. All they could do was attempt to keep active and fight off the enemy of every pilot – panic.

Clark, interested in geography, started looking out of the *Yorktown*'s gunslot-type windows, made of triple laminated plexiglass. Perhaps if he tested himself mentally by picking out features and making quick computations on their . . . hell, he was kidding himself; he was worried sick

– about Adrienne, about himself. He sighed and looked over at Lewis who was rapidly punching numbers into the ship's computer.

On the centre panel of the *Yorktown*'s cockpit were three pyramidically aligned display screens. As Lewis punched the numbers in, his calculations instantly displayed themselves on the screens. In the dimly lit cockpit, the flashing digital displays reflected off Lewis' helmet faceplate, giving him the appearance of a human computer terminal. 'Appropriate,' thought Clark, looking away again, out of the window. 'Coming up on the Pacific, leaving Japan,' he said. He stared at the vista of open ocean. Hawaii had yet to come into view; there was nothing to see but the blue sea below and black sea of space above. 'The devil and the deep blue sea,' he muttered ironically. A feeling of utter desolation, the sensation of being helplessly trapped in the cockpit, enveloped him fearfully. He stared at his gloved hands, at the partially working control panel. His suit suddenly seemed to become claustrophobic. He was tired of wearing it, tired of wearing the helmet. With his left hand he reached for his own computer keyboard on the centre console and tapped in some numbers. The printout on the right-hand display screen told him the atmosphere in the cockpit was nominal and safe to breathe. Mission Control's order to keep the suit sealed up flashed in his mind. He disobeyed it. Simultaneously he reached for the two faceplate release buttons located on the temples of his helmet. There was a solid clunk as the buttons were depressed. He pushed two more buttons, one located in front of his chin, the other in front of his forehead, and slid the faceplate up from his face and back into the top of his helmet. The dual-release mechanism was in itself a fail-safe device, designed to prevent accidental release. Clark inhaled the cabin air deeply.

Lewis looked up: 'Houston said to keep the visor down,' he snarled, emphasizing the word 'down'.

'Screw 'em,' countered Clark, not caring who issued the order.

Jack Lewis looked at his partner for a few seconds and returned to his calculations, deep in thought. After a few more seconds he stopped and slid his own faceplate back and away. 'I can see better without it,' he announced. 'Besides, if the cabin pressure fails ... it won't make much difference what we're wearing.'

Lewis, thought Clark, was right again. Jack never did pull his punches in assessing any situation. Some thought him rude – maybe at times he was. But it was more brutal objectivity than rudeness. Lewis always did call a spade a fucking shovel.

Clark's concern, however, shifted to the present. 'Among other things, I've done a breakdown on our consumables.' He pulled out the standard emergency checklist of items to be used in case of a crash on sea or land. 'We have our emergency rations – check that,' he said, referring to the tasteless dehydrated plastic-bagged stuff. 'There's synthetic food for two meals apiece. There's enough water for 24 hours if we stretch it. There's a life raft ...'

'Great,' replied Lewis sarcastically. 'We can row home.'

'... and some flares, and the rest of those carefully thought out items no two stranded astronauts should be without.'

'In other words, we have food and water for one day.'

'And some more water here,' rejoined Clark, patting the arms and legs of his water-cooled suit.

Lewis winced at the thought. 'I don't think either of us will be that thirsty by tomorrow.'

The voice of Capcom Steve Whitimaker in Mission Control crackled through their headsets. '*Yorktown* and *Columbia*, *Yorktown* and *Columbia*, this is Houston Capcom, do you read.'

'*Yorktown*, go Houston,' replied Lewis.

'Roger, Houston,' replied Bishop above them in the *Columbia*.

'O.K. guys, we wanted to give you an update on tomorrow's docking with the *Atlantis*. We're still working towards a 10:05 central daylight time launch from Vandenberg, docking at 12:03 p.m. We've got a tentative timetable for you. You'd better copy this down.'

Whitimaker read out the procedure and timetable to the crews who, in turn, punched the information into their computers and called the numbers back to the Capcom for confirmation before processing. Check and re-check. It was standard procedure, especially in alien circumstances.

'. . . and finally at 12:20 we have your exit from the *Yorktown* into the *Atlantis*. *Columbia*? Your separation from the *Yorktown* will be scheduled later; we're still working on it,' concluded Whitimaker.

Anxiously Lewis waited to hear how Mission Control planned to transfer them to the Atlantis. But the only sound he could hear through his headset was the soft crackling of an open line. Suddenly it dawned on him that Whitimaker was not going to say anything further.

'Look Houston, have you guys got anything on how Rob and I are going to transfer out of here?' Lewis looked over at a confused and angered Clark.

Whitimaker's reply was slow in coming. 'Ah, *Yorktown*,' he replied, 'not at this time.'

The news angered Lewis. 'Well, Houston, I take it that Mission Control and simulation operations are at least working on it?'

'Roger, that's affirmed, *Yorktown*,' replied Whitimaker sheepishly.

Lewis snapped the communication line closed. 'They don't know how to get us out of here,' he said flatly.

'I know,' whispered Rob Clark. 'I know.'

CHAPTER FIVE

'The hell of it is, we don't know how to get them out – any one of these options might kill them,' said Doug Pierce in exasperation.

Gathered about Pierce's console, the launch vehicle engineer flight activities office, Tex Harwood and Vince Torino studied 3-D cut-away diagrams of the *Yorktown* on Pierce's display screen. The cool green lines of computer-drawn X-ray-like diagrams delineated the *Yorktown*'s key components – the cockpit, main cockpit door, fuselage, wings and tail rudders. With a push of the button, the diagram could be rotated to enable the viewer to see any of the ship's components from any angle.

By 4:20 p.m., Pierce's 'transfer group' had evolved three possible options, but their attitude was far from ecstatic. Each transfer option was risky, totally unproven and potentially fatal to Lewis and Clark. As a manager and director used to dealing with hard data, knowns and givens, Pierce chafed at such vague alternatives and hated the prospect of having to choose one of them with so little to go on.

That Pierce's transfer group had developed the options in such a short period of time bespoke their intimate knowledge of the *Yorktown*'s structure and design. However, none of them could be proud of such an accomplishment. It was *Yorktown*'s design itself which both limited and circumscribed their thinking and thus, the number of options.

The first option, and perhaps the most obvious: enter the *Yorktown*'s cockpit by the main door immediately behind Jack Lewis' left-hand cockpit. But just as obviously, debilitating dilemmas arose.

To enter the cockpit via the main door would require depressurization of the cockpit to equal the vacuum of

110

space. With the suits Lewis and Clark were wearing, depressurization would finish them off. But behind the *Yorktown*'s cockpit was an aft door separating the cockpit from the rest of the ship. The first option required Lewis and Clark to begin a slow depressurization, leave the cockpit and close the interior door behind them. When full depressurization had taken place, the astronauts of the rescue shuttle *Atlantis* would enter by the main door, re-pressurize the cockpit and, after Lewis and Clark donned adequate protective suits, reverse the sequence and leave for the *Atlantis*.

The difficulty was clear, and Pierce seized on it. He reached forward to the screen and traced his finger down the interior door dividing the cockpit from the rest of the ship.

'Will it hold?' he asked. 'Is it strong enough? Could it withstand the vacuum?' Pierce searched the faces of his transfer group.

The launch vehicle engineer spoke up. 'I know the specifications for this plane. The specs on the interior door do not call for enough strength to take a total vacuum.'

'But, uh, shouldn't we verify its strength?' interjected Tex Harwood.

'You don't have to – it's not strong enough,' replied the engineer. 'This first option is no option at all.'

'One down, two to go,' said Pierce.

The second option was as bold as it was dangerous, and involved a system which had had its technical origins in World War II.

The notion of pilot escape from damaged aircraft involved the parachute. No pilot ever liked to bale out, preferring even a rough landing to no landing at all. But the parachute was an option of last resort. Theoretically, the act of baling out was simple: slide the canopy back, undo the safety harness and jump out and pull the ripcord. But even in World War II the rate of successful bale-outs from relatively low-speed propeller-driven fighters, was barely 50%. The onrushing wind would pin the pilot to his seat, and even if his strength was enough to push himself out, the tail rudder claimed many pilots in a cruel, abrupt manner.

After World War II, with the development of higher-speed jet aircraft flying at over 600 miles per hour, the use of ejection seats became an absolute necessity. If the parachute was an option of last resort, the ejection seat came to be used only in the face of imminent death, and even then with great trepidation. Consisting of a rocket charge directly under the pilot's seat, the ejection system literally blew the pilot free of his jet. It was an effective, if bone-jarring solution.

However, as the speeds of aircraft doubled and tripled into four-figure numbers beyond subsonic speed, the ejection seat turned deadly. At speeds in the thousands the pilot would indeed be blown free, but the physical impact on his body would produce grisly results. The effect was comparable to being shot into a brick wall from a cannon. And even if the escaping pilot somehow withstood the impact of the onrushing air, the high altitudes at which the jets travelled were so depleted of oxygen that the pilot more often than not had already asphyxiated by the time he descended by parachute to the ground.

A new system was first introduced during the Viet Nam war. The Airforce's FB-111 swing-wing bomber presented a unique solution. Since the pilots could not leave the cockpit and survive, the entire cockpit was made to leave the ship. The cockpit of the FB-111 was in effect a giant enclosed ejection capsule. When the pilot pushed the 'Eject' button, explosive bolts separated the cockpit from its retaining members. A powerful solid-fuel rocket motor simultaneously boosted the enclosed cockpit away from the rest of the plane. Within seconds, small stabilizing parachutes called 'drogues' were automatically deployed by the cockpit's computer, keeping the ejection capsule stable until it reached an altitude sufficiently thick for the main chutes to be effective. The cockpit capsule was pressurized independently of the rest of the plane and could withstand altitudes ranging from high near-space down to 12,000 feet, where the air was breathable. It contained emergency rations of food and water, survival equipment, radio beacons, smoke bombs and flares and all the other accoutrements of survival that Lewis and Clark had already bitterly itemized.

The same cockpit capsule ejection system had been built into the *Yorktown*.

The three hypersonic jets, the *Yorktown*, the *Hornet* and the *Liberty* had flown in active duty for almost four years without a single crash. The system had never been used. Now, ninety-four miles into space, it had emerged as one of the only remaining ways to save Lewis and Clark.

Tex Harwood and Vince Torino, the two astronauts in Pierce's transfer group, cringed at the prospect of using it.

'For one thing,' said Torino, 'our indicators show that the system has no power – at least we have no telemetry readings indicating power. Don't forget, that's why we didn't use it this morning – that's why we went for a mated orbit.'

Pierce nodded slowly. Christ, he thought, if only the power hadn't been knocked out – if only they could have just blown the bastard free!

'Agreed,' said Pierce, 'but this is theory now; we're assuming we could restore power to the ejection system. We mustn't leave any stone unturned.'

'Even so,' replied Harwood heatedly, 'we haven't considered the implications of doing it in outer space. Don't forget, me and Vince here know what it's like to blow a cockpit away in the atmosphere – we had to do it last year in that F-111 test . . .'

Torino closed his eyes, recalling the bone-jarring blast as the cockpit separated from the F-111 jet. Harwood continued:

'Lemme tell you, it's a kick in the ass. I mean, there's one hell of a powerful rocket blowing the cockpit away from the rest of the ship, and in zero gravity – well, shit!

113

If we got Lewis and Clark to pull the plug, it would send the cockpit spinning into space out of control! The *Atlantis* would have to high-tail after it, corral the cockpit – and God knows how they'd do that – then put it in the *Atlantis*' cargo bay. Hell, even if the *Atlantis* could catch up with the cockpit, Lewis and Clark would probably be dead from the spinning!!'

'Tex. Calm down,' ordered Pierce coldly. 'We're exploring every option.'

Harwood sat in a swivel chair, crossed his legs and brusquely thrust his hands into his pockets. 'Well, I don't like it,' he said angrily.

'Neither do I,' agreed Torino.

Pierce could appreciate the two astronauts' concerns in looking out for the best interests of their trapped colleagues; as astronauts they were more aware than any flight controller of what Lewis and Clark faced.

'I understand your worries,' he said. 'I don't like it any more than you do, so let's consider the next option.'

In the world of technological back-ups, even the cockpit ejection seat had a back-up. It the hypersonic jet was still on the runway and some emergency required the crew's immediate evacuation, the ejection cockpit capsule system would blow the nose off the airplane, turning it in seconds into a billion dollar pile of titanium and aluminum scrap.

A second escape system was therefore designed into the ship. If an emergency escape was required on the runway, the pilot could pull a lever which mechanically opened a 30-inch diameter hatch behind their seats on the floor of the cockpit and another hatch on the underside of the ship's fuselage. Connecting the two hatches was an inclined cylindrical tunnel. Crew members would slide, feet-first, through the tunnel, down the chute to the outer hatch where a flexible plastic slide was already deployed, allowing them to drop the final twenty feet to the ground. There, firemen in asbestos suits would be waiting to throw them bodily into the back of a protective truck which would immediately drive off. Practice sessions had shown that the crew could evacuate the cockpit, slide down the chute and enter the truck in less than ten seconds. In typical NASA acronym fashion, the system was called the GBEES – pronounced *gee-bees* – which stood for 'Ground Based Emergency Escape System'.

The third option thus called for one of the rescue astronauts, either Lyle Gerber or Gordon Alexander, to enter the *Yorktown* via the underside outer hatch, close it behind him, equalize the pressure of the chute and the cockpit, travel up the chute, and open the inner hatch into the cockpit.

The problem, however, was exactly the same as the first option, and Harwood got to it first: 'We don't know if the outer hatch can withstand depressurization! If it blew off . . . Jesus!' he muttered.

Pierce and the group understood Harwood's concern. If the outer chute hatch did blow off, the depressurization would suck Lewis and Clark out into space like meat through a grinder. Pierce glanced up at the chronometer above the world map. It was already 4:30 p.m.

'We're running out of time,' he announced. 'How long until simulation operations can run these through?'

'An hour, two hours,' replied the flight activities officer.

Pierce clicked his tongue in frustration. 'That's shaving it awfully close. Whichever one we choose, we'll have to block it out, plan it, co-ordinate it into the flight plan, and if we're lucky, give Gerber and Alexander some practice time.'

Practice, thought Harwood, leaning his bulky frame back into his chair – always practice. Rehearsals, that was the NASA system – prove it here on the ground before trying it in space.

'Well,' said Pierce, 'none of these options looks very good. In fact they all look bad, but that's all we've got. Tex, get over to Building Five with the sim ops people and start running these options through.'

The astronaut nodded slowly and then spoke in a confidential tone. 'Doug? What if we don't have enough time for Gerber and Alexander to rehearse the chosen option?'

Pierce replied without thinking. 'Then they'll have to do it first time, cold. We may have no option.'

Pierce had meant to say 'no alternative'. But the members of the transfer group were quick to see the aptness of his Freudian slip. The three transfer options they had come up with were all dubious, and the simulation runs might very well show that none of them would work. Indeed, there might be no option at all and no rescue.

Pierce caught their glances. 'Well, you know what I mean,' he said, surveying the reserve control room.

The flight controllers in the other two groups continued to work away on co-ordinating the *Atlantis*' countdown and trouble-shooting problems with the *Yorktown* and *Columbia*. Without positive results from the sim ops their efforts would come to naught; Pierce wondered for a moment just what he would do if the results were bad. He turned and faced Harwood.

'Tex, get going, push it. I need the data.'

'Will do, Doug. Will do.'

Pierce's console rang with an incoming call.

'Pierce here.'

'Doug? Ben Fleck.'

Pierce was more than a little surprised to get a call from his boss, the NASA administrator, yet at the same time he felt some relief. The series of depressing reports on the *Yorktown*'s condition from his flight controllers and his failure to develop a hard-and-fast safe method of transferring Lewis and Clark to the *Atlantis* had perplexed and troubled him. These concerns he had already expressed to his team, but not in the same way that he could confide them to Fleck. Fleck was, after all, his oldest colleague, his mentor, almost a father-figure, someone Pierce could really level with.

'Ben, glad you called. We've been putting together—'

'Never mind that, I've got some news for you.'

The gravity and earnestness in Fleck's voice caused

Pierce to scan his display screen, searching for some change in the data. News? he thought. What could Benjamin Fleck possibly know about the flight that Doug Pierce did not?

'I'm listening,' he replied. 'What is it?'

'Sergei Balderis, Doug – he's on the line right now and wants to talk to you.'

Pierce's eyebrows arched sharply in surprise. 'Balderis?'

Vince Torino shifted in his seat beside Pierce. The name of the Soviet Union's top flight director caught his attention. Balderis. A man whose reputation was so legendary the mere mention of his name prompted attention and memories.

'He's calling from the Baikonur Cosmodrome in Russia—'

'But it's the middle of the night there!' replied Pierce.

'So it is – which prompts me to conclude this is no social call, if I may understate matters. We both know he wouldn't call – check that, *couldn't* call – unless he's had top-level approval: the very top, I might add.'

'Did he say what he—'

'No, just that he wants to talk to you.'

Pierce's mind raced through the possible reasons for the call and through all the experiences he had shared with a man he had once seen as a colleague, but now saw more importantly, as a friend.

'O.K. Ben, patch the call through, I'll handle it.'

'Doug? This is your show. But there may be . . . implications, depending on what he says.'

'I know that Ben.'

Implications, thought Pierce sardonically. The NASA–Soviet Academy of Space Science relationship had once been cordial – witness the 1975 Apollo/Soyuz Test Project. Linking three American Astronauts in an Apollo Capsule with two Russian Astronauts in a Soyuz Capsule. Sure, the televised handshake between astronaut and cosmonaut had been a P.R. gesture. They all knew it. It was politics. What wasn't? But it had also been a beginning to what could have been some kind of sharing and co-operation in space.

Implications. The faltering of détente during the 1976 Presidential Campaign. The cancellation of joint US-Soviet Union High Altitude experiments. The continuing frustrations and watering-down of the SALT II agreements.

The bitterness engendered had even crept into the United States-Soviet Anti-Satellite Weapons discussions during the second round of the Strategic Arms Limitation Talks. The Soviets had called for a halt to the entire Shuttle Program, declaring the shuttle was, in fact, an anti-satellite weapon. The US, of course, dismissed the charge out of hand, the talks stalled in the Senate and with the rejection of SALT II the death knell was sounded to all hopes of future shared missions.

Ten years, thought Pierce, *it's been ten years since I talked to him.*

Crackling interference danced in Pierce's headset.

'This is Doug Pierce speaking.'

'Hello? Pierce?' The accent was thick, the voice huskier than he remembered, with a tired tone to it. But the use of his surname 'Pierce' confirmed the caller's identity.

'Sergei! I read you clearly. How do you read me? And how are you?'

'Clear, Pierce, clear . . . I am good, my friend.'

My friend. It cheered Pierce, after all this time.

'And you Pierce, your flight? Is it not well?'

'No Sergei, my flight is most decidedly not well.'

'We have listened and watched. This project of yours is bold.'

'There are no secrets in science, Sergei . . . Our projects begin at different times and in different places, but the true discoverers should take the credit,' said Pierce.

Balderis took Pierce's remark as it was intended – a compliment. For Balderis was the creator of the Airborn Launch concept tested in today's flight of the *Yorktown* and *Columbia*.

In key areas, the Soviet Union's Space Program had surpassed that of the United States. Like NASA, they had created a re-usable shuttle-like spacecraft as an economical means to explore the heavens. Their ship, the Raketoplan – meaning 'rocket/plane' – was much smaller than the Shuttle – 41 feet long compared with the Shuttle's 122, a 20-foot wingspan versus 78 feet, and at an unfueled 10 tons, over 1/7th the weight of an unfueled 75-ton Shuttle. If the Shuttle was a station wagon, the Raketoplan was a sports car.

Just as NASA had initially tested the Shuttle's in-flight aerodynamics in 1977, by carrying the *Enterprise* on the back of NASA's 747 and releasing it to fly back to Edwards Air Force Base, the Soviet Union had glide-drop tested the Raketoplan from the back of their Tupolev 'Bear' bombers. But the Russians, with their passions for secrecy, had begun the Raketoplan's glide test flight in 1975 – a full two years before the first *Enterprise*-747 test!

Ironically, this news leaked out on March 18th, 1978 – the day the eight space-shuttle astronauts scheduled to conduct the Shuttle's first orbital flights were presented to the media at the Johnson Space Center.

At the accompanying press conference veteran astronaut John Young had told the media that he wished the Russians luck with the Raketoplan but that his job, and NASA's, was to develop the Shuttle Program. And so they did. But NASA in general and Doug Pierce in particular still kept a watchful eye on the progress of the Raketoplan and launching system.

Initially, the Raketoplan was blasted into space using a conventional booster rocket on the launch pad – just like the early years of the space shuttle. But unlike NASA, the Soviets had planned all along to shift to the Airborn Launch concept. The Raketoplan had long since been mated to the back of the Russians' own hypersonic-type aircraft, carried to the edge of space just as the *Yorktown* had carried the *Columbia*, and then blown free to fly alone into space. But there was one major difference between the two systems. The Soviets' Airborn Launch concept worked.

Although the Shuttle had been the first re-usable

spacecraft to fly into space, the inherent versatility of the Raketoplan's Airborn Launch system had enabled the Russians to leapfrog well ahead of the United States. There had been rumours of accidents, but available information and the fact of regular Raketoplan flights verified that the Airborn Launch concept was viable.

While the Raketoplan was smaller than the Shuttle and able to carry far less into space per flight, the Airborn Launch system enabled the Russians to land the Raketoplan, refurbish it and be ready for a second flight within fifty-two hours. The best turn-around time NASA could achieve with the Space Shuttle and its external tank and solid rocket booster was two weeks.

Like Pierce, Sergei Balderis had fought against internal opposition to pioneer the Airborne concept. But Doug Pierce made no bones about it, the genesis of his Airborn Launch development project had come from Balderis: Indeed, there were no secrets in space, they just began in different places at different time: but Balderis had been the true discoverer:

'Your words are taken with appreciation,' said the Soviet flight director, 'and your decision – I know it was yours alone – to seek orbit for both the *Yorktown* and *Columbia* was both brave and scientifically correct . . .'

A prophet is not without honour, thought Pierce. 'That's kind of you to—'

'We deal in facts and figures – kindness is incidental. Had I been faced with the same dilemma again . . . I would have done what you did.'

Pierce's brow knitted in confusion. Balderis' voice had suddenly faltered, as if his words had been tainted with the guilt of a troubled conscience. Had I been faced with the same dilemma *again* . . . There had been word of an early failure of the Raketoplan in which two cosmonauts had been lost just after take-off, but it had never been confirmed; there were no details, just suspicions. Was it a slip on Balderis' part? Or was he trying to let Pierce know that an attempted landing of the *Yorktown* and *Columbia* after the accident would have been fatal?

Something only Balderis could know for sure, *because only he had experienced it*?

Pierce decided not to respond to the remark. Their conversation was being monitored on both sides of the Atlantic. The slip, if it was one, might already have cost Balderis dearly. The line hummed as both men remained silent:

'Pierce?'

'I'm still here.'

'Pierce, I'm authorized to instruct you . . .'

Pierce tensed in his chair. Balderis seemed to be reading from a very carefully prepared script:

'. . . that the Soviet Union can launch the Raketoplan within fifty-two hours of your approval.'

Pierce's jaw dropped open – the Soviet Union helping NASA?

'Jesus,' muttered an equally surprised Vince Torino at Pierce's side. Balderis continued in the tone of an announcer.

'The Raketoplan can be flown by one cosmonaut, leaving room for your men in *Yorktown* to take the remaining two seats. The choice is yours, we are prepared to begin.'

Pierce could barely believe what he had just heard, and hesitated before replying. Given the relationship between the United States and the Soviets, the gesture was profound. If he accepted, if it could be done, it might heal so much! But was it scientifically appropriate? Would it save Lewis and Clark? That was his only concern.

Balderis had said fifty-two hours. It was now 4:31 p.m. Monday, and the *Atlantis* would be ready to launch 11:00 a.m. Tuesday. Fifty-two hours would make it 8:30 p.m. Wednesday before the Raketoplan could even take off.

Pierce thought of the *Yorktown*'s status reports. No way it could hold together until then. No, he could not accept. Besides, he rationalized there were too many other problems other than language. A silence had built again between them:

'Pierce? We can overcome the language problem. The cosmonaut chosen is Kirenkov.'

'I know him,' replied Pierce. 'At least, I've heard him speak – on a BBC documentary . . . Sergei, I have to turn you down. Your offer of help is deeply appreciated, I can say that for everyone here and for the men in the ships. But our rescue Shuttle, the *Atlantis*, will be ready in another eighteen hours . . .'

'I see . . .'

'And the *Yorktown* is badly damaged.'

'Yes.'

'And I just don't know if either of our men would still be alive by the time the Raketoplan could be launched. I know you'll understand the problems I face.'

'Yes, yes, Pierce, again your decision is correct. Nonetheless we will continue to watch and wait. I wish you luck.'

'Thank you, we can use all we can get.'

Balderis rang off before Pierce could even begin to absorb the impact of the call.

Benjamin Fleck cut in. 'It was the only option you had, Doug.'

'Yeah – I guess that conversation will have the Kremlinologists in the State Department busy for a while. You heard his line about doing it over again?'

'I heard it, I don't think it was a slip of the tongue.'

'Neither do I . . . poor bastard . . . I've got a lot to do, Ben.'

Pierce shut off the mike and turned to Vince Torino. 'Quite an idea, Vince.'

'You're telling me! But Ben was right, you didn't have any option.'

Pierce nodded regretfully. He tapped some numbers into his console keyboard and from Vandenberg Airforce Base in California came a picture of the still-empty launch pad awaiting the arrival of the *Atlantis*. *No option*, thought Pierce. *We've got the* Atlantis *and nothing else.*

*

122

Five-thirty p.m. Monday, the simulation operations building, Building #5. Unaware of the call from Balderis, a wholly depressed Tex Harwood sat motionless in a padded swivel chair, staring blankly into the print-up on his T.V. display screen. Reams of paper were scattered about the console. A cold skim had formed on the surface of a cup of coffee, long untouched and long chilled by the efficient air-conditioning. A solitary fly buzzed determinedly, relentlessly above a half-eaten ham and rye sandwich.

All about him there was frantic activity as the simulation operators ran, re-ran and re-ran simulated entrances into the *Yorktown* in conjunction with their counterparts at Vandenberg Airforce Base, California. The data compiled in Houston's computers was patched through the simulations operations building in Houston via satellite to the simulation facilities at Vandenberg. There, in the western launch site, astronauts Lyle Gerber and Gordon Alexander sat in a shuttle simulator and rehearsed the launch and docking of their ship.

Harwood had left the calculation and administration of that simulation to his subordinates. It was effectively 'routine' – at least, as routine as a co-ordination of computer programs over a distance of 2,500 miles, using simulators worth 60 million dollars could ever be. Harwood was not worried about those runs. No – it was the others, the actual transfers of Lewis and Clark from the *Yorktown* to the *Atlantis* that bothered him. Both he and the simulation operators had sought the 'good numbers' that Pierce had requested, but thus far, the numbers had all been bad. he had told Pierce he would have the results in two hours, by 8 p.m. He had the results all right – in just over one hour – but not the ones he expected, and he loathed the prospect of calling Pierce. What he feared was failure; and being by far his own worst critic he hated to admit that he couldn't solve a problem. Three times he had run the simulation on the transfer options. Three times the numbers had not added up. Now he could wait no longer. He gathered up his material and took a waiting JSC taxi to the Mission Control complex, Building #30.

Minutes later, in the reserve control room, Harwood informed Pierce: 'We've completed the simulations on the two transfer options.'

'Already?' replied Pierce, surprised at Harwood's early return.

Harwood frowned in disappointment.

'Yeah, that's the good news.'

'What's the bad?' asked Pierce.

'Both transfer options are technically feasible. We've proven that. But both have problems – big ones.'

Pierce clicked his tongue in disgust. It was always the way. Harwood pulled up a chair and tapped out a code on Pierce's console keyboard. A three-dimensional X-ray diagram of the *Yorktown* appeared on the screen.

As Harwood explained it, the simulations proved what he had feared earlier. The first transfer option, blowing the entire cockpit away from the ship, would send the cockpit and Lewis and Clark along with it, spinning uncontrollably through space.

'I guess we shouldn't be too surprised with such a result. The cockpit jettison system was designed for use in the atmosphere, so there's no control system to guide it in space. Another thing; even if there were no spinning, the *Atlantis* would have one hell of a race to catch up with the cockpit, and even if it did, like I said, she'd have to corral the cockpit and put it in the cargo bay.'

Pierce remained impassive at the findings, as if no news could disturb him further.

'Now it's feasible – I mean, technically feasible – but it would be so damned risky I'd hate to – I mean – I'm glad it's your decision Doug and not mine.'

'You, Colonel Harwood, are a constant source of inspiration,' replied Pierce sardonically. 'What about the GBEES?'

Harwood outlined the mechanics of the second transfer option. The astronauts of the *Atlantis* would approach the *Yorktown*'s underside near the entrance to the escape chute. Inside the *Yorktown*, Lewis or Clark would depressurize the escape tunnel and manually open the outer hatch on the *Yorktown*'s underside, allowing the rescue astronaut to enter the tunnel carrying the two rescue space enclosures necessary to transfer Lewis and Clark out. Once the astronaut was inside the tunnel, the outer hatch would have to be closed and the tunnel repressurized to the same level as the *Yorktown*'s cockpit, so that the inner hatch could then safely be opened up. Then, and only then, could the rescue astronaut enter the *Yorktown*'s cockpit. But while the tunnel was repressurized, an enormous pressure would be placed upon the outer hatch separating Lewis and Clark from the vacuum of space.

'So,' sighed Pierce, 'how long will the outer hatch hold?'

'Fifteen seconds,' replied Harwood.

'Fifteen seconds?!'

'Doug – I don't have to spell it out. The outer hatch was designed for one-time use. Damn it! It's an escape system. Who the hell would figure we'd be using it to get *into* a ship!?'

'No-one,' replied Pierce, 'not you and not me.'

Pierce leaned back in his chair, eyes closed, his mind whirring. If the outer hatch blew before the inner hatch was opened, it was all over. And if it blew while the inner hatch was open . . . he shuddered at the thought. 'The only question is whether or not we can get up the tunnel into the *Yorktown*'s cockpit in less than fifteen seconds. Isn't that right, Tex?'

'Yes, sir.'

'Can we do it?'

'I don't know. We'll have to try it out in the water chamber at Vandenberg; we'll have to try it here at the centre: and we'll have to do more simulations.'

'In any event, I take it your recommendation is to go with the escape chute entrance approach, and not jettison the entire cockpit?'

Harwood scratched the back of his neck. 'Not necessarily . . . there's a problem with it.'

'Sure – the outer hatch can only take fifteen seconds full pressure.'

'No, that's not it,' said Harwood turning back to the console. He tapped at the keyboard once again and one of Adrienne Brooks' long-range pictures of the *Yorktown* came onto the screen. 'This is the best single image view of the *Yorktown*'s underside. You can see the explosion point and the gaping hole.'

Slowly Harwood spun the chair and faced Pierce: 'The damage starts right next to the outer hatch . . . and the only way to determine if it's damaged is to eyeball it. Given the situation, I'd rather not have Rusty or Dick leave the *Columbia* and go for a spacewalk, but—'

'—Well, one thing's for certain. We can't authorize an attempted entrance into the *Yorktown* through the outer hatch system without verifying its reliability,' said Pierce. He pondered a moment, staring into the display screen: 'O.K., we'll have them go for a spacewalk.'

While the necessary preparations for the spacewalk were conducted, Adrienne Brooks continued to work with the launch vehicles engineer's staff to determine the cause of the *Yorktown*'s accident. But they were still no closer to a solution. In fact, given the problems with the transfer plans, Adrienne was beginning to wonder whether it was worth the effort.

Meanwhile, Tex Harwood worked with other astronauts in the immersion tank facility, where a duplicate of the *Yorktown*'s escape chute had been put in position. Dressed in their spacesuits, the astronauts were attempting to duplicate the logistics of entering the chute and reaching its inner hatch in less than fifteen seconds.

At Vandenberg Airforce Base, astronauts Gerber and Alexander, the crew of the *Atlantis*, conducted identical tests. Although they were separated by thousands of miles, both groups were coming up with the same results. None of them could get in the hatch and up the chute in less than seventeen seconds – two seconds too long.

By 7:02 p.m. Bishop, the commander of the *Columbia*, was itching to get on with his spacewalk. Now fully suited up, he concentrated on the data displayed on his control panel screen. The necessary pre-spacewalk preparations were finished.

He pulled his helmet over his carrot-red head of hair, secured it to the collar of his white spacesuit and twisted it, locking and sealing it in place. For a brief moment, he listened to the sounds of his own breath coursing throughout the portable life support system that would be his only protection in space.

'That does it, Dick,' he said to Merriman. 'Houston Capcom, I'm suited up and ready to go.'

'Roger, Columbia,' replied Capcom Steve Whitimaker in Mission Control.

Sitting beside Whitimaker, Blue Team flight director Charlie Egerton's console showed all indicators reading nominal, all systems green and go. The bearded flight director opened a line to Bishop:

'Columbia Commander, this is Flight. I want to reiterate your objective. We want to see the condition of the emergency escape system and the Outer Hatch. Do not spend any more time outside than you have to, do you copy?'

Bishop, the most senior astronaut in the Corps lifted his eyes upward. He took slight umbrage at Egerton's warning. He did not need anyone to remind him of the purpose of his walk, nor of the importance of doing it quickly. He had always thought of flight directors as worry-warts, Egerton especially, but checked his urge to toss out a one-liner.

'Roger Houston, I copy,' he replied.

'And Merriman, keep the remote manipulator arm back from the underside. Do you copy?'

'Jeez,' said Merriman to Bishop, 'you'd think we'd never done this before.' He opened a line to Egerton: 'Yeah, I copy that, Houston.'

Egerton surveyed Mission Control.

'O.K. Blue Team, we're ready to roll – Steve? Give them the go.'

'*Columbia*? Houston Capcom here,' said Whitimaker. 'You're go for your walk and can commence your egress maneuver from the ship.'

'Thank you, Houston!' replied a relieved Bishop. He shut off his microphone. 'Desk jockeys!' he said sarcastically to Merriman, and slid his cockpit seat back and away from the shuttle control panel. 'Don't spend more time than you have to,' he said, mimicking Egerton.

Bishop spun the seat on its base 180 degrees, until it faced the rear of the shuttle's upper flight deck, undid his seatbelt and with a slight controlled kick, vaulted himself out of the chair. In the weightlessness of zero gravity, the kick was sufficient to propel the 200-pound astronaut through the air and he floated to the left-rear of the flight deck and caught hold of the six-rung chromium ladder leading down to the lower deck.

Grasping the top of the ladder, he spun in mid-air, stood on the upper rung and waited for Merriman. Having placed the ship on auto-pilot so that the *Columbia*'s computers maintained the ship's attitude as trimly as possible, Merriman undid his belts and floated back towards Bishop, towards the remote manipulator arm operator's chair. An array of controls on the rear bulkhead were positioned so as to afford the user a rearward view of the shuttle's cargo bay through two 13-inch diagonal rectangular windows. From the chair, Merriman would guide the remote manipulator arm and follow Bishop's spacewalk.

Merriman, still wearing his powder-blue cotton jumpsuit, settled into the chair, fastened his seatbelt, glanced through the rear windows into the pitch black cargo bay where the spindly but powerful arm was located, and turned on the control panel.

'O.K. All set. Let's go.'

Bishop looked down the ladder, held onto the railings and stepped back off the top rung, hovering momentarily in zero G, suspended entirely by the muscles of his wrists like a gymnast in the double rings competition – but with a fraction of the effort.

'Good luck, Rusty,' said Merriman.

'Back in a flash,' replied Bishop.

Effortlessly flicking his wrists upward, he disappeared from Merriman's view, gliding silently down the ladder and landing with a soft *whumph* on the floor of the lower deck. He surveyed the lower deck, replete with storage space, galley for cooking food, zero gravity toilet (a device veteran astronauts of earlier programs were especially thankful for) and the vertically aligned sleeping bags secured to the bulkhead. He approached the airlock separating the lower deck from the dark, cold vacuum recesses of the shuttle's cavernous cargo bay. Bishop opened the 4-foot diameter airlock door and in a mid-air half-crouch floated carefully into the cylindrical 6-foot deep airlock and locked the door behind him.

He felt as if he was in the barrel of a huge cannon. The comparison was apt. If either end of the airlock failed, he would become a cannonball.

'Dick, I'm in the airlock. I'm ready to depressurize. Activate the cargo bay lights, please.'

'Roger, Rusty,' Merriman pushed a series of buttons on the console and the interior of the Bay was suddenly plunged into light. Bishop then activated the airlock's controls and when the readings indicated full depressurization matching the vacuum in space, he gave Merriman the signal:

'O.K. Dick, she's depressurized. Ready to open the outer door.'

With the activation of five switches located around the door, the outer door swung open. Tentatively at first, Bishop ventured into the bay.

'Dick? You can open the doors now.'

'O.K. Rusty,' Merriman depressed the appropriate switches.

Slowly and gracefully, Bishop watched as the twin doors which formed the upper round portion of the ship's fuselage, opened out into space like the petals of a giant metallic flower greeting the sun. The only sound he could hear was that of his own breathing, but as he held the support handles at the base of the cargo bay, he felt through his gloved left hand the reassuring vibration of the hydraulic pumps.

A shaft of brilliant sunlight split through the opening, partially illuminating the cargo bay.

'O.K. Dick, the cargo bay is open – uh, Jack and Rob, I'm going to put on my backpack and go down for a look.'

'Tourists always welcome,' replied Clark in the *Yorktown*.

The backpack, dubbed the manned maneuvering unit, MMU, gave an astronaut the power to fly through space. A white modular unit extended from the shoulders to the waist with two armrests jutting forward contoured to the user's arms. On the end of the backpack's armrests, at the astronaut's fingertips, were twin control stocks which, when activated, released low-thrust cold nitrogen gas propellant, enabling the astronaut to twist, spin, climb, descend and generally maneuver through space with precision and speed. Bishop loved to use the backpack. It was really the closest thing to flying: better than skydiving, better than anything – well, almost anything. A flick of the wrist and you could go up, down, twist, turn, stand on your head, do what you wanted. It was the ultimate freedom machine.

He edged back against the unit secured against the cargo bay's interior wall, pulled the restraint belts around his waist and over his shoulders, tested the controls, then depressed the release switch, freeing the unit from the cargo bay. He flexed his knees and with an easy push he sailed up and away from the wall. With a slight twist of the left control stock, a minute wisp of nitrogen was released, halting his climb, suspending him motionless in the midst of the cargo bay, looking directly at a waving Dick Merriman seated at the remote manipulator operator's chair inside the *Columbia*.

'You're looking good, Rusty,' said Merriman. 'Houston, Rusty's got his backpack on.'

'O.K. Dick,' said Capcom Whitimaker, 'we'd sure like some pictures.'

'Houston, I heard that. I'll get the camera now,' said Bishop.

Flying down feet first towards a storage box adjacent to the airlock, Bishop opened its lid and removed the remote manipulator arm camera, held it in his left hand and with a flick of his right control stock, spun 180 degrees on the spot and flew silently towards the rear of the ship.

Neatly folded in two sections on the left side of the cargo bay floor was the remote manipulator arm, a fifty-foot long electro-mechanical probe. Canadian-designed and built, the arm had the strength to gently, but firmly place twenty-ton satellites along a precisely plotted path through space. Bishop fixed the camera on the wrist portion of the giant arm, the part dubbed in typically pragmatic NASA jargon the end effector, and then backed away and up from the base of the bay until he hovered motionless twenty feet above the ship.

'Dick? The camera is secured. Give her a go.'

'O.K. Rusty. Houston? I'm activating the arm; we'll have a picture for you in a few seconds.'

With the care of a diamond cutter, Merriman twisted one control with his right hand and pulled the other with his left. With dramatic precision the giant arm unfolded and opened. Merriman twisted the controls again until the camera faced the hovering Bishop at a distance of twenty feet, then switched on the camera and turned to the display screen on his control panel.

In Mission Control, the giant Eidophor T.V. screen flickered with horizontal static lines, then the crystal-clear picture of an astronaut in his stark white uniform set against the blackness of space snapped into view, eliciting an immediate gasp from the normally quiet flight controllers.

'Beautiful picture of Rusty. We've got it on our screens,' said Whitimaker.

'O.K. Houston,' replied Merriman.

The indicators in Mission Control all read 'go'. The

picture was clear. The astronaut was ready. The arm was ready.

Flight Director Charlie Egerton pulled at his nose pensively. 'Rusty, we're all ready here. You've got your 'go'. Let's take a look.'

'Roger, Houston,' replied the hovering astronaut.

'Dick, give me a minute before bringing the arm down.'

'Gotcha, Rusty,' replied Merriman.

In the reserve control room Pierce stood, arms folded across his chest, fingers drumming on his biceps: 'Now we should see something,' he said to Torino, without taking his eyes off the screen.

Alone in space; his backpack his only link to the shuttle, Bishop looked at the earth below. A shiver of profound awareness twitched up his spine, reminding him that like the *Columbia* and *Yorktown*, he too was an object controlled by the laws of physics. He too was in orbit. Again he looked down, this time through his feet. Italy. *My boot, Italy's boot*, he thought whimsically. He pushed the control stocks forward and moved silently across the cargo bay, past the doors and away from the ships. Sixty feet out, he spun in mid-space and faced the ships. Jack Lewis in the *Yorktown* spotted him first.

'Rusty? Jack here. I see you!'

'TV or live?' asked Bishop.

'Live!' replied Lewis, then quickly glancing at his display screen, '—and on TV too!'

The astronaut hovered at a distance, determining exactly where his first steps should be.

'Houston? I'd like to inspect the topside of the *Yorktown* before going down to the underside. Do you concur?'

Whitimaker looked at Egerton for approval. The tall, thin flight director of the Blue Team nodded slowly and then decided to answer directly himself:

'Rusty? Charlie Egerton here. 'I'll give you the Go for topside inspection, but shake a leg – it's the other side we're worried about.'

'I just want a complete picture, Flight,' replied Bishop.

'So do we, but our immediate concern is the underside

and the condition of the emergency escape hatch. That's the purpose of your walk.'

'O.K. Houston, I understand. I'm going in for a closer look.'

Bishop pushed forward on the backpack's control stock, and silent jets of nitrogen gas quickly propelled him toward the *Yorktown*'s portside cockpit windows. He pulled back on the control's stock and stopped six feet from the cockpit of the big black jet.

'Hi guys!' He moved closer until he could see both Lewis and Clark peering out at him. God, they looked haggard. 'How are you guys doing?'

'Considering everything – so-so,' replied Lewis.

'I'd like to come in and get you—'

'So would we,' replied Clark.

'But I'll have to leave that to Gerver and Alexander tomorrow.' He looked longingly at their haggard faces, wanting desperately to be able to take them back to the *Columbia*, but knowing that this was impossible. *Get on with it*, he said to himself. 'O.K. Dick, follow me with the camera and we'll start the checkout.'

Bishop moved cautiously along the *Yorktown*'s fuselage, then down to the support structure assembly which held the two ships together, scanning for damage. 'Houston, the support structure on the portside looks O.K. I'm going over to the starboard.'

'Roger,' replied Egerton in Mission Control.

Approaching from the starboard side, Bishop examined the support structure assembly.

'It appears to be all right,' he reported with relief. If anything had happened to the structure assembly, the *Yorktown* could have broken free.

Bishop pulled away from the ships and hovered for a moment above the *Yorktown*'s massive port wing, preparing to examine the underside. The Blue Team's flight surgeon noticed that Bishop's heart and respiration rates were well above normal. Within the confines of his own suit, Bishop also could hear his own heartbeat, accelerated not only by the thrill of flying but also by a mixture of fear and anticipation of what he was about to see below.

In the Reserve Control Room Doug Pierce paced anxiously up and down behind his console. Merriman's pictures, taken via the remote manipulator arm camera and displayed on the front TV Eidophor screen, did little to calm him. Bishop, looking for all the world like a stuffed marionette, seemed to be simply hovering motionless above the ship.

'Come on Bishop,' muttered Pierce as he walked back and forth. 'Get on with it, get on with it.'

The floating astronaut hesitated another moment, inexplicably feeling real dread and a desire to go no further, and yet willing himself to overcome his nerves and get moving. In Mission Control, Egerton noted the delay: '*Columbia* Commander, we would like you to begin please.'

'Uh, Roger, O.K. Houston,' replied Bishop.

In the *Columbia*, Merriman watched his TV display screen as Bishop moved away from the leading edge of the *Yorktown*'s wing and then slowly, agonizingly slowly, dropping beneath the giant swept-back black wings and disappearing totally from view. Merriman maneuvered the controls of the giant arm so that like a snake charmer's python following the moves of the charmer's pipe, the arm with its camera in place followed Bishop's descent. As Bishop disappeared from view at the edge of the wing, Merriman, following express instructions not to venture the arm to the underside of the *Yorktown* until given the green light, brought it to a halt. Like his colleagues in the *Yorktown* and like his associates in Mission Control and the Reserve Control Room, Houston, Merriman waited impatiently for the first word from Rusty Bishop. After long seconds, Egerton could wait no longer and was about to call the astronaut when Bishop's voice shattered the silence.

'Oh, Jesus!'

'What do you have, Rusty?' asked Egerton.

Bishop did not reply immediately, but through the

flight controllers' headsets all could hear him exhale a long breath of resignation.

'Dick?' he said coldly, 'you can bring the camera in for a look. Keep her back a good distance though.'

His brow knitted in concern, Merriman quickly activated the arm and brought it purposefully down past the wings until the image of the *Yorktown*'s underside appeared on the Eidophor screens in the two control rooms. The transmitted pictures prompted muttered curses and a few audible gasps. The *Yorktown*'s underside looked like the scene of a demolition team's retreat and destroy drill.

'Houston?' asked a sobered Rusty Bishop. 'Do you have this in view?'

'Roger, we've got it,' replied Charles Egerton.

Onboard the *Yorktown*, Lewis and Clark viewed their own screens in stunned silence. The damage was awesome and overwhelming, far greater than they had ever thought possible.

'Christ, look at it!' said Lewis.

'Not much left,' muttered Clark.

Beneath them Rusty Bishop began a monologue in the sanguine, objective tones of a coroner presiding over the autopsy of a particularly bloodied corpse.

'Houston, I'll call out the damage as I see it, O.K.? The underside is ripped away pretty good.' *Be specific, damn it!* he chided himself, *they can see that!* 'Uh, the main area of damage extends from the aft underside by the engine, to . . . uhm, I make it out about twenty-five to thirty feet. Do you have this in view, Dick?'

'Yeah, Rusty,' replied Merriman, swinging the camera around.

Bishop continued. 'Houston, I make the opening to be about ten feet wide at the rear and, uh, well it tapers to about three feet at the forward point – kind of a rough V pattern.'

'What about the escape chute hatch?' asked Egerton. 'Is it all right?'

'The hatch . . . the hatch appears to be O.K., Houston!

135

The explosion point begins about eight inches behind it!' cried Bishop.

In the Reserve Control Room, Doug Pierce sank back and mopped his brow with relief. The hatch was intact. Lewis and Clark's transfer was now at least technically feasible.

'Jack? Rob?' called Bishop, sliding his glove over the outer hatch. 'Did you hear me? The hatch is O.K.'

'We heard you, Rusty!' said an elated Rob Clark.

'We're still in business,' grinned Jack Lewis.

'Damn right we're still in business!' replied Bishop. He backed away from the underside and cautiously maneuvered the backpack until he hovered at a discreet fifteen feet away. He continued his description. 'There's, uh, there's a lot of pipes and hoses dangling down from the guts of the ship and I, uh, just a sec – I think I'd better go in for a closer look.'

'Not too close,' whispered Doug Pierce in the Reserve Control Room.

'Rusty,' said Capcom Whitimaker in Mission Control, 'keep your distance. We advise that you do not, repeat, *do not* touch any of the ship's components, damaged or otherwise.'

'Don't worry, Houston, don't worry. Not with a 10 foot pole . . .'

'Dick? Can you bring the camera in for a closer look? How about another six feet?'

'Will do, Rusty,' replied Merriman, gingerly nursing althe arm forward and pointing the camera directly up into the shattered underbelly.

In relation to the ships, the arm was now aligned like a letter V lying on its side, out and down twenty-five feet from the shuttle and then back twenty-five feet in towards the damaged underside. Bishop stared up into the ship's mechanical innards, a heap of twisted and broken pipes and tanks, and shook his head in disbelief: 'Houston, it's pretty hard to tell what's intact – it's like a parts bin!'

In the Reserve Control Room a shaken Doug Pierce sat down at his console chair, wondering how the *York-*

town had even held together. One thing was clear: with so many pipes and hoses dangling from the underside, and with 4,000 pounds of turbine propellant still in the *Yorktown*'s tanks, any direct docking with the *Atlantis* would be exceedingly risky, if not downright impossible – unless, *unless* . . . But there was absolutely no alternative. Pierce pulled out his flight log and jotted down his impressions of the extent of the damage.

Bishop activated his backpack and soared a hundred feet away from the ships to take one last look before rejoining Merriman in the *Columbia*. He hovered and stared at the two craft – one black, one white – hanging against the blackness of space. It was a totally incongruous sight. The *Yorktown* – in space! 'God! This is nuts,' he muttered to himself. 'O.K. Houston,' he said aloud, 'anything further you want me to—'

Suddenly his voicebox froze in a moment's stab of fear. His eyes immediately swivelled to the controls of his backpack, wondering if he had set himself into a spin by accidentally firing off some nitrogen gas. No, that wasn't it. he hadn't touched the controls at all. He wasn't spinning. But if *he* wasn't, then . . .

In the *Columbia*, Dick Merriman felt a distinct jolt and was pitched face-first towards the control panel, flinging his arms inward in an instinctive bid to protect his eyes. In the *Yorktown*, Lewis and Clark were flung forcefully back into their seats.

One hundred feet away in space, Bishop's eyes widened at the horrifying sight of a quickly-growing cloud of gas spewing from the *Yorktown*'s underside.

'Propellants! Houston! *Yorktown*'s venting propellants!'

The two ships were cartwheeling crazily, nose-first, end over end, tumbling through space.

'Houston! Houston! We're pitching down,' yelled Jack Lewis in the *Yorktown*, as the earth appeared to rise past the cockpit window.

In Mission Control, a succession of rapidly changing numbers flashed across the flight controllers' panels as the shuttle's computers relayed telemetric information to Houston indicating how and where the ships were tumbling. Horrified, alone, Bishop could only watch. Lewis and Clark could do nothing; it was now all up to Merriman.

'*Columbia* pilot,' cried Egerton to Merriman, 'we've got venting from the *Yorktown*, venting from the *Yorktown*!'

But before Egerton had completed the message, Merriman had already depressed the buttons marked 'Auto' and 'Return', thereby ensuring that the giant arm would repackage itself back into the shuttle's cargo bay automatically.

'On my way, Houston!' said Merriman. In one swift twisting motion he spun from the chair, sailed across the flight deck and clambered frantically back into his cockpit seat.

'Dick,' shouted a terrified Jack Lewis, 'slow her down! Slow her down!'

Hastily Merriman strapped himself into his seat and pulled back on the *Columbia*'s control stock. The shuttle's reaction control system jets fired, attempting to counter the force of the spin. The venting was now accelerated and the ships were spinning end over end, faster and faster, performing a complete rotation now every 1½ seconds. With each rotation the support structure assembly holding the *Yorktown* to the *Columbia* came under severe strain, while inside the *Yorktown* the force was almost sufficient to pull the two astronauts out of their chairs.

As Merriman pulled backwards on the control stock of the shuttle, the reaction control system fired blasts of propellants downwards from either side of the *Columbia*'s nose and on either side of the rudder. Yet still the ship would not stop tumbling. And with every second, gallons of precious propellants needed for a safe re-entry were being drained out into space.

The earth appeared to pass by the cockpit window again and again and again in a dizzying progression as the

138

Columbia and the *Yorktown* tumbled on. Bishop watched in horror from 100 feet away.

'Keep firing, Dick! Keep firing!' he screamed.

'Houston! She's not responding! Not responding!' cried Merriman in the *Columbia*.

'Maintain your thrusters, *Columbia*,' replied flight director Egerton, 'you'll have to ride it out!'

A feeling of horror ripped through Dick Merriman. He had felt it only once before. It was just like his crash, the crash that had nearly ended his career as an astronaut, and nearly killed him.

It has been a routine training flight in a T38 jet. In the pilot seat sat Dick Merriman. Behind him, his co-pilot Frank Branscom. They were on their final approach to the runway. The landing gear had descended and been locked in place. The skies had been clear, the sun still blazing, mid-afternoon bright. Merriman had just glanced at his air/speed indicator – 140 miles an hour – when the engines flamed out, shut down, cold dead, and the jet dropped like an elevator with its cables cut, and hit and skidded and slid and skidded and the last thing Merriman remembered before blacking out was plowing through a fence.

When he awoke he had no sense of pain; in fact he had no feeling at all. But when he undid his harness and tried to get out of the cockpit, bolts of pain ripped through him and he realized his legs were broken. And God, how it hurt.

'Frank' he cried to his co-pilot. 'Frank!?' No answer. Merriman slumped back into the seat. He was distantly aware of rescue vehicles trundling and bouncing across the field towards him, then Airforce personnel scrambling up to the cockpit. The first one there took one look at Frank Bramscom and threw up. One of the fenceposts had impaled the dead pilot right in the face.

Merriman saw the man retch and knew the score. At least it had been quick. Merriman passed out. In the seconds of the crash he had been racked with the same empty feeling he felt now. No control! He couldn't control the spinning of the two vehicles. No control! Damn it! Damn it! Damn it! Not again!!

Merriman pulled back on the control stock desperately. There was nothing left to do but pray that the force of the small reaction control system jets in the *Columbia*'s nose and tail would work. *They had to!*

A hundred feet away, Bishop could only hover and watch, praying to God that the spin would stop. If the venting did not stop before the *Columbia* ran out of propellant, the two vehicles would cartwheel into the atmosphere, and he, Rusty Bishop, would be left alone in space – with only one hour's air.

But as suddenly as it had begun, the venting stopped, and Merriman's firing of the *Columbia*'s engines slowly brought the spin to an end, until the *Yorktown* and *Columbia* hung, nose down, pointing towards the earth. Small, golden nuggets of frozen propellant trailed away and out in a crazy, spiralling pattern, forming a frozen, glittering frame of light around the two vehicles. Merriman reactivated the *Columbia*'s engines until both craft were brought aerodynamically trim, horizontal to the earth.

'Houston,' said Merriman, 'we've stopped it, we're stable.'

'Jack and Rob,' asked Whitimaker, 'are you all right?'

'Roger, Houston,' said Lewis weakly. 'We're O.K., but that was some ride.'

'I sure hope we don't have a replay,' added Clark.

'If we do,' replied Lewis coldly, 'you can kiss it all goodbye.'

Still hovering at a distance, Bishop could hear his heart pounding, and feel the blood pounding at his temples. He had to get into the *Columbia* fast. Racing his backpack at full acceleration, he plowed through the solidified gas cloud, the particles hitting and bouncing off his suit like hailstones. He was petrified by his narrow escape. He had come within an ace of being left up there all by himself.

The pelting stopped. He had cleared the field of solidified gas and was now approaching the entrance hatch to the cargo bay's airlock. God, that hatch looked beautiful! He reached for the door, but then stopped. A mental alarm bell sounded in his mind. The support structure assembly! He could not enter the *Columbia* without checking out the assembly holding the two ships together.

Up, out, down and around, he flew from the cargo bay to the assembly. It needed only one look.

'Shit!!' he thought, clenching his jaw. He said nothing and flew back to the cargo bay.

'Dick, I'm coming in.'

Although the flight controllers in Mission Control continued to monitor their consoles in an outward appearance of calm, the venting incident had shaken them badly. It had all happened so suddenly, so unexpectedly! And there had been so little that they could do to help! In the reserve control room, Pierce began to wonder how much more his men could take, and how much more the ships, especially the *Yorktown*, could take. And the *Columbia* – what of its own propellants?

As if in answer, the propulsion engineer flashed the data onto Pierce's display screen. In the attempt to bring the spin under control, the *Columbia* had used up all but 5,833 pounds of propellant fuel supply. In order to land and return safely to earth, the ship required 4,140 pounds of propellant. The *Atlantis* would still carry the *Yorktown* to a safe altitude, but one more spin, one more tumble, or one more vent to be brought under control., and the *Columbia* would have too little fuel to land. Like the damaged *Yorktown*, it too would have to be abandoned.

Chilled by the data, Pierce turned to Vince Torino and pointed to the screen. Torino saw the figures and understood.

Pierce opened the line to the propulsion engineer: 'I have your numbers on the *Columbia*. What about *Yorktown*'s propellants? Is there anything left? Are we going to have another super spin?'

The engineer shrugged, whistling a long, low note of frustration at his inability to provide a relatively routine answer. 'Doug, all we know is that before the venting there was 4,000 pounds of turbine fuel in the *Yorktown*. It's hard even to guesstimate how much got dumped during the vent. The only thing I can suggest is to take the amount of propellant the *Columbia* used to counter-act the spin and try to give you a rough-cut figure on how much was leaked out of the *Yorktown*. But it really will be a rough number.'

'Is there any possibility it was all used up?' asked Pierce, hoping against hope the engineer would say yes. Another venting at the moment of docking and . . . Pierce pushed the thought out of his mind.

'Is there any *possibility*?' the propulsion engineer said, repeating Pierce's question. He sighed and shook his head, perplexed again at his inability to respond to an essentially routine request. As a scientist he was used to dealing with precise data and it frustrated him to find himself reduced to playing hunches. His response was matter-of-fact: 'We have no incoming telemetry on the *Yorktown*'s propellant supply. We have no telemetry on how much was vented. We do know the venting lasted for 96 seconds and we know that the venting could have come from any one of four different points. Unless we know what size the leak was and from how many points – well, your guess is as good as mine. Look Doug . . .' his voice was distraught, barely controlled, '. . . I wish to God I could give you something to hang onto, but I can't.'

'O.K., it's O.K.,' said Pierce with a wave of his hand. He closed his eyes and kept them closed a few moments and tried a new approach. 'So we do know how much propellant is left in the shuttle, right?'

'Yeah – 5,833 pounds combined on both the reaction control system and the orbiting maneuvering system.'

'And the minimum for a safe landing is 4,140 pounds,' stated Pierce.

'Allowing for separation from the *Yorktown* and re-alignment for a re-entry path – yes.'

'Four thousand, one hundred and forty pounds. But that's a minimum, right?'

'So, in other words we have . . .' The propulsion engineer punched numbers into a desk calculator, '. . . 1,693 pounds of propellant left in the *Columbia*, and that's all.'

Pierce shook his head and groaned softly. 'Sixteen hundred pounds – that's awfully low.'

Torino, sitting to his right, did a quick mental computation. The combined weights of both ships was 750,000 pounds or 375 tons of aluminum, chromium, reinforced carbon and other alloys. If the *Columbia*'s propellant levels dipped below the minimum, Pierce would be forced to order Bishop and Merriman to abandon ship, transfer to the *Atlantis* and leave both the *Columbia* and the *Yorktown* to burn up.

'Maybe if they come in over water . . .' said Venerolli absentmindedly.

Pierce glared at him. 'And if they come in over land? A city?' His mind flashed back to Skylab in 1979 – and Skylab had only weighed 85 tons.

Onboard the *Columbia*, a shaken Rusty Bishop stowed his suit away in the lower deck, stripped off his underwear and changed into an orange Nomex casual flight outfit as bright as his carrot-red hair. Disturbed by what he had seen of the starboard support structure assembly, he pulled himself up the *Columbia*'s ladder from the lower deck of the shuttle to the flight deck, where Dick Merriman sat, still gripping the control stock, fearful that if he let go the spinning might start again.

Bishop strapped himself into the commander's left-hand seat, exhaled deeply and exchanged a furtive glance with Dick Merriman. 'Thought I'd almost lost you guys – hell of a sight.'

Merriman's expression was ghost-like, and his voice a low whisper. 'I thought we were going to spin right into the atmosphere. I didn't know if I could pull it out, Rusty.'

'You did, Dick, you did. Like I said this morning, once you get up here, it all comes back. Let me take the controls for a change.'

Merriman quickly acceded and sat back as Bishop

143

grasped the control stock. In his heart Merriman knew he had performed well. It had been his first big test since returning to active duty from his jet crash, and he had passed. Rusty's words meant a lot.

'I used up all but 5,800 pounds propellant fighting the spin, Rusty; we've only got 1,693 left.'

'Sixteen hundred – that's cutting it awfully thin.'

'If we have to try and keep both ships trim, aerodynamically trim that is, we'll use it all up . . . that's if the *Yorktown* doesn't spring another leak first . . .' His words trailed off.

Bishop stared straight ahead. 'The *Yorktown* had better not vent any more, because there's a six-inch crack on the starboard support structure assembly.'

The news stunned Dick Merriman. 'What? You said there was no damage!'

'That was before the spin. I checked it out again before coming back in.'

'Oh, Christ! Are you sure?'

Bishop glared at him, his look serving as an answer.

'Do we tell Jack and Rob?' asked Merriman.

'No,' replied Bishop, shaking his head vigorously. 'There's nothing they can do about it. There's nothing we can do about it. It's a crack, a big one, and it was caused by the spin. If we have another one, the *Yorktown* could break free. Jack and Rob have enough to sweat about already.'

'We'd better call Houston,' said Merriman.

'On a closed line,' said Bishop, not wanting Lewis or Clark to hear the conversation.

Bishop piped the call through on a biological communications channel beyond the *Yorktown*'s capacity to hear. That alone keyed Doug Pierce for bad news. But even so he was unprepared for the seriousness of Bishop's message.

'. . . so before I came back into the ship, something told me to take a look – instinct, I guess. There it was, a six-inch crack. Sorry to keep dumping bad news on you, Doug.'

'Forget it, Rusty. I'm the one who should be apologizing to you. We just have to hold it together until tomorrow.'

Neither Bishop, nor Pierce, nor anyone else knew, nor would they ever discover, that over 1,000 pounds of propellants still remained in the *Yorktown*'s broken innards.

It was 9:48 p.m. In twelve minutes the Gold Team's shift would end. They had been on duty since 4:00 a.m. and could take little more. But still there were nagging questions left unanswered. In spite of the efforts of Harwood and the simulation operations team, it remained unclear whether the outer hatch could withstand the pressurization level necessary for a rescue astronaut to enter the ship.

At the left-hand console in the second row of the reserve control room, one man was oblivious to the passing of time and to the impending Team transfer – the flight surgeon. Brow knitted in concentration, he watched his console display of Bishop and Merriman's heart and respiration rates. Both were close to normal. But for Lewis and Clark he still had no information, no telemetry coming through, thus no data on the *Yorktown* crewmen's condition. Relying entirely on ears, he keyed on Lewis and Clark's conversations with the Blue Team's Capcom Steve Whitimaker in Mission Control, trying to determine their physical state.

Whitimaker was reading up data to them. They in turn tapped the data into their computers, first reading the numbers back to Whitimaker before processing the information to guard against error. Their exchanges sounded like a group of chartered accountants comparing debit columns:

'. . . and the last one is 5911,' said Whitimaker.

'O.K., and it's 9511,' replied Jack Lewis.

'No Jack, that's a 59, again 5911, preceded by 6337.'

'O.K., 59 and, uh . . . I just, I'm sorry, I just didn't get the one before that.'

'It's O.K., Jack, it's O.K.'

The surgeon had heard enough. He rang Pierce.

'Flight, this is the surgeon. If you're not doing so already, listen to Blue Team's Capcom uplinking data with Lewis and Clark, will you?'

The surgeon's 'will you' carried the ring of an order. Pierce listened to the astronauts' conversations for a few moments.

The surgeon cut in again. 'Flight, unless there's something damned important that they have to know, I want them to try to get some sleep. They're tired and thirsty and hungry, and they need rest.'

'O.K.,' replied Pierce, removing his glasses and rubbing his own tired eyes, 'I'll pass it on. I guess we could all use some sleep.'

At 10:03 p.m. the Red Team, led by flight director Joe Gibbs, took over the active flight duty from the Blue Team in Mission Control. The Red Team's 10:00 p.m. to 6:00 a.m. shift was the least envied in NASA. Some of the flight controllers wore small buttons on their jackets featuring a cartoon character, eyes bloodshot, headset askew, with the caption, 'Guess what shift I have?' Others, feeling humour was inappropriate, had quietly removed the buttons.

With the Red team now taking over, Charlie Egerton in the Blue Team would soon arrive in the reserve control room to continue the pre-launch preparations through the night. Egerton's last order before handing it over to the Red Team was to relay the surgeon's message to the crews. Clark's reply had been typically laconic. 'We'll get some sleep all right – at least some part of us will.'

By 10:20 p.m. the three Flight Teams, Gold, Blue and Red, had completed an orderly transfer of responsibilities. In Mission Control on the second floor of Building 30, the incoming Red Team's flight controllers hoped desperately that their shift would be routine and uneventful, unlike the preceding two. On the third floor in the reserve control room, members of the Gold and Blue Teams formed up into spontaneous groupings around the various consoles of each of the four rows, as the Gold Team members sought to convey key points of information to

146

their counterparts. As always, the hub of activity was the flight director's console in the centre of the third row. Joining the group now was Benjamin F. Fleck, the Administrator for NASA, a strong, tall, white-haired man with an imposing, imperial presence. Fleck, Pierce and Egerton could almost have stood for three generations of the space program: Fleck, at 56, former flight director from Apollo days; Pierce at 43, flight director during Skylab and early space shuttle missions; and Egerton, 37, the youngest, a flight director only after NASA had begun the shuttle missions. Only nineteen years separated them, but for NASA those years had seen three distinct generations of technological advance.

'No word from Harwood?' asked Pierce.

'No, not yet,' replied Egerton.

'Well, let's get on with it.'

Pierce ticked off the scheduled countdown on a chart resting on his lap. 'O.K., we're still working at an 11:08 *Atlantis* launch and rendezvous at 12:36, and no transfer option has yet been verified by Harwood.' He looked up at the bearded Egerton. 'You'll have to choose one of the options tonight, Charlie. Gerber and Alexander won't have any practice time. I'm afraid whatever option you choose, they'll have to get it right first time.'

Egerton's face was expressionless. The timing of the shifts and failure of simulations operations to verify the feasibility of a transfer plan had both shoved responsibility for decision-making from Pierce to Egerton.

Inside Pierce, two factions warred on. One chafed bitterly: it was *his* mission and he wanted to make the decisions. The other faction was relieved: at least if the chosen option didn't work, the responsibility for failure was no longer his.

'Whatever you decide Charlie, I'll back you. It's your show.'

Egerton nodded and Pierce looked at Benjamin Fleck, realizing he had said just what Fleck had told him that morning – that the show was his.

'Gentlemen,' said Fleck, 'I suggest we let Charlie and the rest of the team get on with it.'

Pierce thought it was the best suggestion of the day. The Gold Team began to disperse, their bodies aching for rest. But before giving up his chair, Pierce wanted one last look at Vandenberg Air Base. He pushed the display button on his console and his screen flickered to life.

From 2,100 miles away on the Pacific Coast came the image of the SLC-6 launch tower at Vandenberg Airforce Base, lit up to a harsh white by bank upon bank of Klieg lights. The tower seemed eerie as dozens of white-coated helmeted technicians moved with deliberate haste, appearing and disappearing like ghosts as they stepped out of the pitch black shadows into the bright, white light. He deactivated the picture on the screen, pulled his headset off, placed it in the top drawer on the right of the console, stood, pulled his jacket off the back of the chair, and draped it over his right shoulder. His day was over.

'Good luck, Charlie.'

'Thanks, Doug.'

Pierce walked slowly down to the front of the reserve control room and then looked back across the rows of consoles, again fully manned, this time by a team of fresher minds. He pondered for a moment. They had done all they could, but would it be enough?

On board the *Yorktown*, Jack Lewis dozed fitfully, his exhausted body craving rest, his mind unable to switch off. Beside him, an equally beat Robert Clark had converted his flight plan into a makeshift diary in which he scribbled his observations and feelings. The exercise was more for mental therapy than for historical purpose; Clark knew as well as anybody that there was a very real probability that neither he nor his notes would long survive . . .

'I have never known such utter fear or exhaustion in my

life. Accident. Explosion – didn't think we'd make it into orbit, or that we would be alive.

To be alive! To have survived! Never known such fear or exhilaration – repeating myself – tired. Like going to the gallows, then reprieve – now maybe to the gallows again. Shit. Pierce – entering Yorktown *by escape chute – Christ, what a mess!'*

His eyelids heavy, Clark stared out the *Yorktown*'s forward window at the Earth's horizon – a bolt of bright light appeared to rise above it turning the skim of the Earth's atmosphere into a brilliant spectrum of purple, blue, red, orange and yellow hues. The sight inspired him . . .

'Sunrise. Beautiful. One every 96 minutes – really lost track of time – 10:30 p.m. Houston, Monday "night". It feels like Tuesday or something – God, it's beautiful up here. Jack is sleeping. I miss . . .'

His eyes stung and he bit his lower lip to plug the formation of tears. *'I miss her, I miss home . . . we both knew it could happen.'*

In the reserve control room, Adrienne Brooks walked up to Capcom Steve Whitimaker's console. The test she had helped run had long been completed, albeit unsuccessfully. 'Are they asleep yet?' she asked.

Whitimaker looked up from his writing, surprised to see her. 'Oh, hiya Adrienne, ah, let's see, Dick Merriman is sleeping while Rusty's flying the *Columbia*. He'll be at the controls till four a.m. We think Jack Lewis is asleep in *Yorktown*, at least we haven't heard from him in an hour, but there was some conversation between Rob and the flight surgeon about twenty minutes ago so he's probably still awake.'

Brooks nodded slowly, assessing her next request. 'Can I talk to him?' she said quietly.

'Rob?'

'Yes.'

'Sure – ah, here's my headset,' he said, rising and handing it to her. 'I'm going for a coffee, I'll be back in ten minutes.'

'Thanks, Steve,' she said appreciatively, knowing that Whitimaker never drank coffee.

She sat down at the console. Cheer him up, she thought. Keep it short, don't choke up.

Onboard the *Yorktown*, Rob Clark jerked, startled at the chiming of the incoming call bell. His eyes darted to the still sleeping Jack Lewis and with a quick stab of his right hand, Clark silenced the bell. '*Yorktown* Pilot,' he said softly so as not to wake Lewis, 'What is it Houston?'

'Hello Robert Clark,' said the soft affectionate voice.

Clark sat up straighter, smiling at the sound of her voice. 'Hello Adrienne Brooks,' he replied with a warmth that could not begin to reveal what he felt in his heart, 'I was hoping you would call . . . sorry about standing you up for dinner.'

'That's all right . . . just don't make it a habit.'

'I won't . . . am I keeping you up? What time is it down there anyway?'

'About 10:30 p.m.'

'Every ninety-six minutes, another sunrise, up here.'

'Pretty?'

'Very, and uh, I've been writing some things in my diary . . . you know, thoughts, observations.'

'About me?' Christ! what did I say that for, she thought.

'Yeah,' he laughed, 'some of it was about you.'

'Rob? . . . we're really working on it – for you and Jack . . .'

'Yeah, sure . . .' His eyes stung once more. He couldn't continue. She sensed what he felt – there was so much they couldn't say.

'The countdown is on schedule,' she said, '*Atlantis* is almost ready.'

'Right. Gerber and Alexander are good guys . . .' God, how I love you! he thought.

'I've been working on the cause of the accident . . . with the launch vehicle engineer and his staff.'

'Any luck?'

'Not yet – but I'll find it.'

150

It doesn't make much difference; he thought – 'Yeah, I'm sure you will . . .'

Brooks saw Whitimaker slowly walking back towards the console, a styrofoam cup of milk in his hand. 'I have to go now – when you get back tomorrow, we can talk – I'll make dinner.'

'I'd like that – really I would.'

'You take care of yourself, get some sleep.'

'Good night, Rob.'

'Yeah, O.K. and Adrienne? . . . I love you.'

'And I love you,' she replied in a scarcely audible whisper.

Whitimaker approached the console. She shut the microphone off, stood abruptly and handed him the headset. 'Stay on your toes, Steve.'

Utterly exhausted, Doug Pierce fumbled with the keys to his car, locked it and trudged up to the front door of his unlit home. Living in Clear Lake City had certain advantages, not the least of which was being 5 minutes from the Space Center.

He stooped to pick up the morning and afternoon papers, neither of which he had seen. Inside he noted the headline. The morning *Houston Post* proclaimed, 'SHUTTLE SET TO GO'. He then looked at the evening *Houston Chronicle*. The headline was in thick, black, funereal letters, 'DISASTER IN SPACE!'. He cursed and pitched both sets of papers onto a nearby chair.

PART TWO

Tuesday, May 12th

CHAPTER SIX

The explosion of sound was simultaneous. The bedside radio alarm clock and white princess-style telephone both sounded at exactly 4:00 a.m. – the radio blaring the climax of the William Tell Overture, and the phone set on loud ring. Doug Pierce was suddenly wide awake. He had asked Steve Whitimaker, the Capcom, to ring him in case his alarm clock failed. Just another back-up by a man used to dealing with back-ups.

Throwing the covers off, Pierce spun from a prone to an upright sitting position, silencing the radio alarm clock with his left hand and grasping the telephone's handle with the other.

'Pierce here,' he said crisply, giving no indication that seconds before he had been dead to the world.

'Doug,' enquired Whitimaker, 'are you up?'

Pierce, feeling as if he had been shot from a cannon, stood cradling the phone between his neck and right shoulder and stretching his arms high above him. 'I am now. How's it going?'

'Fine,' replied Whitimaker. 'A quiet night, no new problems. They're still asleep.'

Pierce's mind quickly shifted to the continuing overnight simulation runs by the simulation operations team, trying mightily to lengthen the time that the *Yorktown*'s Outer Hatch would hold shut during today's transfer attempt. 'And the sim ops, how about them?'

'No progress, Doug. Still fifteen seconds.'

'Damn,' replied Pierce, 'O.K. Steve, I'll be right over.'

As Pierce drove quickly through the pre-dawn darkness to the Space Center, his mind was already ticking off the duties of the day. He was tired, very tired. *Another twelve hours and you can sleep all week long, if you want to.*

Taking the elevator to the Mission Control level, Pierce

emerged and practically bowled over a startled Adrienne Brooks. Instinctively he grabbed onto her, saving her from a fall, but knocking file folders flying.

'Adrienne! Sorry! Are you O.K.?'

'Yes, I'm all right. Just a bit tired.' She regarded the pile of scattered papers then stooped to pick them up.

'Let me,' Pierce scooped up a handful.

'That's O.K.,' she said. 'I was hoping I'd find you . . . I found the cause of the accident.'

The news shook Pierce. 'You did! When?'

'About an hour ago – 3:30 a.m. to be exact. We worked on it all night. Got the data down the hall in the launch vehicle staff support room.'

Pierce looked at his watch. 4:30 a.m. 'I'll make time for this one, Adrienne. Let's take a look.'

The launch vehicle engineer's staff support room, directly opposite the entrance to the Mission Control Room consisted of two rows of computer consoles. Although empty of personnel now, the room had surged with activity throughout the night as Adrienne Brooks and other NASA personnel traced down all of the *Yorktown*'s incoming telemetry, from the moment of take-off to those split-milliseconds after the accident when the force of the explosion had knocked out all incoming data.

Brooks tapped some numbers into the keyboard as Pierce drew up a chair.

'I'm calling up a profile right now. We ran this through, backwards and forwards – couldn't make sense of it until . . . here it is.'

The display screen showed a matrix of columns of numbers aligned in a 5 by 5 grid pattern.

'Pressurization levels of *Yorktown*'s fuel system, right?' asked Pierce.

'Right. Now, we've frozen the numbers moments before the explosion. The numbers in the top left-hand corner are the minutes and seconds into the launch.'

Pierce nodded slowly as he interpreted the figures. 'They all read normal.'

'At this point, yes.'

Adrienne pushed the console's 'Run' button and the numbers began changing slowly, consistently, predictably. Some of the columns decreased in value, indicating depletion of the *Yorktown*'s hydrogen propellants others increased in value, indicating the corresponding increase in flow rates.

'Keep watching,' she said. 'This is ten seconds before the bang. Now watch the centre column . . . There!'

The numbers plunged. Pierce groaned. Brooks continued, pointing at the centre column. 'With loss of pressure in that tank, the propellants flooded the compartment. I don't have to tell you what happened next – ignition upon contact, causing the explosion.'

The numbers continued to decrease rapidly for a few more seconds, then stopped.

'That's the end of the run,' Brooks said. 'All of that damage from just one tank!'

Pierce focused on the number of the flawed tank. '7833–1. Who built it?' he snapped.

'Pacific Dynamics.'

'Bastards! The design specs of the entire system were set at three times potential pressurization. When that tank blew it was barely at 904 of its minimum acceptable level!'

'I know. Pacific Dynamics engineers are in the vehicle analysis room. They say the tests at their Los Angeles plant went perfectly.'

'Sure they went perfectly!' he replied sarcastically. 'They always do until something goes wrong.' Pierce stood, shaking his head in disbelief, and glowering at the screen. 'Run that again, Adrienne.'

Brooks observed his brooding presence and activated the display screen one more time. 'Here it is.'

Again the numbers ran, and again at the precise moment of the explosion the centre column figures plunged rapidly.

'Damn!' he said, shaking a finger angrily at the screen. 'That tank - that tank should not have failed!'

157

'But it did fail, and when it did it started a chain reaction.'

'Jesus, Jesus,' muttered Pierce, trying to calm himself.

'At least,' reflected Brooks, 'we know what caused the accident. At least it's not a design flaw in the hypersonic jets themselves. That particular tank may be flawed, but the ships themselves are not.'

'How do we know that?'

'Because I had Edwards run identical tests on the *Hornet* and the *Liberty*. Their tanks check out perfectly.' Not that it does Rob and Jack any good, she thought.

'All this money, all this work, all this preparation and some damn fool doesn't check out one fucking tank properly!'

His language surprised her. Doug Pierce never swore.

'Sorry.'

'Don't apologise,' she said.

Pierce shook his head and smiled in exasperation. 'I've said sorry to you twice this morning, when I should be congratulating you.'

'The messenger usually does get blamed for the bad news,' she replied, shutting off the terminal.

'Yeah, all too often.' Pierce noticed her haggard appearance. 'You must be exhausted, Adrienne. Go get some sleep. 'I'll have someone call you before the *Atlantis* launches.'

'I'd rather stay.'

'That's an order,' he said with a smile.

'Well, if it's an order, that's different.'

Pierce crossed the hall into Mission Control. In less than an hour the Red Team would hand over flight responsibilities back to Pierce's Gold Team. Through the night, Charlie Egerton's Blue Team in the reserve control room had continued the countdown check-out with Vandenberg Airforce Base. All was well. At 9:08 Houston time, 7:08 Vandenberg time, the shuttle *Atlantis* would be launched.

Pierce sat down beside Joe Gibbs, the Red team's flight director, a short excitable Briton in his mid-forties. Pierce

158

noted Gibbs' standard attire of neatly pressed gray slacks and sporty tweed jacket.

'Ah! Douglas!' said Gibbs, reaching for his flight log, in which he had penned his observations of the preceding shift. He handed it to Pierce. 'I should think it safe to say weak plot, but exciting reading nonetheless.'

Pierce smiled, said nothing and absorbed the document's contents, allowing Gibbs to continue monitoring the flight without interruption. That was the NASA system; the man on duty, be it flight director, surgeon, or avionics engineer, was the man in charge. Pierce, of course, was the lead flight director, since his Gold Team was the lead team; but hierarchy notwithstanding, if at 5:59 a.m. one minute before he came on duty, there was a decision to be made, it would be made by Gibbs. Unless otherwise instructed, the incoming flight controllers looked over their colleagues' shoulders as unobtrusively as possible.

The first few moments after a new team begins its shift of on-duty flight responsibility are easily the most critical. The incoming team members, having attempted for the previous hour or so to absorb as much of the present essence and status of the mission, are naturally eager to get down to business. The outgoing team, after eight hours of activity, just as naturally wish to leave their consoles, their positions, in the best possible shape.

The transfer itself usually took no more than two minutes, during which headsets were unplugged by outgoing members, plugged in by incoming members, a few quick words of encouragement were exchanged and incoming colleagues given last-minute briefing on critical points. This morning was no exception. But in another sense it was special. Joe Gibbs and the Red Team would not in any sense be going off duty. Instead they would move immediately up to the third floor reserve control room to replace Charlie Egerton's Blue Team for the final countdown to the launch of the *Atlantis*.

One floor above in the reserve control room, a tired Charles Egerton was relieved to see Gibbs and the Red

Team arrive to take over the countdown responsibilities. He had already decided to take a JSC taxi to his home a scant half-mile from Pierce's in Clear Lake. Frankly, he was just too tired to drive and was confident Pierce and Gibbs would hold it all together until he and the Blue Team reported back to duty at 2 p.m. that afternoon.

To Doug Pierce, however, 2 p.m. was far in the future. He had a real sense that the battle was finally joined. Capcom Torino sat eagerly beside him. Together with the Gold Team, Pierce and Torino began the standard review of the mission's status.

In the fourth row of consoles behind Pierce and Torino, Benjamin Fleck sat at the NASA HQ console, studying the final version of the flight plan evolved during the night. Gibbs and the Red Team would run the final countdown along with Vandenberg control. At the moment of the *Atlantis*' launch, control would shift from the Red to the Gold Team and from then on it would be Pierce's responsibility to guide astronauts Gerber and Alexander in the *Atlantis* to the rendezvous with the *Yorktown*. On paper the plan was simple. Execution would be a different matter.

The status reports came in quickly. Trajectory stated that the ship's orbit had declined during the night to a low of 91·06 miles, down from a high of 94·7 the previous day. On Pierce's display screen, the trajectory engineer displayed a flowing green altitude graph covering four days, Monday to Thursday; the horizontal axis represented the days, the vertical axis the altitude in nautical miles. A yellow horizontal line cut dramatically across the graph, curving gently down through Monday to the late Wednesday afternoon section. At Thursday the line began diving sharply down, indicating that by 1:30 Thursday afternoon the *Yorktown* and *Columbia*, unless rescued, would ultimately hit the earth's atmosphere and burn up. It was, as everyone knew, an open-ended projection, and it assumed that the *Columbia* would not separate from the *Yorktown* and that the *Atlantis* could not carry the broken *Yorktown* to a safe altitude. But

Pierce had no time for projections past this morning. His sole concern was 12:20 p.m., the scheduled docking time. According to trajectory estimates, the altitude of the two craft would be a safe 90.89 miles.

More numbers came in, reassuring numbers. The propulsion engineer's readings of the *Columbia*'s propellant levels were 5,730 pounds – well above the minimum 4,140 and more than enough for a safe de-orbit manoeuvre. Pierce was comforted; the figures indicated that the *Columbia* would be able to come home.

The flight surgeon noted that the crews had slept poorly. Bishop and Merriman had not dropped off until 1 a.m. and Bishop had awoken shortly after 3. Rob Clark had slept about six hours. Jack Lewis, despite orders to the contrary, had stayed up to do calculations on the *Yorktown*'s computer until after 3 a.m. Houston time.

'What kind of calculations?' asked Pierce of the computer engineer.

'Trajectory, altitude and consumables consumption rates,' replied the engineer. Each was a key aspect of survival. Pierce was not surprised at Lewis's concern, nor could he begrudge him his actions.

As the reports continued, it was clear that the mood in Mission Control was distinctly different from the unhealthy tension that had prevailed twenty-four hours earlier. Pierce noted a sense of urgency in his men, a no-nonsense attitude, a feeling of 'let's do it right this time'.

The accident had shaken them all, but they had responded as he had known they would. Their pride had been stung, lives were at stake – that was their top concern. But also at stake, and no less a motivating factor, was the natural desire of competitive people to atone for a past failure or defeat.

And the *Yorktown*'s accident had been a defeat. It didn't matter that none of the flight controllers of the Gold Team were personally responsible. The accident was a defeat for all of them. Now they had a second chance, a chance to prove themselves to their colleagues, their superiors, and to the corps of astronauts they worked

161

with, and indeed to the whole world, a chance to prove that no problem for which they were responsible could, in the last analysis, beat them.

Pierce listened in on the various conversations between flight controllers. Their tone was not arrogant, nor cocky, but clearly determined and confident. He allowed himself a smile before calling Vandenberg Airforce Base to check when the *Atlantis*' crew had been awoken. *We're going to do it*, he thought.

He punched in the call button to Vandenberg and queried the flight controller there.

'Roger, Flight. We awoke Gerber and Alexander five minutes ago. Right now we're backing the *Atlantis* up to the external tank on the launch pad.'

Pierce quickly pushed the display button so that he could see the action from the launch site in California. In the pre-dawn darkness the launch pad was still bathed in the Klieg lights, and the *Atlantis* and the bullet-shaped external fuel tank were slowly drawing closer together.

The controller at Vandenberg rattled off his up-date and Pierce alternately watched the screen and jotted the key points down on his flight log. Dozens of technicians moved about the launch pad, about to connect the *Atlantis* and the external tank. Pierce found his curiosity made it difficult to concentrate on recording information in the log.

'Do you want me to repeat those numbers?' asked the flight controller at Vandenberg.

'O.K.,' replied Pierce, 'just the last two sections, though.'

'O.K. then, here it is – 7, 6, 4, 3, then there's a space, 5,—'

The line clicked twice in Pierce's headset and then went dead.

'Vandenberg? Do you read me?' asked Pierce. Maybe the flight controller had inadvertently cut the call off. The picture on his screen had turned fuzzy, and he reached forward to adjust it. No, it wasn't fuzzy. The picture was – well, it was *vibrating*.

'Hello Vandenberg, Vandenberg! This is Houston Flight. Do you—'

Pierce stared at his screen, his mouth open in disbelief. The whole launch site was shaking; technicians were falling off the gantry towers. Pierce stopped adjusting the screen. There was nothing wrong with the picture.

'Vince!'

Torino glanced over at Pierce, wondering first why he was calling him out loud, and second why he wore such a stunned expression. He followed Pierce's line of site to the console's screen, then stood transfixed at the view.

'Holy Mother of God!'

The screen went blank. Pierce jabbed at the console call button. Joe Gibbs – he had to know what was happening. But one floor above in the reserve control room the Red Team's consoles were out cold. No images, no telemetry, nothing from Vandenberg. It had been cut off with a snap. It was as if the western launch site had simply, suddenly, ceased to exist.

In the three seconds since Pierce's conversation with Vandenberg had been interrupted, NASA Administrator Benjamin Fleck had sprinted down from his console in the third row:

'Have you got Gibbs?' he asked excitedly.

Pierce said nothing. The line had just been cleared.

'Joe! What the hell's going on at Vandenberg?'

Pierce's console was lit up with flashing orange call lights from his team's flight controllers. Everyone had experienced the same thing – a sudden cessation of communication.

'Joe! Are you there?'

'Doug – I – the line – they just went dead.' Gibbs' voice conveyed an uneasy mixture of fear and shock. Both he and Pierce had seen the same sight on their respective console display screens.

Twenty thousand feet above Vandenberg Airforce Base, an F18 Hornet on an early morning reconnaissance patrol was about to begin its descent. The sun was beginning to illuminate the base, far off on the horizon. The pilots chattered in a breezy manner. The flight had been routine to the point of boredom.

'O.K. Bobby,' said the pilot, 'I'll call the base. Vandenberg, Vandenberg, Airforce 603, do you read?'

Silence.

'Vandenberg, Airforce 603 on frequency 72 requesting permission to land. Do you read?'

Nothing.

'Bob?' said the pilot, 'I can't raise them. You try it.'

'O.K. Ken – Vandenberg, Vandenberg, this is Airforce 603, do you read?'

The sleek jet had descended from 20,000 down to 18,000 feet and the Vandenberg Airforce Base loomed larger and larger on the horizon.

'Ken, I get no response either. I'll change frequencies.'

Frequencies were altered, but still no reply came. Accordingly, both men immediately began standard Airforce procedure for such circumstances. They continued their descent, their landing lights were activated and they took a low-level flypast of the base at a sedate 180 miles per hour at a low altitude of 1,500 feet.

In seconds they passed the *Atlantis'* launch pad.

'Jesus,' said the pilot, pulling back on the rudder and banking left for another look, 'did you see that?'

'I saw it,' said the co-pilot in a crushed voice.

'What in God's name are we going to do?'

CHAPTER SEVEN

Pierce's mind raced. Someone had to know the answer. He would try the instrumentation, navigations and communications officer.

'INCO, can you re-establish contact with Vandenberg?'

'Flight, we're working on it – it's like everything was cut!'

'Keep working on it,' replied Pierce.

'Doug,' said Torino, 'Edwards Airforce Base can't raise Vandenberg either. What do we do?'

'We try the NESR,' he said forcefully.

Acting on a hunch, he immediately punched the call button through to the Natural Environment Support Room above them on the third floor, NASA's clearing house operation for world-wide atmospheric operations.

'NESR, this is Flight,' said Pierce, pronouncing the acronym as 'Ness-sir'.

'Roger, Flight,' said the NESR officer in a voice that gave no hint of the urgency and fear gripping Mission Control. 'What can we do for you?'

'Do you have anything, I mean absolutely anything out of the ordinary at Vandenberg?'

'Vandenberg, Vandenberg,' repeated the officer calmly, as if he was running his eyes down a routine checklist. 'Flight, we have nothing unusual. The temperature right now at Vandenberg—'

'Forget the temperature!' Pierce snapped, 'I said anything unusual!'

'Sorry, Flight,' replied the officer apologetically, 'I – wait a minute, wait a minute . . . . I have some unconfirmed readings from Vandenberg.' Pierce heard a sudden note of panic in the man's voice. 'Our readings are that: Vandenberg and environs were hit at 4:20 a.m. Pacific

Time with a tremor registering 5.7 on the Richter Scale—'

'An earthquake!?'

'No sir, a tremor. At 5.7 there should be no more than minor structural damage, if anything at all.'

'Thank you,' said Pierce. 'I want confirmation on this as soon as you have it.'

'Roger,' replied the officer, 'NESR out.'

Pierce was stunned, his face ashen. Fleck and Torino equally were lost for words. Silently the three of them contemplated the potentially disastrous implications unfolding before them.

'We've got to establish communications,' Pierce said, thinking aloud. 'We've got to get positive confirmation.'

The excited voice of the communications engineer cut through. 'Flight, I have Vandenberg!'

Pierce touched the appropriate buttons:

'Vandenberg, this is Houston. Do you read? Do you read?'

Pierce's headset crackled angry feedback into his ear. '. . . – ston – . . . enberg Contr—. . .' The reply was inaudible.

'Say again, say again! You're breaking up. You're breaking up,' said Pierce.

'Houston, Vanden– Control, we read you.'

'What's going on out there,' stammered Pierce. 'What happened? How's the *Atlantis*?'

The reply was infuriatingly disjointed, but as if to complete the picture Pierce's display screen suddenly flickered into life again, blinked, flickered again and came in focus. The image of devastation before him made his heart sink. The space shuttle *Atlantis* stood at a precarious 65° angle to the launch pad, and even worse, the huge external tank lay on its side, broken in two places, seemingly cleft in two by a giant axe.

Over the headsets communications with Vandenberg continued to be broken by earshattering whines and deafening crackles, dismembered sentences and phrases.

But by now the extent of the damage was all too depressingly clear.

'– . . . tremor – . . . may be quake . . . damage severe . . . on the base – ship is broken – . . .'

Maddened by the high-volume barrage of interference, Pierce ripped his headset off angrily and slammed his fist onto the console. He stared at Torino and Fleck, enraged and totally helpless.

The call button from the *Columbia* lit up on his console, accompanied by a gentle chiming sound.

'Mission Control? *Columbia* says good morning.' The voice was Rusty Bishop's. 'Dick and I are awake up here and ready to go; we were wondering if you guys had forgotten us?'

Torino pushed the reply button, his voice utterly defeated. '*Columbia*, this is Capcom. No, we haven't forgotten you.'

Bishop looked at Merriman quickly. 'Vince sounds like he's been punched in the head.'

'So ask him what he was doing last night,' chuckled Merriman.

'Hey Vince,' said Bishop, 'what's the matter? You sound kinda down in the mouth.'

Torino grabbed his forehead with his right hand and stared at Pierce. 'What in God's name do I tell them?'

'Hey Vince? Do you copy?' asked Bishop.

Pierce pulled his headset back on. 'Rusty? Doug Pierce here.'

Pierce's uncharacteristically informal use of first names alerted Bishop to the possibility that something was wrong.

'Doug? What's going on down there?'

'Guys, we got a real problem here. The, uh, the *Atlantis* can't come to get you by 11 a.m.'

'O.K. – a little delay. We can hold out for a few more hours.'

'No. It's not a delay; it's a hold – a scrub.'

'What's scrubbed?'

'The rescue launch. Vandenberg was hit by an earth

167

tremor. The external tank is destroyed and we have no official report on the *Atlantis*.'

'Are we broadcasting to the nation?' snapped Bishop.

'Negative,' replied Pierce, 'it's a closed line.'

'All right then. Do Jack and Rob know about this yet?'

'Negative Rusty,' replied Pierce, 'they're still asleep.'

'O.K. then. Now what Dick and I want to know is whether or not you've got an option left for them.'

Bishop's use of the term 'them' hit Pierce like a sledgehammer. He was right; it was the *Yorktown* that was the problem. The *Columbia* could still separate and return to earth safely. The *Yorktown*? Never.

'Uh, Rusty, we're moving on that right now.'

'What about the *Challenger*?' asked Merriman, referring to the shuttle that had returned to earth two days earlier. 'Or even the *Enterprise*?'

'Rusty, Dick – we just don't know at this point.'

As Charles Egerton walked up to the front door of his home in Clear Lake, he felt totally exhausted. The door swung open and there stood his wife. Egerton began to smile until he saw his wife's expression: a mixture of fear and panic.

'There's been an accident,' she said.

Her words riveted Egerton to the spot. 'Where? What happened?'

'The rescue ship – it's been destroyed.'

Egerton bolted past her to the kitchen, grabbed the telephone, but stopped dialling as the voice on the radio cut through with a report. He listened and then hung up and turned to face his wife.

'I'm going to try to get some sleep. I've got to be back on duty in seven hours.'

Six-thirty a.m. Joe Gibbs burst into Mission Control and ran back to Pierce's console. His face was the picture of desperation, his appearance that of a man desperately seeking to control himself.

'Damage report,' he said, catching his breath. 'We're standing down upstairs – here's why.'

He handed Fleck a single page of paper. Fleck pulled on his thick, black horn-rimmed glasses and read the report aloud in a dull monotone:

'. . . two dead, ten injured, five seriously; all deaths on the gantry of the launch pad. Astronaut Lyle Gerber—' Torino winced, fearing the worst '—broke his leg. Astronaut Gordon Alexander received second degree hot water burns to his left arm and chest.' Fleck looked up at the assembled group of flight controllers. 'They were showering when the tremor hit.' He read silently for a few seconds and then continued aloud. '. . . the external tank was destroyed. *Atlantis*' rudder is cracked in five places. The starboard wing was broken off at its root.'

He pulled off his glasses and looked at the still heavily breathing Gibbs and at Pierce and Torino.

'It's no good. The ship will take months to repair.'

Pierce punched up the trajectory engineer's latest graph analysis of the *Yorktown* and *Columbia*'s descent from orbit.

'They hit the atmosphere Thursday at 1:33 p.m. There's nothing we can do.'

The flight controllers of the Gold Team sat in silence, stunned, almost hurt, their spirit numb. The NASA system, the most effective, most efficient managerial system for the co-ordination of the most complicated technology ever devised, had been broken. The NASA people, the flight controllers, the astronauts – their spirit had been crushed. What had happened was simply not supposed to happen!

First the mission of the *Yorktown* and *Columbia* and now that of the rescue shuttle *Atlantis*, lay in scattered fragments. The flight controllers' confident morale and proud spirit, those qualities which separate mediocrity from excellence, which divide the shoddy and lacklustre from the brave and polished, were now reduced to the burnt ashes of defeat and despair.

'The cause', that operational manifestation of idealism

169

which was an essential vibrant reality of NASA itself was irrevocably lost.

For the first time in NASA's history, for the first time in Doug Pierce's career, a crushing helplessness hung ominously in the air: the hopelessness of defeat that no 'system', no 'technology' could cope with. Now Doug Pierce, his flight controllers, NASA and the world would be forced to wait in frustrating, bitter, spirit-wrenching agony and watch the deaths of two, possibly four men.

Deep within Doug Pierce's mind, there flashed a memory from long ago; his first training lecture on being a flight director. The words of a younger Benjamin Franklin Fleck, then Director of Flight Operations, announced themselves in his mind's ear:

'You must never forget that when you are on duty in Mission Control, when there are astronauts in space, when your team of flight controllers are at their consoles, you as Flight Director, are God. At that moment, no-one else in the world is more powerful nor weighed down with greater responsibility. Whatever the challenge, it is you, the Flight Director, who must always, always lead.'

Pierce inhaled deeply, inflating his chest. He drew himself up, punched open the P.A. line and cleared his throat:

'Flight Director to Gold Team – Flight Director to Red Team in the reserve control room. Our present plan is no longer feasible. Maintain your present positions. Four men continue to depend on us. Give me status reports. We're not going to quit.'

Pierce looked at his control panel. A gently chiming sound attracted his attention. It was Lewis and Clark.

'Houston, this is *Yorktown* Commander,' said Jack Lewis. His voice sounded upbeat. 'We're wide awake up here and want to know if we're still matching the flight plan? Are we still going for an 11:08 launch?'

'Ah, dear God,' muttered Pierce, staring blankly at the contingency flight plan. No longer a plan of attack, it was now merely a hopeless prediction of what should have been.

170

Lewis called again: 'Houston? Vince? Do you read?'

Awash with fears and confusion, neither Torino nor Pierce knew what to say. The seconds hung long in the air.

It was, in truth, Vince Torino's responsibility as Capcom to field the incoming call. But the circumstances seemed, in an unspoken way, to transfer the responsibility to Pierce, the man in charge. Unable to resist his duty any longer, Pierce reluctantly and tentatively reached forward and depressed the green square answer button on the console and opened a line between himself and the crew of the *Yorktown*. He pushed his glasses back into place, his voice only partially masking his emotions.

'*Yorktown*, this is Lead Flight Director.'

The fact that Pierce, not Torino, had answered, combined with the less than immediate response and its ambiguous tone, caused Jack Lewis' brow to furrow with concern.

'Doug? Has Vince taken the day off?' asked Lewis.

'Ah, no Jack, he's here – we're all here. But, uh, there's been some developments at this end.'

'Like what?' Already Rob Clark sensed problems.

'*Yorktown* – you and the *Columbia* are going to have to stay up there a little bit longer.'

'No thanks,' interrupted Lewis tersely, 'we're ready to come down.'

Pierce took a deep breath, drawing upon emotional reserves he was not certain existed any more. 'Jack and Rob, we've had a problem with the *Atlantis*—'

'What kind of problem?' interjected Lewis, increasingly angered at Pierce's evasion.

Pierce, sensing both their growing hostility and now emboldened by that curious surge of inner strength that somehow accompanies messengers of cold, ugly realities, looked at Torino for a fleeting second, knowing that if he were in their position he would want the truth.

'Gentlemen, at 6:10 a.m., Houston time,' Pierce looked

171

at the chronometer; it was now 6:45, 'Vandenberg was shaken by an earth tremor registering 4.8 on the Richter Scale.'

'Four point eight! Doug that's nothing; it couldn't—'

'The external tank, Jack – it was being mated to the *Atlantis* when the tremor hit . . .'

Two seconds of numbing silence were followed by a single word from Clark.

'And?'

A second of silence.

'And, uh, the external tank was jarred loose onto the pad and broken in half.'

'Oh, great, just great,' snapped Clark sarcastically.

'Houston,' asked Lewis with icy calm, 'can you fly in another external tank?'

'Negative, *Yorktown*,' replied Pierce, rubbing his forehead. 'The *Atlantis* suffered structural damage that appears to be irreparable within the timeframe.'

'Houston, you mean, before we re-enter Thursday morning, don't you?'

'That's affirmative, *Yorktown*.'

In the cockpit of the *Yorktown*, Rob Clark shook with fear and anger, but Lewis' jaw was clenched as a succession of thoughts whirled through his mind. *A test pilot doesn't panic; he keeps thinking his way out of the problem. If he panics, he's dead.* 'Houston,' he said, 'do you have positive confirmation on the damage status? If so, what alternative options do we have?'

Lewis' objective tone offered Pierce, Torino and Fleck a small ray of hope. They were, at least, still thinking.

'Jack, the damage is confirmed – I'm sorry.'

'So are we, Houston – so what about the options?' said Lewis.

'*Discovery* and *Enterprise*,' interjected Clark, 'they're all that's left, huh?'

'Roger, we're plotting out timelines for both of them.

'How long before you know?' asked Lewis.

'As soon as we know, you'll know,' replied Pierce.

For the first time Doug Pierce began living the nightmare which had plagued him throughout his professional career: he had lost control of the mission. His team of flight controllers were confused, frightened, desperate for answers, for direction, for leadership. Pierce perceived the despair on their faces and thrashed his mind for options. He snapped himself physically to attention in his chair, as if that would shake the uncertainty away and restore an air of control he did not feel.

'Alright, we're without a flight plan. Now we earn our pay. I want you all to keep monitoring your systems. We're going to be winging it for a while, so stay on your toes. All we've got left is the shuttle *Discovery* at Kennedy. Its next flight is scheduled for ten days' time—'

'Ten days!' said Gibbs. 'All we've got is barely forty-eight hours before the *Yorktown* burns up . . .'

'I know that,' said Pierce. He turned to Torino. 'Vince, call the Kennedy Space Center. We have to know the earliest that the *Discovery* could be ready to go.'

Torino placed the call. Pierce turned to Gibbs. 'Joe, we don't have a flight plan. Your job, the Red Team's job is to start putting one together.'

'But Doug—'

'I know, I know, we've no timelines, no idea when, or even if the *Discovery* could be ready.' Pierce clutched the contingency flight plan binder and waved it at Gibbs. 'You're going to have to rip this baby apart and block out a plan; when we hear from the *Discovery*, we'll have to plug in the times.'

'Doug! That's like building a shuttle from a pile of parts on the floor.'

'I know that, dammit. Would you rather just sit here and wait for them to burn up?'

Gibbs fumed through clenched teeth. 'That's low, Pierce – really low.'

Pierce shook his head in regret and held up his hands in a gesture of mock surrender. 'I'm sorry, Joe, I shouldn't have said that. But all we can do is make plans for a launch. We have to assume the *Discovery* can do it.'

Torino pulled off his headset. 'Kennedy says they'll be able to tell us by 7:45.'

'My team can have a lot done by then,' said Gibbs with grim confidence. 'We'll get a new flight plan under way.' The Red Team's flight director hurriedly left Mission Control, stunned by Pierce's comments, but determined to get on with the job.

Pierce turned to Torino. 'Vince, did they have any idea, any hunch . . .'

'No, they can't say, Doug; we'll just have to wait.'

It was Fleck who broke the thoughtful silence.

'Is there no other alternative?'

'Such as?' asked Pierce.

'The Russians? Balderis? He said they could have the *Raketoplan* airborne in fifty-two hours.'

Pierce's eyebrows arched in drawing awareness and he jabbed open a line to his trajectory engineer. 'What's your latest fix on *Yorktown*'s eventual re-entry?'

The trajectory engineer plotted the ship's declining orbit path and reported back. 'My latest data shows a re-entry no later than 1:20 p.m. That's Thursday afternoon.'

'How many hours is that?' snapped Pierce.

'Fifty.' Two hours too late.

'Thank you, trajectory,' replied Pierce in a crushed voice. He turned to face Torino and Fleck. 'The *Discovery* will have to be ready.'

'What could he do? What did they have left? Were there any options he had left unturned? The *Challenger* had returned from space on Sunday and there was simply no way that the shuttle could be refurbished in time for a Thursday morning launch. The *Discovery*? They would have to wait another half hour to find out. The *Atlantis*? Destroyed. The *Discovery* was the only remaining option.

Why had he not accepted Balderis' offer? Had he done so, the Russians could have launched within twenty-four hours. Instead he had dealt away a valuable card – he had dealt away a back-up. He saw the folly of it now, only too clearly.

'Doug?' asked Torino, 'what if the *Discovery* can't be ready – what do we do then?'

Back-up, thought Pierce, *we've got to have a back-up*. 'We still have the *Enterprise*.'

'No way,' said Fleck. 'The *Enterprise* is sitting on top of the *Hornet*. Its mission is a duplicate of the *Columbia* and *Yorktown*'s. I don't have to remind you that that mission failed, that that concept of getting them into space simply didn't work. No way do we risk four more astronauts' lives!'

'You said it was my show,' replied Pierce, firmly.

'It is, unless you give me reason to make it otherwise,' said Fleck.

'It's your privilege, at any time, to make such a determination,' said Pierce. 'But right now, I intend to call Edwards Airforce Base.'

Fleck nodded slowly. 'Very well then.'

Pierce placed his call. 'And now,' he said, 'we wait.'

Pierce's request to the base had been simple and concise. His question had been as follows: if every single corner was cut off the preparations and the countdown, and if work continued round the clock, when could a launch of the *Enterprise* take place? The question might have been simple, but the answer was not.

At the Kennedy Space Center, the *Discovery* was being readied for its next standard launch pad blast-off, ten days hence. At Edwards Airforce Base in California, the *Enterprise* sat atop the hypersonic jet *Hornet*, being readied for the Ninth Airborn Launch Development Test Flight – the duplicate of the failed *Columbia* and *Yorktown* mission.

The respective control rooms in Florida and California responded to Pierce's and Torino's calls immediately. Because the Kennedy Space Center was in the Eastern Time Zone, it was only 7:50 a.m.; NASA's eastern launch port thus had a considerable headstart over Edwards Airforce Base, where it was only 4:50 a.m. Pacific Time.

In Florida, the morning shift of technicians and flight controllers had already been at their respective jobs for

175

almost an hour. At Edwards Airforce Base, the *Enterprise* sat with the hypersonic jet *Hornet* in the Number 2, Mate/Demate Device, looking forlorn and forgotten. The ground crews had been dispersed with the cancellation of the Ninth Airborn Launch Development Test Flight, moments after the *Columbia* and *Yorktown*'s accident, but within moments of Doug Pierce's call to the head crew chief at Edwards, word spread to the ground team like wildfire. The news was electrifying: 'We may have a second chance!'

But determining which of the ships could be made ready sooner was nearly as complex a task as actually launching them. In order to determine the readiness of the *Discovery*, the ground team at Kennedy Space Center had to relay information requests through sixteen major computer systems. Within these sixteen systems were 106 sub-systems. When both were combined and interrelated over twenty thousand associated tests could be run. In the *Discovery* alone, (as in its sister ships, the *Atlantis*, *Columbia*, *Enterprise* and *Challenger*) there were over seven thousand different test parameters. In the Apollo program in the late 1960's and early 70's, a similar checkout would have required 250 engineers working for over six months. There never had been a rescue back-up for the Apollo program, as an emergency launch was technologically impossible under those circumstances – even for NASA.

Now, a scant decade later, Doug Pierce had asked for an equally difficult checkout to be carried out not in six months, but in just over an hour. The *Columbia* and *Yorktown* would re-enter the atmosphere on Thursday morning. Time was their enemy now.

But the present generation of flight controllers had an enormous technological advantage over their Apollo predecessors. Utilizing Honeywell's H6680 Large Scale Host Computer, engineers at Edwards and Kennedy were able to employ a technique called 'Exception Monitoring' to calculate the earliest possible launch time. In the past, such calculations called for teams of engineers to scan yards of strip chart recording paper to find out which measurements within the Apollo capsule system were malfunctioning or 'out of tolerance'. Now, however, the shuttle's pre-defined tolerance values were pre-programmed into the computers and as each system was checked only those values in error or 'out of tolerance' were displayed on the computer screens. Eternally competitive, both sets of ground crew teams now raced to find the answer.

It was 7:15 a.m. In Mission Control, Pierce scanned the rows of consoles. The flight controllers were now monitoring their controls in what effectively had become a holding pattern. Telemetry continued to pour in from the *Columbia* to the Real Time Computer Complex in the basement and then up to their display screens in Mission Control. The Controllers continued to process the information in a desultory manner. But the prevailing mood was one of gloomy resignation.

It shouldn't be long now, Pierce thought. *Edwards and Kennedy – they'll have an answer soon.* Beside him was Vince Torino and Franklin Fleck. The three sat in silence, their collective intellects seemingly rendered useless. One by one, suggestions were ventured as each tried vainly to get their thinking process functioning again. They knew in truth, however, that there was nothing they could do, absolutely nothing, until Edwards and Kennedy reported back. Clearly, it was the forced inaction during the wait that chafed at them all.

In the *Columbia*, Rusty Bishop's wisecracks, his normally upbeat demeanour, had long been stifled. To him too the situation was infuriating: his ship was functioning perfectly – it was that damn *Yorktown*! If only Jack and Rob had been kitted out in space suits instead of pressurized flight suits! Hell, they could have had them transferred up to the *Columbia* in ten minutes. They could have been home by noon Monday. But recriminations served no purpose now.

Attired in standard issue cotton coveralls, Bishop looked about the cockpit as Merriman manned the

Columbia's controls. He stared at the control panel, at the label on the switch which read 'Auto Sep'. All it would take was one jab at those two buttons and the *Yorktown* would be blown away from the *Columbia* and sent spinning into space. He paused thoughtfully, then reached into a storage drawer beneath his seat and pulled out a roll of two-inch-wide masking tape, ripped off a six-inch strip and wrote on it.

'What are you doing?' said Merriman.

'What I should have done yesterday,' replied Bishop coldly.

Eyes widening in horror, Merriman watched as Bishop reached for the Auto Sep switch. *My God!* he thought frantically, *Rusty's cracked!* Frantically he reached for Bishop's right arm, but was too late.

'There!' announced Bishop grimly. The tape had been placed over the 'Auto Sep' switch. There was one word on the tape. The word was 'NO'.

Below them in the *Yorktown* a pensive Jack Lewis wriggled in his seat, cramped and uncomfortable; his throat was dry, the last rations having run out a couple of hours earlier.

'Fucking dry air!' he sniffed.

Clark frowned. 'What do you mean?'

'I mean the life support system in this bitch really sucks! It's as dry as a desert in here!' He slammed his hands on his non-functioning control stock in frustration, his cold blue eyes staring witheringly at the controls as if by a conscious act of the mind he could will the ship back into its normal condition. His taut, tight face was expressionless.

Suddenly he was aware of Clark's gaze, and looked up apologetically. 'Sorry, Rob.'

'It's O.K.,' replied Clark, 'it's O.K.'

Lewis' mind ran back over the past. How long had it been? Twenty-three years? Yes, he had been sixteen when he had decided to become an astronaut. He smiled, thinking back. At sixteen he had had enough nerve to write to NASA and inform them that he planned to be an astronaut – not wanted to, notice, but *planned* to. Such confidence! Such arrogance! So he had left his home in Pennsylvania to attend Annapolis Naval Academy. That was the first step: attend Annapolis, get his Navy commission and then apply for test pilot at Patuxent, the home of the Navy Test Pilot School. After surviving seven years at Patuxent, in spite of seeing dozens of his colleagues die in crashes, he had still had no doubts when he applied as an astronaut candidate to NASA. The testing? It had been nothing more than a necessary inconvenience to him, so sure was he that he would make it. Everything he had ever done, he had done with confidence, and he had won. Until now.

In Mission Control, Doug Pierce's eyes focussed fixedly on his console screen, deep in thought. At his command was the entire power and technology of the United States Space Program. At a touch of a button he could be put in contact with any NASA station throughout the world. With the touch of a button he could command any piece of information stored in NASA's computers. He looked around at his flight controllers, each responsible to him, each gifted with talents. Pierce's orders were law. He was in total command. And yet he felt totally helpless – a giant trapped by circumstances, his power useless to save the men.

Pierce rallied, fighting his feelings of powerlessness by re-assessing the entire situation. He looked at the Real Time Chronometer: it was 7:09. He called up data on the ship's trajectory: The orbit had fallen to an altitude of 90 miles, 22 from re-entry. The *Columbia*'s fuel was down to 5,500 pounds, a mere 1,460 pounds above the acceptable minimum for a landing attempt. He glanced at the clock again, 7:10 a.m. Questioning doubts swirled around in his mind. Which shuttle could be readied for a rescue? What if neither rescue shuttle could be readied? Would he have to order the *Columbia* to separate from the *Yorktown*, killing Lewis and Clark in order to save Bishop and Merriman? He shuddered physically at the thought and felt sick to his stomach.

The time was now 7:11 a.m. Another four minutes and he would have a report on the *Enterprise* and the *Discovery*.

The call button on Vince Torino's console rang. The Capcom answered it. 'Doug? We've got a report from Kennedy.'

Pierce opened the line. 'This is the Lead Flight Director. What do you have?'

The report was terse. The *Discovery*, scheduled for a routine launch pad blast-off from the Kennedy Space Center, Florida, ten days hence, could be rush-readied for a rescue launch by 3:00 a.m. on Thursday – a whole nine hours before the *Yorktown* and *Columbia* would burn through the atmosphere. Torino grinned at Pierce. Rendezvous with the ships could be made by 4:30 a.m. The *Yorktown* and *Columbia*'s altitude would be 80 miles by then – 12 miles from burn-up.

Torino's console rang again. It was Edwards Airforce Base, with their own report. Pierce interrupted the call from the Kennedy Space Center to field the news from Edwards.

The analysis from Edwards, where the *Enterprise* remained secured to the *Hornet*, was equally blunt. The *Enterprise* could be launched by 6:20 a.m. Thursday morning, less than three hours before the *Yorktown* and *Columbia* burned up. Altitude for rendezvous would be a mere 72 miles only 6 miles above the burn-up point. All systems of both ships could be verified as ready to go by 6:20 a.m. Thursday.

'So we go with the *Discovery* at Kennedy,' said Torino. 'Nine hours versus three hours, 80 miles versus 72. It's pretty clear, Doug.'

Ignoring the comment, Pierce resumed contact with the Kennedy flight controller and asked him to finish his report. There was a problem. In order to launch by 3 a.m. Thursday, the Kennedy Space Center would have to drop 4½ hours of checkouts from the countdown. Pierce frowned. The flight controllers at Kennedy had justified the move on the grounds that the systems involved were

180

highly reliable and unlikely to malfunction. There was a risk, but in their view a risk worth taking.

'And what if you ran a full and proper checkout?' Pierce asked, 'when could you be ready?'

The answer was 7:30 a.m. Less than two hours before re-entry. Pierce looked at Torino. 'It's pretty clear, is it Vince?'

It was now 7:25. Both launch times predicted by Kennedy and Edwards had been predicated on the assumption that they would have authorization to begin the countdown by 8 a.m. Doug Pierce, the last man in the decision chain at NASA, had 35 minutes to decide. Each minute of delay through indecision on his part subtracted a crucial minute at the other end during the rescue rendezvous, when the *Yorktown* and *Columbia* would be moving ever faster, ever closer to burn-up.

Pierce agonized over the facts before him. Intangibles were suddenly assuming importance out of all proportion. The *Enterprise* at Edwards was an experimental launch – a near duplicate of the failed *Columbia/Yorktown* mission. The *Discovery* at the Kennedy Space Center, however, utilized the conventional launch pad system, the system tried and true. But in order to have a chance to rescue Lewis and Clark the *Discovery* had to be launched without certain critically important checkouts. The *Enterprise*, on the other hand, would have all of its systems checked – but its systems, like the launch itself were experimental. Pierce agonized. Time was moving all too quickly for him.

If he chose the *Enterprise* and the Ninth Airborn Launch Development Test Flight, he could be accused of trying to protect his concept, the concept of the *Yorktown* and *Columbia*'s launch – which had already failed. If it failed again at any point during the launch, the entire program would be killed stone dead. If he chose the *Discovery* and *it* failed, he would be accused of authorizing the flight of a ship not fully prepared. The question was simple: which shuttle was more likely to save the men? But was either of them likely to save the men? After all, the transfer manoeuvre rehearsed by Harwood and the sim ops team had yet to be verified.

He decided to call the crews. It was his decision, but he wanted their opinion. He wanted to leave the door open for them either to support it or demand the alternative . . .

He spoke to the four orbiting astronauts. 'So with all of those timelines, all those factors, my feeling is to go with the *Enterprise* at Edwards.' He paused for a moment, 'I'd like your concurrence on this one, guys, and I'm open to suggestions.'

A long silence fell between the crews and Mission Control.

'Damned if you do and damned if you don't – right, Doug?' said Jack Lewis in the *Yorktown*.

Right, thought Pierce, not replying.

'Give us a minute will you, Flight?' asked Lewis.

'You've got it, Jack, but it's 7:45. I want to move before 8:00,' said Pierce, turning off his mike. He looked at Torino.

In the *Yorktown*, Jack Lewis and Rob Clark sat in stony silence. Lewis' mind tripped through the technical alternatives, weighing the pro's and con's coldly, fighting a gnawing doubt that neither would work. Rob Clark tried to think logically, determining the advantages and disadvantages of each alternative as well, but he could not forget that if the *Enterprise* flew, it was Adrienne who would be flying it. *Exactly what I didn't want to happen*. He bit his lip in frustration.

Lewis broke the silence. 'Do you believe in this project, Rob?' He looked at Clark, his face stubbled dirty by a day's growth of beard.

The question confused Clark.

'The project? Yes. The ship? No.'

'Same here. I think . . . I think Pierce is right. I don't care which shuttle they launch first, even if it's by elastic band, as long as it gets up here.'

Clark's grim visage remained unchanged. His voice was low, full of trepidation: 'But if it doesn't work, if there's another accident—'

'Then four more get stuck up here . . . only by then we'll be dead.' He sighed and sagged back into his chair. 'Every time a pilot or astronaut climbs aboard, he knows, she knows, what the risks are . . .' Lewis snapped his fingers. 'There's always the risk it could end just like that!'

Clark nodded in agreement. Lewis radioed Bishop and Merriman above them in the *Columbia*.

'Rusty? Rob and I have talked it over. We think Pierce is right. We want the *Enterprise*. It's a gamble, but it's my ass and Rob's on the line.'

'And our's too,' volunteered Bishop.

'Uh, uh, Rusty – just me and Rob.'

Bishop looked at the 'NO' taped over the auto separation switch. Lewis was infuriatingly correct.

'The *Enterprise* then,' said Bishop.

Lewis called Pierce. 'Houston? Tell the folks at Edwards to get moving. Rob and I want to see the *Enterprise* up here damn fast.'

'Jack, I'll give them the go right now,' said Pierce. He looked at Torino: 'Call Edwards, get them moving.'

It was 7:55 a.m.

Adrienne Brooks could hardly believe that the phone was ringing. She had slept barely four hours. In the pitch darkness she fumbled for her bedside phone, knocked the main set off the table with a crash, but held onto the receiver.

'Hello!'

'Adrienne? Vince. Pierce told me to call.'

She opened her eyes wide sensing the urgency in Torino's voice. 'What is it Vince? What's happened?'

'There's been an accident.'

Fear shot through her. '*Yorktown*?'

'No. They're still all right. It's the *Atlantis*.' Torino hurriedly explained the situation. '. . . so it's you and Tex, and the *Enterprise*, Thursday morning.'

'Have you called Harwood?' she asked.

'No, not yet. I'm about to though.'

'Tell him I'll pick him up in ten minutes and we'll be there in fifteen.'

Adrienne Brooks' silver-gray Jaguar XJS Sports Sedan screeched to a halt in front of Tex Harwood's home and before its shock absorbers had fully dampened the rocking motion, Harwood, clad in his NASA jumpsuit, had sprinted across the lawn and jumped in.

'Hold on,' she said, slamming the powerful auto into a neck-snapping first gear. Harwood grappled for the seatbelt, but before he had locked it into place she had already ripped the racing auto through three gears.

Harwood's face turned white. 'Careful, they've got radar all over the place.'

'They'll have to catch us first.'

'What do you mean "us"?'

The car tore through the back streets of Clear Lake City and onto NASA One Boulevard. The first car they passed was a police car. Siren screaming, lights flashing, the cruiser pulled alongside.

'Pull over!' bellowed the policeman in the passenger seat.

Foot still on the accelerator, Brooks glanced to her left. 'The Space Center! It's an emergency!'

The angry expression of the officer's face dissipated into one of recognition. *He knew who she was!*

'We'll give you an escort!' the officer yelled.

'Thanks!'

She dropped one gear, stomped the gas pedal and left the police car far behind.

'Get your face on TIME magazine – it works wonders.'

'Remind me to try it in Traffic Court,' replied Harwood.

In Mission Control the final roll of the dice was underway. Pierce's face was drawn with fatigue, his eyes hurt from strain. His exhausted body sagged in his chair as Torino ticked off the rescue procedure. Pierce usually found Torino's energy an infectious stimulant; now it was an annoyance. He was having trouble keeping up and it bugged him.

184

'After rendezvous between the *Enterprise* and the *Yorktown*,' Torino continued, 'Harwood will take the two rescue enclosures and spacewalk them over to the *Yorktown* . . .'

'But Harwood is the Commander of the *Enterprise*,' interrupted Pierce, neither looking up nor uncovering his eyes.

'I know.'

'Standard procedure, Vince. Pilots do the walks. Commanders fly the shuttle. Tex is the Commander, Adrienne is pilot.'

'I know that too,' said Torino in a low voice.

Pierce exhaled a tired breath and glanced at the clock, annoyed at Torino's faulty assessment of crew responsibilities.

'So that means Adrienne should take the rescue enclosures to the *Yorktown* – not Tex.' Pierce smiled weakly and raised his eyebrows, thinking that Torino had confused the roles of the astronauts somehow.

Torino looked back in silence, his expression grim and unchanged, a mask which said he was unwilling to accept Pierce's verdict. Pierce's brow became furrowed. Torino barely moved his lips. 'Doug, I believe Harwood should do it.'

Overhearing the exchange between the two men one or two flight controllers began to exchange anxious glances.

'Vincent . . .' Pierce only used Torino's first name when he was angry with him, a characteristic Torino was well aware of. Torino quickly pressed home his argument in confidential, urgent tones.

'Harwood is bigger and stronger than Adrienne, Doug. It'll take all his strength to get the enclosures over to the *Yorktown*, into the ship and transfer two men – *two* mind you – back to the shuttle.

Pierce sat in silence, frustrated at Torino's logic. Brooks would be furious, but good sense indicated Torino's argument was correct. He nodded resignedly. 'O.K. – Harwood does it. Adrienne will fly the shuttle.'

Moments later Brooks and Harwood themselves

entered Mission Control. The situation was quickly reviewed, and Harwood informed that he, not Brooks, would conduct the spacewalk.

'Me?' asked Harwood incredulously.

'Yes, you,' replied Pierce crisply.

Harwood was nonplussed. 'But, I'm Commander of the *Enterprise*. Pilots do the emergency spacewalks.'

'And I'm the pilot,' said Brooks angrily.

'And I, Dr Brooks, am the Flight Director,' said Pierce. 'Tex is seven inches taller than you, and stronger. He stands a better chance than you. Period. You don't have to agree. Just follow orders, or be replaced.'

Fearing Brooks would say something she would regret, Tex Harwood took her arm and squeezed it restrainingly. 'We agree,' he said, turning her away. She shot a withering glance at Pierce, who already regretted his outburst, but was convinced his decision was correct.

Brooks left Mission Control in a cold rage. Throughout her training she had put up with petty insults and cutting remarks about 'women pilots'. Always her talents had served to silence her critics and to win grudging respect, even from the hardline sexists. Throughout it all she had thought of Doug Pierce as the one person she could count on for a square deal. But to find herself cut off at the knees at this, the most critical assignment in her career, was too much to bear.

Almost as confused as she, Tex Harwood lumbered after her. He could figure Pierce's logic, but the logic had trampled Adrienne's pride – and that too he could figure. He grabbed at her arm from behind as she strode down the hall outside Mission Control.

'Adrienne!'

'Let go of me!'

'No, wait a minute!' he said, spinning her around.

'Bastard!' she spat, her face red with anger.

'Look, you can call me what you want—'

'Not you. Pierce!' she replied, pulling away from him.

Harwood grabbed at her arms again, forcefully, harder than he had ever held any woman:

186

'O.K.! That was a dirty, low blow! But Adrienne, damn it! Pierce is right!'

'The hell he is! You let go of me!'

'Only if you'll listen to me! I'm on your side!'

Harwood relaxed his grasp. 'Adrienne, if you were Commander of the *Enterprise* and I was pilot and Pierce needed a smaller person for the job – like you – he'd choose you and not me, and I'd be just as pissed as you are.'

'That's easy for you to say!'

'Yes, God damn it! It is. Listen: I'm sorry he gave you the shaft, but he made the choice on merits alone, not because you're a woman and I'm a man. Adrienne, listen. We're a team – a damn good team. You're a damn good astronaut and you're going to be the first woman shuttle pilot in space. Don't screw it up now! Jack and Rob have their asses on the line and we have to save them!'

Jack and Rob. Temporarily the over-riding reality of their plight had been pushed from her mind. Harwood's reminder pulled that reality back and with it the realization that maybe Pierce had chosen Tex instead of her for the precise reasons Tex had just confronted her with. In fact, maybe she had read Pierce all wrong. Perhaps Pierce's choice represented the ultimate acceptance of her as an astronaut. But right now, this very moment, Tex was right: there were other things to think about. The disciplined self of Dr Adrienne Brooks over-ruled all other concerns. She and Tex had to hustle over to the immersion test facility.

She looked up at Harwood: 'Come on – you've got a date at the pool.'

By 1:10 p.m. the *Yorktown* and *Columbia*'s eighteenth orbit of the earth had begun. Their altitude was now 89 miles, down by four miles since Monday at 10:31, and now only 21 miles above the point in the heavens where sensible traces of atmosphere begins and space ends, the point where the lives of the crew, if not rescued, would end.

Onboard the *Yorktown*, Rob Clark made a further log entry:

'*1:20 p.m., Tuesday, last emergency food rations gone – tasted great. Never thought I'd ever say that about pre-packaged chemicals! Water almost gone: two days before* Enterprise *can arrive.*'

He closed his eyes and thought for a moment: could the *Enterprise* really arrive?

Closing his log he tucked it into his left knee-pouch and wriggled in his seat.

In fact, thirst was not his only problem. But who should he call? When in doubt, start with the Capcom – Vince Torino.

'Vince? I've ah, got a problem here with the liquids.'

'*Yorktown*, this is Capcom. How's your emergency water supply?'

'Yeah, well, Vince . . . that's not quite what I'm worried about right now. Could I speak to the flight surgeon?'

Torino's curiosity was aroused. 'Rob? You want the surgeon? O.K. Patching you through . . . Capcom to Surgeon,' said Torino, quickly transferring the call, 'I've linked you through to the *Yorktown*. Rob Clark wants to speak to you.'

The surgeon, who was more aware than any other flight controller of the physical and psychological strain on the two stranded astronauts anticipated the worst, but did his best to make an upbeat response. 'Rob, this is the surgeon. Sorry I can't make any housecalls, but can I be of any help?'

'Yeah, Doc. I wish you could make a house call too. Er, look, I don't want to be indelicate but, ah, I just don't want to wet my pants.'

'Say again, Rob?'

The explanation was simple. Clark had to urinate. The *Yorktown*'s pilots had been equipped with a simple tube and funnel arrangement in the cockpit, known universally as the 'relief tube', leading directly to a urine dump in the hold of the ship. But by now they had been in orbit for over twenty-six hours, and the dump was full.

For a few moments the flight controllers debated the problem. Given the life-and-death situation the crew faced, this problem seemed so ludicrous that inevitably jokes started to fly about the room.

Eventually Pierce cut in. 'Hey guys, this *is* a problem.' The jokes stopped.

Pierce was not overstating the issue. In space, liquids present a real problem. In the zero gravity of space, liquids do not spill but form up into spherical droplets. Whether water or urine, the droplets float randomly about the cockpit, thereby threatening dangerous short-circuiting in the electrical panels and air-conditioning systems. As a result, stringent safeguards were brought in for the early Mercury and Gemini Programs. Drinkable liquids were stored in flexible bags equipped with pre-attached rubber straws with one-way flow valves allowing the astronauts to suck their drinks safely. Urination involved a simple rolled elastic cuff attached to a flexible hose leading to a storage tank. With the longer duration Apollo flights, the elastic cuff remained but was connected to a diaphragm which led to a urine receptacle and then to a large storage bag. From this bag, which also held contaminated water from the batteries and air-conditioning system, the liquids were simply dumped into space.

Bowel movements presented a different problem. On the short Mercury mission the astronauts could simply be placed on high protein diets prior to the flights, thereby reducing the need for in-flight bowel movements. But on the week-long Gemini and Apollo flights the problem could no longer be avoided and the simplest route was taken – diapers. In short order a new problem predictably arose – diaper rash. So a disposable diaper was developed, featuring an adhesive surface which the astronaut stuck to his buttocks. However, since cabin pressure in the Apollo capsule was only five pounds per square inch, there was a real risk that pressure from decaying fecal matter could actually explode the bags. To avoid this particularly messy situation, the bag was first sealed and then emptied into a germicide pouch which both neutralized bacteria and prevented explosive 'outgassing'.

Fortunately for Lewis and Clark, they had been placed

on a high protein diet, had had bowel movements before take-off and with their severely limited diet of the last twenty-six hours, felt no need for any more.

Above them in the *Columbia*, astronauts Bishop and Merriman faced no such problem, as the shuttle was equipped with a zero-gravity toilet using a pressure differential and vacuum system to keep both urine and fecal matter from leaving the toilet. If nothing else, the shuttle's toilet made space travel a more comfortable experience.

But still Clark's delicate problem remained unsolved.

'How about the motion sickness bags?' suggested the flight dynamics officer. 'They could go in them.'

'Well,' replied Pierce, 'I guess necessity is the mother of invention. It should work.'

Pierce forwarded the idea to the surgeon who concurred with the essential simplicity of the proposal and radioed the suggestion to Clark: 'Your motion sickness bags . . . can you use them?'

'I got you,' replied Clark.

'Rob,' said Pierce, 'remember it's zero gravity up there.'

'Don't worry,' replied Clark, 'don't worry.'

Clark pulled out a motion sickness bag from its secured position beneath his chair and slipped it under his arm. He shut down the valve for the urine, undid his suit, pulled the diaphragm off his penis, and clamped the bag tightly around it.

'Jack? Did you ever see that NFL football game on TV? Gee, it must have been ten years ago. There was this lineman, both hands broken, both hands in casts, and the announcer says, "there's so-and-so leaving the field. I guess when he gets to the urinals at half time he'll find out who his real friends are".' Lewis broke up. 'No kidding!' continued Clark, laughing out loud, 'I heard it myself!'

Relief. The bag was half full. Clark sealed the end with great care, wincing as a few drops of urine floated up past his face.

'Houston? Tell the Doc that the, ah, evacuation man-oeuvre has been completed, successfully.'

Shortly after, Lewis duplicated what was quickly dubbed an E.M. – a tiny, humorous wedge easing the unrelenting tension both in Mission Control and on board the ships.

Pierce wanted the mess out of the way immediately and suggested the urine bags be stowed in the engineering section behind the cockpit. Lewis and Clark agreed, and Lewis, undoing his seatbelts extracted himself from his seat and wriggled in zero gravity back to the engineering door, eight feet behind the seats, and opened it.

Clark, carefully holding the bag of urine, turned to face Lewis.

'Ready?'

'Yeah,' said Lewis. 'Pitch it in.'

Gingerly, with a gentle shove, Clark sent the first bag floating back towards Lewis, who carefully deflected it through the open door and into engineering. The second time, Clark's aim improved and the bag, toppling end over end, glided past Lewis and through the door.

'Two points!' announced Lewis with a smile, closing the door.

'Two points? From this distance it's a field goal – three points!'

'O.K.,' chuckled Lewis, 'three it is.'

Lewis stretched and twisted in mid-air, enjoying the sensation after the hours of sitting, and looked down at the inner hatch of the emergency escape chute. *When they come to get us*, he thought, *that door will be all that separates us from outer space*. He shuddered.

Back in Mission Control, the surgeon sat at his console at the left-hand end of the second row, commiserating with the other members of the medical flight staff. Their voices were low, their countenances grave. The surgeon, like the other flight controllers, had no incoming data on the condition of the *Yorktown*'s pilots, and could only rely on experience and judgment in making his next recommendation to Pierce.

191

'Flight, this is the flight surgeon. I'm afraid we're running into a real problem with Lewis and Clark.'

Pierce frowned, uncertain as to what the surgeon was getting at. 'Go on,' he said.

'The problem is that Lewis and Clark have gone for over a day with only emergency water, which is now almost gone. They will now begin to experience the effects of dehydration.'

'Well, they'll be thirsty by the time the *Enterprise* gets up there Thursday, there's no question of that.'

'That's only part of it. Their ability to function will become increasingly impaired because of lack of water. The electrolyte count in their brains will drop steadily.'

'Electrolytes?'

'Yes. In order for the brain to function properly there has to be sufficient fluid in the body for the brain impulses to complete the thinking action process. In other words, Lewis and Clark's ability to function, to conduct even the simplest mental actions, is deteriorating and will continue to deteriorate much more rapidly as time goes on. Without some liquids . . . well, I'm thinking about Harwood entering the *Yorktown* through the emergency escape chute. Am I correct in assuming that his entry will depend on co-ordinated action on Lewis and Clark's part before he can get into the ship?'

'Affirmative. Jack or Rob will have to open the inner hatch at precisely the moment Tex Harwood goes up the chute. It will require split-second timing. Oh, Christ,' muttered Pierce, sizing up the surgeon's point. 'What you're saying, then, is that they may be functionally unable to open the hatch – unable to let Harwood into the ship?'

'That, indeed, is my fear. Is there anything onboard that they can drink? Anything at all? Anything in the systems of the ship itself?'

Pierce shook his head. 'No, nothing that they have access to. Nothing that's drinkable.'

'What about their flight suits. They're water-cooled, aren't they?'

Pierce was horrified. 'Cut into their suits?' he stammered.

'Yes,' replied the surgeon, 'if necessary. And I think it *is* necessary.'

Pierce mulled the notion over a moment. He was very reluctant to authorize the move, yet at the same time, if the surgeon's observation of Lewis and Clark's ability to think was correct . . .

Pierce confronted Vince Torino. 'Vince. Ask the flight activities officer to get onto his staff support people to see if the water in the suit coolant system is at all drinkable.'

The report was quick in coming, essentially fingertip information. Torino relayed the information to the surgeon: 'Doc? They say that the water in the suits is flat, distilled and tasteless, but it is water and it is drinkable.'

'How many ounces are there in each suit?' asked the surgeon.

'Twenty-eight ounces apiece,' replied Torino.

The Surgeon groaned. 'But Flight, the human body requires 32 ounces of liquid per day to stave off dehydration. They've had barely 12 ounces in the last day and a half. Twenty-eight ounces over the next two days isn't nearly enough.'

'I'm afraid 28 ounces is all we have. I don't want to destroy their suits if I don't have to.'

'I can appreciate that, but I most strongly recommend that Lewis and Clark be authorized to cut into their suits.'

'O.K. Doc, I read you,' replied Pierce, 'I read you.' But for a moment he hesitated. The surgeon was the only flight controller in Mission Control who could, at least technically, pull rank on the flight director when it came to the health of the crews. Yet Pierce's instinct and natural caution militated against taking such an irreversible measure. Once the suits were cut into, they would be totally useless and offer no protection. Despite the surgeon's repeated insistence, he held off issuing the order. "Doc, I'll determine the appropriate time, later . . . Flight Director out.'

Over my dead body! thought Pierce.

193

The immersion tank facility was no swimming pool in the ordinary sense – as its 60-feet depth and underwater observation windows, its mechanical arms and fixtures and brightly-shining under-water lights indicated. The tank's purpose was to simulate on earth the effects of zero gravity.

Generations of astronauts had used the pool to rehearse spacewalks and practise construction techniques, wearing duplicates of the suits they would wear later in space. But the underwater rehearsals could only approximate to the conditions of space. Buoyancy, of course, gave the illusion of weightlessness, but the unalterable fact remained that in space, unlike water, a kick of a foot or wave of a hand resulted in only those actions and no corresponding reaction of movement. The hours Tex Harwood had spent rehearsing in the clear, bright waters of the immersion tank, could thus only hint at whether or not the manoeuvres he was practising would work in space.

Even as Pierce had ordered Harwood and Brooks to the tank, another order had gone out to the manufacturers of the emergency escape chute system – Lone Star Aeronautics of Dallas, Texas. Prime contractor for the hypersonic jets' emergency systems, the Lone Star technicians and engineers had anticipated the possible need for an underwater simulation and had flown a copy of the cylindrical tunnel leading from the *Yorktown*'s cockpit floor to the ship's underside outer hatch to the Johnson Space Centre.

Tethered securely at the 25-foot mark, the cylindrical shaft now rested horizontally in the water. Flitting around it, aqua-lunged NASA divers positioned themselves once again, as for the umpteenth time Tex Harwood, replete with a space suit identical to the one he would use to try

to enter the *Yorktown* on Thursday, attempted to enter
the chute. His task was to carry the personal rescue
enclosures for Lewis and Clark up the chute and through
the other end in less than sixteen seconds. In those crucial
sixteen seconds the *Yorktown*'s emergency escape chute
would have to be depressurized to a vacuum so that Harwood could enter; Harwood would then close the outer
hatch behind him and repressurize the chute to the full
atmospheric level of the *Yorktown*'s cockpit, so that he
could then enter the cockpit itself to save Lewis and Clark.

'Sorry, Tex,' said the controller at the 20-foot level
observation window. 'That took twenty seconds.'

'Damn! Double damn!' replied Harwood, thumping a
gloved fist against the pitch black inner wall of the chute.

'You want to come out and try it again?'

'What time is it?' asked Harwood.

'Twenty seconds.'

'Naw, I know that! I mean real time!'

'Seven p.m.'

'Awright, open the hatch – I'm coming up.'

Two divers approached the outer hatch door and
opened it, allowing Harwood to glide out, feet first. With
cumbersome kicks and thrusts he swam to the surface,
grabbed at the chromium runged ladder, clambered out
of the tank and plopped himself onto the edge, his feet
dangling listlessly in the water.

Adrienne Brooks in a powder-blue, zip-up jumpsuit,
crouched and tapped his helmet. He turned, and she saw
his perplexed, frustrated expression. Harwood removed
his helmet and handed it to her.

'Twenty goddamned seconds, Adrienne. Twenty!'

'It's O.K.,' she said, patting his right shoulder. 'You
started at 27, remember?'

'And I'm stuck at 20.' He sighed aloud. 'God, I'm tired.'

Harwood stared between his feet at the chute below,
where the divers were resetting the outer hatch for
another entrance attempt. There had to be an angle.
There had to be something he'd overlooked.

Adrienne stood, walked over to a doorway behind them and slumped against the door jamb, still holding Tex's helmet. *So we get up there, so we rendezvous with the Yorktown. What's it matter if Tex can't get into the cockpit before the outer hatch buckles and blows off from repressurization?* She clicked her tongue at the dilemma and tried not to think of Jack and Rob being sucked out into space. *Just like a meat grinder . . .*

Through the P.A. system on the deck level, the Controller called out from his 20-foot level underwater observation post. 'Tex? How about another go?'

Harwood turned to face the microphone speaker unit on the wall beside Brooks. 'Yeah, O.K. Just let me—'

He stopped and studied Adrienne Brooks. He was 6' 2"; the doorway was 6' 3". It had to be! He had ducked instinctively upon entering! But Adrienne was only 5' 6"! That was the angle! That's what he had forgotten, what Pierce had forgotten!

Quickly he swung his feet from the pool, walked over to Brooks and grabbed his helmet back.

'I'm not going to need this! Get your suit on!'

'What do you mean, get—'

'I said, get your suit on! You're going for a swim!'

'But Pierce said—'

'Forget what Pierce said. Look kiddo, I'm seven inches taller than you are and 60 pounds heavier.'

'Seventy,' she corrected.

'All right, seventy,' he grinned. 'Let's give it a try, it's getting late.'

As the long second day of the mission wound to a close, the world watched the unfolding story with rapt attention. ABC, CBS and NBC had had their portable trailer studios positioned at the Space Centre since Monday to give full coverage of the ill-fated launch of the *Atlantis*. Now that the Vandenburg earthquake had turned the crisis of the *Yorktown* and *Columbia* into a fully fledged disaster, the networks' top anchormen had been flown from New York and Washington to the Space Centre to conduct their respective evening news broadcasts. Biographies and background footage of the crew had been hastily packaged into mini-reports. Standard programming had been reshuffled and the entire nation watched and waited on the news from NASA.

During the day, flight after flight of private and military jets had flown into Ellington Airforce Base adjacent to the Space Centre, bringing with them teams of experts employed by the corporations who had built the hypersonic jet *Yorktown* and the space shuttle *Columbia*. The vehicle analysis room adjacent to Mission Control had quickly become so overcrowded with experts that other staff support rooms of lesser importance had to be reassigned for use.

The tragedy had touched the nation. At Houston International Airport, the president of Metro Airlines, a small company offering 15 mini-connecting flights to Clear Lake each day, announced he was rescheduling all flights to the Space Centre for the convenience of incoming scientists, technicians and employees. At the small Metro Airlines Airport in Clear Lake the owner of Red Top Cabs, a small husband-and-wife company of two taxis, volunteered their services free in order to drive people to the Space Centre. The Days Inn, Holiday Inn and Ramada Inn opposite the Space Centre on NASA One Boulevard had been engulfed with the arriving experts and responded by offering free rides to and from the Centre.

Some NASA employees on vacation returned simply to be a part of the Mission and to offer whatever help they could. Every man and woman on the flight teams felt both dread and concern, but beneath all their fears and worries was a firm and deep commitment to the Airborne Launch Development Program, the value of the flight of the *Yorktown* and *Columbia* and in the last analysis the value of human life.

In Rome, speaking in English, Polish and Russian, the Pope offered a special prayer for the safe return of the

197

men in an address broadcast throughout Europe. In London, the Archbishop of Canterbury held a special service asking God's blessing for the lives of all involved. In the United States, the Commissioner of Baseball instructed team owners to observe a minute's silent prayer before the start of all baseball games until the Mission was safely completed. The owners, to a man, complied. In Canada, the National Hockey League's seventh and deciding game of the Stanley Cup Final in the Montreal Forum, between the Canadians and the Chicago Blackhawks, was preceded by a bilingual invocation.

In Mission Control itself, the flight activities officer plotted the latest projections of the *Yorktown* and *Columbia*'s re-entry point on Thursday. Through the facilities of the Federal Aviation Administration and the Department of Defence, preparations were made to ground all U.S. commercial air traffic from 6 a.m. to 12 noon on Thursday. There was a real possibility that the *Enterprise* or the *Columbia* might not be able to land at the Kennedy Space Center or at Edwards Airforce Base and would have to put down at a commercial airport instead. The major U.S. airports and the potential landing zones geared up their emergency crews. The United States of America readied itself for a return flight that might never occur.

Adrienne Brooks and Tex Harwood had told the immersion tank staff that they wanted to break the news to Pierce themselves. It was well after 11 p.m. before the two exhausted astronauts entered the reserve control room. Clusters of haggard-looking flight controllers from Pierce's Gold Team and other controllers, scientists and engineers grouped around their consoles. It was late, but much remained to be done. Maddeningly, the countdown at Edwards was falling behind schedule. There were problems with the *Enterprise*'s guidance system. Minor but frightening aftershocks from the Vandenburg earthquake had rippled through Edwards – nothing serious enough to damage the equipment, but strong enough to scare, and to conjure up a 'what next' attitude.

Through it all, Doug Pierce pressed on, pushed his team on. He was tired, desperately tired. He saw Brooks and Harwood approach.

'Finished?' he asked.

Harwood pulled up a chair and lowered his hulking frame into it. Brooks stood behind him as Harwood leaned forward:

'We've got the entrance time into the chute down to fourteen seconds.'

'Pierce's eyes lit up, and a broad grin displaced the weariness of his face. 'Fourteen! A two second margin!' He slapped his thighs resoundingly. 'Beautiful! I knew you could do it, Tex!'

Harwood looked around at Adrienne Brooks who was staring at the floor, then back at Pierce. 'Ah, Doug, it wasn't me who did it.'

Pierce's face went blank. His eyes darted from Harwood to Brooks and back to Harwood.

'I did it,' said Brooks, looking up. 'In fourteen seconds.'

'And the best time I could get was twenty,' added Harwood.

Pierce nodded slowly, reassessing his earlier decision to go with Harwood and his bitter confrontation with Brooks. He pondered momentarily how it was that his logic had been proven incorrect. Then he took a deep breath. 'The objective is to save them. We go with whoever can do it best.' He looked at Brooks squarely. 'Adrienne, that means you. We've got a lot to do tomorrow. You two have simulated take-offs and rendezvous beginning at 07:00. Get some sleep. That's an order.'

Brooks and Harwood took the elevator and walked in silence to the lobby of the Mission Control complex, deserted save for the ubiquitous guard waiting to demand identification from anyone without an authorized plastic NASA identity badge. They stepped outside into the cool Texas night and star-filled skies and walked to the brightly-lit parking lot.

199

'Tex, I'm glad you stopped me from taking Pierce's head off this morning.'

'No problem, except, ah . . .' he chuckled in embarrassment, 'I don't have a ride home.'

A Johnson Space Center taxi station-wagon sat nearby.

'You want to take the taxi?' Adrienne asked. 'Or shall I give you a lift?'

Harwood glanced at her silver-gray Jaguar XJS, the machine she piloted rather than drove. 'Only if you keep it below a hundred miles per hour,' he said. 'Promise,' she replied.

Shortly before midnight, Pierce turned off the engine of his Chevrolet station-wagon and trudged up to the front door of his darkened house.

He picked up the morning and evening newspapers. Inside the house he scanned the headlines: 'SHUTTLE RESCUE TODAY – NASA SCRAMBLES', followed by 'ATLANTIS DESTROYED'.

Pierce scanned the report describing the effect of the earthquake on the *Atlantis* at Vandenberg. The accompanying picture of the shuttle sickeningly canted over beside the debris-strewn gantry tower and shattered external tank, turned his stomach. He dropped the papers back onto the mat and looked at his watch. Midnight. He had four hours' sleep ahead of him.

In the bedroom he reset his alarm clock, lay back on the bed fully-dressed and in seconds was fast asleep.

The chatter between Lewis and Clark, Bishop and Merriman and Joe Gibbs' Red team, continued to be heavy, despite the late hour. Driven by nervous exhaustion and fighting the effects of only three or four hours' sleep, Lewis and Clark continued to call down an essentially routine series of requests, not wanting, it seemed, to break off their only link with earth. In the *Columbia*, Rusty Bishop and Dick Merriman seemed to prefer to call it a day and good-naturedly kidded Lewis and Clark to stop the talk with Houston.

The surgeon of the Red Team sensed that fear was keeping them talking, and knowing the conversation was largely inessential, made the unusual request to flight director Joe Gibbs to speak directly with Lewis and Clark. Gibbs acceded and patched the surgeon through.

'Jack and Rob, it's 1:10 a.m. down here. You're going to have a lot to do tomorrow getting ready for the rescue and so on. I'd like to suggest you call it quits. Leave the driving to us and get yourselves a few hours' shuteye.'

Lewis and Clark reluctantly agreed and the conversations became increasingly sporadic, then stopped. In the *Columbia*, Rusty Bishop moved down to the lower deck, zipped himself into his sleeping bag affixed to the side of the bulkhead, and dozed off. Dick Merriman had drawn the late shift and kept a watchful eye on the ship's controls. 'Don't spin on me, babe,' he said, peering down at the *Yorktown*.

Lewis and Clark attempted unsuccessfully to recline their seats to a more comfortable position and groused about the discomfort. 'It's like sleeping in the front seat of a Volkswagen,' said Clark.

From the *Columbia*'s flight deck, Dick Merriman looked ahead and down through the starboard side window, and watched the *Yorktown*'s cockpit light dim considerably, until only a weak, red glow emanated through the black hypersonic transport's gunslot type windows.

Finally, overcome by exhaustion, having been ordered to get to sleep and knowing Merriman in the *Columbia* would be at the controls, Jack Lewis and Rob Clark drifted off to sleep.

At 1:31 a.m. the ships began their twenty-seventh orbit, at 87 miles altitude. In the *Yorktown* Lewis and Clark both slept. In the *Columbia*, Merriman could hear an occasional snore from Bishop's sleeping bag on the lower deck, and kept himself busy by monitoring his controls. Communications with Houston became increasingly sporadic and routine, and to while away the hours Merriman turned on a pre-recorded tape of Handel's Water Music. The second long night had begun.

At 1:55 a.m., twenty-four minutes into the twenty-

PART THREE

Wednesday, May 13th

CHAPTER NINE

Rob Clark dreamt. It was a silly dream – the kind he knew was only a dream even while he was dreaming it. He was sitting in a kayak wearing a spacesuit. The kayak, a large Eskimo type made from the skins of caribou, restrained him. He couldn't move. In the bizarre world of his dream the kayak sat perched on a snowbank beside his home in Houston. That's stupid. Snow in Houston? It had to be his parents' home in Chicago. People were passing by, waving, wishing him luck. He paddled on, moving nowhere, and it was getting cold. He felt the cold, and kept paddling on. *It's only a dream* . . .

By 4:16 a.m. the *Yorktown* and *Columbia* had descended another half mile to 86·5 miles altitude. Merriman felt a slight cramp in his right leg, unbuckled himself, slid his cockpit seat back and carefully stood up. The cramp eased. The *Columbia* was on auto-pilot. *I'll go down for a piss*, he thought, *and be right back.* He looked out the cockpit window; the British Isles were covered in cloud – *typical*. His eyes scanned the *Yorktown*'s cockpit and he almost missed it. He stared, this time searching for details. Something was wrong. Or was there? He frowned, sat down, buckled himself in again. It didn't make sense, or did it? No, damn it, it didn't! He hit the wake-up button.

'Rusty! Get up here! Fast!'

Without a word, Bishop ripped open the sleeping bag and bolted up the ladder leading to the flight deck, pulling himself hand over hand, sailing prone across the flight deck floor and grabbing the back of the Commander's left-hand chair:

'When you hit that buzzer, I thought my head was coming off! This had better be import—'

'Take a look at the *Yorktown*'s cockpit.'

Bishop floated above the seats, steadying himself on the control panel and squinted out at the *Yorktown*. 'Holy shit. Holy shit!' he whispered, pulling himself into his cockpit seat. 'How long's it been like that?'

'Don't know. Just saw it.'

'Have you called Houston?'

'No – I said, I just saw it!'

'O.K., O.K., I'll handle it . . .' He pulled on his headset. 'Houston, Houston, this is *Columbia* Commander. Do you read? Do you read?'

In Mission Control, the Red Team's Capcom, Navy Captain Russell McDonald, fielded the call, surprised to find Bishop paging him at 4:20 in the morning. He had been scheduled for sleep until 6 a.m.

'Roger, *Columbia*. We read you. What's up?'

'Houston, there's no light coming from *Yorktown*'s cockpit.'

The statement caught McDonald off guard and his reply was not fully thought out. 'Yeah, well, *Yorktown* is in a sleep mode. They've probably cut the lights back—'

'Houston, the *Yorktown* is pitch black!'

'Roger, *Columbia*. Will you hold a minute?' McDonald turned to the Red Team's flight director, Joe Gibbs. 'It's Rusty and Dick. They say there's no light from the *Yorktown*'s cockpit and—'

'*None?*' responded Gibbs, intrigued, but not overly concerned.

'No, sir.'

Gibbs punched open a communications line. '*Columbia*. This is the Flight Director.'

'Joe?' said Merriman. 'I was just eyeballing the *Yorktown* and there's no light from the cockpit.'

'Yes, so the Capcom tells me. Now, I should think it's entirely probable that Jack and Rob had powered down their lights—'

'Flight, I'm aware of that – they *did* power down, before going to sleep. There was light from the cockpit at that time.'

'But is it not—'

'No! It is not!' said Merriman. *Damned desk jockeys! They don't get it!* 'Houston, I'm going to call them . . . *Yorktown, Yorktown,* this is *Columbia.* Do you read? Do you read?'

The call startled Jack Lewis wide awake, and two impressions registered immediately on his mind. First, he was bitterly cold and second, the cockpit was pitch black. Everything was out, no lights, no power.

'What the hell . . .' said Lewis out loud.

'Jack, do you read?' asked Merriman.

Lewis reached over and pushed at Clark, awakening him with a start. The cold blackness of the cockpit mixed with Rob Clark's evaporating memories of the kayak dream.

'Jesus, it really is cold! Who killed the lights?' Clark asked.

'*Yorktown, Columbia* here, do you read?' asked an increasingly worried Dick Merriman.

'Dick, the power's out down here,' said Lewis curtly, starting to flip the switches on the console in front of him.

'*Yorktown,* this is the flight director,' said Gibbs.

But the cockpit remained in darkness. It meant one thing.

'Houston,' said Lewis, 'all of our lights are out. We have no power.'

The message chilled Gibbs. '*Yorktown,* I say, repeat please.'

'*We have no power!*' said Lewis. He stared at Clark, fear etched on his face. With no power to produce oxygen they would soon be dead from asphyxiation.

The bedside telephone's loud ring startled Doug Pierce awake. He fumbled for the phone. *Four-thirty,* he thought, turning on the light. *What now?*

'Hello,' he said sleepily, picking up the telephone.

'Doug? Russ McDonald,' said the Capcom excitedly. 'We've got a real problem here.'

Hearing the urgency in McDonald's voice, Doug Pierce spun from his bed. 'What's happened?'

'We've lost all power in the *Yorktown.*'

207

'Jesus,' muttered Pierce. 'When?'

'We don't know. It was on as of 1:20. Merriman first saw that there were no lights at 4:16.'

'And Jack, and Rob?'

'They're all right – at least, they're still with us.'

'Have you traced it back to anything? Any idea what happened?'

'Negative, Doug, negative. All we know is that sometime between 1:20 and 4:16 the power stopped cold.'

'But main Battery A is supposed to have a 72-hour back-up capacity.'

'I know that, Doug, but it's cut out.'

The implications dawned on Doug Pierce forcefully. 'Then they're running out of air,' he said quietly.

'Yes, sir,' replied the Capcom.

'Have they shifted to Main Battery B?'

'Negative,' replied the Capcom. Battery B was the sole remaining potential back-up. 'Our thinking is that if there's a leak somewhere we'd just drain that one out too.'

Pierce's mind raced. 'O.K. Now look, Russ, call Vince Torino and get him over to Mission Control. I'll be right there.'

Pierce sprinted to the washroom, brushed his teeth, applied some spray deodorant, decided to skip shaving, combed his hair hurriedly into place, then rushed out to his car. Pushing his Chevrolet into the high 80's, he raced through the pre-dawn darkness of Clear Lake to the Space Center, stopping at red lights only long enough to see if the way was clear. He arrived in record time. When he parked his car, the air surrounding his vehicle had the acrid stink of scorched rubber. He sprinted past the guard into Building 30, found no elevator waiting on the main floor and so bounded up the stairs to Mission Control. Red Team flight director Joe Gibbs and Capcom Russ McDonald were at their consoles in the third row, surrounded by half-a-dozen colleagues, including a dishevelled Torino dressed in a track-suit, studying 3-D cutaway diagrams of the *Yorktown* on their display screens.

It was 4:45 a.m. The atmosphere in the room was charged; in the mind of every man present was the prospect of Lewis and Clark's imminent choking death. All thoughts of the rescue had been blown away. This was a problem requiring an immediate solution. Gibbs was plainly doing his best to remain cool, but amid all the tension his face was becoming redder and redder.

'Right then. What we have is one hypersonic jet, completely without electric power in its main emergency Battery A, and two men, Lewis and Clark, with one half-hour's breathable oxygen in the cabin and their suits. If we can't get some electricity into the *Yorktown*'s system, then that one half-hour is all they have left.'

'But do we know how much air they actually have in the *Yorktown*'s cabin?' asked Pierce.

'I can't tell you that because we're unable to determine exactly when the power died,' replied Gibbs.

'Damn! So they might have an hour, or they might have five minutes,' said Pierce.

'Houston, this is *Yorktown*,' called Lewis.

Capcom Russ McDonald broke away from Pierce and Gibbs' conversation to answer. 'Roger, *Yorktown*.'

'Houston, I – I can't be sure, but . . . the air seems to be getting kind of thin in here.'

'Roger, *Yorktown*.' The Capcom shut off his mike and informed Pierce and Gibbs.

'It's already started,' said Pierce. 'We don't have an hour!'

'But do we have five minutes?' replied Gibbs.

A priority alarm rang on Gibbs' console: an emergency call from the *Yorktown*. Pierce reached forward to the console and opened it to broadcast Lewis' angry, strained voice:

'I told you the air is getting thin. Don't put us on fucking Hold again! We want to shift to Main Battery B. It's our only chance.'

The *Yorktown*'s power supply was generated through

209

the ship's environmental, mechanical and electrical system and in emergencies such as this, through a dual 72-hour system of back-up batteries – Main Battery A and Main Battery B. Main A had failed – but how? From the moment orbit had been achieved on Monday, they had all been aware of the potential delayed-effect damage. That potential had now become real. No other explanation even seemed feasible. The *Yorktown* had been using Main Battery A since 11 a.m. Monday, far short of the 72-hour power reserve limit. Lewis' request to shift to Main Battery B was no more than a desperate gamble: if the power loss had indeed been caused by a short circuit, then would Main B drain as well?

'Houston? I say again, can we go to Main B?'

Gibbs waved off McDonald and spoke directly to the astronauts. 'Jack and Robert – give us a few minutes here—'

'Look, Joe,' snapped Clark, 'we told you the air is getting thin. Now we're going to try Battery B and that's that.'

Gibbs looked at Pierce fearfully. 'If the main lines have been cut, and if they shift to Battery B it'll drain right out – that means they'll be left only with what's in their suits.'

Pierce chewed on his lower lip, concentrating hard. 'Let's give it a try – if Battery B dies, it dies. Either way, we're down to almost nothing.'

Gibbs nodded grimly. There was, he realized, no other option.

'*Yorktown*. We concur with your request to implement Main Battery B. But I must advise you that—'

Clark snapped off Gibbs' response. 'Forget it, Joe. Either it'll work, or it won't.'

Gibbs looked dejectedly at Pierce who shuddered at Lewis' and Clark's ability to confront their predicament.

'*Yorktown*,' said Gibbs, 'you are go to fire Main Battery B.'

'Roger, Houston,' said Lewis, turning to face Rob Clarke. 'O.K. Rob, here goes,' he said, reaching for the Main Battery B button.

Harsh sunlight now streamed through the cockpit windows, illuminating the instrument panel. Even so, Lewis hesitated a second, to make certain it was the right button he was about to push. Holding his breath, he pushed it.

The instrument panel glowed back to life. The environmental system whooshed anew as air surged into the cockpit. The computers hummed. Power restored! But both Lewis and Clark remained silent, watching.

'*Yorktown*, do you read?' asked McDonald in Mission Control.

Lewis and Clark studied their indicators, saying nothing, waiting to see if the restored power was mirage or reality.

'*Yorktown*, do you read?'

The flight controllers crowded around Pierce's console. All work stopped. They waited.

In the *Columbia*, Rusty Bishop bit on his left index finger; Merriman closed his eyes, praying silently. In the *Yorktown* the indicators were holding steady and Jack Lewis felt a slight flutter of hope. His lips began to form the faintest of smiles.

'Houston!' he exulted, 'we have . . .' But his voice died in mid-sentence.

'*Yorktown*?' asked Capcom McDonald. '*Yorktown*?'

The cockpit had suddenly sighed back into darkness. The environmental systems shut down. The humming computers groaned to a halt. The whoosing air stopped. The lights faded.

'Houston? This is *Yorktown*,' said Lewis, in a voice so utterly dejected that the flight controllers knew the rest of his message. 'Main Battery has dropped out. This ship . . . is dead.'

And so are we, he thought. It was 4:50 a.m.

Pierce looked at his colleagues, their faces drained ashen with resignation.

'I fear there are no options left to us,' said Joe Gibbs softly.

'The hell there aren't,' replied Pierce. 'We have to *find* some options!'

Gibbs, Torino, McDonald, the flight dynamics officer and environmental engineer all looked at him, wondering at his seemingly fruitless defiance.

'I said,' reiterated Pierce forcefully, 'let's find some options. We haven't brought them this far to lose them because of some damn battery!'

Pierce snapped open a line to the *Yorktown*, speaking with a boldness fuelled by anger and desperation.

'This is Lead Flight. Now keep cool. We're on it at this end. I want you to stay as still as possible. Conserve oxygen.'

'We're not going anywhere, Houston,' said Clark bitterly.

'Neither are we, Rob, neither are we. Hang in there.' Pierce shut off the line and stared at his colleagues.

Torino, standing in his light-blue track suit, seized on an idea. 'What if we separate the *Columbia* from the *Yorktown*?' Catching his colleagues' withering glances at the suggestion, he went on. 'No – let me finish. Separate, re-orient the *Columbia* underneath the *Yorktown* and then go for an emergency transfer out the chute?'

'Vince, that's no good,' replied the flight dynamics officer. 'Lewis' and Clark's suits wouldn't keep them alive in outer space for five seconds. Besides, the *Yorktown* has no way to control its attitude. If the *Columbia* separated from the *Yorktown*, the sheer movement of separation would set the *Yorktown* spinning. We couldn't control it. Neither could they.'

Torino plowed on with another idea, scrambling frantically. 'O.K. then. What about a suit transfer?'

'What kind of transfer?' asked Pierce.

'Merriman is the tallest and biggest of the four. Bishop takes Merriman's suit, leaves the *Columbia* and enters the *Yorktown* as we planned for Brooks to do tomorrow – that is, up the *Yorktown*'s emergency escape chute outer hatch. Jack and Rob would then put on Merriman's suit and transfer back to the *Columbia*—'

'But the hatch,' said Pierce, 'the hatch is barely strong enough to withstand one entrance. You might get one of them out that way, but not both.'

'I wasn't suggesting it would get both of them out. We'd only get one out.'

Pierce's mouth opened slowly at the suggestion. 'Wait a minute. I don't want to get into a situation where we're choosing for the short stick.'

'We're *already* choosing short sticks,' snapped Russ McDonald. 'Better lose one than both!'

'Look, Doug,' said Torino, 'Jack and Rob are both my friends. Don't think I'm saying it's an easy suggestion – it isn't. What I'm saying, is that if I was in that mess, I'd want to try anything that would save one of us.'

Pierce bit back a reply, but Russ McDonald, the other astronaut present, spoke up. 'I agree with Vince – better lose one than lose both.'

'Houston? This is *Yorktown*,' radioed Jack Lewis. 'Rob and I have been kicking an idea around up here – about, uh, about trying a suit transfer. Maybe Rusty or Dick, bringing a suit over . . .'

The words caught everyone's attention. The two stranded astronauts had reached the same conclusion as their astronaut colleagues McDonald and Torino. Pierce began to see no escape from the sickening decision before him.

Joe Gibbs handled the reply. 'Roger, *Yorktown*, we've been trying that one out here too.'

'Yeah,' said Lewis, 'it's a square peg in a round hole.'

'Indeed, *Yorktown*, it is,' replied Gibbs.

Square peg, round hole. Something clicked in Pierce's mind. Apollo 13, 1971? No! It was 1970. Yes, Apollo 13. The Apollo 13 service module had been knocked out by an explosion, and the three astronauts, Haise, Swiggert and Lovell had faced imminent asphyxiation from the loss of electrical power. The lunar landing module with which they were scheduled to land on the moon had been undamaged by the explosion, and the air supply was still working, but the systems in the Apollo capsule and lunar module were incompatible and had been built by different contractors; one ship's air systems hoses were squared, the other's rounded. And so the astronauts had improvised. Facing death at any minute, the three men had patched together the hoses linking the two systems, and it had worked!

Umbilicals, compatibility. It all fell together. *Oh, Jesus! It has to work!* Pierce lunged at the console and opened a line to the crew. '*Yorktown*, Lead Flight. Forget any suit transfer. I want you both alive! I want you to start thinking about using your G.M.P.'s.'

Ground Maintenance Ports? thought Torino. Then it clicked. 'Right!' he said aloud. '*Right!*'

Gibbs correctly sensed that if Pierce had to waste time explaining this brainstorm more than once, Lewis and Clark might end up dead. So he stood, stepped back from his chair and motioned to Pierce by a quick sweep of his arm to take command. Pierce did not hesitate for a second.

'Don't leave, Joe,' he said, sliding into place. 'Back to your positions,' he ordered his colleagues. 'This is going to be close.' It was 4:55 p.m. '*Yorktown* and *Columbia*, this is the Lead Flight Director in Houston. We're going to link the *Columbia*'s umbilicals to the *Yorktown*'s Ground Maintenance Ports. I'll explain it to you and *Columbia* and Mission Control simultaneously.'

Subsequent to the investigation following the near-fatal accident aboard Apollo 13, NASA had implemented unit standardization throughout the space program wherever feasible. Hoses, switches – every conceivable item which could potentially interact had been standardized. The standardization had extended to the Ground Maintenance Ports, small openings the size of a silver dollar located on the left side of *Yorktown*'s cockpit immediately behind Jack Lewis' seat.

To keep the internal environmental system of a ship like the *Yorktown* functioning while routine ground maintenance was being carried out would have been wasteful. Accordingly, the ports allowed for portable environmental systems to be plugged into the ship from the outside, thereby providing a comfortable and safe inflow of air. The ports featured a dual-lock valve system allowing the portable environmental system's connecting hose to be pushed in and locked into place. A measuring device inside the hull then verified first that the hose was securely affixed, and secondly, that there was an air supply being forced through. Then, and only then, would the inner valve on the inside of the cockpit wall open up.

Standardization had also extended to the umbilical cords used by astronauts to connect them to the ship during spacewalks. To prevent the cords becoming entangled with any satellites, telescopes, or other experimental equipment, they were connected to the base of the cargo bay, each umbilical cord locking onto the other, so as to form a single longer cord. In the nick of time Pierce had recalled that the astronauts' umbilical cords were compatible with the ground maintenance ports on the *Yorktown*, his plan being to link Bishop's and Merriman's umbilical cords and connect them to the *Yorktown*, thereby providing Lewis and Clark with a safe, uninterrupted supply of air from the space shuttle itself.

'Christ, will there be long enough?' stammered Clark, hoping Pierce knew. But Pierce did not know.

'Let's just get on with it.'

'In the *Yorktown*, Jack Lewis opened his faceplate and inhaled a painful breath. The cabin air was now virtually unbreathable. He looked at his suit's gauge.

'Houston, I've got twelve minutes' air left in my suit. There's nothing left in the cabin.'

'Fourteen minutes for me,' said Clark, checking his gauge.

In the *Columbia*, Merriman slid his seat back. Bishop stared at him. 'My turn, Rusty,' he said.

Bishop nodded in agreement. 'Houston, Dick's getting suited up.'

'Rusty, it's Jack – tell Dick to hustle.'

'He's moving, Jack! Hold on.'

Merriman dove headfirst down the ladder to the lower

deck of the shuttle and donned his suit in record time. By the time he had fully checked and readied himself, a full seven minutes had elapsed.

'Rusty ... Dick ... I've got five minutes left,' said Lewis.

'On my way,' replied Merriman.

'Flight Director? This is the surgeon. Tell Jack and Rob to stop talking. They're wasting air.'

'Roger,' replied Pierce. '*Yorktown*, the surgeon advises you not to speak in order to conserve oxygen.'

'O.K., O.K.,' snapped Lewis testily.

'Houston,' said Merriman, closing the airlock door behind him, 'I'm about to enter the cargo bay.'

It was 5:01 a.m. The fully-suited Dick Merriman now began depressurizing the airlock. In seconds he would be outside, and he would have only seconds in which to act.

5:02 a.m. Four minutes left in Lewis' air supply. Six minutes in Clark's. The *Columbia*'s airlock opened.

'Rusty, open the cargo bay doors!'

'O.K. Dick,' said Bishop, pushing the cargo bay door switch wide open.

As the doors arched back and open, exposing Merriman to the brilliant sunlight the astronaut pulled on the manned manoeuvring backpack, secured himself by buckling up, then darted up and away from the shuttle.

At the base of the cargo bay sat a modular box holding the umbilical cords. By the sunlight flooding the bay Merriman saw the umbilical box, jetted down, lifted its lid and snapped it open against the inner bulkhead.

'O.K. I've got the module open – connecting the umbilicals.'

The umbilicals, looped around an axis in the centre of the module, extended up the two-foot height of the box and branched out three prongs designed to prevent the cords from accidentally floating out. Merriman quickly connected his umbilical cord to Bishop's. For the moment he wasn't worried about air; his own portable backpack had a four-hour supply and a half-hour reserve.

Grabbing one end of the umbilical, Merriman headed

216

up and out of the bay, extending the white umbilical cords to their full length.

In the *Yorktown*, Jack Lewis feebly attempted another transmission:

'Hou-ston,' he gasped, his lungs aching for air.

'Houston,' yelled Clark, 'Jack is almost out!'

'Move it, Dick,' said Pierce urgently, 'Jack's slipping!'

'On my way!' said Merriman, backing up from the ships.

Clark's air supply had now dwindled virtually to nothing and the astronaut felt himself passing out. Each breath was increasingly difficult and painful. Lewis now lay slumped motionless in his cockpit seat.

Having extended the umbilical cords to their full length, Merriman firmly held the cord in his left hand, controlling the backpack with his right, and raced out of the shuttle's cargo bay and down to the *Yorktown*. As he blasted the backpack to full speed and approached the ground maintenance port, he could hear Rob Clark's dying gasps over his headset. Now just forty feet from his target, Merriman raced on, closing quickly. He knew what he had to do: stop just short of the *Yorktown*, bring the backpack to a halt and plug in the cord. *Plenty of time to slow this thing down*, he thought – but before he could react, a scant four feet from the *Yorktown*'s fuselage, he felt himself spun around as if cracked by a whip and smashed into the hull of the ship. Dazed, Merriman felt like he had been hit by a truck, and bounced off the fuselage like a rag doll, his legs and arms flopping uselessly as he struggled to re-orient himself. He saw the dangling snake-like cord hanging limply. Then he sized it all up. The umbilical cord was too short!

Inside Rusty Bishop had felt the thud of Merriman's body plowing into the *Yorktown*. 'Dick? What's happened? Are you alright?'

A shaken, still dizzy Dick Merriman reached for the dangling cord:

'The cord! It's too short!'

'It can't be!' replied Bishop.

217

'I'm telling you it's too fucking short!' retorted Merriman, pulling at the hose, sweating like a pig, racking his brains for an answer.

On board the *Yorktown*, Rob Clark gasped what he feared would be his last words. 'Houston . . . Jack's out – hurry!'

'The module!' cried Merriman aloud.

Playing one last hunch, he blasted the backpack to full power again, soared up from the *Yorktown*, banking at a 45° angle over the space shuttle's cargo bay door, his legs hanging like outriggers, and zoomed to the umbilical cord's restraint module.

There it was! The last section of cord loop had been caught on one of the three prongs from the axis of the box. With a single tug he ripped the cord free.

'Houston, I've got it!' he yelled, activating the backpack.

'Can't – breathe,' gasped Clark.

'Dick, *hurry!*' said Pierce coldly. 'Jack? Rob? Open your masks. You'll have air in the cockpit in a few seconds.'

But there was no reply from Clark. Merriman pivoted over the side of the cargo bay and flew towards the end of the dangling umbilical cord. Grasping it in his left hand, he moved towards the ground maintenance port.

'Rusty!' he yelled, 'when I signal you, hit the air!'

Bishop's hand already gripped the environmental supply switch, waiting to pump air through the umbilical cord to the *Yorktown*.

'I'm ready,' he replied.

'Jack. We're almost there – open your mask!' cried Pierce again. But once more there was no reply. Both Lewis and Clark had their masks down, and were sealed off from the cabin's depleted atmosphere. Soon Dick Merriman would pump new air into the cabin, but if both men had already passed out, visors down, the new air would merely circulate around two cold, dead bodies.

Approaching the *Yorktown* a second time and once more blasting through space at full speed, Merriman jammed the cord into the porthole with room to spare. The nozzle snapped and locked into place. As soon as he felt the clunk, Merriman screamed: 'Hit it Rusty! Hit it! She's in! She's in!'

Bishop had slammed the button down before Merriman had even shouted his name, and by the time he had said 'She's in!' currents of air already flowed through the cord, flexing and bending it like a giant garden hose whipping from the force of rushing water. But from the *Yorktown* there was only a deathly silence.

'Rob, you've got air! Open your mask!' called Pierce.

Merriman flew to the front of the *Yorktown* and stared into the darkened cockpit, sickened at the sight of the motionless Lewis and Clark. He yelled at them:

'Rob! Jack! You've got air in the cabin! Open your masks.'

As he slipped into the gentle arms of death, Clark seemed to hear Merriman's words echoing in his mind like a distant foghorn. The words were an annoyance, an interruption of this final flight into forever. Frantically Merriman gestured to Clark, pounding on the fuselage of the *Yorktown* with his fists, screaming:

'Rob! You Goddamned sonofabitch! Open the fucking mask!'

The words pulled at Clark's waning consciousness. Dimly he peered through the cockpit window and saw the white-suited, ghostly figure of Merriman, wildly waving his arms. Almost instinctively, he raised his faceplate and felt oxygen surge painfully into his lungs; the ghost became his colleague, his friend Dick Merriman, and he gasped back into reality.

'Now open Jack's mask! Open it!' screamed Merriman.

Clark inhaled and struggled, and exhaled, his face distorted from lack of air as he fumbled with Lewis' mask. He couldn't get it open! His hands slipped, and slipped again.

'I think he's stopped breathing!' said Clark, his lungs still heaving, trying to shake Lewis, but to no avail.

'Open it! Do something! Anything!' bellowed Merriman.

Success, finally. Then, with all the force he could muster, Clark slammed his right fist into Lewis' stomach, doubling Lewis up and forcing him to take a sudden gulp of the air now circulating through the cabin. Clark prepared to rain in another blow, but Jack Lewis' hand caught it in mid-flight:

'I'm O.K.,' he coughed.

'He's breathing!' cried Clark, and then with a delirious half-laugh: 'I'm breathing too!'

Pierce pulled off his headset and sat back in his chair. He looked at Gibbs, numbed. The room fell silent.

CHAPTER TEN

Pierce flung a sheet of print-outs onto his console. 'I think we've just leapt from the fat to the fryer,' he said in disgust.

Joe Gibbs exchanged an uneasy glance with Bob Sanders, flight director of the Green Team, whose flight controllers were now preparing to begin their 6 a.m. shift. Pierce's analogy if unpleasant, was apt. The exhilarating relief of Dick Merriman's life-saving spacewalk had been short-lived. Engineered by Pierce's quick thinking, the spacewalk had forestalled Lewis and Clark's imminent death, but, as the latest print-outs showed, the end result of the *Yorktown*'s wholesale power shutdown had raised an equally deadly possibility, far more cruel than asphyxiation.

Every answer Pierce and the flight controllers came up with seemed destined to be followed by a new and more pernicious dilemma. Each step forward somehow seemed to precede a step and a half backward. Pierce thought aloud, checking off the plusses and minuses:

'I guess we should be grateful the *Yorktown*'s emergency radio transmitter can still be picked up by the *Columbia* and relayed back to earth. At least we can still talk to them. But with loss of power, the *Yorktown*'s environmental support system can't function. Sure, we can keep them breathing with air from the *Columbia* and the *Columbia* has oodles of power to keep pumping oxygen through the hoses . . .' He banged his fist on the console. 'But damn it, we can't get any heat into the *Yorktown*.'

Up to now, as they moved relentlessly towards the fiery burn-up in the atmosphere, Lewis and Clark's ultimate enemy had been time; but now a new deadly enemy had emerged. Already exhausted from lack of sleep, emotionally and psychologically pummelled by the psychic strain and physically diminished by hunger and dehydration, Lewis and Clark's new enemy was the bitter cold of space – a cold which could kill them.

'According to our nearest estimate, it's now 46° Fahrenheit in the *Yorktown*'s cockpit,' replied Gibbs softly. 'In their condition, that's already cold enough. But you can be damn sure it's going to get colder than that.'

'And one-half of each orbit is behind the earth, relative to the sun, so for each 96-minute orbit they'll spend 48 minutes in the shade,' replied Bob Sanders.

'So we only have 48 minutes of sunlight to work with for each orbit. What do we do?' asked Gibbs.

'We could put them into a bar-b-que mode,' said Sanders.

'A slow roll? Have the *Columbia* rotate the *Yorktown* for maximum exposure to the sun?' asked Gibbs.

'Sort of. Not a complete roll. We could have just a three-quarter roll to the left and a three-quarter to the right.'

'Fuel,' interjected Pierce. 'If we do that, we burn up the *Columbia*'s re-entry fuel. She won't have enough left to separate from the *Yorktown* after the transfer, re-orient her position, or ride out the re-entry to land.'

'Right, then,' replied Gibbs. 'Have we considered putting the *Columbia* into, how should I call it, a corkscrew roll? Set a continuing, gentle roll in motion and the *Columbia* would then merely have to exercise slight course corrections. I reckon the propellant savings are obvious, are they not?'

'They are,' replied Pierce, 'but there's another problem. Setting up a continuous roll to heat the *Yorktown* evenly will automatically increase the ship's drag and speed up their rate of fall. As it stands right now, trajectory's best estimates are that Brooks and Harwood will rendezvous on the *Yorktown*'s second-to-last orbit before burning up. We're cutting it very close as it is. If we authorize the *Columbia* to begin a roll, it may very well mean the

Yorktown's orbit will collapse before Brooks and Harwood can even get into space.'

'Pierce? May I speak bluntly?' Gibbs asked confidentially.

'Of course.'

'If we don't consider using a roll to heat the *Yorktown*, the whole exercise becomes pointless. If we don't do something, Lewis and Clark will freeze to death long before their orbits decay.'

Pierce stared fixedly at Gibbs, aware that the tiny Englishman had described their predicament with precision.

Bob Sanders, the Green Team's Flight Director broke the uncomfortable silence. 'It's 6 a.m. guys. My team is ready to take over here.'

Pierce and Gibbs rose from their chairs. Pierce faced Sanders. 'Bob? I'll have trajectory and flight dynamics crank out some reliable numbers on the effects of the roll. I'll be upstairs in the reserve control room if you want me.'

'The temperature is falling in the *Yorktown*, Doug. We don't have much time.'

Pierce nodded in slow resignation, and he and Gibbs left Sanders and the Green Team to their duties and walked from Mission Control in silence.

Entering the elevator, Gibbs pushed the third floor button. 'Douglas? You are aware, are you not, that by ignoring the surgeon's suggestion yesterday to open up Lewis' and Clark's suits for water . . .'

Pierce leaned back against the elevator, his legs crossed at his ankles, his arms folded across his chest, and studied Gibbs' face quizzically.

'. . . You are aware,' continued Gibbs, 'that it saved their lives, aren't you?'

Had their suits been cut open, had Pierce taken the obvious step to provide the men with water, Lewis and Clark would have asphyxiated before Merriman could have attached the umbilical cords to the *Yorktown*.

Pierce said nothing, his face expressionless as he

223

thought and pondered. The elevator door opened and the two men walked to the reserve control room. Why had he made that decision to ignore the surgeon's request? He could hardly claim it was a logical decision; no – it had been a hunch, no more, no less. But it had also saved lives.

They stopped at the door to the Reserve Control Room. Pierce spoke matter of factly. 'I guess if I had made that decision to cut their suits . . . I guess I would have killed them.'

Pierce's candor formed a lump in Gibb's throat. 'This is a wretched business, at times.'

'Not often,' replied Pierce, 'but at times, yes. Take this question of conducting a roll; you realize that if we do start a roll we've got ourselves another problem?'

'Which one?' Gibbs was taken aback.

'The crack in the support structure assembly holding the *Yorktown* to the *Columbia*. The roll will put greater stress on it. The *Yorktown* could very well break free and we could lose Lewis and Clark altogether.'

Pierce realized that until now his decisions throughout the flight had been relatively clear-cut. Unpleasant? Yes. Difficult? Yes. But also straightforward. They had been yes-no, go-no-go choices, each independent of the other in cause and effect. But now, each alternative course of action intermeshed and entangled itself with other choices, each causing damaging ripple effects which spread to all other parts of the flight.

While his team in the reserve control room continued to assemble the myriad timelines and the correlated sequence of events necessary to conduct tomorrow morning's final rescue attempt, Pierce authorized the flight dynamics officer to plot out the merits and demerits of putting the *Yorktown* and *Columbia* into a slow roll.

In minutes, he had the evidence before him. As always, the numbers on his screen never lied. If he ordered the roll, the resultant increase in drag due to a reduced aerodynamic attitude would mean that the *Yorktown* and *Columbia* would burn up at 10:17 a.m. Thursday – one full orbit and 74 minutes earlier than they had calculated. If he didn't authorize the roll, the *Yorktown* and *Columbia* would remain aloft until 11:31 a.m.

Burn-up at 11:31 if no roll; burn-up at 10:17 if Pierce ordered the roll. *Seventy-four minutes extra*, thought Pierce; *and enormous fuel savings for the* Columbia. Not only that, the extra time would give plenty of leeway for Brooks and Harwood to come alongside the *Yorktown* and retrieve Lewis and Clark. With no roll, the *Columbia* would still have enough fuel for Bishop and Merriman to put the abandoned *Yorktown* into a steep re-entry pattern – steep enough almost to guarantee its total burn-up in the atmosphere; even if some parts did survive, they would fall harmlessly into the Indian Ocean.

But – and it was a big but – if the ships weren't rolled and the *Yorktown*'s cockpit kept as warm as possible, Lewis and Clark would likely be dead by the time Brooks and Harwood got there. The cold of space, unrelenting, unyielding. A roll would keep the *Yorktown*'s cockpit temperature around 40° Fahrenheit. Without it, the temperature would be below freezing.

There were other factors to be considered too. If a roll was started, not only would the orbit decline faster, not only would the re-entry burn-up point move from 11:31 to 10:17 a.m., the *Columbia*'s fuel supply would be too low to put the abandoned *Yorktown* into the steep dive and thus ensure a debris-free burn-up. Worst of all, the earlier re-entry time of 10:17 would mean that the *Yorktown* would begin to burn up over the Hawaiian Islands, with the 'footprint' of debris potentially extending 250 miles inland, starting at Los Angeles.

Simply put, Bishop and Merriman in the *Columbia* would not have enough fuel left both to put the *Yorktown* into a steep dive and then attempt to re-enter themselves and land. If he authorized the roll, Pierce might very well seal the fate of the *Columbia*. Like the *Yorktown*, it too would burn up. And most assuredly the West Coast of the United States would be sprayed with the fiery remnant chunks of the ships.

Pierce stared hard at the numbers, cool green digits on his display screen. He probed the flight dynamics officer with challenging questions as to the veracity of the computations, trying to shake out any discrepancy. But there were none. The numbers were absolute.

The loneliness of decision-making came upon him like a cold hand on his shoulder. It was his choice and his alone. Could Lewis and Clark be kept from freezing by a roll? Perhaps. Would both the *Yorktown* and *Columbia* have to be abandoned? Would he lose both? Would subsequent debris hit Los Angeles or San Diego, or both? What if a building were hit? What if citizens were killed? Hell, with Skylab he had at least had a measure of control over its re-entry. But now? No way.

What would this do to NASA, to the entire space program? He thought of the Tuesday evening paper's headline: 'ATLANTIS DESTROYED'. Would it become 'NASA DESTROYED'? Were the lives of two men worth that? And what would happen to his career? The Airborne Launch Development Project was his project, after all, it was his ambitions that had got him into this mess. Would there be another headline: 'PIERCE FINISHED'?

He was wasting time. He had the data before him. Every second he delayed, the *Yorktown*'s temperature dropped further. He looked up for a moment and abstractedly watched the flight controllers going about their duties, wondering if his next decision would destroy all their efforts. His eyes closed. *God help me*, he prayed, *I may kill two good men.*

Now at 85 miles altitude and falling, the *Yorktown* and *Columbia* were only 90,000 feet away from re-entry and burn-up, and the computations just completed by the *Columbia*'s onboard computers had done nothing to improve Rusty Bishop's disposition.

'If Pierce doesn't give us the go for roll, Jack and Rob will have their asses frozen.'

'Asses frozen? You mean dead.'

226

'Yeah, but that's not all. If we do roll, the computer says that by the time Tex and Adrienne get up here, we'll only have 4,100 pounds of propellants left.'

'That's 100 below minimum!' said Merriman, 'We can't land this ship with under 4,140 pounds! 4,140's the minimum!!'

'We'll be below the minimum only if we do the roll . . but if we don't, Jack and Rob are dead.'

'If we do, we can't land . . .'

Bishop and Merriman stared at each other, a sickening realization touching them both. Bishop's voice sank to a whisper. 'All this time we've been thinking about Jack and Rob – they're in the broken ship, not us! It's been the *Yorktown* that's been in trouble. They're the ones without the space suits! We've got them! But if Pierce orders us to start the roll . . .'

'I know,' interjected Merriman.

'It's not just Jack and Rob who'll be trapped . . .'

Merriman shivered at the thought.

CHAPTER ELEVEN

'Resistance to the cold differs from individual to individual' said the flight surgeon as Pierce listened in. 'Lewis, for instance, showed only average resistance in his training, while Clark scored very highly. He skis in Vermont in the winter quite regularly. Were you aware of that?'

'No, and it doesn't interest me except insofar as it affects his ability to take the cold.'

'I mention it for that very purpose,' replied the surgeon. 'Are you leaning towards no roll – having Lewis and Clark tough it out?'

'I'm considering it. There's a truckload of complications if I don't.'

'I see. Among your load of complications, I trust you've included their dehydrated state and lack of sleep?'

'I've accepted those as given.'

'With all due respect—'

'Wait a sec, Doc. If you've got something to say, forget the respect, just lay it out.'

'Alright. As flight surgeon I can state with great certainty that unless Lewis and Clark get some liquids soon, you won't have to worry about the *Yorktown*'s outer hatch holding up when Brooks tries to get in.'

'What are you saying?'

'That because they're so dehydrated, so exhausted and so cold, Lewis and Clark will simply fall asleep some time tonight and won't wake up. They'll drift off and die. Now, yesterday, I urged you to have them cut into their suits. You chose to deny my request. Fortunately, Lady Luck smiled and they had air to breathe when the power cut out. But if you go against me this time, I'm telling you straight – you'll finish both of them off.'

'And if they cut into their suits to get those crummy twenty-eight ounces of water—'

'They'll have a chance.'

'But their suits will then give them no warmth.'

'I suppose not.'

'So I have to order the *Columbia* to start a roll to heat them up?' In which case the orbit would decay faster. And the *Columbia* might not have enough fuel. And the *Yorktown* might scatter debris on the West Coast.

Pierce, was the only one who could decide. He radioed Rusty Bishop and gave the order.

Minutes later, Bishop radioed back: 'O.K. Houston, here goes.'

Rusty Bishop inched the *Columbia*'s control stock to the left a prescribed distance, calculated by the ship's computers to produce a roll giving the maximum heat advantage. With slow certainty, the mighty *Columbia* and the battered *Yorktown* rolled to the left about its longitudinal axis. Through the Commander's window to his left, Bishop saw the earth appear to move; if he looked left and out the window, the blue-green ball of life in space now appeared directly below him. For two long seconds it disappeared from view and blackness returned, then the planet reappeared. The ship performed one complete roll every four seconds: a slow motion pirouette in the heavens. The *Columbia*'s fuel gauge numbers began to drop.

Having taken that last desperate step to keep Lewis and Clark from freezing, Pierce listened in on the astronauts' exchanges with Vince Torino in Mission Control, hoping that by starting the *Yorktown*'s roll he would have helped raise their spirits. Instead, their voices sounded dispirited; they were like sailors caught in a pounding gale, frantically pitching everything overboard to lighten the ballast, yet finding that still the waves pounded and still the ship floundered. One by one their defences had been stripped away. First the accident trapping them in space; then the crushing disappointment of the *Atlantis* and the venting incident; then finally the loss of power. Now there was a haunting, hollow echo of utter despair in their exchanges with Mission Control; the proceedings were infected with hopelessness. Lewis and Clark were exhausted, desperately thirsty, and cold.

Dying, thought Pierce, *they know they're dying*. He turned to Vince Torino. 'If you were in their spot up there, I mean would you want to talk to someone other than here in Mission Control?'

'You mean family?'

'Yes, exactly, family.' Pierce sighed and rubbed his face in concentration, suddenly remembering he had yet to shave this morning. 'I don't want them to think we've given up, or we've stopped trying . . .'

'One last cigarette and farewell to the world?'

'Exactly. But you're the astronaut, Vince, not me. You tell me.'

Torino hunched forward in his chair, folding and unfolding his hands, speaking in low, confiding tones. 'It's lonely as hell up there, Doug. You feel like a part of the universe, yet at the same time you know that only a handful of people in the history of man have ever seen what you're seeing or felt what you're feeling. You feel, well . . . god-like. You're looking down, *physically* looking down on the world; you know there's war down there, and murder and death and fights over borders and over energy. But when you look up, there's no borders, just infinity. No war, just silence. And yet the earth's still home and always will be. Right now, if I was up there, yeah, I'd want to talk to someone.'

Pierce nodded slowly: 'Bishop and Merriman's wives are no problem, and Adrienne's already talked to Clark. It's Jack Lewis, though . . . his parents are gone. What's his wife's name?'

'Charlene – his *ex*-wife, actually.'

'Is she still living in Houston?'

'I don't know. Jack's tight-lipped about the whole thing. The last thing I heard she was still working for TWA.'

'If she's still with TWA, we'll find her.' Pierce exhaled a long, tired breath. 'Oh, and we can't put off cutting into their suits any longer. Give Jack and Rob the go on that, and I'll get Fleck to call the families. Ben's a tactful old bastard, he'll handle it.'

Torino acted promptly on Pierce's order and called the *Yorktown*.

Regarding your water situation, guys, we think it's advisable to cut into your suits—'

'I'd prefer a daiquiri, Vince,' said Clark.

'Wouldn't we all,' smiled Torino. 'Listen there's eight ounces of distilled water in each of your suits and we think you'd be best advised to use your survival knife to make a one-inch incision on the interior side of the ankle – the left ankle, that is.'

'Ugh,' said Clark to Lewis.

Lewis licked his cracked lips with a tongue that felt almost as dry: 'Vince, we'll take that under advisement. *Yorktown* out.'

Clark looked at the Commander of the *Yorktown*. 'Well, Jack. What do we do?'

'I'll cut mine open, and we'll share it,' he replied.

'Wait a second. If you cut yours open, I'm cutting mine. There's no way we don't do it together.'

'Rob, I'm the Commander of this bus—'

'And fourteen ounces of water apiece is nothing,' interrupted Clark, 'Jack, it's been three days. All we've had is the emergency rations, and we've got another twenty hours to go—'

Lewis looked at his chronometer. It was 11:10 a.m. 'Twenty-two hours,' he corrected.

'Alright, twenty-two hours then! What the hell difference does it make?'

Lewis sat motionless, unblinking, for six long seconds, thinking hard of the implications of destroying both suits.

'Both, then,' he said finally.

In the weightlessness of zero gravity and the cramped conditions of the tiny cockpit, getting out of their suits was an exhausting trial comparable to undressing in a sleeping bag. As they struggled with their zippers, their floating helmets bounced around the cockpit. Clark took

231

a grab at one, missed, and his bare hand touched the starboard window, the coldness chilling him to the bone.

Now, sitting in their long john-type undergarments, they wrestled with the limp, floppy suits.

'Ever tried to fold a blanket underwater?' asked Lewis in rhetorical frustration. 'You got your knife?'

First Clark, then Lewis cut into the suits and sucked the horribly flat but beautifully wet, water. It was 11:30 Houston time, over twenty hours to the rescue. The last of their water had now been consumed.

Before Brooks and Harwood got thirty feet down the hall, the simulation operations chief, a short, stocky man with a crew cut, emerged from a side entrance leading into the Simulation Operations Facility. He wasted no time over hellos.

'Dr Brooks, Colonel Harwood?'

Quickly, he briefed them on the simulation team's preparation. Deep in technical discussion, the three of them passed hundreds of computer terminals and banks aligned in neat geometric sections like a huge array of giant toy blocks. After walking past the equivalent of half a football field of computers, they stopped at the base of the simulator, a two-storey-high replica of the shuttle's cockpit, the size of a two-car garage, secured atop six powerful hydraulic legs capable of tilting and twisting the cockpit into a near infinity of simulated flight positions.

Surrounding the simulator, a four-foot-high metal fence forty-foot square prevented the wayward from accidentally being crushed by the mechanical legs during operation. By the gate to the enclosure hung a prominent "NO SMOKING" sign, and beside it sat a gray cylindrical garbage can filled half-way with sand and labelled in military white lettering, "BUTTS ONLY". On the floor behind it lay a pressurized black rubber mat. It was impossible to get to the stairs leading up to the simulator without stepping on it, and any unauthorized person doing so immediately triggered off alarms loud enough to wake the dead.

The sim ops chief opened the gate. 'Hank?' he said to an assistant, 'we're going up.'

The assistant shut off the alarm system and the three climbed the narrow twenty-five-step stairway up to the deck of the sumulator. Another metal "BUTTS ONLY" can stood in their path. Stepping around it, they approached the simulator's hatch.

The chief leaned back against the fence surrounding the simulator's upper deck. 'Hank! Give us some power!'

'It's on!' came the reply, as the assistant flipped a series of switches on the crescent-shaped console around the simulator's base. The chief opened the hatch door and Brooks and Harwood ducked and squeezed through, stepping from the platform into an exact duplicate of the shuttle's cockpit. The sim ops chief followed.

'Just like home,' he said with a grin.

Brooks said nothing and took the right-hand pilot's chair, Harwood the left-hand Commander's chair. They strapped themselves in, not as an attempt to enhance realism but to prevent them from falling out during the pitching of the simulator, which was capable of duplicating an 80° climb, a 70° dive or a 120° bank to the left or to the right.

'O.K. We're in,' said Brooks.

'All right,' replied the chief, 'give me a minute and we'll crank her up.'

As the chief left the simulator and shut the hatch door, Brooks and Harwood powered up the cockpit. Harwood pulled on his headset: 'Harwood to simulation control.'

'Control to *Enterprise* Commander,' replied the chief, taking up his position at the crescent-shaped console. Harwood liked the use of the term '*Enterprise* Commander.' The chief was playing it real, right from the start.

'Ready to commence roll-out,' replied Harwood.

'O.K. *Enterprise*,' said the chief, pushing a button marked 'Visual Systems'.

233

Instantly, the windows of the simulator, not black like the night but the dull blank gray of a de-activated television set, were transformed by a computer projection to give a faultless simulation of Runway 22 at Edwards Airforce Base. For all intents and purposes, the view enjoyed by Brooks and Harwood *was* the view from a space shuttle sitting atop a hypersonic jet on the benchmark of Runway 22.

'*Enterprise*, this is simulation control. We'll start roll-out on your command, going for a full power climb with separation at seven zero point one miles nautical.'

'Copy. Ready?' he asked Brooks.

'Ready, let's go.'

'Control, this is the *Enterprise* Commander ready to commence roll-out. On the mark, . . . mark, 3, 2, 1, commencing roll-out.'

The cockpit began to vibrate slightly, the hydraulic legs of the simulator pumping up and down in a near perfect duplication of a hypersonic jet space shuttle take-off. As the ship appeared to gain speed, the images of Edwards Airforce Base sped past the simulator cockpit windows. Far down the simulation operations building, on a huge relief map of Edwards Airforce Base, a tiny camera, co-ordinated with the computers and the simulators, moved a fraction of an inch above a miniature landscape of Edwards. Once the 'field' was 'cleared', animated images were projected onto the simulator cockpit's windows.

The ride was so realistic that it was not unknown for inexperienced visitors to be made airsick, and even hardened pilots facing a pre-programmed 'disaster' would black out in abject terror of supposedly impending doom. Once in fact, the simulation chief's assistant had opened the simulator hatch only to find one such pilot sitting in the cockpit, mouth open, eyes glazed, suffering a severe spasmodic twitching in his neck and gripping the control stock so hard that his knuckles had turned white.

Above the crescent-shaped console control panel at the base of the simulator, a neatly-framed sign urged all NASA employees to "REMEMBER THE CARTHAGINIANS!" In truth, the business of simulation had began during the Romans' attempt to combat the marauding power of the Carthaginian Empire. Rome had no real navy, and in order to survive the Carthaginians' challenge of world dominance, desperately required a full-fledged battle-tested naval force. Some unknown genius whose name remains lost in the dust and mists of history arrived at the notion of building land-based full-scale models of Roman and Carthaginian ships. There were, of course, no computers, no screen projections, no mechanical aids in those days. Such illusions of reality were undertaken by slaves moving the landed crafts closer together until the Roman soldiers had practiced and perfected the act of pitched battles against the enemy on the high seas. The rest was history. To the victor went the world. But the vehicle to victory had been effective simulation.

No comparable advance in simulation techniques came until 1930, when another genius, the American Ed Link, put a rudimentary opaque-windowed plane cockpit on a rotating, pivoting base. Once sealed inside the cockpit, the pilot's only contact with the outside world was his instrument panel.

In terms of technological development, the Link Trainer was hardly more complicated than its Roman progenitor. But whereas the days of navy vessels pulling alongside enemies and boarding them in battle were long gone, the era of the airplane had just arrived with each advance in speed and altitude and technical complexity, came greater and greater financial costs and higher physical risks in training student pilots. Clearly, the need for more accurate and realistic simulators, was acute.

With the development of the computer, the realism of the simulators took a light year leap into the future. What the shuttle was to the Wright brothers' craft at Kitty Hawk, the shuttle simulator, all sixty million dollars' worth of it, was to Ed Link's original. Link's was the first, the shuttle simulator the latest.

Brooks and Harwood, faced with the task of taking off from Edwards and making a rendezvous with the *York-*

town and *Columbia* over the South Atlantic, needed all the realistic rehearsal they could get if Lewis and Clark were to be saved. The simulated climb to 70 miles altitude, the point in space where the *Yorktown*'s flawed tanks had failed, went perfectly. The roar and vibrations of the engines filled the simulator's cockpit. The viewing screens had long since darkened themselves into the azure blue-black of near-space and the earth's horizon now distinctly filled the lower portion of the simulator's cockpit windows. All was exactly as Brooks and Harwood hoped it would appear on Thursday morning.

'O.K. Houston, we're at the separation point,' said Harwood.

'Roger, *Enterprise*. Houston copies,' replied the chief, getting caught up in the exercise.

'On launch heading, ready to fire main engines,' said Brooks.

'Clear to fire, you are go.'

As the switches were depressed, the simulator jolted forward, duplicating the force of shuttle main engine ignition.

'Clean burn – go for separation,' said Brooks.

'Clear to separate, you are go, *Enterprise*.'

The separation switch, a replica of the one Rusty Bishop had taped over with a 'NO', clunked into place under the pressure of Harwood's right index finger, and just as they hoped they would feel Thursday morning, their shuttle jerked upwards, compressing them into their seats.

'O.K. We're clear of the *Hornet*,' reported Harwood. The imaginary hypersonic vehicle had been left behind; now they were on their own.

'The race is on,' said Brooks.

To the chief, Adrienne's words were well chosen. It *was* a race. To get the shuttle into orbit was a piece of cake; but now the task was to chase the *Yorktown* and *Columbia*. Unless they made the rendezvous in mere minutes, they would be too late even to attempt a transfer.

'Maintaining full power!' announced Harwood, feeling the simulator continue to vibrate.

'Roger,' replied the chief, studying the changing matrices and graphs on his console display screen. The chief, Harwood and the simulation operators had built into the computer program of the flight an imaginary 'blip,' to be picked up on Brooks' and Harwood's control panel screen.

'Do you have a targeted radar fix?' asked the chief, knowing full well what the answer should be.

'Negative,' replied Brooks, 'nothing on our screen.'

The chief frowned, quickly punched a display screen stopwatch, and shut off his microphone to Brooks and Harwood. 'What the hell's going on?' he snapped to an assistant. 'They should be picking up the *Yorktown* and *Columbia!*'

The assistant was nonplussed. 'I . . . I know . . . it doesn't—'

'Still nothing on our screen,' reiterated Brooks.

The stopwatch ticked on: 30 seconds, 40 seconds, 45 . . .

'Houston, we've got a reading,' cried Harwood.

The chief stopped the clock at 47 seconds. 'Suggest you go to visual,' he said, annoyed at the inexplicable discrepancy in time. Brooks and Harwood should have had radar contact in 5 seconds, not 47.

'Going to visual,' said Brooks, expecting to see an X in the sky or some alpha-numerical figure representing the *Yorktown* and *Columbia*.

'Negative on visual,' she said.

The chief bit his lip angrily and punched on the stopwatch again. Ten seconds, 15, 16 . . .

'I don't believe it,' muttered Brooks. 'Look!'

Harwood looked up from his controls in amazement. There in the distance appeared a perfect replica of the *Yorktown* and *Columbia*!

The chief shut off the clock again: 18 seconds.

'Thought you'd like that. I worked all night on it. Figured it would be better than closing in on a number.'

'O.K.!' exulted Harwood, 'we're closing in on the *Yorktown*! Estimated rendezvous in—'

Suddenly the simulation cockpit screens beaming the images of the earth, the heavens and the *Yorktown* and *Columbia* into Brooks and Harwood's consciousness clunked to a dead blank gray. Brooks released her control stock and angrily slammed herself into her chair.

'Shit!' spat out Harwood. 'What the hell's happened now?'

'*Enterprise*?' said the chief, 'you took 47 seconds to acquire radar contact and 18 for visual. That's 65 seconds too long. If you'd attempted rendezvous, allowing 10 minutes to transfer Lewis and Clark out, you'd have been too late. Let's do it again.'

He pushed the reset button. In the cockpit the screens came alive again. In a twinkling they had left the blackness of space and been transported back thousands of miles to the runway at Edwards.

'Once more, from the top' said Brooks resignedly.

The point in time at which the real *Enterprise* could be launched was fixed; but so was the decay time of the *Yorktown* and *Columbia*'s orbit. Neither could be altered. And this first simulated launch and climb had fallen 65 seconds short of the intersecting position in time and space where the *Enterprise* and *Yorktown* were due to meet. Simply put, Brooks and Harwood had failed. The shuttle itself had travelled fast enough – they had powered it to its maximum – but the *Hornet*, the sister ship of the *Yorktown*, would just have to go faster – *much faster*.

The simulation operations chief sat with a scowl on his face, anxiously considering how much further the *Hornet* could be pushed. 'Yeah,' he said, 'once more from the top.'

At 4:15 p.m. in the reserve control room, Vince Torino stepped back from his console and assisted a petite, attractive brunette into a chair. He adjusted her headset and told her to wait one minute.

'*Columbia*? Houston Capcom here. Dick? We have a

238

call for you. You're on a closed line. There's someone here who'd like to talk to you.'

Torino motioned to Mrs Dick Merriman, unplugged his headset and stepped away, allowing the two some privacy.

'Dick?' asked a familiar voice. Despite a brave front, her tone was frightened, desperately concerned.

Nervously and with some self-consciousness, Merriman cleared his throat. 'Hi! How are you? Glad you could call,' he said, trying to project a confidence he did not feel.

As they spoke, Dick Merriman's emotions welled up within him, and with them the memory of their last parting . . . It had been last Friday. It seemed longer. They had spoken little. Words could not be rehearsed for such moments, because such moments were best shared in touches, in tones, in scents: the softness of her lips; the slight taste of the lipstick which had remained on his tongue; the feel of her hair through his fingers; the brush of her cheek against his. And then all too quickly, it had been time to leave . . .

'We're going to be O.K., honey – I promise, said Dick finally, 'I'll see you tomorrow.'

Drumming his fingers on his oaken desk in the seventh-floor office of the Administrative Building, Dr Benjamin Franklin Fleck sat, eyes closed in concentration. His calls to Mrs Rusty Bishop and Mrs Dick Merriman had been made and their conversations with their husbands had not produced what he had feared – an emotional outburst. Fleck actually felt relieved to contact the families; it gave him an emotional release of his own to reassure and console people under great strain themselves. But Charlene Lewis – that was another matter. Jack and Charlene Lewis' marriage had been a desperately brief one. Charlene still lived in Houston; in fact, they hadn't yet begun the messy process of divorce. Why, Fleck didn't know. Should he call her? Or would it be better to contact

Lewis' father instead? He shook his head negatively and with some frustration. Logic said it would be a mistake to contact Mrs Lewis. It was a decision he didn't want to make, but time was forcing his hand.

His concentration was broken by the buzzer on the intercom link to his secretary's outer office.

'Dr Fleck? Mrs Lewis to see you.'

Fleck raised his bushy white eyebrows, surprised and caught off guard. *That solves that*, he thought. But what would he say to her? What *should* he say?

'Thank you. Send her in.'

Charlene Lewis, dressed in a stunning navy-blue pant-suit set off by her long, gently-curled blond hair, entered the office. At once Fleck's eyes were drawn to hers: eyes that had quite clearly been red with tears. Her thin face was made up neatly but bore the unmistakable signs of great stress. He smiled and shook her hand.

'Charlene, good to see you again. I wish it was under different circumstances.'

She smiled weakly and nodded. 'May I sit down?' she asked faintly.

He gestured to a pair of padded high-backed chairs in front of a small reception table by his desk.

'Can I get you a coffee? Perhaps some sherry?'

'No, thank you,' she said politely. 'Dr Fleck, are you going to get them back?'

Her bluntness rocked him. She stared at him firmly. He opened his mouth to reply, but no words would come out. The agonizing silence, he knew, was giving her an answer in itself. 'Mrs Lewis, . . .' he began, in a stronger voice.

First it was Charlene, now Mrs Lewis. *Make up your mind*, he told himself.

'Charlene, I'm not going to try to fool you, or to be unnecessarily pessimistic—'

'Are they going to die?' she said with polite but measured force.

'I don't know. I don't think so. But it's going to require a huge effort from all of us, Charlene. They're all very tired men. We're trying to keep their spirits up. We can only do so much on the ground. They themselves are very much in control of their own destiny – at least once we get the *Enterprise* up there and—'

'Can I talk to Jack?' she interrupted. Her voice was calm, and there was quiet authority in her eyes.

'That's something we've been working on.'

She pulled out a pack of 100-millimetre filtered cigarettes. Fleck stopped speaking and pulled out a Lucky lighter from his pocket. He didn't smoke, but once had; he now kept a lighter as a constant reminder that he had stopped.

'Thanks,' she said, exhaling a long stream of white smoke off to the side. 'You're probably asking yourself if I'm the best person to talk to Jack right now.' She shifted her gaze from the floor and back to his face.

'Well, I have given it some consideration, yes.'

'Dr Fleck. Do you know why we separated?'

Fleck felt a slight pang of unease. 'Really, I don't think it's important that I—'

'It *is* important,' she said with emphasis. 'We separated because *I* couldn't take it. Not Jack, *me*. I'd seen this whole business as glamorous; it never crossed my mind that Jack's flights could ever go wrong.'

She took another drag on the cigarette. Fleck, noticing the lengthening ash, picked up a flat, clear glass ashtray from his desk and placed it on the reception table beside her.

'Thanks,' she said. 'The flights never did go wrong – until now, of course. But somehow things became different between us – I couldn't adjust, and he couldn't accept the fact that I couldn't. I still love him, Dr Fleck. Maybe he needs me now more than I ever needed him.'

Fleck nodded. He looked at his watch. 'We can go over to Mission Control right now' he said.

'The hell of it is,' sighed Doug Pierce, flopping shut and hefting the thick black binder onto his console, 'the real hell of it is that so many of these times will stay in a state of flux right up to your take-off.'

Brooks and Harwood said nothing. What could they say? They had spent the whole day in the simulation operations facility and were now an hour late for their departure to Edwards.

Brooks tried to be reassuring. 'It'll coalesce, Doug.'

'I hope so.'

'No. It will. It'll just take more time.'

'But there are so many unfixed variables . . . so much I can't control . . .' Pierce's voice trailed off.

'Let's start with the givens,' interrupted Brooks. 'Tex and I have come as close as we can to a perfect launch.'

'By pushing the hypersonic jet to its limits,' said Pierce in a correcting tone.

'Yes. To its limits. But the *Hornet* can take it. Noonan and Schacter have been running *Hornet* simulations all day at Edwards. They think they can do it too. So do I.'

'Me too,' chimed in Harwood. 'Lookee here, Doug,' he drawled, 'you and your boys just keep the *Yorktown* up there and me and Adrienne will do the rest.'

Pierce smiled at Harwood's bravado.

'Never let you down before, have I Doug?'

Pierce nodded with a grin. 'No, you haven't. So, we deal with the givens.' He reached through the black binder and thumbed through it. 'Right now, the *Yorktown*'s orbit is 81 miles. At 68, they re-enter. Trajectory says that'll happen at 10:14 tomorrow morning. Edwards say they'll be ready to launch you and Tex at 8:10 a.m. By then the *Yorktown* and *Columbia* will be starting their final orbit. You'll have to rendezvous with *Yorktown* no later than 41 minutes after take-off over the South Atlantic. You'll have exactly ten minutes to get Lewis and Clark out, because by that time you'll have to fire your rockets by 9:46 a.m. to slow the *Enterprise* down. If you don't get Lewis and Clark out in ten minutes and if you can't fire your rockets before 9:46—'

'Then we won't be able to land at Edwards, right?' said Harwood.

Pierce nodded. 'So ten minutes it is,' he reiterated.

'Doug? What about the *Columbia*'s propellant levels?' asked Brooks.

'At this point, the roll is burning up the *Columbia*'s propellants to within .5 percent of our estimates.'

'Low or high side?'

'Low, I'm afraid.'

'Are Rusty and Dick going to have enough propellants left to attempt a landing?'

'Too close to tell. Won't know until just before take-off at Edwards.'

'So there's no way to tell if we'll have to get Rusty and Dick into the *Enterprise* as well?'

'Right. They may have to abandon the *Columbia* along with the *Yorktown*.'

'What are the odds on this happening, Doug?' asked Harwood.

'The odds? No numbers. Just look at it this way: it's odds-on that you'll have to bring Bishop and Merriman aboard the *Enterprise* as well.'

'And their orbital decay?'

'On target – damn it.' said Pierce. 'The roll is slowing them up, no question, and we're only just keeping the *Yorktown*'s cockpit above freezing as it is.'

For a moment Harwood paused to consider the implications of both the *Yorktown* and the *Columbia* being abandoned. 'God! That'll be a lot of hardware coming through the atmosphere!'

We've programmed a delayed auto manoeuver into the *Columbia*. If they do have to leave the shuttle, we'll have a chance of plowing the ships back in. The debris should fall short of the West Coast. It all comes down to how long you take to get Lewis and Clark out of the *Yorktown*, Adrienne. If you can beat ten minutes, even by seconds, it'll make a big difference.'

'I can do it,' she said.

'That's one of the few things I am certain of,' he replied.

Adrienne smiled, and Harwood pulled himself to his feet.

'We've got a date at Edwards, and we're late,' he said.

Pierce rose to shake Tex Harwood's hand and clapped him on the back. 'Watch yourself, cowboy.' He turned. 'And Adrienne . . . just do it like we rehearsed it, O.K.?'

'I will, Doug.' She reached forward and gave him a hug.

Pierce watched them walk to the front of the reserve control room past the rows of flight controllers. One of them – Pierce didn't catch who it was – said in a voice loud enough to be heard by all: 'Go get 'em!' Brooks and Harwood, startled by the cry, stopped in their tracks, seeking who had called out.

First one, then two, then dozens of the controllers began to applaud. Pierce smiled broadly and joined in the growing ovation. They had all slaved to improve the odds of rescuing four trapped men. Brooks and Harwood were their agents: two astronauts who would try to translate the flight controllers' work into results. The gesture was for good luck, but everyone in the room, especially Brooks and Harwood, realized it might also be for farewell.

Half an hour later, Vince Torino placed a call to Jack Lewis. 'O.K. Jack, we've got somebody down here who wants to say hello.'

In the *Yorktown*'s cockpit, Jack Lewis knitted his brow. What in God's name was his—

'Jack? Can you hear me?' said a soft voice tentatively.

'Charlene!' he replied, totally stunned, totally surprised. It didn't make sense.

Rob Clark, just as surprised to hear her voice, caught the shocked look on his colleague's face. Exercising discretion, he disengaged his communications link. 'I've got to test some . . . ah . . .' He looked at the incredulous Lewis, then dropped the pretence: 'Go on! Talk to her!'

'Charlene – I . . .'

'Jack? It's alright.'

'Are we on closed line?'

'Yes – at least, they said it was private.'

'Did Fleck ask you to speak?' As the words came out, Lewis in his confused state realized she would probably take the question the wrong way.

She had, and the words had hurt her. 'No, I asked him.' There was a long silence before she spoke again. 'Jack. There's so much I want to say.' Tears were forming in her eyes. Torino looked away from her. 'As soon as I heard – I wanted to—'

She was making no sense. Her carefully prepared thoughts had collapsed under the force of his presence, one felt even over the phone. Suddenly they were two people, desperately wanting to communicate, neither able to find the words, and each afraid of what the other might think.

'Jack – I – I still love you—'

'No, Charlene, please – I, uh . . . I really appreciate it that you called and . . .' He inhaled, forcing back tears: '. . . and I'm going to be alright and I've got a lot of things to do so I'm going to have to go now. O.K.? Look, you take it easy . . .'

'I love you,' she repeated softly.

'. . . because I know . . .'

'Jack?'

'. . . you kind of work too hard for your own good, you know that Charlene?'

'Jack?' she asked again. Her voice was stronger. He could no longer ignore her.

'Yes.'

'I need you. I want you to know that.'

The words hit hard at Lewis, words he had not heard in a long time. A man whose emotions never broke through to the surface, Lewis suddenly wrestled with his contradictory feelings. He was copping out. *She'd* had the guts to call, and here he was cutting her off. But she had been the one who copped out of their marriage. A sudden pain fanned Lewis' desire to retaliate. Something deep within him longed to make a fresh start with her. Something else told him he would never see her again, one way or the other, and that maybe it was just as well. *But she had said she needed him.* Again and again it echoed in his mind. The feeling of longing returned. He suppressed it, pushed it back down, told himself that now of all times he could do without the aggravation.

'Charlene. Thank you for calling. Good luck.' He depressed the cut-off button.

'Jack!' she cried vainly. She waited for long seconds, covered her mouth then removed the headset and placed it on the console.

Torino walked over and placed his hand on her shoulder.

'I'll never see him again,' she whispered.

'Don't worry, Charlene. We'll get him home,' he said, trying to reassure her.

She nodded at him. 'I'll never see him again.'

Torino, totally unaware of the nature of their conversation, could only guess at her meaning as he watched her leave. Someone handed him a note, and he passed it to Pierce. The two F-24 Condor jets had just left Ellington Airforce Base adjacent to the Space Center. Brooks and Harwood were on their way.

11.30 p.m. Verification of the *Enterprise*'s link-up with the hypersonic jet *Hornet* had just been received. The countdown continued, straining the computers to the limits of their theoretical tolerance. Ten working days of testing and re-testing had been condensed and compressed into one 'yes-no' checkout.

In the reserve control room, Pierce reviewed the countdown checklist verified by the computers in the Real Time Computer Complex on the first floor of the Mission Control building. The huge burden of responsibility, the heavy psychological strain, the unrelenting twists and turns of the mission, weighed down upon him. Vainly he sought to restore some measure of discipline to his thinking as he stared at the blinking numbers on his console display screen – an infinity of numbers, most changing, some constant.

Suddenly, Pierce was overwhelmed with the realization

that the fate of the men largely depended on the workings of these machines. His role was simply to mediate between man, machine, and the inflexible physical laws of the universe.

The laws of physics are precise and predictable. Because e always equals MC^2, never MC^3, and because every action has an equal reaction, never a greater reaction, any machine which interacts with those laws must function equally precisely and predictably. Thus, the imperfect, imprecise, fallible abilities of man must be made specific and precise through the computer. Only the computer, able to command an engine to ignite at the precise split-millisecond in time necessary for proper firing, only the computer can stand in man's stead and act as a refining filter, a perfecting agent more perfect than its creator, and interact with the physical laws governing such complex operations as space travel. To push the proper sequence of buttons on the computer's keyboard and order the computer to direct the actions of an orbiting machine was no mere physical act. It was, in the highest truth, a momentary but intimate embrace with the perfect order of the universe. An embrace sometimes beautiful and uplifting, but sometimes, like now, ugly and cold.

Pierce hesitated from his computations, immobilized and disturbed by his thoughts. His actions were dictated by the numbers on the console display screen. If they didn't add up, if their sum was not *the* sum necessary to achieve his desired goal, then no amount of human desire could alter the conclusion. If the numbers were not exactly right, then neither his talents and abilities nor those of all the control teams in Mission Control and throughout the world could save Lewis and Clark and Bishop and Merriman.

And the numbers were not right. They were not adding up. They were running out of time.

The *Yorktown*'s orbit had fallen to 84 miles. Because of the continuing rolling motion necessary to keep Lewis and Clark from freezing, it was decaying much too rapidly. Fight it as he might, Pierce now had a real sinking premonition that all his efforts and those of Brooks and Harwood would be too little, too late.

A question from Torino pulled his consciousness back into the realm of the immediate present. His mind had been elsewhere. The question was neither technical nor empirical, but rather was one of raw emotion.

'Do you think we can save them?'

The forty-three-year-old flight director stared at Torino's face, a face now revealing something Pierce had not seen in any astronaut's face before. Torino was as trained as any, as professional as most, and calmer than all but a precious few. Yet his eyes now revealed unmistakable fear.

Pierce swallowed, not wanting to answer. 'We'll give it our best . . . Vince, I'm going home – catch a few hours' sleep.'

'Good idea. There's not much more you can do tonight. I'll stay, though. We'll have the final timelines for the launch by the time you get back.'

'Good man.'

Pierce rose to leave, but an incoming call stopped him. It was Benjamin Fleck, the NASA Administrator.

'Doug, can I see you before you leave?'

'Benj? Is it important? I'm cross-eyed.'

'It's important. I'm in my office.'

Pierce sighed. 'O.K. – be there in five minutes.'

The Administrator for NASA sagged in his chair, feeling as low as he had ever felt in his life. Fears, doubts and uncertainties rumbled around in his mind like angry storm clouds. Pierce's project, the Airborn Launch Development Project was not only in jeopardy; it now threatened NASA's very survival.

Fleck viewed the future with dread. Here was NASA in the middle of a crisis, just when it stood on the verge of resolving much of the nation's energy problems. The solar power station concept would work – the demonstrations had proved it. And if the Airborn Launch Concept could be made to work too, if space shuttles could be launched via hypersonic jets, then full-scale 15 by 5 kilometre solar power stations were feasible. The nation was on the verge of real electrical energy independence!

Thanks to NASA, the development of hydrogen to replace fossil fuels was just around the corner too. Non-polluting, more powerful than gasoline or diesel fuel, hydrogen also had the advantage of a totally inexhaustible supply, since it could be drawn from water. Such was only one lasting benefit of the Apollo Project, but that development alone was surely worth the 24 billion dollars spent to get a man to the moon. For now, more and more and cars both in the United States and throughout the free world were using exactly the same fuel as had powered the Apollo capsule. At least the historians could accurately record that it had been because of NASA.

Yet in spite of that, NASA's yearly budget was barely enough to run the Department of Health and Human Resources for less than seven days – even though, according to various independent economic studies, every dollar spent on space research, both manned and unmanned, returned ten dollars to the economy. Fleck groaned. Unfortunately, the *Yorktown*'s accident gave a perfect pretext for some bright-ass senator or self-appointed public watchdog to stand up and claim that space travel wasn't worth it, or that the money should be spent 'on Earth'.

That one – 'spend it on Earth' – always rankled Fleck. He looked to the ceiling in disgust at the thought. *All we ever promised was to search for knowledge, and we kept our word. What we brought back was knowledge: new knowledge, new systems, new products and devices to improve the quality of life.*

Didn't those critics who wanted the money spent on the problems facing mankind, like energy and food production, realize that in addition to bringing greater knowledge with which to solve problems, space travel guarantees, *guarantees* mind you, immediate return benefits? Didn't they realize we live in a technological world?

If NASA, with its publicly scrutinized programs and annual budget review and congressional control, wasn't allowed to be the leading edge of technological development, who was it to be? The clowns who built the Three Mile Island nuclear power station? The guys who dumped P.C.B.s throughout Michigan? The Love Canal and Hooker Chemical people in New York? Did they want some multinational corporation leading the way? Fleck sighed. Always, always, always, there were vested interests who would fight the explorers, the innovators. It was a lesson of history.

Fleck's office door swung open and a pasty-faced Doug Pierce, his tie dangling limply about his neck and jacket slung over his shoulder, entered the room.

'Sit down, Doug.'

Fleck crossed over to a small cabinet, which opened to reveal a small but well-stocked bar.

'Bourbon, isn't it, Doug?'

'Yeah – but no thanks.' Pierce slumped into one of the high-back chairs.

Fleck poured out two glasses of the amber coloured liquid, no ice. 'Here, you can use it.'

'Ah, what the hell,' said Pierce with a feeble smile.

Fleck leaned against the front of his desk, feet crossed, and faced Pierce squarely. 'Doug, I want it straight. Are we going to make it?'

'Are we going to make it?' Pierce replied bitterly. He stared hard at Fleck: 'Yeah, . . . we'll get the *Enterprise* up there, and if we're lucky, the *Columbia* might have enough fuel to land . . .'

'And the *Yorktown*? What's its burn-up and potential debris area?'

'If left alone, the debris will come very close to hitting Los Angeles; in fact, it's probable. If Bishop and Merriman have enough fuel left, they'll be able to guide the *Yorktown* into the Pacific. If not, they'll put the *Columbia* on auto pilot and switch to the *Enterprise*, in which case it should still fall short of Los Angeles. We think.'

'I don't have to tell you I've been getting calls about that from the President on down.'

'We'll be O.K.'

'What about Lewis and Clark? What are the odds?'

'Of getting out alive?'

'Fifty-fifty?' asked Fleck.

'Thirty-seventy. That's against, by the way.'

'That bad?'

'That bad.'

Fleck stared at the green carpeted floor and spoke resignedly. 'I'll prepare two announcements for tomorrow then.'

Pierce finished off the bourbon in a shot and handed Fleck the empty glass. He glanced at his watch: almost midnight. A few more hours and he'd be back on duty, leading the rescue flight, maybe the last flight for a long, long time . . .

The All-News Radio Station helped keep Pierce awake as he drove home. As he pulled into his driveway, one report caught his attention. He turned the engine off but left the radio going and closed his eyes, leaned back and listened:

'. . . And so tomorrow, the first true rescue attempt in the history of the United States Space Program will take place, as two astronauts, Dr Adrienne Brooks and Colonel Tex Harwood will be launched from Edwards Airforce Base in California, to rendezvous with the men in the stricken vessels in outer space. America has never yet lost a man in space, but there follows a special list of men who died in training:

'Major Charles A. Bassett of the United States Air Force in 1966. United States Navy Lieutenant Commander Roger B. Chaffee in 1967. United States Air Force Captain Theodore C Freeman in 1964. Edward G. Givens in an auto accident near Houston in 1967. Lieutenant Colonel Virgil I. Grissom of the United States Air Force in the Apollo Spacecraft fire of 1967. Eliott J. See in 1966. Edward H. White III, a Lieutenant Colonel in the United States Air Force in the same Apollo Spacecraft fire. And Clifton C. Williams, a Major of the United States Marine Corps in 1967.

'Of these men, only Virgil Grissom, America's second

man in space and Ed White, the first American to walk in Space, ever conducted space missions.'

Eight men, thought Pierce, heading for his house. *And no more!*

On board the *Yorktown*, Jack Lewis looked out the port window and stared off into space for several moments, allowing his mind to go completely blank, soaking up the tranquil nothingness before him. His eyelids were heavy with physical exhaustion. His beard had reached an uncomfortably itchy state. His undergarments had the clammy stickiness of three days' wear. He licked his lips. At least his salivary glands still worked, providing small but welcome relief to his throat. He would have to tell Mission Control about that: thinking about food seemed to help relieve thirst. But what difference did it make anyway? What difference did *he* make either, or the mission – any mission?

'Stop it asshole,' he said aloud, chastening himself. He glanced quickly over at Clark, worrying whether or not he had awoken him. No, he had not.

'*Columbia*,' he said in a barely audible whisper. 'Dick, are you still awake?'

Merriman had drawn the last shift at the controls while Bishop slept in the *Columbia*'s lower deck. Merriman looked at his chronometer. What was Jack doing awake? 'Yeah, Jack. I'm here,' he replied.

'Oh, it's nothing,' said Lewis in a desultory tone, 'just wondering.'

'Try to get some sleep, Jack.'

'Sure, Dick. Sure.'

Lewis looked out the *Yorktown*'s port window again. The ship continued to roll. They were passing over the southwest United States. The lights of hundreds of cities, towns and villages seemed strung together in a cobweb-like pattern covering thousands of miles. He studied the peculiar geometry of the lights. They were like the stars above, now coming into view once more as the ship rolled. Jack Lewis felt terribly alone.

He glanced over at Rob Clark sleeping soundly, hands

floating weightlessly in front of him. He wasn't alone, Rob was with him. But he felt alone.

His stomach grumbled hungrily, and in the awesome silence of space, he became increasingly aware of the sound of his body – the slight ringing in his ear, the thumping of his heart, the sound of his own breathing.

The loneliness seemed to start in his chest and work out pervasively through his limbs.

More than loneliness, perhaps a part of loneliness, he felt a deep longing in his soul, a desire to touch, to hold, to embrace all things terrestrial.

An untrained person would have felt trapped in such circumstances, but Jack Lewis felt lost. Everything that he had worked for, trained for and planned for seemed to have turned on him viciously, pummelling his very essence. He looked down upon the Earth again. The lights of Denver – yes, it was Denver – flickered anew and repressed memories deep from within him surfaced. *Denver*. He had met Charlene in Denver. He had fallen in love in Denver.

'Damn,' he muttered.

PART FOUR

Thursday, May 14th

THE FOURTH DAY OF THE MISSION

CHAPTER TWELVE

THE FINAL ATTEMPT

4 a.m. Mission Control

Doug Pierce arrived at the Johnson Space Center shortly after 4 a.m., two hours before he and his team would begin the final shift, the last attempt to save the crews of the *Yorktown* and *Columbia*. Adrenalin pumped through his veins, counteracting his bone-tiredness. Today of all days he had to be on top of things.

But the news from Joe Gibbs presented graphically on his console display screen sent him reeling in disbelief.

'These numbers – they can't be right!' he spluttered. 'They *can't* be!'

'I'm afraid, old man,' replied Gibbs, 'their accuracy is beyond dispute.'

Pierce stared into the screen, juggling the figures in his mind, adding, subtracting, trying to disprove the sums. Yet the facts remained.

From the moment the *Yorktown* and *Columbia* had achieved orbit at 10:31 Monday morning until moments ago at 4 a.m. Thursday, the stricken ships' altitude had consistently but gently declined from 94 to 84 miles, a fall of 20 miles in 66 hours.

'It works out to a third of a mile every hour,' said Gibbs.

But in the last hour, from 3 a.m. to 4 a.m. the orbit's altitude had dropped from 84 to 81 miles! Not one-third of a mile an hour but three miles! The *Yorktown*'s orbit was now declining in a gently consistent arc towards the burn-up altitude of 68 miles. It was collapsing before their very eyes.

Gibbs went on. 'The *Enterprise* is scheduled for launch at 8:54. If the decay continues at its present rate, the

Yorktown and *Columbia* will have burned up before Brooks and Harwood even leave the ground.'

Like everyone present, Pierce had known that ultimate consequence of putting the *Yorktown* and *Columbia* into a slow roll would be that the increased friction would slow the ships and thus speed up the rate of orbital decay. But lacking any reliable figures on the actual drag on a space shuttle and hypersonic jet in orbit, he had had no way of determining the interim consequences of the roll; that is, the actual moment a rapid decay would begin.

'I *had* to start that roll,' said Pierce softly, thinking back. 'Otherwise Lewis and Clark would be frozen by now.'

'Yes, yes. Quite. However, the roll is costing the *Columbia* propellants dear. At present rates of consumption, the *Columbia*'s propellant supply with fall below 4,100 in another three and a half hours, and it will therefore—'

'Be unable to negotiate its own re-entry.'

'Precisely. We are, I suggest, on the verge of losing both crews before the *Enterprise* can even launch.'

'And if we stop the roll and conserve the *Columbia*'s propellants?'

'The rate of orbital decay would, of course, be arrested somewhat.'

'Enough?'

'Not calculable. At least, not with any reliability.'

'Would the *Columbia* at least have sufficient propellants to attempt re-entry?'

'The propulsion engineer indicates that with stringent propellant conservation, the *Columbia* would end up at a level of 4,050 pounds – 50 below minimum.'

'We've got four and a half hours until the *Enterprise* takes off. If we stop the roll, and thus stop heating the *Yorktown*, Lewis and Clark will freeze.'

'I should think so, yes.'

'So we could end up losing two, or even four men. Both crews, both ships.'

Gibbs nodded grimly. Slumping back in his chair,

Pierce removed his glasses and rubbed his sore, bloodshot eyes, deep in anxious thought.

'Douglas, we have one further consideration. The minimum acceptable altitude for the type of spacewalk Brooks will have to perform lies, of course, between 75 and 80 miles . . .'

Pierce looked up, startled that he could have forgotten so obvious a fact, and now fully aware of what Gibbs was about to say.

'. . . so that even if we slow the roll, the *Yorktown* and *Columbia*'s altitude may be too low for Brooks to attempt a transfer.'

'How close can we go?'

'If the roll is stopped, trajectory plots the *Enterprise*'s rendezvous with *Yorktown* and *Columbia* at 75·4 miles. Brooks will have . . . less than ten minutes to transfer Lewis and Clark to the *Enterprise*.'

'But we've projected five minutes per man, per transfer.'

'It'll have to be less.'

'Does she know?'

'No, not at all. All of these numbers—' he waved his hand across the display screens '—came together just before you arrived.'

'Either way, it looks like we lose the *Yorktown* . . . and the *Columbia*.'

'I had hoped not, but yes, it appears we shall.'

'Do either of the crews know about this yet?'

'No, they don't. I've held off giving them the data until I . . . we, have determined a course of action.'

'Good move.'

'However, they're acutely aware, even obsessed, with the numbers on their own screens. Quite frankly, I'm surprised we haven't heard from them.'

High above, but closer then ever to earth, the *Yorktown* and *Columbia* continued their orbit. Neither Lewis' nor Clark's sleep had been sound. Through the long last night, they had enjoyed little more than brief, fitful periods of unconsciousness. Every now and then they would jerk back into an exhausted awakened state, fearful of some fresh disaster.

'Hey, ah, *Columbia*? How's our altitude?' radioed Rob Clark.

'I'll take it, Rusty,' said Dick Merriman. 'Just a sec, Rob, I'll punch up the numbers.'

The *Columbia*'s pilot tapped into his keyboard and the cathode ray tube screen printed up 81.6 miles. Immediately he shut off his line to the *Yorktown*.

'Rusty? What was your last altitude reading?'

Bishop leaned back in his chair sleepily, hands folded behind his neck, and gave the tired sigh of a student being asked to recite the times table. 'Three a.m. Houston time, altitude, 84 miles.'

'Well, look at this. It's now 81!'

Bishop straightened up smartly. 'What!'

'It's on the screen! Look at it!'

'Holy Christ!'

Meanwhile the delay in answer to his question annoyed Rob Clark. It was a simple enough request. 'Hey! Are you guys having a tea party, or what? Give me the altitude.'

Bishop's mind absorbed the ugly implications and he looked at Merriman. They both knew. He swallowed hard: 'Hiya, guys. Right on the money. Didn't know you were in a hurry. Old Dick here sloughed it off on me! Like I said, right on the money.'

'Yeah, but what's our altitude?'

Merriman shook his head from side to side, mouthing a 'no' to Bishop.

'Just below 84, Rob.' *By three stinking miles!*

Clark's reply was slow in coming. Bishop's answer of 'just below' had puzzled him; it seemed a curiously imprecise response for one who prided himself on precision. Or was he overreacting?

'That's a relief,' he said.

'Try to rest, Rob,' counselled Bishop firmly. 'Brooks and Harwood will be up here soon! You're going to have to be on the ball to open the hatches for her!'

'We'll be here. *Yorktown* out.'

Angrily Bishop punched open a private line out of Lewis and Clark's hearing. The buzzer rang on Gibbs console.

'Closed line,' he said. Pierce plugged in his headset. Gibbs started to identify himself: 'Hous—'

'Gibbs? You hear me?' Bishop allowed no reply. We've just lost three miles in the last hour! Now what the hell's going on down there?'

'Rusty, we were about to—'

'The hell you were!'

Bishop's outburst stunned Joe Gibbs. Pierce grabbed his shoulder and spoke in blunt, firm tones. 'Bishop. This is Pierce – you keep your mouth shut until I'm finished explaining . . .'

Pierce pulled no punches. For the next five minutes he gave Bishop ahd Merriman a full account of the new facts of life. '. . . So if Gibbs or I had had the computations any sooner, we would have called. Right?'

Gibbs made a rolling motion with his hand, and then stopped.

'And *Columbia*? Stop the roll. Keep the ships super-clean trim. Got it?'

'Yeah,' said a chastened Rusty Bishop. 'I got it. Joe? It's been a long flight. Sorry.'

'Right, Rusty. As you say, a long flight. Have you told Lewis and Clark?'

'Negative, Houston. Save it until you have to . . .'

'Right. Mission Control out.'

Bishop nursed his control stock to the right and the *Columbia*'s reaction control jet thrusters fired, then fired again, and the rolling motion ground to a halt. Bishop fired the jets again briefly, thus placing the *Yorktown* and *Columbia* belly-down relative to the earth.

'Correction completed, Houston. We're trim as a pin.'

Onboard the *Yorktown*, Rob Clark had pondered Rusty Bishop's uncharacteristically vague response to his earlier request, and had made nothing of it. Nothing, that is, until the roll was stopped. Suddenly, with the two

261

incidents taken in conjunction, Lewis and Clark were able to size up the situation and realize its meaning. Asphyxiation or incineration – it mattered not, for it was clear they were now doomed.

In Mission Control, the trajectory engineer called Gibbs. 'I have an update on the *Yorktown* and *Columbia* re-entry.'

'Roger,' replied Gibbs, motioning to Pierce. 'Patch it through.'

'O.K. These numbers are 95% accurate, assuming that *Columbia* maintains a minimum drag attitude . . .'

The trajectory engineer's report concerned time – several times in fact, fixed points in the very near future which in absolute and unalterable terms would dictate the sequence of events. Pierce, his flight controllers, the crews in space, and Brooks and Harwood – all would soon have to follow and obey.

One of the Newtonian laws, perhaps the most fundamental, certainly the most sublime, declared that for every action there was an equal and opposite reaction. Transposing action into time conveniently explained the bedrock upon which the Trajectory Engineer's report rested.

At the near end was the time of 8:54 a.m., the time scheduled for the *Enterprise*'s take-off from Edwards Air Force Base. At the far end was the Real Time Computer Complex's final calculation of 10:47:17 a.m., the moment set for the *Columbia* and *Yorktown*'s burn-up at 400,000 feet. This far end, the burn-up, had been deliberately turned into NASA jargon as Entry Interface – the interrelated points in time and space where the ships would enter the atmosphere.

The take-off of 8:54 a.m. could not be brought forward. The re-entry of 10:14:17 a.m. could not be slowed. Between these near and far ends were 80 minutes and 17 seconds of time, each second of which had now been plotted out and assigned a corresponding activity for the crews and Mission Control.

Within these parameters the rest fell into place. At 8:54

a.m. the *Enterprise*, atop the hypersonic jet *Hornet*, would take off. At 9:14 the *Enterprise* would ignite its main engines, and 30 seconds later would attempt to separate from the *Hornet*. If successful, it would have to achieve orbit by 9:20, and rendezvous with the *Yorktown* and *Columbia* by 9:34. The transfer of Lewis and Clark and Bishop and Merriman would then have to be completed by no later than 9:46, in order to leave time for the entire re-entry procedure.

To survive re-entry and avoid smashing into that Entry Interface wall, the Enterprise had to slow itself to reduce the friction-heat level by firing its orbiting manoeuvring system engines.

But slowing the ships was no matter of merely firing the engines, for re-entry was merely the beginning of a complex process, ending with a landing at a specific point on earth. The re-entry and touchdown process was, in fact, a complex equation of time, distance, altitude and speed, lasting 31 minutes and 55 seconds, whose starting time and altitude and speed automatically dictated the distance they could travel.

Once entering the atmosphere, the shuttle became an unpowered glider which could travel no further than 4,100 miles. Whenever the orbiting manoeuvering system engines were fired, 31 minutes and 55 seconds later, and 4,100 miles further, the space shuttle would land, be it on mountain, river or city core.

The computers had verified that the *Yorktown* and *Columbia* would hit the atmosphere at 68 miles and burn up at exactly 10:14:17, just above the Marshall Islands, 1,500 miles south-southwest of Hawaii. If Brooks and Harwood were to be able to get Lewis and Clark out of the *Yorktown* and Bishop and Merriman out of the *Columbia* and land at Edwards Air Force Base, the rescue transfer would have to be completed by 9:46 a.m

'Those are our numbers,' concluded the trajectory engineer. 'That is our schedule.'

Certainty. Utter certainty. In this mission where things seemed anything but certain, the numbers should have relieved Pierce, but instead he sat near-immobilized. There was no margin of error. None. And the unalterable march of events began with the supposition that the *Enterprise* would be ready by 8:54. It *had* to be. A delay of even a few minutes would push each subsequent event that much further into the future.

Three points in time fixed themselves and glowed, hot-white in Pierce's mind:

The *Yorktown* and *Columbia* would start burning up at 10:14:17 a.m.

If that fiery sentence was to be commuted, the *Enterprise*'s retrofire would have to occur no later than 9:46 a.m.

If the order to retrofire was ever to be given, the *Enterprise* would have to be launched at exactly 8:54.

The laws of gravity declared burn-up time as unalterable. The laws of aerodynamics predetermined the time for the retrofire burn. Human limitation could not change the take-off time of 8:54.

Shortly before 6 a.m., Joe Gibbs prepared to hand over the duties of flight director to Doug Pierce. The fresher members of the Gold Team had already plugged in their headsets one last time and received backslaps, handshakes and final reminders from their tired Red Team partners. But despite their mental exhaustion, and despite standard operating procedure, the Red Team remained in Mission Control, to a man.

At the middle console in the third row, Joe Gibbs requested one last look at the *Columbia*'s propellants. Instantly the numbers came up on his screen, and he relayed them to Pierce.

'Four thousand and ninety-four pounds, Douglas. The projection for *Columbia*'s propellants supply by 9:34, rendezvous time, is 56 below landing requirement. But it's higher than I'd thought it would be. And very close to the minimum . . .'

Pierce caught the obvious hint of intrigue, perhaps hope, in Gibbs' voice. 'Bishop and Merriman have their orders, Joe. The *Columbia*'s computers are programmed to dive it and the *Yorktown* into the atmosphere as soon as they're safely on board the *Enterprise*.'

'Quite. However, mightn't we—'

'Another thing, we cannot, under any circumstances, risk the debris from the *Yorktown* and *Columbia* hitting the West Coast. We're talking about more lives than just four men.'

'Yes, quite. But if, after the transfer from the *Yorktown* and *Columbia* to the *Enterprise*, there were still sufficient propellants for Bishop and Merriman to land the *Columbia* safely? Are you willing to let a perfectly functioning space shuttle burn up?'

Pierce arched his eyebrows at Gibbs.

'I should think it prudent,' continued Gibbs, 'for my Red Team to move up to the reserve control room – on standby – just in case the *Columbia* can land. The contingency landing sites have been placed on alert. Like you said, Douglas, it's always worth keeping your options open, eh?'

'Nothing like quoting someone's words against them, Joe,' smiled Pierce.

'It is an effective debating tool.'

'O.K. Move your men upstairs. But remember: I'll write off every shuttle in the fleet rather than have another Skylab. You make the announcement to your team.'

Gibbs, pleased at having talked his superior round, turned and addressed his crew over the P.A. 'Red Team? Red Flight here. We shall not be watching the launch from Mission Control . . .' Audible groans of disappointment filled the room. 'There is a chance the *Columbia* will require our services from the reserve control room . . .' Gibbs savoured the pause '. . . for re-entry.'

The declaration served as a shot in the arm for the tired Red Team flight controllers, and the groans were replaced by a muted yet enthusiastic response.

'Good luck, Douglas,' said Gibbs, shaking his hand.

'Thanks. You too.'

'We'll be ready.'

As Gibbs and the Red Team left Mission Control,

Charlie Egerton and his Blue Team and Bob Sanders and the Green Team came in, creating a minor traffic jam at the main door. Having worked so hard and so long, all felt compelled to be physically present in Mission Control, right now the centre of their universe. Suddenly the room seemed inundated with personnel drawn to be present for the denouement.

6:00 a.m. Pierce depressed the P.A. button. Here we go, last chance.

'O.K. We're kind of crowded here so let's keep the chatter to a minimum. Here's what we're up against.' The room fell silent as Pierce flashed the final take-off, rendezvous, transfer and re-entry times on the far left-hand Eidophor screen. Audible gasps and curses of disbelief punctuated the silence at what, to the Blue and Green Team members, was an entirely new set of numbers. 'As you can see on screen 1, we're working against some pretty fine timelines. We cannot, I repeat, cannot have any delays. The procedure has to be faultless.' Pierce hesitated but a moment: 'Gentlemen, we've come a long way. Keep cool. Stay sharp – and let's bring 'em home, alive.'

Pierce's Gold Team began. A certain awareness, a certain knowledge seemed to permeate Mission Control; even an outsider would have been aware of a distinct surge of emotion and purpose among the flight controllers. Here were men who were used to back-ups, used to working within clearly prescribed margins or error. But here, today, Thursday morning, there was no margin, no allowance for error. At 10:14:17, ready or not, transfer completed or not, the *Yorktown* and *Columbia* would burn up.

On board the *Yorktown*, Jack Lewis sat in stony silence, trying to come to terms with the terrifying hours ahead. Beside him, Rob Clark continued writing in his makeshift diary:

'*This log shall not survive me, but if by some cruel twist of fate it does, I want it known we did our best.*'

He stopped, anguish gripping his face, eyes closed, and prayed in silence.

When his eyes opened again he found Jack Lewis looking at him curiously.

'What are you doing?'

'Praying,' replied Clark in a bare whisper. 'Join me.'

'No . . . I . . . no, I don't, I mean . . .'

'It's all right, I've prayed enough for both of us – all of us. If it happens, it happens.'

Lewis studied the bleak serenity of Clark's face. 'You can say that? With such calm?'

'My faith, Jack – I believe.'

'Up here? In this?'

'Especially here. I've had . . . a full life . . . I've loved.'

Not me, thought Lewis, looking back at his controls. He had used people like he had used machines, to get from point A to point B. Ever since that hospital bed in his teens, he had longed to be number one; now he was number one, and he was exactly the same as when he started out: alone. He could not change that. But perhaps he could summon the will for a last gesture towards peace of mind . . .

He radioed Vince Torino in a voice which surprised the Capcom, revealing none of its characteristic arrogance or certainty.

'Vince? Would you do me a favour, please?'

Please? That was one word Vince Torino had never heard from Lewis before.

'Sure, Jack.'

'Call my . . . my wife, Charlene . . .'

'O.K.'

'And tell her I'm sorry. That's all. Just, I'm sorry.'

Lewis' voice was on the verge of breaking. Torino swallowed, and motioned to Pierce who tapped in on the call. 'Sure. I'll . . . I'll call her, Jack.'

'No. Not later. I mean right now. Before . . . I mean, right now.'

'Listen, ah, Jack, I can have you patched through to her . . .'

'No! Sorry, no . . . Listen Vince, I . . .' Tears flooded Lewis' eyes, and his voice cracked.

Torino himself fought his emotions. 'Jack? It's O.K.'

'I really dumped on her a lot and, ah, she was the only one who cared, and I'm sorry . . . do it for me, Vince.'

From the cold stinking cockpit of the broken hypersonic jet *Yorktown*, Lieutenant Commander Jack Lewis drew himself up to full military bearing and regained enough control to say firmly: 'This is the *Yorktown*'s Commander. Over and out.'

'Roger, *Yorktown* Commander. Read you,' replied Torino softly.

'Call,' said Pierce in a low voice. '*Now*.'

Torino nodded and dialled the residence of Charlene Lewis . . .

'. . . and that's all he said? Just, I'm sorry?'

'Yes, ma'am.'

'Thank you, Vince. One thing . . .'

'Yes?'

'If they do make it, where will the *Enterprise* land?'

'Edwards—'

'Thank you.'

The line clicked in Vince Torino's ear. He felt as if he had just delivered the death notice for a good friend, but there was no time to reflect upon this or other personal matters. he tapped back into the propulsion engineer's conversation with Pierce.

The propulsion engineer's first report had done nothing to improve Pierce's disposition. Despite the savings in propellants achieved by ending the roll and keeping the ships in an aerodynamically trim attitude, the *Columbia*'s propellant supply was approaching dangerously near the minimum.

'4,613 pounds – that's all they have left,' said the engineer. 'At present consumption, Dick and Rusty will have less than 4,100 pounds by the time the *Enterprise* arrives.'

'Gibbs showed me a projection of 4,094 by rendezvous,' said Pierce.

'Roger, 4,100 is an update.'

'Well 4,140 is the minimum,' snapped Pierce. 'The *Columbia* can't even think of landing with less than that.'

In the *Columbia*, Rusty Bishop checked the propellant level: 4,610 pounds. Meanwhile Dick Merriman adjusted the shuttle's trim by again firing the reaction control system rockets in the nose of the ship.

'Jesus! Go easy on it, Dick!' said Bishop.

Merriman turned round, surprised at the outburst. 'I've got to keep our attitude trim,' he snapped.

'Sorry, Dick,' sighed Bishop, 'but we're cutting it awfully close.'

'*Columbia*? This is Houston flight director,' broke in Pierce. 'We've got a reading of 8,202 pounds and project you to be at 4,100 pounds by *Enterprise* rendezvous time.'

'Roger, Houston,' replied Bishop, his voice noticeably downbeat.

'All right, *Columbia*, we won't make a decision yet on whether you two will transfer over to the *Enterprise*, but I want to confirm two points . . .'

Pierce was keen to establish, first, that Bishop and Merriman were indeed wearing their spacesuits, so as to be in a position to leave the *Columbia* the moment Lewis and Clark were transferred out of the *Yorktown*. Time would be of the essence. His second query was far less palatable. Had the *Columbia*'s computers been programmed to start a cartwheeling spin into the atmosphere as soon as Bishop and Merriman had left the *Columbia* for the *Enterprise*?

'Roger, Houston. We've put that program together,' replied Bishop. He snapped off the communications line and stared at the controls, pondering for several moments in silence.

'Vince Torino and I once landed the *Challenger* with 4,050 pounds.'

'I was thinking of that too,' replied Merriman.

In Mission Control, the summary from the flight activities officer was brief. The few words it contained, however, gave little indication of the immense physical upheaval going on behind the scenes.

'All commercial air traffic west of the Mississippi is grounded effective 6 a.m. this morning; all commercial and military airports in said areas are on alert status, preparatory to possible landing by either or both the shuttles *Columbia* and *Enterprise*. Designated landing site for the space shuttle *Enterprise* is Edwards Air Force Base. Back-up landing sites include San Francisco International Airport, Los Angeles International Airport and Fairchild Field, San Diego.'

'It's *all* grounded?' asked Pierce, '*all* the air traffic?'

'Yes sir,' said the flight activities officer. 'There isn't a plane in the sky. There's plenty of room up there.'

'We may need it,' replied Pierce.

The logistics were mind-boggling. For over five hours, not a single plane would enter or leave the airspace of the continental United States. The loss to Eastern Airlines and TWA alone was pegged at over five million dollars.

Pierce was blasé about the inconvenience to the airlines. Without NASA's technological contribution, none of their planes, their guidance systems, their flight systems would have been developed. At least, not until years later. They owed NASA this one.

6:12 a.m., Edwards Air Force Base.

'Houston Flight Director?' The voice was that of Edwards' chief flight controller. 'Just about to wake Brooks and Harwood.'

'Roger. Tell me when they're in the suit room,' replied Pierce, activating a video picture from the launch site.

On Runway 22 at Edwards Air Force Base, the convoy leader had already assembled his armada of escort vehicles and was pacing up and down in front of his diesel flat-bed truck, an unlit cigar jammed in his mouth. Since Edwards was two time zones ahead of Houston, the sun had not yet risen above the horizon and a cold breeze cut across the tarmac, causing the convoy leader to zip his white coveralls up completely. He looked across the field at the two ships, the *Enterprise* and *Hornet*, both waiting in the Mate/Demate device. He watched the teams of technicians racing to complete the final pre-launch checkout The Klieg lights which flooded the entire Mate/Demate device were so bright that the technicians scurrying about the ships seemed to glow in the desert darkness. He bit down on the cigar and rolled it with practised efficiency from one side of his mouth to the other. *This time!* he thought defiantly. *This time!*

In Houston, Dr Benjamin Franklin Fleck had made certain that the crews' families would not be alone in the VIP Room at the rear of Mission Control. Each group was accompanied by an astronaut to explain the mission and to help sustain their spirits. Fleck, as usual, was pragmatic. If the rescue failed, he didn't want the media besieging the families at their homes.

Looking back through the glass partitions separating Mission Control from the VIP Room, he saw Dick Merriman's wife and their two children, along with Rusty Bishop's wife Helen, and Tex Harwood's wife and son Ken. He looked for Charlene Lewis, but in vain. William Cranston, the astronaut assigned to accompany her, shrugged his shoulders and shook his head negatively. Unsurprised by her absence, Fleck nodded and turned back in his swivel chair.

Adrienne Brooks, pensive, deep in thought, gave the suit technician a desultory 'thumbs-up' as her helmet thumped solidly, reassuringly into place. The morning had gathered its own procedural momentum, giving her little opportunity to consider the magnitude of the task before her. She and Tex Harwood had awoken, showered, eaten breakfast with NASA's Deputy Administrator and the pilots of the hypersonic jet, Schacter and Noonan, been briefed along with pilots of the chase planes and now, at last, were alone with their thoughts. Sitting in her bulky padded spacesuit and waiting for the technicians to finish with Harwood, Adrienne should have felt elation. It was her first flight into space, and she was the first

271

woman space shuttle pilot in history. She had trained and sacrificed years of her life just to reach this point. This was to have been the peak of the mountaintop, the final climb to the pinnacle of success.

But elation had long since been replaced with a mixture of gritty determination and, although she would barely admit it to herself, trepidation. All that mattered was whether or not she could save the lives of two colleagues, one of whom she dearly loved. If she failed, the stain of defeat would never leave her.

Maybe she could cope with personal failure: she was, after all, just one cog in this vast machine. But to lose Rob Clark! She shook her head and closed her eyes. *No*, damn it! She wasn't going to lose him.

She looked up and fixed a steely gaze on Harwood. 'Tex? We're going to take off at 8:54 on the dot.'

Harwood understood her meaning. 'Eight fifty-four,' he replied, 'ready or not, we go.'

A surgically garbed technician entered the room to announce that the van was waiting to take them to the *Enterprise*.

Doug Pierce monitored the progress of the countdown from his console in Mission Control with growing anxiety. Reams of checkouts had yet to be completed and the clock was ticking on relentlessly to 8:54. The time required for the checkout had been based on the assumption that there would be delays and corrections required. The complexity of the system virtually ensured that problems would appear, and appear they did. Somehow, inexplicably, there seemed to be fewer than anticipated. At 5:00 a.m. the final checkout had been 10 minutes behind schedule. By 6:00 a.m. the gap had narrowed to 6 minutes, 2 seconds behind schedule. By 7:00 a.m., 4 minutes, 11 seconds behind, and now at 8:00 a.m., a tantalizing 90 seconds behind. They were catching up. But would they catch up in time? One major delay, even one minor but unavoidable delay, could erase all their efforts. The race would continue right up to 8:54.

Jack Lewis and Rob Clark shivered uncomfortably in

the *Yorktown*'s cockpit, Clark swinging his arms in front
of him in a vain attempt to generate some heat. Lewis
stared through fatigued, red eyes out the window at the
earth below. His throat was cracked dry, it hurt him to
breathe, his stomach ached, and it was as cold as hell.
Altogether he didn't have much left.

'*Yorktown*? This is Mission Control.' The voice was
Torino's.

Lewis, his hands lodged under his armpits for warmth,
turned to Clark and reached for the answer switch. 'Go,
Houston, this is *Yorktown*.'

'O.K. *Yorktown*, Adrienne and Tex are at the
Mate/Demate device. We're 54 minutes from take-off.'

'O.K.' Muttered Lewis, his voice barely audible.

'Say again, please *Yorktown*,' replied Torino.

'I already said!' snapped Lewis, but then calmed
himself. 'O.K. Houston, we read, 54 minutes.' He gritted
his teeth. Fifty-four minutes to take-off; two hours to
burn-up.

Brooks and Harwood plowed on through the checkouts
from the cockpit of the *Enterprise*. Below them in the
Hornet, pilots Noonan and Schacter co-ordinated their
own checkouts. With practised efficiency, orders were
given and acted upon; the exchanges became clipped with
urgency and utterly devoid of the banter and wisecracks
which usually enlivened the procedural yes-no, off-on
monotony. Although this was an experimental flight, a
rescue, it was also a duplicate of the flawed take-off of
the *Yorktown* and *Columbia* – a flight whose preparations
had been far more thorough.

As the convoy leader's fleet of diesel vehicles pushed
the *Hornet* and *Enterprise* back out of the Mate/Demate
device and towed them onto the benchmark at the top of
Runway 22, Brooks, Harwood, Noonan and Schacter
stole not a glance at the blue skies or the expanses of
desert, their eyes remaining fixed on their display screens.
At 8:29, they reached the benchmark and the convoy
pulled back and away, leaving the *Hornet* and *Enterprise*
alone on the field. The convoy leader now radioed the

crews with a final message of good luck, while Brooks and Harwood looked up and out the *Enterprise*'s windshield, down the length of Runway 22 and out onto the horizon.

The chase squadron of F24 Condors were given their 'go' for launch and roared past the *Enterprise*, down the runway and into the heavens, leaving chase planes 5 and 6 on the ground ready to take their place behind the *Hornet* and *Enterprise*.

8:36 a.m. eighteen minutes from take-off. The *Hornet*'s five turbine engines were ignited, tested, and found to be firing perfectly. The *Enterprise*'s auxiliary power units 2 and 3 were activated and checked out. The space shuttle's flight controls systems were tested and verified. The tail rudder and speed brakes were tested and verified. The countdown was now only twenty-six seconds behind schedule.

8:52 a.m.: two minutes to take-off. Chase planes 1 to 4 approached the base, holding at 2,000 feet. At 30 seconds to take-off the *Hornet* would soon throttle up to full power.

'Houston,' said hypersonic jet pilot Noonan, 'we're ready to throttle up on the mark of 30.'

'Roger. You are go,' said Pierce.

'Roger, and . . . Mark! 30 seconds! Throttling up on engine 1, engine 2, engine 3, engine 4, 5 . . .'

'Good burn on all five, Flight!' said the launch vehicle engineer to Pierce. The mighty ship began rocking up and down from the force of the exhaust from the turbines.

'Firing on five,' said Noonan in the *Hornet*.'

'O.K. Adrienne and Tex,' said pilot Irv Schacter. 'Just about ready for brake release.'

'Roger,' snapped Harwood.

In Mission Control the numbers on Pierce's console suddenly fell into place. They had finished the checkout on schedule! They had caught up! Grinning, he turned to Torino and pointed triumphantly to his console display screen.

A red flight flashed and a droning buzzer sounded.

One of the *Enterprise*'s four rate gyros had failed, and all of the countdown clocks except for the Real Time Clock stopped dead.

'Hold on the count!' cried Pierce. 'We have a hold!'

'Screw the hold!' replied Brooks from the *Enterprise*. We're go for take-off!' Her tone was half plea, half assertion. '*Give us the go!*'

Pierce hastily assessed the situation. There were four sets of rate gyros onboard the *Enterprise*. The shuttle could still fly with only one, but first Pierce had to determine that the other three were not in jeopardy. As had been discovered through flight simulations, with all four gyros gone, the space shuttle was like a sailboat without a keel.

New information was quickly flashed onto his display screen: the other three gyros were still functioning and according to indications, would continue to function. Scarcely seven seconds had passed, but it had seemed like an eternity.

'*Hornet/Enterprise*', said Pierce, 'you are go! *Hornet*! Count it down to brake release!'

'Counting it down, Houston!' said Noonan, the *Hornet*'s engines still surging, 'On the mark! 10, 9, 8, 7, 6, 5, 4, 3, 2, 1, Brake release!'

Slowly, agonizingly, the vehicles lurched and lumbered forward, gaining speed with apparent reluctance, but travelling faster and faster and gobbling up the runway, as if unwilling or unable to leave the earth. Then the nosewheel came free and the *Hornet*'s nose arched up, followed by the rear wheels. For long seconds the two ships hung there in the sky before finally climbing, clawing up and away.

The convoy leader's binoculars remained riveted on the two craft until mother-ship and passenger had shrunk to tiny specs on the eastern horizon, leaving tracing white contrails behind them.

For fifteen minutes the *Hornet* carried the *Enterprise* higher and faster, higher and faster, until, at 9:09 a.m., at an altitude of 89,000 feet, the *Hornet*'s air-breathing turbine engines strained to find oxygen to turn their turbo fans. The first threshold had been reached. It was now time.

'Ready for hypersonic ignition,' said *Hornet* pilot Noonan.

'Go for ignition,' replied Pierce.

As the *Hornet*'s ignition switches were hit, the hydrogen-powered engines lit up, belching flames and power and Brooks and Harwood were slammed back into their seats. The chase planes now fell farther and farther behind their escaping targets and the *Hornet* pulled away into the darkening atmosphere towards that point in the skies where speed met time and distance, where the *Yorktown* had failed on Monday, where today the *Hornet* had to succeed.

'Coming up on separation,' announced Harwood from the *Enterprise*.

The declaration, as matter-of-fact as a stockmarket report, only twisted the screws of tension one notch further in Mission Control.

'Launch vehicle engineer? This is Flight,' said Pierce, with growing apprehension.

But Pierce's call was not completed. The launch vehicle engineer, the man who first learned of the *Yorktown*'s explosion, had anticipated the request and kept an eagle eye on the *Hornet*'s telemetry.

'It's O.K., Flight. The *Hornet*'s fuel line is green — perfect flow, perfect pressure.'

'Roger,' replied Pierce.

At 71 miles altitude, Pierce gave the crucial order: '*Enterprise*. You are go for main engine ignition.'

Brooks and Harwood had awaited the moment. Once acted upon, the responsibility for the flight would fall to them alone.

'Roger. Go for main engine ignition. Thanks for the ride, *Hornet*.'

'Copy, and Godspeed, *Enterprise*,' replied *Hornet* pilot Pete Noonan.

Meanwhile the countdown to main engine ignition ticked away on Vince Torino's console display screen.

'O.K. *Enterprise* – ignition in 10 seconds, on the mark . . . mark 10, 9, 8, 7 . . .'

Brooks placed her hand on the ignition switch to light the *Enterprise*'s troika of engines.

'. . . 2, 1, Ignition!' cried Torino, and Brooks jabbed the switch on. In micro-milliseconds, the *Enterprise*'s computers translated the electrical impulse generated by the pushed button into a command to fire the shuttle's three main engines. Before Brooks had time to remove her finger, the shuttle's three main engines had flamed power into the rapidly diminishing atmosphere, their collective brute force jerking her hand back from the console and rudely slamming both astronauts into their cockpit chairs.

'Houston, we have ignition. Firing on all three,' she announced in a clear, rapid voice.

Pierce watched his console. The numbers were perfect. 'Roger, *Enterprise*. You are go for separation – go for separation!'

The sheer power at Adrienne Brooks' fingertips exhilarated her, sending her heart racing at 122 beats per minute. Harwood's grip on the control stock was gentle, but firm. His own heart pounded at a nerve-tingling 140 beats per minute.

'Roger, Houston,' she replied firmly, 'initiating separation sequence. From 5, on the mark . . .' her gaze was riveted on her control panel '. . . Mark 5, 4, 3 . . .'

As her right hand grasped the control stock with measured strength, her gaze shifted and she flipped open the Auto Separation switch.

'*Separation!*' she cried.

Simultaneously, the restraining bolts of the support structure assembly holding the two ships together exploded, and with a fluid, forceful, deliberate and controlled motion, the white space shuttle *Enterprise* and the *Hornet* parted company.

'We have separation!' Harwood cried.

Wide-eyed in amazement, the crew of the *Hornet* watched the *Enterprise* whisk off into space. 'Beautiful burn, Houston!' said *Hornet* pilot Noonan, 'She's got a beautiful burn!'

By now the clock in Mission Control read 9:15:30 a.m. It had been a historic moment – a space shuttle had been carried to the edge of space by a hypersonic jet. Pierce's theory, the concept of the Airborn Launch Development Project, had been shown to work. The years of research, planning, practice, sweat and heartache, had been proven out. But the flush of success was momentary and the grin on Pierce's face quickly disappeared. There would be no real celebration until Brooks could save Lewis and Clark and Bishop and Merriman.

The job now complete, Noonan and Schacter set the *Hornet* into a shallow right-hand dive, gently, gently, banking around and back to the west, to land at Ellington Air Force Base in Houston. Brooks and Harwood's job had begun.

'O.K. *Enterprise*,' said Pierce, '*Yorktown* and *Columbia* lie dead ahead. You should soon acquire radar contact.'

'Roger, Houston,' rejoined Harwood. 'Altitude 92 miles, radar scanning – negative on target acquisition.'

The *Enterprise* raced on. Minutes of routine communication exchanges flew past until, at 9:21, Harwood's boisterous voice boomed throughout Mission Control:

'Houston, Houston! We have radar contact! *Yorktown*? *Columbia*? Roll out the carpet! Get your landing lights on! You guys have got visitors!'

Rob Clark's teeth chattered in the cold, but the joy of the news steadied him, if only momentarily. 'No can do with the carpet, just get on in here!'

Also shaking and shivering with cold, Jack Lewis cut in with a question. 'Houston? Our altitude? What's our altitude?'

'78·95 miles – on schedule,' replied Capcom Torino.

'Close,' thought Lewis, 'and short, too short. Not just altitude, but time! We've got to be out of the *Yorktown* by 9:44!'

Radar contact now allowed the *Enterprise*'s computers

278

to lock onto their target, and the space shuttle plunged on down towards the falling *Yorktown* and *Columbia*.

'Any second now, Adrienne,' said Harwood scanning the space before him. 'Any second . . . *There!* Adrienne! Right there!'

'Houston! We have a visual on the *Yorktown* and *Columbia*!' cried Brooks. Not a second could be wasted. Immediately she scrambled from her seat. 'Hold it steady, Tex.'

'I will. Go get 'em, kid.'

Bounding weightlessly through the cockpit, Adrienne Brooks leapt to the top of the ladderway and slid down weightlessly to the *Enterprise*'s lower deck, landing with a thump. She swung open the airlock door, clambered into the transfer tunnel leading to the Spacelab, and secured the door behind her. Inside the space laboratory, which had its own pressurized atmosphere independent of the shuttle, Brooks pulled on her backpack and fastened the neatly-folded personal rescue enclosures to her chest. Depressurizing the spacelab to a vacuum level, she looked up at the ceiling hatch through which she would soon leave for her one shot at saving Lewis and Clark.

'Tex? I'm ready to go. Get the bay doors open.'

'One hundred yards and closing,' radioed Harwood to Mission Control. He depressed the cargo bay activation switch. 'Bay doors opening.' Slowly the curved doors swung out, exposing the cigar-shaped Spacelab to the sun.

'Fifty yards. *Enterprise* camera's coming on,' said Harwood hitting the switches.

Adjusting his black-knobbed control stock, Harwood slowed the *Enterprise* to a crawl and then to a complete stop, a scant 40 feet from the *Yorktown*'s port wing.

'Houston? We have rendezvous. Adrienne, open her up! We're here.'

'O.K. Adrienne,' said Pierce. 'We're 15 seconds behind. You now have 9 minutes 45 seconds to get them.'

The spacelab's round hatch-like door swung up and open and, powering her backpack, Brooks popped up into space like bread from a toaster, pivoting in mid-space to face the *Yorktown*. Her heart raced as she rocketed to the *Yorktown*'s shattered underbelly and stole a glance at the explosion point.

'Jack? Rob? You read me?'

'Loud and clear, baby,' said Lewis.

'Alright, I'm just below the outer hatch.'

'*Enterprise*? Your altitude is 78·9 miles; 8 minutes, 40 seconds left,' said Pierce.

'Roger, Houston,' replied Brooks. 'Jack? Open the outer hatch.'

'O.K. Opening now,' replied Lewis, throwing the manual lever switch with a clunk. The *Yorktown*'s outer hatch, the door that was designed only to be opened for emergency escapes onto the runway, now slowly arched open towards her. She stared into the pitch-black chute, and cautiously, gingerly nursed her way in, the backpack and her suit brushing awkwardly against the sides of the escape chute.

'Tight fit, Houston! I can barely move!' Her heart pounded as she looked down through her feet at the earth below. Her throat was dry with tension. 'O.K. Jack. You can close the hatch!'

A scant ten feet above her, separated only by the inner hatch on the floor behind his cockpit chair, Lewis reversed the lever and the outer hatch swung and locked shut, sealing Adrienne Brooks inside the tubular chute. She felt and fought the immediate instinct of fear in the nightmare blackness.

Meanwhile, shivering and nauseous, Rob Clark positioned himself above the inner hatch, at the ready, his hands numbed from the cold.

'O.K. Jack,' said Brooks, 'now pressurize the chute.'

'Adrienne, I'll start counting off the seconds as soon as you're pressurized,' said Vince Torino in Mission Control

'Roger,' she replied quickly. 'Let's go, Jack.'

Lewis now activated the chute's pressurization switch. 'Houston, coming up to full pressurization . . . full pressure!'

This is it! thought Pierce. They had sixteen seconds before the outer hatch of the *Yorktown* buckled from the pressure of a full atmosphere. The simulation runs had predicted sixteen seconds – but that was simulation. Brooks' rehearsals in the underwater tanks had only taken fifteen seconds – but that was underwater.

Brooks slithered up the chute, disorientated in the darkness.

'O.K., counting off,' announced Torino, '5, 6, 7, . . .'

Suddenly, without warning, Adrienne Brooks' helmet hit the hatch at the top of the chute. For a moment she thought that she had hit some unknown obstruction, but then realized that in the weightlessness of space, movement was much easier and much faster than in the underwater tank.

'I'm at the top!' she cried in total surprise. *Seven seconds! Way ahead!* 'Rob! Open it! Open the hatch!'

Clark twisted at the wheel-like handle, but in his exhausted physical and mental state, he had not braced himself sufficiently to compensate for zero gravity, and the force of his muscles sent him spinning backwards away from the inner hatch: Unable to stop himself, he flipped backwards and his head smashed with a crack against the floor, stunning him into unconsciousness.

'10 seconds, 11 seconds,' said Torino in Mission Control.

Jack Lewis stared in horror across the cockpit. '*Rob!*' he yelled. Frantically ripping off his seatbelts, Lewis exploded out of the seat and in a twisting burst of force propelled himself towards the inner hatch like a high-diver aiming at a target on the water below.

'What the hell's going on?' screamed Brooks. 'Open the hatch, Rob! Open the Hatch!'

'12, 13,' continued Torino, his words echoing in her headset.

'What's going on!' screamed Brooks, her heart pounding.

Grabbing at the handle and twisting it with every ounce of power he had left, Jack Lewis screamed in agony as a searing pain tore through his left shoulder and throughout

281

his body. Clutching the shoulder, he reached down again, now with his left hand, and turned the handle.

'14, 15 . . .'

The inner hatch opened with a pop, and Brooks powered up the backpack, propelling herself out of the chute and past Jack Lewis and the unconscious Clark.

'Close it, close it!' she screamed. Lewis slammed the Hatch down . . .

'16, 17 . . .'

. . and locked it shut:

'18 . . .'

Two seconds beyond simulation's predictions, the *Yorktown*'s outer hatch blew off and spun crazily like a wobbling silver frisbee, end over end into space.

'O.K. Houston! I'm in the *Yorktown*!' cried Brooks.

In Mission Control, Doug Pierce, sweating profusely, his mouth dry from nervousness, opened his microphone. 'You are at 78·6 miles altitude. You have seven minutes.'

Adrienne Brooks squinted, trying to adjust to the dim cockpit. Her stomach turned at the sight before her. 'Rob!' she gasped. There, floating limply before her, was the unconscious body of Rob Clark, suit torn, face stubbled dirty by days' growth of beard, lips cracked dry, mouth gaping open. Lewis, his face contorted in agony, was clutching himself, broken and helpless.

'Good to see you, Brooks,' grimaced Lewis, 'sorry for the delay.'

'Jesus! What happened?' she said, pulling the personal rescue enclosures off her suit and inflating them into 3-foot diameter balls.

'Hit his head . . . that's why we took so long.' He grunted in pain. 'Ripped my shoulder, too.'

'Can you get into the enclosure?'

'Do I have any alternative?' Lewis smiled painfully.

Grabbing at the enclosure, he zipped it open and pulled it over his head, tucking his legs up into a crouch and, wincing at the pain, zipping the armless, legless space-ball shut. His only visual contact was now through a small, rectangular viewing point.

Brooks grabbed at the second floating enclosure and with increasing frustration, tugged at the motionless body of Rob Clark.

'Come on, Rob. Wake up!' she said, slapping at his face and shaking him. '*Rob!*'

Clark's eyes blinked, and he perceived in dreamlike disbelief and confusion the helmeted face of Adrienne Brooks.

She shook him again. 'You've got to help me get you into the enclosure! I can't do it without you. We're running out of time!'

Head aching, disorientated, Rob Clark grasped what had happened. 'Sorry, Adrienne. Sorry I didn't get the door open. How did you—'

'Forget it! Now climb in!'

Clark bent down in a foetal position and crammed himself into the enclosure, zipping the space-ball shut.

'Take him out first!' snapped Jack Lewis, now floating upside down.

'Alright. I'll be back,' she said, connecting up a safety cord from her suit to Clark's mechanical womb. His head still pounded, but he smiled wanly. He had thought he was dead. Brooks had given him his life again.

Brooks radioed Bishop in the *Columbia*. 'Rusty? Kill the air to the cockpit – Jack and Rob are in the enclosures.'

'Roger, Adrienne,' replied Bishop, shutting down the air supply which had kept Lewis and Clark alive for two days.

'Alright, I'm depressurizing the *Yorktown*,' said Brooks, pushing the appropriate sequence of buttons and switches.

In seconds, the little remaining atmosphere in the cockpit was purged out into space. She could now open the inner hatch and carry them to safety.

'Adrienne? We are five minutes from re-entry,' said Pierce anxiously.

'O.K. Rob, here we go.'

With that, Brooks stepped into the black chute, pulling

Rob behind her, down, down and out into space. Powering her backpack and holding Rob's enclosure in her arms, she approached the *Enterprise*'s cargo bay, unlocked the safety cord and shoved Clark into the spacelab.

'Don't open the enclosure,' she ordered him, 'there's no air in there.' She closed the hatch.

'Houston. Rob's in the spacelab. I'm going back for Jack.' So saying, she sped back towards the *Yorktown* and up again into the blackened chute.

Lewis continued to float about the *Yorktown*'s cabin. 'Brooks . . . Brooks! Can you hear me?' he stammered, increasingly terrified at his totally helpless state. 'Brooks! Where are you?'

'Right here,' she said, powering herself up the chute and into the cockpit. 'Had another delivery – hold on,' she replied, taking hold of a carrying strap.

Jack Lewis took one last look at the *Yorktown*'s interior. *Goodbye, you bitch*, he thought, *and thanks*.

'Four minutes to de-orbit,' said Pierce.

'Four it is,' said Brooks, emerging from the chute with Lewis in tow. She approached the spacelab a second time.

'Houston, I'm opening the spacelab's hatch – hold on, Jack.' She shoved Lewis' tumbling, round enclosure down into the Lab.

From the *Columbia*'s flight deck, Rusty Bishop saw Adrienne Brooks stuff Lewis into Spacelab and then wave to get on over to the *Enterprise*.

'O.K. Rusty, we're waiting. There isn't much time!'

'Bishop!' radioed Pierce from Houston. 'What's the delay? You've only got three minutes!'

Bishop, his forehead furrowed in thought, stared at his control panel. The *Columbia* had 4,090 pounds of propellants left.

He turned to Merriman. 'Dick, we don't know how much debris will be scattered if we just let these two ships burn up. We're 50 pounds below minimum for a landing. No-one's ever brought a space shuttle through the atmosphere with less than 4,050 in the tank.'

'I read 4,002 . . . let's do it.'

'Bishop!' repeated Pierce. 'Do you read? Move it on out. Set your computers for the dive and move over to the—'

'Negative, Houston. We're bringing the *Columbia* home!' cried Bishop.

'Pierce?' chimed in Merriman, 'there's no time to argue!'

'But your fuel is too low!'

'Even if we put it on Auto, we can't be sure what survives re-entry won't be a killer . . . it's our decision!' snapped Bishop.

'One minute left,' said Torino flatly.

Pierce inhaled, his jaw clenched. It wasn't their decision. It was his! But it was their lives .

'Bishop? Cancel the transfer order,' he replied. 'Bring the *Columbia* home.'

'Roger, Houston,' cried Bishop. 'Adrienne? Tex? Move the *Enterprise* outa here. Give us some room!'

'45 seconds,' said Torino.

Pierce radioed Joe Gibbs above in the third floor reserve control room. 'Joe? You got that?'

'Right, Douglas! The Red Team is go! You chaps land the *Enterprise* – we'll take care of the *Columbia*! This one's mine, Doug!' The thick Oxford tones of Gibbs' voice filled Bishop and Merriman's headsets, as Gibbs' team undertook to bring in a space shuttle woefully low on propellants. Now on a different radio frequency to avoid confusion, Pierce had to forget the *Columbia* and Bishop and Merriman. He had but one concern – the *Enterprise*.

Adrienne Brooks had descended into the spacelab and closed the hatch door behind her, stripped off the backpack and then hit the spacelab's pressurization controls, flooding it with breathable air. A green indicator light had flashed: the atmosphere in the spacelab had been restored.

Lewis and Clark scrambled out of the enclosure, Lewis still clutching his shoulder.

'Come on,' said Brooks, 'up to the cockpit.'

Lewis and Clark, their muscles stiff from the days of inactivity, pulled themselves along through the cylindrically-shaped spacelab and into the shuttle's lower deck, gliding up the ladder to the flight deck, where Clark helped Lewis strap himself in one of the two seats positioned behind Brooks and Harwood.

Harwood, guiding the *Enterprise* away from the *Yorktown* and *Columbia*, was shaken at their appearance, but masked it with bravado. 'Howdy boys! Glad to have you aboard!' He handed them pairs of virtually opaque sunglasses. 'Here, you'll need these in a few minutes.'

Adrienne Brooks pulled back on the control stock, firing up the *Enterprise*'s engines.

On board the *Columbia*, Rusty Bishop watched the *Enterprise* move off, then looked back at the 'No' he had taped over the Auto Separation switches controlling the support structure assembly. Abruptly, he ripped the tape away. Bishop, the best in the business, knew exactly what he had to do.

'55 seconds,' announced Torino. It was now 9:45:15, and 45 seconds remained before the scheduled de-orbit burn – the firing of the oribiting manoeuvring system engines which would slow the *Enterprise* down so as to allow it to survive re-entry. To fire the engines after 9:46 would mean overshooting Edwards Air Force Base. To fire before would mean coming in short. And now there were two space shuttles attempting re-entry. An additional hazard was the *Columbia*'s unwelcome passenger, the *Yorktown*, which still had to be blown away before the *Columbia* could attempt re-entry, yet blown away in such a manner as to prevent it from burning up in the *Columbia*'s flight path, thus leaving a fiery trail of flaming remnants for the *Columbia* and the *Enterprise* to fly through.

The *Columbia* and *Enterprise*'s flight path, trajectory and altitude were virtually identical and they were now only a hundred yards apart. If both fired their engines at the same time to slow the ships for re-entry, they would be dangerously close to each other in their descent. In space, wing-tip to wing-tip flying presented no problems, but in the thickening atmosphere aerodynamic shockwaves or trailing wake vortices would be created. These were invisible flows of turbulent air streaming back in a funnel-shaped flow from the lead space shuttle's wingtips, creating buffeting turbulence for the craft behind. Because the vortices generated by large aircraft could create dangerous turbulence for smaller aircraft, the Federal Aviation Administration required a 3 to 6 miles spacing between aircraft approaching for a landing. But here there were two spaceships a scant football field behind one another, travelling more than twenty times faster than jets, and there was still the *Yorktown* to dispense with! Clearly, breathing space had to be made between the two. One shuttle would have to fire its engines *on* schedule and thus be vectored and aligned to set down at Edwards Air Force Base. The other would have to fire its engines *off* schedule to create a safety margin between them. But to do so, the second craft would be incapable of landing at Edwards.

The first space shuttle to fire would be the first to land – that much was a law of trajectory and aerodynamics; and the other space shuttle would still race on at over 13,000 miles per hour. If the *Enterprise* fired first, the *Columbia* and *Yorktown* would race past it and then both would have to re-enter through the debris left in their path by the burning *Yorktown*.

On board the *Columbia*, Rusty Bishop had already determined these facts and their ramifications. Without hesitation, and with Vince Torino's warning of 45 seconds to de-orbit burn still in his ears, he announced 'Columbia will fire de-orbit burn in 15 seconds. We're going in first!'

Bishop was about to commit the *Columbia* to a re-entry he knew to be too early, a re-entry which would make a landing at Edwards Air Force Base physically impossible. But before his shocked colleagues on the *Enterprise* and an equally shocked Doug Pierce in Mission Control could respond, the *Columbia* and *Yorktown* began pitching forward in an end-over-end tumble. By all appearances the two craft were wholly out of control; in reality both were under the firm guidance of Rusty Bishop.

A hundred yards away in the *Enterprise*, Harwoods, Brooks, Lewis and Clark watched in disbelief.

'What the hell's he doing!' said Clark, looking over Harwood's shoulder.

'He's giving us a chance,' replied Harwood somberly.

If the *Yorktown* merely separated from the *Columbia* and coasted, it could very well skip off against the atmosphere like a flat stone skimming across water, travelling closer and closer to the West Coast of the United States, and thus enormously increasing the risks of debris hitting the earth.

But if Bishop set the *Yorktown* into an end-over-end tumble, the *Yorktown* would gouge into the atmosphere violently, stabbing in like a tumbling metal bar into water and break up over the Pacific between Hawaii and California. To set the tumble going, however, meant burning up more of their precious fuel supply, and with each pound of fuel burnt off, cutting back their chances of survival.

The *Columbia* continued to pitch, nose-down, end-over-end, and spun again and again, faster and faster.

Bishop reached for the Auto Sep controls. 'Initiating Auto Sep sequence!' he said, throwing the first switch. 'O.K. Phase I!' Power coursed through the separation system for the first time. With indicator lights glowing green, Bishop hit the second switch and cried: 'Phase 2! Pull it!'

With a powdery explosion, the explosive bolts of the support structure assembly which had held the *Yorktown* to the *Columbia* for four days disintegrated and the shattered hulk which had once been the world's fastest aircraft, blew away from the *Columbia*, cartwheeling earthwards, sickeningly out of control. The entire cartwheel manoeuvre had chewed up a mere fifteen seconds of time.

'30 seconds to de-orbit burn,' said Vince Torino

With that, Bishop re-oriented the *Columbia* until it faced backwards, its rear engines now pointing in the direction it flew, and fired the *Columbia*'s orbiting manoeuvring system, thereby abruptly slowing the ship.

The *Enterprise*, having now climbed over a half mile above the *Columbia*, soared past the slowing ship below and the still tumbling *Yorktown* until it was safely clear of both. At 9:46, right on schedule, Tex Harwood, flying backwards, ignited his own orbiting manoeuvring system engine.

Both de-orbit burns were timed to last 2 minutes and 26 seconds, long enough to slow the *Enterprise* and *Columbia* to a speed at which re-entry would be survivable. In Mission Control, Doug Pierce's concern for Bishop and Merriman in the *Columbia* had been wrenched away by the demands of his own task, that of guiding the *Enterprise* home. But the last indication from the *Columbia* chilled him. At 2 minutes, 13 seconds into the *Columbia*'s slowing burn, a full 13 seconds too soon, its orbiting manoeuvring system propellant supply had run out.

Bishop had gambled that even after using up propellants to cartwheel the *Yorktown* into a full-scale burn-up, he would still have enough fuel left to slow down the *Columbia*; the gamble, it appeared, had failed. The *Columbia* continued to race towards the atmosphere, well above the theoretical speed limit necessary to survive re-entry.

On board the *Enterprise*, Adrienne Brooks began the countdown to OMSCO – Orbiting Manoeuvring System Cut-Off. The engines roared, the vibration tingling throughout the ship. For Lewis and Clark, the sound flushed their souls with hope. For four days, they had been passengers aboard a dead ship. They were still passengers, but this ship, the *Enterprise*, was alive and ticking.

'10 seconds to cut-off,' announced Brooks. She reached for the manual cut-off button as back-up to the auto cut-off and as the countdown clock hit zero, punched the button.

Silence – the engines died. The speed indicator read 10,117 miles per hour, a survivable re-entry speed.

With the *Enterprise*'s wings now level with the earth, Harwood re-orientated the ship, twisting it round until the nose faced forward and the brown wastes of the northeast coast of Australia presented themselves below, surrounded by the vivid blue of the coral sea.

The *Enterprise*, meanwhile, had begun free fall, a 22-minute plunge towards Entry Interface, the contact point in altitude, time and space, 68 miles high, where the speeding space shuttle would first make contact with the atmosphere.

In space, only the rotation of the earth and the speed of the ship gave physical indication of motion. To look up at the blackness of space was like travelling at night on a commercial jet; it tricked the mind into believing, if only momentarily, that one was actually stationary. On board the orbiting space shuttle the impression enhanced itself further, since the earth's horizon always appeared below the ship's nose, with black space filling the windows above. But free fall swept that false impression away, as the earth's horizon lay a full 12° above the astronauts' direct field of vision. Even without reference to their instruments, which would have told them that they travelled at 25 times the speed of sound, the astronauts knew, their senses told them, that they were coming down.

For Brooks and Harwood the 22 minutes flew seemingly as quickly as the ship. Brooks spent the time rattling off a 40-item checkout of key shuttle systems and running a hydraulic fuel thermal conditioning exercise, a procedure designed to ensure that the ship's hydraulic fluid had sufficient fluidity to activate the space shuttle's surface elevons, the rear body flaps beneath the engines and tail rudder.

At exactly 10:14:27 a.m., 40,000 feet directly above the Marshall Islands, south-southwest of Hawaii, travelling at 16,700 miles per hour, the *Enterprise* shuddered and groaned, indicating that Entry Interface had been reached. The thickening atmosphere ground at the *Enterprise*'s underside and the ship vibrated as if Adrienne Brooks had double-clutched her Jaguar sports car and dropped down two gears.

In but 4 minutes, the *Enterprise*, nose-high, plunged from 4,000,000 to 260,000 feet, and the heat on its surface soared to over 2,000° Fahrenheit. It began to glow hot from friction. Harwood and Brooks slapped their tinted helmet visors down, and bright orange plasma light flooded the cockpit.

'O.K. boys,' cracked Harwood to Lewis and Clark, 'get your sunglasses on.'

Now a glowing orange wedge plowing through the atmosphere, the plasma clouds searing the ship grew greater and greater. The combination of heat and speed increased the ion count surrounding the ship, interfering with communcations between the *Enterprise* and Mission Control.

'Houston? We're on target,' said Harwood, 'But, ah, – wel – had—'

The communications line crackled as the ion count rose higher, but even so, Mission Control heard an alarm ring in the *Enterprise*'s cockpit.

'Say again, *Enterprise*! You're breaking up!' replied Pierce.

In a brief break from the crackling, Brook's voice cut through. 'Houston! Auto rate gyro 2 has just failed!'

The second of four gyros had now gone. Pierce was about to request confirmation, but before he could speak, Harwood cut through:

'Picking up – some vibration—'

The line crackled furiously, and this time did not clear. The ion count surrounding the *Enterprise* had reached such proportions that all radio contact between Mission Control and the ship had been lost. The re-entry communication blackout had begun – 21 minutes of silence, in which the *Enterprise* would plunge to a mere 160,000 feet. No further communications could be re-established until then. There was nothing Pierce or anyone else could do.

'We wait,' he said to Vince Torino, 'we wait.'

'It's a good trajectory,' replied Torino.

'*Enterprise*, yes. But *Columbia* . . .'

Pierce opened a line to Joe Gibbs above them in the reserve control room. If the *Columbia* was running on schedule, it should have begun its blackout ahead of the *Enterprise*.

'Joe? What's the word?'

'Douglas . . . I . . .'

'They're all right, aren't they?'

'When we lost radio contact with the *Columbia* she was still travelling much too quickly . . . I can give you the numbers.'

'No. Don't . . . Will they make it?'

'It is, I fear, entirely in their hands. If they can dive and bank the *Columbia* to dissipate the heat sufficiently, then there's a chance they'll at least survive re-entry.'

'What do you mean "at least"?'

'We have them plotted to land at Los Angeles International Airport, but in order to slow the *Columbia* sufficiently it may mean they have to land short, too short . . .'

'Oh, God. Is the Coast Guard standing by?'

'And the Navy too.'

'Pray, Joe. Pray.'

'My dear Douglas,' Gibbs replied in a half-nervous chuckle, 'what makes you think I ever stopped?'

An eerie silence enveloped Mission Control. Pierce stood up, removed his headset, and gulped down a half cup of cold coffee. This was easily the worst part of his job – waiting for the communications blackout to be completed. No communications, no contact. Mission Control, like the families, the TV audience and the rest of the world, could do nothing to help the crews. Like all the rest, they could do nothing but wait.

Pierce looked up at the chronometer: 10:21 – another 19 minutes at least. He exhaled a deep breath, turned and looked back at NASA Administrator Fleck in the fourth row, flashing him a 'thumbs-up' sign. Fleck responded with a fingers crossed gesture. Pierce smiled weakly and nodded.

At Houston Intercontinental Airport, 25 miles north of the Johnson Space Centre, work had come to a complete standstill. Calls had stopped coming in for reservations half an hour earlier. At the American Airlines counter, a reservations agent along with her colleagues and dozens of passengers, were glued to the TV coverage.

'I'd like to reserve the next flight this morning to Los Angeles,' said a woman.

The clerk, although fully trained in customer relations, could hardly bear to look away from the screen. 'Er, ma'am, I'm afraid our scheduled flights have been delayed due to the landing of—'

'I know that!' came the curt and forceful reply. 'When's the first flight to Los Angeles?'

'Ah, yes ma'am. One moment, please.' The clerk moved to her reservations terminal, a plastic smile on her face, and tapped in a request. Moments later she turned back to the woman: 'Flight 408, Houston to Los Angeles, leaves at 10:30 this morning. Will that be first class or economy?'

'I don't care . . . alright, first class.'

The balance of the information was taken down:

'And your name please?'

Hearing the answer, the clerk raised an eyebrow in surprise, smiled unrestrainedly, printed the name on the ticket, longing to ask another question, but not daring to. 'Fine, you're booked onto Flight 408, Houston to Los Angeles, leaving Houston at 10:30 this morning.'

The clerk stared at the woman and the name on the ticket and tapped the shoulder of a fellow reservations agent watching the TV.

'Look at this,' she said.

The name on the ticket was Mrs Jack Lewis.

10:30 a.m. The communications blackout continued. The *Enterprise*'s scheduled re-acquisition of radio contact would not take place for another two minutes, but the *Columbia* was overdue. Pierce and Vince Torino listened in to Joe Gibbs' calls from the reserve control room.

'*Columbia. Columbia.* Red Team flight director. Do you read?'

The sound of crackling interference, electronic nothingness, filled their headsets.

'Trajectory?' asked Gibbs, 'Any fix yet?'

'Negative, Flight,' came a dispirited reply.

Pierce felt a sinking sensation in his stomach. In the VIP room, the astronauts assigned to Bishop and Merriman's wives were explaining with conviction that the blackout was normal, that difficulty in re-acquiring the signal was normal, and that there was no cause for alarm. But their guts churned with anxiety; both were aware that there was a distinct possibility that Bishop and Merriman had already burned up.

10:31 a.m. *It's too long*, thought Pierce. *We've lost them both.* 'I shouldn't have let them try it, Vince. I should have ordered them to leave the *Colum—*'

'Shshh!! Listen!'

Pierce frowned and shut his eyes, concentrating on a sound from his headset. He could hear a very faint gurgling sound – or was it words?

Above, in the reserve control room, Joe Gibbs called out again. '*Columbia.* Red Team flight director. Do you read?'

Silence.

'*Columbia*, do you—'

'. . . ston . . . *bia*!'

More interference. Then, as clear as day: 'Houston? *Columbia*! We have Los Angeles in sight! Do you copy that Houston?'

It was Rusty Bishop. A deafening roar erupted throughout Mission Control. Exulting cheers, then just as quickly, silence. The *Columbia* still had a long way to go.

'*Columbia*, this is Gibbs. We copy and have Chase Squadron 13 at 90,000 feet.'

'Got 'em on our screen!' replied Merriman, scanning the radar blips on his control panel.

'Right then, *Columbia*. You're clear for landing at Los Angeles International, Runway Two Zero.'

'Two Zero. Copy! How long is it?'

'10,000 feet.'

'10,000? A little tight. No sweat. Lots of freeways just in case!'

Pierce looked at his own chronometer: 10:32. *The Enterprise should soon be clear*, he thought. 'Try it, Vince.'

'*Enterprise*, *Enterprise*. Houston calling *Enterprise*. Do you read?'

This time there was no delay, no hesitation; just the soft voice of Dr Adrienne Brooks, coming over loud and clear.

'Houston? *Enterprise*. We read.'

'Roger!' exclaimed Pierce. 'You're clear for landing at Edwards Runway 22.'

'Houston,' said Brooks, 'tell everyone Jack and Rob are fine . . . glad to be coming home and—'

A buzzing alarm sounded off, filling Pierce's headset. The *Enterprise*'s third of four rate gyros had just failed.

Out over the Pacific, west of Los Angeles, the *Columbia*, now escorted by a squadron of ten F24 Condors, continued its descent.

'There's still a lot of water between us and L.A.' said Bishop. 'Houston, we're down to 13,000 feet. How does our energy look? I'm showing maybe a little low.'

In the reserve control room, Gibbs could not reply immediately, as new data had just crammed his display screen. At 13,000 feet the *Columbia*'s problem was as simple as tossing a ball in the air. Once tossed in the air, the ball's energy is directed vertically. The higher it travels, the more gravity decreases its vertical velocity, slowing the ball down until at the peak of its climb, for a split-second, the ball is dead in the air, its vertical energy zero. At the same moment, the ball has enormous potential downward energy, and as it falls that potential is converted into the energy of motion – kinetic energy.

Like the ball, the falling unpowered space shuttle, now

a glider, was converting its own potential energy into kinetic energy and most critically, seeking an equilibrium between the two, the equilibrium being sufficient lift to propel it to Los Angeles. Dick Merriman was right. The *Columbia*'s energy was low – perhaps too low to make it to Los Angeles.

Gibbs scanned his screens, absorbing the data. At 13,000 feet he would normally have recommended 30 per cent speed brake, but they were too short. 'Recommend . . . 10 per cent speed brake.'

'O.K. Boards coming open to 10,' replied Merriman. He activated the *Columbia*'s controls and the ship's wedge-like tail rudder split open at the rear and flared out 10° on either side.

'10,500 feet,' announced Gibbs. 'We now recommend 20 per cent speed brakes – two zero.'

'8 miles out,' announced Bishop curtly, 'copy 20 per cent speed brakes.'

The city with its brown haze lay ahead, the airport's runway lights flashing bright, even in the morning light.

'*Columbia*, we show you 8 miles out and 8.1 potential,' said Gibbs.

'Point one potential?' said Bishop.

'Roger.'

'Not much of a margin . . . Down to 7,920 feet. Speed 280,' replied Merriman.

'Not much room, Rusty.'

'One shot, Dick – that's all we've got. L.A. International? Space shuttle *Columbia*, requesting permission to land.'

The traffic controller at Los Angeles Tower focused on the approaching space shuttle, now at 4,000 feet, accompanied by the F24s. Used to dealing with 767s, 757s, the liquid hydrogen L1011 Transport and other aircraft, he was startled by Bishop's request. Astronauts in a space shuttle? Requesting permission to land? 'Ah . . . Roger,' he spluttered, 'permission granted! Runway 20 is all yours.'

'Runway 20 in view . . . 2,300 feet . . . now 2,000 feet . . . speed brakes coming open – 1 mile out.'

'*Columbia*! Energy potential is .95 of a mile,' cried Gibbs.

'O.K. Houston – flaps still closed! I can see the numbers on the field.'

Fifty feet to the left of the falling *Columbia*, the chase leader, well versed in the life-and-death decisions involved in test flights, took charge. More than once in his career he had guided in disabled ships. More than once he had known the bitterness of failure. There was determination and authority in his voice.

'Chase Squadron! I've got it. *Columbia*? I'll count you down. You're at . . . 300 feet . . . down to 290.'

'O.K. Thank you, Chase, Gear coming down at 270 . . .'

Unlike most craft, the space shuttle's landing gear was neither hydraulically operated nor machine controlled. When the switch was pulled, gravity simply allowed the gear to fall and snap-lock into place.

Bishop released the landing gear switch. Three green lights glowed on his control panel, one for the nose gear, the others for the left and right rear gear.

'O.K. *Columbia*, gear down at 250 feet.'

Suddenly Bishop was aware of a red light on his instrument panel.

'Red light on the nose gear!'

'No! It looks good!' replied the leader.

Not again! thought Merriman, his mind flashing back to the crash that had left his legs broken and had almost finished his career.

'One half mile out,' said the leader. '. . . 200 feet. Quarter mile at 180 feet . . . get your nose up 1°! You're short! You're short!!'

'Nose, 1°!' snapped Bishop.

Falling, falling, vectoring to the outer edge of Runway 20, at 40 feet off the surface, the space shuttle *Columbia* cleared the end of the runway, and Bishop pulled back on the control stock, raising the *Columbia*'s nose further.

'Rear wheels at 30 feet!' cried the Leader, '10, 5, 3, 2, 1 . . .'

With a screeching squeal, white clouds plumed off the scorching tires.

'Rear wheels on the ground! Nose at 10 feet! 5, 4, 3, 2, 1! You're down! You're down!'

Instantly, Bishop opened the tail rudder speed brake:

Brake open full! Slowing! Slowing! Body flap down! Handling beautifully . . . beautifully!'

Fifty feet off the ground, the chase leader followed them down the runway, waggling his wings in victory. Fire trucks raced after the *Columbia* quickly catching up with the slowing spaceship.

In the reserve control room, triumphant bedlam reigned. Gibbs beamed. 'Well done, *Columbia*! Well done!' he shouted over the roar.

'Team effort, Joe,' cried Bishop. '*Columbia* thanks you guys. What about the *Enterprise*?'

One floor below the reserve control room, totally oblivious to the fate of the *Columbia*, Doug Pierce in Mission Control was fighting a battle of his own. Gibbs tapped into the communications, but as he sat back and listened, the look of triumph was punched off his face. The *Enterprise* had lost its third rate gyro.

Thirteen thousand feet out over the Mojave Desert, Brooks and Harwood wrestled with the controls. If the fourth rate gyro failed, all control of the *Enterprise* would be lost and the ship would be put into a final and fatal roll, from which not even Brooks' and Hayward's skills could save it.

Now, above Roger's Dry Lake, and with the Salton Sea behind and to the right, Harwood banked the *Enterprise* slightly to the left and aligned it to Runway 22. At 330 miles per hour, he dropped the *Enterprise*'s nose to 16° below the horizon, a descent angle five times steeper than that of a commercial jet. Simultaneously Brooks armed the space shuttle's landing gear system. The *Enterprise* was now plunging down at 200 feet per second, unpowered, and streaking earthward.

'O.K. Down to 12,712 feet,' said Harwood.

'*Enterprise*? Get your speed brake to 50 per cent please,' said Vince Torino.

The microwave landing system had locked onto the *Enterprise* at 18,000 feet, registering the ship's altitude to within 12 inches. But Harwood, confident in his instincts and training, had decided to bring it in on visual. He had landed space shuttles dozens of times. Gritting his teeth, he forced the thought of a potential fourth rate gyro failure from his mind.

'Opening speed brake to 50,' he announced, 'coming open at 20°, 30°, 40°, 50°!'

'Energy potential looking good,' said Torino. '7 miles out, 8 miles potential.'

'Altitude 7,888, speed 290,' said Brooks.

'A little high!' said Torino.

'O.K.,' replied Brooks, opening the speed brakes a further 5°. 'Speed now 280.'

'5,690 feet,' said Harwood.

The lakebed loomed ahead. This was the final approach.

'O.K.! Over the lakebed!' said Brooks.

The leader commanding Chase Squad 5 joined in the final landing assistance count:

'*Enterprise*? Chase leader here. I have you at 3,000 feet.'

'3,000,' repeated Vince Torino in Mission Control. '*Enterprise*, get your speed brakes closed!'

Plunging 200 feet per second, nose down 16° below the horizon, the *Enterprise* reached 1,700 feet. Harwood pulled back on his control stock, raising the ship's nose to 1½° above the horizon. Right up to the pre-flare landing manoeuvre, Brooks rattled off the altitudes in a numerical duet with the chase leader, to ensure that Harwood's final pull-up came exactly as scheduled. To overshoot the pre-flare would mean a pull-up, possibly overstressing the shuttle and splattering the ship onto the runway. Now, 15 seconds from touchdown, any error could be fatal.

Dead ahead, the black, block numbers 22 lay on the dusty brown surface of the runway.

'You're at 300 feet!' said the chase leader.

Brooks activated the landing gear. 'Gear going down.'

'They're down!' cried the chase leader.

An alarm rang in the cockpit. Brooks thought her heart would stop. Pressure had built up in the orbiting manoeuvring system used to slow the ship in space – but it was no factor in the landing. 'Ignore it!' cried Harwood.'

The Chase Leader counted it off: 'O.K. Your gear is down. You're at 80 feet . . . 60 . . . 50 feet! Speed 220! Down to 30! 20! Holding at 20!'

Another alarm droned. It was the fourth rate gyro. The shuttle lurched to the right violently. Brooks slammed the control stock to the left.

'Hold on! This is it!! she yelled.

'10 feet! 5! Picking up dust!' cried the chase leader.

The *Enterprise* slammed into the Runway, sending clouds of dust billowing up beside and behind its rear landing gear.

'Rear gear down!' cried the pilot.

But the *Enterprise* bounced up, airborne again, then slammed down once more, the nose gear smacking into the surface. The *Enterprise* skipped 50 yards, but the landing gear held. The ship was intact!

The chase leader grinned. 'Home again! We'll see you babe!' Pulling back on his own control stock, he blasted his jet into a spiralling, vertical victory roll.

'Speed brake open, Houston!' cried Brooks. 'The *Enterprise* is home!'

In Mission Control, four days of pent-up frustrations and tensions burst forth in unrestrained cheers, Dixie rebel war whoops and backslapping. The Red Team had raced down from the reserve control room to join the bedlam and Joe Gibbs pumped Doug Pierce's hand in delirious joy. 'Well done, well done,' he repeated over and over to everyone, and Pierce, speechless, tears of joy

300

and relief in his eyes, nodded, hardly able to believe it was over.

American flags seemed to sprout out of thin air, waved triumphantly by the flight controllers. NASA Administrator Benjamin Fleck approached Pierce, grabbed his hand, then hugged him. 'Excellent, Doug! Excellent!' He reached into his jacket pocket and pulled out the media release he had prepared to read, had the worst come to the worst, and tore it in half. 'You did it,' he said to Pierce.

And the celebrations continued.

At Los Angeles International Airport, surrounded by rescue vehicles, their headsets still on, Bishop and Merriman sobered, tired and numb, sat in silence. Rusty Bishop spoke quietly:

'The first time I thought we had pulled this whole thing off, was when our wheels touched the runway.'

Dick Merriman amended the observation: 'Not me. When the wheels stopped rolling and we stopped, right here.'

'Yeah,' sniffed Bishop.

'Let's get a drink. I'm buying.'

The two astronauts shook hands on the proposition and undid their seatbelts.

Eighty miles north of Los Angeles at Edwards Air Force Base, a horde of pilots and medics had scrambled onboard the *Enterprise* and up the ladder to the flight deck. Lewis' shoulder was attended to and Tex Harwood helped him down and out to the waiting van.

Suddenly Adrienne Brooks and Rob Clark found themselves alone. As she helped him undo his harness, her eyes flooded with tears of joy. He looked up at her, saw the tears in her eyes, his lips trembling with emotion. Painfully he stood, holding onto her for balance. Tears streamed down her face and she held him, clutched him, and he kissed her.

'Dear God, how I love you!' she said.

'No more flights. That was the last one for me,' he said,

enfolding her against him, holding on as if he would never let go.

'The project. It's over,' she said.

'And we've just begun.'

In Mission Control, the celebration continued. Pierce pulled open his console drawer to stuff his headset away, and there in a plastic protective cover, was the insignia for the flight of the *Yorktown* and *Columbia*. NASA tradition called for each mission insignia to be hung up immediately after the successful completion of the flight.

'Come on, Doug! Party at my place!' said Torino.

'Not yet, Vince – there's one small step left,' replied Pierce.

And he took the plaque from its cover and holding it fondly, firmly, walked to the left-hand wall of Mission control. Without hesitation, he hung it in its deserved place. The room erupted with roars of approval and a hundred voices cheered Doug Pierce. Someone had begun singing the National Anthem, quickly joined by dozens of voices.

> *'What so proudly we hail'd,*
> *At the twilight's last gleaming . . .'*

'Damn, I'm proud of this agency!' said Torino, 'and I'm proud of this country!'

'Nobody else could have done it, Vince. Nobody,' replied Pierce.

> *'. . . And the rocket's red glare . . .*

Doug Pierce savoured the moment of victory. His concept worked; the solar power stations could be built. And space shuttle flights would be cheaper; more research could be carried out; more knowledge could be gained – knowledge that would improve the quality of life for all people. And there was the call from Balderis, the Russian. The omens were good.

And his own career, the post of Administrator was

assured. He, Doug Pierce, would be running NASA. And he had so many ideas. Amidst the cries of approval, the future opened up for him.

> *'O'er the land of the free,*
> *And the home of the brave*

In California, at Edwards Air Force Base, it was business as usual. Once more, dozens of screaming jet aircraft roared through the skies. Crossing the base's perimeter at 400 feet, this time defiantly oblivious to the noise, a lone eagle with vanquished game locked dead in its talons, beat its wings and screeched for the sake of screeching and headed for home.